Ripples of the Past
The Pages of Time Book 2

Damian Knight

For my parents

The story so far...

After suffering a traumatic brain injury in the crash of Flight 0368 – a shocking terrorist attack that killed his father and left his mother in a coma – sixteen-year-old Sam Rayner wakes in hospital to discover that he has developed seizures during which he is transported into the body of his past or future self.

Sam collapses at his father's funeral and suddenly finds himself flung several hours ahead, where he learns of a bomb blast at Thames House, the headquarters of the British Security Service. Upon returning to the present, he tips off the police, thereby preventing the atrocity and inadvertently drawing the attention of Lara McHayden, head of the Tempus Project, a secret government organisation investigating people with alleged time-travelling capabilities.

McHayden offers Sam the chance to control his ability and help track down rogue MI6 agent Esteban Haufner, the man responsible for both the foiled Thames House bombing and the sabotage of Flight 0368. Using Tetradyamide – a drug originally developed during the Vietnam War by McHayden's long-lost fiancé, Isaac Barclay – Sam begins training at the Tempus Research Facility, a subterranean complex outside of London.

He is not, however, the only person to have developed such abilities. In 1969, Michael Humboldt, a horrifically injured soldier, escapes from a secure military hospital in California under mysterious circumstances. After almost half a year in hiding, Michael embarks on a murderous rampage and returns to San Francisco intent on coercing Isaac Barclay into providing him with a continued supply of Tetradyamide. In a desperate bid to escape Michael's clutches, Isaac destroys his research into the drug before going on the run himself.

Back in the present day, McHayden believes Humboldt is responsible for corrupting Haufner, and asks Sam to help confirm his location prior to a missile strike. Unwilling to become responsible for the destruction of an innocent village, Sam tries to leave the Tempus Project and is sucked into a bloody conflict with McHayden and her foot soldier, George Steele, which threatens everyone and everything he holds dear. On the night of Christmas Eve, Sam travels back to the day of his father's funeral and reverses his decision to alert the police to the Thames House bombing, creating a new timeline in the process.

Now, in *Ripples of the Past*, we rejoin Sam as he struggles to adapt to a reality in which he has no recollection of the last month, and journey back to 1970s California as the deadly feud Michael Humboldt and Isaac Barclay comes to an explosive head.

Not read *A Trick of the Light* yet?

Get a free ebook copy when you join my new releases mailing list. Just visit the website, sign up and start reading today!

http://www.damianknightauthor.co.uk/free-book

CONTENTS

Chapter I

The Homecoming

1

November 1916

Stephen Rutherford's dream of a lazy afternoon in the garden of the family cottage was shattered by a distant thunderclap. He twisted in his hammock to see the rusted walls of the cabin shakily illuminated by a lantern swinging from the ceiling. Joseph, his older brother, was already up and on his feet in undershirt and breeches, his eyes like pools of shimmering liquid in his oil-streaked face.

'What the devil was that?' Stephen asked.

Joseph wiped his forehead with the back of his hand, smearing muck about. 'You don't suppose we're under attack, do you?'

'No. Fritz wouldn't dare, not with the escort we've got.'

'What about U-boats?'

Stephen swallowed the lump in his throat. Hoping that the fear spreading through his gut wasn't also painted across his face, he threw his blanket back and dropped barefooted to the floor. Over the last year or so U-boats had become an ever-growing threat to British merchant vessels as the German navy sought to tighten the stranglehold of its blockade, but before he could take measures to reassure his brother, the ship was rocked by a swell that sent the pair staggering. Stephen's tankard slid along the ledge by his hammock and clattered to the floor, while Joseph lost his footing and toppled onto his backside, landing with a huff.

'No time for rest,' Stephen said, and reached down to haul him upright. 'Come on, let's take a gander up on deck.'

For a moment Joseph remained seated, his brow creased as he prepared to voice some objection or another.

'Would you rather stay down here?' Stephen asked. 'It's no safer if we are under attack, I can promise you that.'

Joseph nodded his reluctant consent, gripped Stephen by the wrist and clambered to his feet. Once the pair had pulled on their oilskins and boots, Stephen paused to snatch his father's fob watch from the hook beside his hammock before bundling his brother through the cabin door.

The dank, dimly lit corridor echoed with shouts and cries as they made their way to the stern of the ship. A volley of heavy gunfire sounded somewhere nearby, shaking the hull as though they had run aground. On reaching the far end, they ascended the treacherously slippery metal steps and emerged into the biting cold of the main deck.

'Look,' Joseph said. He was pointing to the north side of the convoy, where the darkness of the blackout was broken by a pillar of fire that cast reflected flames onto the water as it rose high in the night sky. '*The Earl of Sussex*, I wager.'

'Poor bastards.'

Joseph swallowed, his bottom lip quivering. 'I'm scared, Stevie.'

'Don't be,' Stephen said, and laid a hand on Joseph's shoulder. 'I'm right here with you. I won't let anything happen.'

Although younger by two years, to Stephen it often felt as though he were the older of the brothers. Their father had been killed in an industrial accident in 1903, leaving Stephen, who was only three at the time, with little more than a handful of hazy memories and the gold fob watch bequeathed to him. Growing up, Joseph had suffered a series of ailments that had stunted his growth and left him permanently short of breath, and as a result Stephen had had little choice but assume the role of man of the household, taking on a variety of errands and odd jobs in order to supplement their mother's meagre income while his brother stayed in bed, mostly reading. By the age of thirteen, Joseph was fluent in five languages, including Latin and ancient Greek, and spoke both French and German without the trace of an accent (a talent that had already earned him the suspicion of their crewmates). Coupled with his slight frame, Joseph's preference for the company of books over that of people had made him an easy target for the other boys at their school, and Stephen, who by then had already developed a reputation as a fighter, had habitually returned home sporting the cuts and bruises earned defending his older brother.

As they watched *The Earl of Sussex* burn, Stephen's hand on Joseph's shoulder, a barrage of fire erupted from the guns of a nearby cruiser, throwing further light onto the scene. No more than three hundred feet from where they stood, the turret of a German U-boat broke the surface of the water.

As the full bulk of the enemy vessel emerged, Joseph let out a whimper. Gripping him by the collar, Stephen began tugging his brother towards the row of lifeboats positioned along the port side of the deck.

Suddenly Joseph's body went rigid, his feet scraping over the deck. 'T-torpedo!' he stammered.

Stephen glanced back to see a long, thin shadow carving through the waves towards them, a wake behind it that lead back to the bow of the surfaced submarine. He yanked Joseph's collar hard enough to lift him clean off his feet and, dragging him along like a dead weight, made for the nearest lifeboat.

After only a couple of steps there was an ear-splitting boom, followed by the screech of tearing metal. The world inverted on its axis, and Stephen briefly found himself bouncing head-over-heels.

He came to lying on his back, seemingly unscathed. Thick, tarry smoke choked his lungs and stung his eyes. His ears were filled with screams of dying men.

'Joe?' he called out, and rolled onto his knees, groping blindly over the surface of the rapidly tilting deck. 'Where are you?'

There was no reply.

At that moment a gust of wind blew a hole in the smoke, granting Stephen a fleeting glimpse of the moon shining down overhead. Calling his brother's name over and again, he scrambled to his feet and staggered to the handrail. The torpedo had struck two-thirds down, severing the bow from the rest of the ship. Directly below where he stood, Joseph's oilskin hat bobbed on the surface of the sea.

Stephen laid his head on the handrail and began to weep, rendering him unaware as the U-boat launched a second torpedo.

2

July 1976

It was a warm summer's day with only the faintest of breezes to the air. Rapping the tip of his white cane along the edge of the path, Isaac approached the hulking concrete monstrosity that was Stribe Lyndhurst Military Hospital. The building and surrounding grounds seemed somewhat shabbier than he remembered, as though the significance of the events played out there had coloured his recollection, making his memory of the place more impressive than it actually was (although the funding cuts since Nixon had pulled out of Vietnam three years earlier might have also contributed to the flaking paintwork and weed-clogged flowerbeds).

Yesterday he had reached San Francisco buried among a heap of muddy potatoes in the car of a freight train, thus re-entering the city for the first time since the small hours of New Year's Day, 1970. On that fateful night Isaac's life had been altered beyond all recognition, dividing the time before from everything that had followed like a line in the sand. With smoke from the fire he had started choking his lungs, he had stumbled from the Bereck & Hertz building to the sound of fireworks. Tetradyamide still burned through his veins, turning the world into a flickering, disjointed imitation of itself. Glancing down, he'd realised that his tuxedo was spotted with Michael Humboldt's blood, so he had climbed directly into his car, dropped Michael's briefcase and the paper bag containing the last batch of Tetradyamide in existence on the passenger seat and then driven through the night.

The first day of the new decade had passed in a meandering blur of changed clothes and snatched sleep. At some point he'd glimpsed the front page of a newspaper on the rack at a gas station. There were two photographs beneath the headline *ARSONIST DOCTOR WANTED FOR DOUBLE HOMICIDE*, one of fire fighters tackling the blaze the night before and the other of Isaac at his graduation from medical school in '65. Without bothering to collect his change from the attendant, he had jumped back in his car and continued east, only stopping when the dial on the fuel gauge hit empty again.

During more than six years on the run, he had travelled the length and breadth of the continent several times over. Much had changed in that time, not least his appearance. The tailored suits and expensive Italian shoes had been replaced by stained corduroy pants, a ripped overcoat and a pair of scuffed army boots. A thick, scraggly beard now covered his chin, and his hair, which at thirty-six years of age was streaked with grey, hung in a matted clump that stopped halfway down his back. Over time he had learned to whittle his possessions down to a bare minimum, carrying everything he owned – a dented aluminium canteen, a rolled blanket and an eight-inch hunting knife for protection – in a drawstring bag over his shoulder.

There had been times of abject hardship along the way, but his new lifestyle was also liberating, making him realise that, once you stripped everything back to the essentials, all a person really needed in life was food in their belly, a warm and dry place to sleep and, most importantly, a purpose.

It had taken Isaac close to four years of exile to rediscover his. While working as a farm hand in Montana during the fall of '74, he had stumbled upon an article in the business pages about a merger between Bereck & Hertz Pharmaceuticals, his former employer, and a company called Harrison Industries. All innocuous enough at first glance, but then he'd scanned down and found the owner listed as Michael Harrison, a man in his twenties who had apparently overcome extensive childhood injuries to make a fortune betting on sports results before diversifying into business and property acquisition. It was all too much of a coincidence and, after some digging, Isaac's worst fear was confirmed: not only had Michael survived the fire at the Bereck & Hertz building but, in the years since, he had somehow found a way to utilise his ability without Tetradyamide, assuming an alias and setting up what by all accounts sounded like a thriving young business empire, while Isaac himself remained on the run, wanted for the other man's crimes.

Isaac hadn't stopped moving in the two years since, rarely staying more than a week in any location. Evading the charges against him was no longer his priority, for he had a new purpose in life: stopping Michael Humboldt.

Although almost completely unrecognisable from the man he had once been, he wasn't taking any chances on his long-overdue return to California. He hadn't bathed in two weeks and had picked up a white cane and dark glasses while passing through Phoenix four days earlier, which, when combined with a tin cup containing a handful of change, created a convincing blind beggar disguise.

As he got closer to the hospital entrance, two young candy-stripers approached from the opposite direction, so absorbed in conversation it seemed they might walk straight into him.

Rather than break character, Isaac continued on his course, rattling his cup a little louder and muttering, 'Spare some change?'

One of the pair glanced up just before crashing into him. 'Ewwie, gross!' she exclaimed, wrinkling her nose and yanking her friend out of the way.

Isaac allowed himself a wry smile.

As a result of his previous employment, he knew the building as well as anyone, and had already decided entering through the front lobby was too risky. Instead he cut around to the service entrance at the rear. On turning the last corner he found Thomas, one of the orderlies on the Lincoln Ward and a man with whom he'd shot the breeze during many a slow night shift, leaning against the wall, a half-smoked cigarette dangling from his lips.

Isaac just about managed to suck back a gasp before it escaped his mouth. Staff turnaround had always been high at the hospital, and although he'd expected to encounter a familiar face or two, to run into one so soon into his venture was a sizeable slice of misfortune.

Hoping his reaction hadn't betrayed his surprise, he continued on his way, tapping his cane with his head tilted toward the sky.

'You lost, old timer?'

Isaac straightened up, recalling that Thomas was, in fact, three years older than him. 'You tell me, son,' he said, and turned to gaze roughly a foot to the side of his former colleague's face. 'This the main entrance?'

'Nope.' Thomas took a step closer, then grimaced and recoiled as Isaac's stench assaulted his senses. '*Jesus*! Look, man, you can't be back here, okay? It's staff only. Just go back the way you came, you can't miss it.'

'Much appreciated.' Isaac rattled his cup again. 'Care to help a veteran out? I lost my sight in a bomb blast in '72 and—'

'Yeah yeah.' Thomas dropped his cigarette, pulled a handful of change from his pocket and deposited it in the cup. 'Get yourself something to eat on me. And a bath while you're at it.' With that he disappeared through the service door, kicking away the brick he'd used to wedge it open.

Isaac sprang forward and caught the handle just before the latch closed. He counted to thirty and slipped through, finding himself in a deserted corridor where several trolleys of dirty bed linen had been lined against the wall, awaiting collection.

Dropping the blind-man act, he hurried ahead, taking a left turn and then a right and then a left again before shoving open the door to the emergency stairwell. Here he removed his dark glasses, folded his cane away and started to climb.

The air-conditioning system didn't extend to the stairwell, and although Isaac was in the shape of his life, perspiration was flowing freely down his face by the time he reached the sixth floor. He wiped his brow with his sleeve, eased the door open and peeked out through the crack and onto the Lincoln Ward. There was a nurse barely old enough to be out of school at the main desk, plus a few other medical staff milling about near the office, none of whom he recognised.

He let the door swing shut, then climbed the next two flights, arriving on the eighth and final floor, home to the Hoover Ward, a specialist plastic surgery unit that had still been under construction during his time at the hospital. Once again he stopped and opened the door a crack. Finding the main desk unoccupied on this occasion, he snuck out and crept down the corridor to his left. There was a public restroom halfway down. On the wall next to the door was a fire alarm. After a quick glance about to check that the coast was clear, he drove his elbow into the glass panel and tugged the lever.

Nothing happened for a couple of seconds and then a loud ringing sounded from several directions at once.

Almost immediately it was accompanied by raised voices from the ward.

Isaac sprinted back down the corridor and into the stairwell before anyone arrived. Instead of descending, he continued to climb. The only thing above him was the roof, the door to which was always kept locked. It was, however, one of the few places no one would think to look in the event of a fire. He squeezed himself into the recessed doorway, from which he had a restricted view of the landing on the floor below.

A minute or so passed before the first people began to make their way down from the Hoover Ward, mainly patients deemed fit enough to walk unaided. They were followed by several others, each accompanied by a member of staff. Finally the fire warden, an anaesthetist named Hobbs, emerged and made his way down too.

Isaac gave it another minute just in case anyone was straggling behind, then descended the three flights to the Lincoln Ward. As he'd been counting on, the main desk was now unattended. He left the stairwell and hurried over, the memory of watching Apollo 11 touch down from the very same spot briefly flashing through his mind. With a wistful shake of his head, he stepped through the door of the office behind the desk; he was here for a purpose, and there was no time for reminiscing.

Patient records were stored in several tall filing cabinets at the far end of the room. The first two were reserved for current patients, so Isaac headed straight to the third, where he lowered his bag and pulled out his hunting knife.

Over the last two years he had conducted numerous dissections, moving on from the brains of cattle acquired at abattoirs to those of humans, a good source of which had been found in an undertaker of questionable morals in Nebraska. Unfortunately, these experiments had all confirmed only one thing: without Michael's medical records, there was no chance of recreating his brain injury and therefore no hope of understanding and thus blocking his ability. And those records were stored in one of the cabinets in the office of the Lincoln Ward, where they were supposed to remain for seven years after a patient's discharge – or, in Michael's case, escape – before being transferred to a central vault in the city. That would happen in just over one week's time, after which any chance of recovering them would be lost, prompting Isaac's belated homecoming in spite of the dangers involved.

With the fire alarm still ringing loudly around him, he unsheathed his hunting knife, slid the blade into the gap above the top drawer and jimmied the lock until it popped open. After placing the knife on the cabinet, he began flicking through the files within. They were organised primarily by date, with subject dividers denoting the year of discharge, and then subdivided alphabetically according to the patient's last name.

Isaac worked his way through the third cabinet and moved onto the forth, once again jimmying the lock with his knife. Located in the second-to-bottom drawer was a divider marked *1969*. He sifted through the individual files until he reached a section marked *H*. Close to the back was a file with the name HUMBOLDT, M in the top left-hand corner.

He pulled it out and opened it, a smile spreading. Everything was there, from the field report written by the doctor who'd operated on Michael in Vietnam right down to Lara's last update, completed just a few days before Michael's escape.

Isaac withdrew the field doctor's report and skimmed through the text. A third of the way down were the words, '*...fragment of metal, approximately half an inch in* *length, embedded in basal ganglia region of brain. Extensive damage to body of caudate nucleus. Initial attempts to remove foreign object successful, however resulted in heavy bleeding and the likely formation of extensive scar tissue. Chances of full recovery: minimal to non-existent...'*

He moved on to Lara's initial report, completed on Michael's arrival at Stribe Lyndhurst just a week later. *'...it may have taken three visits, but the patient has finally allowed me to examine his wounds, and the rate of tissue regeneration around the incisions at the base of his skull is phenomenal, unlike anything I've ever seen. I've double-checked the attached field doctor's report, and can only assume the date of surgery must have been recorded incorrectly, since such extensive healing could not possibly have taken place in only one week...'*

He closed the file and, lifting the back of his coat, slid it behind the waistband of his pants. Could it be that Michael had survived an injury that would have killed an ordinary person, and the resulting scar tissue had somehow altered the way his brain processed the passage of time?

After a final glance around the office, Isaac closed the cabinet, sheathed his knife and made his way back to the emergency stairwell. He descended to the ground floor and stepped out into the same corridor through which he'd entered, pausing to unfold his cane and put his sunglasses on before following the signs to the nearest fire exit and emerging into a bright sunlight and a sea of people.

The first fire truck had already arrived on the scene, and several fire fighters were working their way toward the building. Tilting his head to the sky, Isaac started tapping his cane again as he circumnavigated the crowd.

Along the way he could make out snippets of conversation:

I can't see any smoke, can you?

Gus told me he was going to the bathroom just before the alarm sounded. You don't think he's still in there, do you?

My shift finished ten minutes ago, you know. You think I'll get paid overtime for this?

Isaac rounded the corner of the building and reached the path that led down to the gates and out onto the street beyond. Stopping to glance back one last time, he saw something that suddenly rendered him immobile: Lara McHayden, the woman who could have been his wife if things had panned out differently, was standing at the edge of the crowd, talking to a male doctor whom Isaac failed to recognise.

He lowered his dark glasses and stared, his disguise forgotten. Apart from a sad, slightly jaded look to her eyes, she appeared the same as ever, and his heart skipped a beat as a thousand emotions swept over him in the same instant. What was she doing back here after all these years? She had, as far as Isaac was aware, returned to Britain in 1970 after her visa expired. It made no sense, but then he remembered reading about a memorial service last month that his parents had arranged in his honour. Lara would have been invited, of course, so it was entirely possible she had opted to stay on in California for a few weeks afterward.

Without intending to do so, he found himself retracing his steps toward her. What would she do if he revealed himself? Would her reaction be one of joy, relief, anger or some hybrid of the three?

But no. Patting the file hidden down the back of his pants, Isaac reminded himself that he had a purpose that transcended his personal feelings. And if he was ever to win Lara back, not to mention everything else that had been taken from him, stopping Michael Humboldt was the first step.

He stood watching her a moment longer, drinking in the sight of the woman he loved, and then turned back toward the gate.

'Isaac? *Isaac Barclay*?'

Betty Mclean, one of the nurses on the Lincoln Ward, was standing a couple of yards farther down the path, watching him with a stunned expression on her heavily made-up face. He stared back, then cleared his throat, slid his dark glasses on and continued on his way.

'Isaac?' Betty repeated, suddenly by his side. 'It *is* you! I'd recognise those eyes anywhere.' She paused as the incongruity of his bum's outfit dawned on her. 'Hey, what happened to you anyway?'

'Must have me confused with someone else,' Isaac muttered, and strode away.

He only glanced back at the gate. Betty was standing where he'd left her, watching him with the same stunned expression.

3

Michael leaned back in his chair at the head table in the banqueting hall of the newly constructed Sandstone Springs Resort and surveyed the three hundred guests quaffing his champagne and filling their bellies with his food. Among their number were several prominent local businessmen, the drummer from a fading rock band, a minor movie starlet and the politician whose palm he'd needed to grease in order to secure planning permission for the development; a hotel, golf course, spa and casino complex set across two-hundred acres of Nevada desert.

As the brass band struck up a rendition of Ritchie Valens' *La Bamba*, Lynette, the latest in a long line of girlfriends, leaned over from the chair beside him and held out a miniature pancake with a mound of caviar balanced on top.

'What *is* this stuff?' she asked. 'It smells kinda funky.'

'It's caviar,' Michael explained. 'They're fish eggs. Sturgeon, I believe.'

She eyed her caviar with disgust. '*Fish eggs*? You are kidding me, right?'

'No, princess. They're a delicacy.'

'You mean all those icky black balls come outta a fish's butt?'

'Not its butt, technically. And those "icky black balls" cost over a hundred bucks per pound. Why don't you give it a try? I promise, you won't regret it.'

Lynette shook her head and returned the pancake to her plate. 'Uhuh, won't catch *me* eating something that's come outta a fish's butt, no siree!'

Michael sighed and waved a passing waiter over to refill his glass. There was no denying that Lynette was beautiful, with a shapely body, long auburn hair and green eyes that sparkled just as his one true love Rachel's once had, but these assets increasingly failed to compensate for what she lacked between the ears.

As she continued to speak, he feigned interest, smiling and nodding at the appropriate pauses while his mind drifted off to faraway places. In addition to the completion of the new resort, there was another, more significant reason for today's celebration; one that only Michael was aware of. Next week would mark the seven-year anniversary of his escape from Stribe Lyndhurst, the day the bird had flown its cage, and he felt a justifiable sense of pride about everything he had accomplished since.

At twenty-six years of age, Michael Humboldt was already a millionaire several times over. In the first few weeks of 1970, his seizures had returned. Although limited and uncontrolled without Tetradyamide, often dropping him a day or two into the past or future with little prior warning, these episodes had represented his only means of travelling through time. After his winning streak at the racetrack, it had dawned on him that they could be used for his own financial gain and he began studying the sports results in case a seizure came on unexpectedly and he found himself back the day before, where he would place a flurry of bets. He had also adopted the habit of keeping a newspaper close at hand, so that if he suddenly found himself flung into the future, he could then check the sports pages, allowing him to place bets when he returned to the present.

In this manner he had amassed a small fortune over the first two years of the decade before realising that an even greater source of income could be tapped by applying the same methods to the rise and fall of stocks and shares in the business section of the papers. It wasn't long before he had set up Harrison Industries under the alias he'd been using since 1969 and, in due course, started taking on a small staff.

As his earnings spiralled and the company grew, he had come to recognise a pattern to his seizures. More often than not they were linked to his emotions, with feelings of anxiety, anger and fear being far and away the most effective triggers. While inducing a seizure remained more of an art than a science, there was, however, a fail-safe, a memory so guaranteed to get his blood boiling it brought one on almost every time. That memory was of the look on Dr Barclay's face as he had tried to cave in Michael's head before leaving him for dead in a burning building on the night of New Year's

Eve, 1969. Dr Isaac Barclay, the man who, through his unauthorised testing of Tetradyamide, had given Michael a taste of the power that might be his and then snatched it away. For although the ability to see a day or so into the future or bring knowledge back to a day or so into the past was enough to make a killing on the stock markets and sports results, it was only a fraction of what Michael was truly capable of. He could only speculate as to what might be possible with an unlimited supply of Tetradyamide, but with the ability to alter the distant past or see weeks, months or even years ahead, he would no longer have to hide in the shadows and use aliases to conceal his true nature; the world would be his for the taking.

Lynette suddenly giggled at her own joke, jerking Michael's attention back to the moment. He laughed along rather than ask her to repeat what she'd just said. Perhaps, like the others before her, her time by his side was approaching an end. Still, there would be no shortage of substitutes to take her place; his scars had improved so much that, with a touch of make-up here and there, it was getting harder and harder to spot them. And besides, if there was one lesson he had learned over the last six years, it was that the lure of money and power far outweighed that of good looks.

'Excuse me, sir.'

He looked up to see Donna, his assistant, standing behind his chair, a frown lining her doughy face beneath a fuzz of brown curls.

Donna was the first applicant Michael had interviewed when Harrison Industries began taking on staff. In many ways it was a miracle he hadn't replaced her yet; she was a slow typist, had no head for numbers and couldn't make a decent cup of coffee to save her life. But what Donna *did* possess were the two attributes he valued above all else, namely loyalty and a blind eye to his indiscretions.

'Donna!' he exclaimed, grateful for the interruption. 'Join the party, why don't you? Grab a glass of champagne, something to eat.'

'There's a telephone call for you at reception, sir.'

'Take a message then.'

'I believe the call is rather urgent. It's Mr Winters.'

Michael dropped his serviette and pushed his chair back. By the fall of '74 he had finally accumulated enough wealth to purchase a controlling stake in Bereck & Hertz Pharmaceuticals. However, it had soon become disappointingly apparent that Barclay had made a remarkably thorough job of his sabotage, the fire at the old head office having destroyed almost all of his research. Undeterred, Michael had continued to pump funds into the project in the hope that one of the chemists on his payroll might be able recreate the lost work, but none so far had demonstrated the necessary skill to fit the pieces of the puzzle together again. Last year he had even set up the Harrison Foundation, a scholarship programme aimed at recruiting the brightest young chemists from across the land, but all to no avail, leading him to the conclusion that his only real hope of recreating Tetradyamide lay in apprehending Barclay. To that end he had devoted so much time and effort that the manhunt had turned into something of an obsession. At great expense he'd employed a nationwide network of informants and private investigators but, aside from a false sighting in Alaska a year and a half ago, Barclay seemed to have vanished into thin air.

Mr Winters was the lead investigator in the search, and a telephone call at a time like this could only mean one thing. Ignoring Lynette's calls for him to wait up, Michael followed Donna out of the banqueting hall, across a cream-carpeted lobby dominated by a piece of modern art that looked like a giant ball of wool woven from stands of metal and into the office behind a long mahogany reception desk.

A telephone lay unhooked on one of the tables. He snatched up the receiver and, dispensing with formalities, demanded, 'Barclay, where is he?'

There was a pause on the other end of the line, then: 'San Francisco, Mr Harrison. A fire alarm was triggered at Stribe Lyndhurst Military Hospital a little over an hour ago. One of our informants identified him in the crowd.'

'Stribe Lyndhurst? You mean the turkey's come home to roost?'

'So it would seem.'

'I never dreamt he'd be so stupid. Who was the informant?'

'Nurse Mclean.'

Michael chuckled, remembering the cruel, po-faced bitch all too well from his time on the Lincoln Ward. 'Good. And she's sure it was him?'

'Positive. Although she said he was dressed up like a hobo or something.'

'Figures, the man never did have any sense of style. Make sure Nurse Mclean is suitably rewarded, would you?'

'Yes, of course.'

Michael hung up and turned to Donna, who looked up from wiping her nose on a tissue.

'Good news, sir?'

'You bet your life it is! Listen, Donna, I'm going to need a few minutes alone time, if you catch my drift. Make sure I'm not disturbed, would you?'

'Certainly,' she said, and backed through the office door, closing it behind her.

Michael flopped into a cushioned leather chair and shut his eyes. The web he had patiently spun had at long last snared its prey, and the spider was ready to pounce.

As always when it really mattered, he went with his old faithful, casting his mind back to the look on Barclay's face as he'd raised a Bunsen burner high into the air. Almost immediately his pulse began to quicken, his cheeks filling with heat. The lights in the room appeared to flicker, but this was no electrical fault.

Although Michael had no control over the exact time and place a seizure would take him, with experience he had learned that he could influence the direction in which he travelled simply by thinking of times past for back- ward or a future date, such as his birthday next year, for forward. As the seizure took hold of his body, he summoned childhood memories, happy times with his mother and his brother Eugene – rest their souls – when Pa was already passed out drunk.

Suddenly he felt himself swept back like flotsam on a wave. He saw himself stand and turn to face the door as Donna came in again. Things got steadily faster, and he briefly glimpsed himself picking up the phone before all detail was lost to a storm of shape and colour. An unconnected moment passed, his mind and body two separate entities, and then the images began to slow before stuttering to an abrupt halt.

Michael blinked and discovered he was now lying in bed, looking up at the stucco ceiling of the presidential suite on the top floor of the Sandstone Springs Resort. Lynette lay on her stomach beside him, lipstick smeared across the silk pillowcase and her face buried beneath a tangle of hair. A glance at his new, state-of-the-art digital clock revealed that the time was 05:38.

He threw back the covers and jumped out. Lynette rolled over, blinked at him with bloodshot eyes, mumbled something he couldn't make out and then rolled back the other way with the sheet over her head.

Without bothering to attach his prosthetic arm, he strode from the suite, naked as the day he was born. 'Donna?' he called, stepping into the hall. 'Donna, you up yet?'

The door to the next suite opened and Donna stepped out in a pair of men's pyjamas, her hair up in rollers. She rubbed her eyes, gasped and covered her mouth. '*Sir*, you've got no clothes on!'

Michael glanced down and then looked back up. 'Yeah, never mind that,' he said, making no attempt to cover himself. 'Get dressed, then get Bruno out of bed and tell the driver to ready my car.'

'Is everything all right? You told me never to wake you before nine.'

'Everything's just peachy, Donna. We're taking a road trip.'

4

Isaac hurried through the hospital gates, a deep fore-boding in the pit of his stomach; he had been recognised, just as he'd believed he was home dry. This was bad news – there was no getting round that – but he had long ago decided the potential rewards of returning to San Francisco far outweighed the risks. The main thing was he had what he'd come for, and in a few hours the city would be far behind him, by which time Betty Mclean would, with any luck, be left wondering if she had imagined their encounter.

Patting the lump at the back of his coat that concealed Michael's medical records, he turned right onto the side-walk. After only a single step, a heavy hand clamped down on his shoulder. He spun around to find a large man with a sloping forehead standing directly behind him.

'Dr Barclay?'

Isaac sank his teeth into the man's index finger, causing him to yelp and release his grip, then took off at full sprint. Six years on the run had stripped away the excess fat his body had accumulated during his late-twenties, leaving a sinewy network of muscles in its place, and not many people could match him over distance.

To the sound of blaring horns, he charged through a DONT WALK light and across both lanes of traffic, narrowly missing the fender of a braking sedan. He reached the opposite sidewalk without slowing. There was an alleyway between two squalid apartment blocks a short way up ahead. A quick glance over his shoulder revealed his assailant struggling to pick his way through the messy knot of cars now blocking the road.

Turning sharply into the alley, he found himself running down a gloomy, urine-reeking passage. His feet crunched over broken beer bottles and discarded needles: the all-too-familiar hallmarks of vagrancy. The alley turned to the right about fifty yards down, where it presumably met the road on the perpendicular side of the block. He put his head down and kept going, ignoring the burn of lactic acid in his calves. Suddenly a wino reared up as if from nowhere and lurched into his path, a bottle in a crumpled paper bag gripped in one hand. As the dishevelled man staggered forward, Isaac shoved him in the chest, sending him flailing into a cluster of trashcans, and then rounded the bend.

A strip of daylight beckoned up ahead. Pushing himself ever harder, he closed the gap to freedom one long stride at a time.

The sidewalk was less than ten yards away when a stretch limousine pulled up, blocking his exit.

He skidded to a stop. Looking back, he saw his pursuer emerge round the bend, a handkerchief wrapped around his bloody hand.

Isaac was cornered, but hanging directly above him was the fire ladder of the apartment block to his left. He dropped his bag, bent his knees and sprang to one side, vaulting off a dumpster and then clawing for the bottom rung. The fingers of his left hand closed around it. He heaved himself up one-armed and grabbed the rung above with his right hand. But before he could reach the third rung, someone tackled him around the legs and dragged him back down.

As he fell, Isaac's chin connected with the bottom rung, and the next thing he knew he was on his back, the big man towering over him. He had, however, landed next to his bag, and through the loose drawstring could make out the handle of his hunting knife. He pulled it out, but before he could unsheathe the blade, the man withdrew a gun from a holster beneath his suit jacket.

Isaac stared back for a second, then dropped the knife. The man reached down, picked him up, slung him over his shoulder and carried him over to the waiting limo, where he deposited him on his feet.

As the blacked-out rear window lowered, Isaac found himself face-to-face with Michael Humboldt.

5

Michael's seizure slowly fizzled out. He blinked three times and opened his eyes. Instead of returning to the office behind the resort's main desk, he found himself in the leather-lined back seat of his limo. While these transitions as reality bent to fit around his alterations were occasionally disorientating, he had by now grown accustomed to them as an unavoidable side effect of meddling with the past.

Donna was seated beside him, staring absently out of the window. Sitting across from them were his body-guard, Bruno, who was nursing a bandaged hand, and Isaac Barclay, the man Michael had spent the last six years searching for.

It had worked: Mclean's tip-off had been accurate and the manhunt was finally at an end.

A smile began to spread across Michael's face until he registered the atrocious odour radiating from Barclay's body. 'Yikes! That you, Isaac?' he asked as he whipped out a silk handkerchief with his initials – *M.H.* – embroidered in one corner and pressed it over his nose. 'Donna, open the window, would you? It smells like the elephant enclosure at the zoo back here. When did you last take a bath, Isaac?'

Barclay remained staring down at his hands, which lay loosely curled in his lap. The pampered young man Michael remembered was almost completely unrecognis-able, with tatty clothes, a greying beard and long, filthy hair that hung past his shoulders. It was a most gratifying transformation; although Barclay couldn't have been more than ten years older than Michael, he looked at least twice that.

'Boss, he had this on him,' Bruno said, and passed Michael a faded green folder with the name HUMBOLDT, M in the top corner.

'What's this then? Doing some homework?'

Panic flashed across Barclay's eyes, but the look faded as quickly as it had arrived and he returned to the study of his hands.

With a sigh, Michael opened the folder and looked inside. On top was a grimy, hand-written document that appeared to be the write-up by the field doctor who had performed surgery on him after his injury in Vietnam. Beneath was a thick wodge of sheets, all typed on the same thin paper, all with either Barclay's or Dr Mac-Hayden's signature at the bottom and all dated between March and July of 1969.

'So, it really is homework,' he said, looking back up. 'Care to explain what you're up to?'

Barclay straightened in his seat, his hands balling into fists. He opened his mouth as if to speak, then decided against it and, with a slight shake of his head, lowered his gaze again.

'Didn't think so.' Michael closed the folder. 'Allow me to hazard a guess, if I may. You've spent the last six years plotting my downfall, and you think the answer's somewhere in here. What's the plan then? Recreate my injury in yourself? Or maybe find a way of blocking it?'

Barclay maintained his defensive silence, motionless apart from a slight narrowing of his lips.

'Donna, give this to Sebastian when we get in, would you? Never know, might be something useful in there.' Michael handed her the folder and turned back to Barclay. 'The silent treatment is wearing a little thin, Isaac. We've got a long drive ahead of us, and you're going to have to talk at some point. How about a game of twenty questions to pass the time? I'll go first. Right, I'm thinking of an object. I'll give you a clue, it's something in this car. First question, if you please.'

Barclay looked up, his features distorted by hatred of the purest kind. 'What, are you out of your freaking *mind*?'

'Ho, it speaks!'

Barclay tensed like he was about to swing for Michael, but a snarl from Bruno settled him back in his seat. 'You ruined my life,' he muttered through gritted teeth.

'No, Isaac, I offered you fame and fortune, the chance to help me change the world. As for ruining your life, *you* did that when you took the decision to leave me for dead in a burning building.'

'If it's revenge you want then why don't you get it over with and kill me?'

'Oh, I've got no intention of *that*!'

'Then what do you want?' Barclay asked, looking genuinely confused.

'Why, the same thing as ever,' Michael said. 'Tetradyamide.'

Michael passed the remaining hours of the journey shivering against the cold air circulating through the open windows of the limo, his handkerchief pressed over his mouth and nose in an attempt to lessen the impact of Dr Barclay's odour. Dawn was almost upon them by the time they finally began up the resort's long, crushed-stone driveway. The party – which he guessed he must have missed in this timeline – should have ended at midnight, but there were still a few guests milling about, including a couple necking on the edge of the marble fountain near the hotel's grand front entrance.

Instead of stopping, Michael instructed the driver to follow the maintenance road that looped around the entire site. They pulled up beside a low concrete hut on the far side of the golf course, close to where the artificially maintained fairways gave way to a rocky outcrop that climbed high into the steadily lightening desert sky.

The driver opened the rear door and Michael climbed out, followed by Donna. Barclay, however, made no attempt to move until Bruno elbowed him in the ribs hard enough to nearly knock him out of his seat.

'Okay, okay,' he said, rubbing his side. He paused after stepping out as he failed to hide his amazement at their surroundings. 'Where *are* we?'

'The Sandstone Springs Resort, Nevada,' Michael said, beaming with pride. 'About an hour west of Vegas, to be exact. So far the project's cost over a million dollars and two years of my life to complete, but I think you'll agree it was worth the effort. We've got a golf course, spa and casino, all on-site. Work will begin on a sister resort in Florida when the land purchase goes through next week, and I'm already looking at sites in Texas and Hawaii, too. You play golf, Isaac?'

'In a former life,' Barclay muttered with a shake of his head. 'So this is what you've been up to all these years, building golf resorts in the desert? Hardly changing the world, is it?'

'Sideshows and distractions,' Michael said, dismissing the jibe with a wave of his hand. 'Let me show you the annex. I know it doesn't look like much from out here, but just wait till you get inside!' He pulled a set of keys from his pocket and unlocked the reinforced steel door of the hut, which opened onto the dark, humid room that housed the resort's elaborate sprinkler control system. 'Come on,' he said and hit the lights. 'No need to be shy.'

Barclay remained by the door, again unmoving until Bruno shoved him in the back and sent him stumbling in. He regained his footing on the other side and blinked at the array of clicking and whirring equipment before him.

'What is this place?'

'The annex serves two functions,' Michael explained. 'The first is to control the resort's sprinkler network. Believe me, when you're maintaining two-hundred acres of grassland in the middle of a desert, irrigation becomes a serious issue. The second function is a little more… confidential, let's say.'

He crossed the room to what looked like a patch of damp staining the concrete of the far wall a slightly darker shade of grey. There was a faint click as he pressed his hand to it, and a concealed panel swung open to reveal a recessed keypad hidden behind. After punching the code in, he turned back. A couple of seconds passed and then a deep rumbling noise started up, building as multiple counterweights and gears shifted and moved in the foundations. The floor began to shake as if the aftershock of a distant earthquake were rocking the place.

Barclay took a step back, his eyes wide, but Bruno was on hand to clasp him around shoulder.

'Relax, we're perfectly safe,' Michael said. 'Look!'

With a grinding of stone against stone, the wall began to inch back, gradually revealing an inky chasm below. It took a full minute to move the yard and a half necessary to uncover the top of a flight of rough concrete stairs that descended into blackness, at which point it stopped with a bone-shuddering thud. A series of lights flickered on beneath them, illuminating the entrance to a tunnel.

Michael trotted down, a light-hearted spring in his step. He paused halfway to wave the others along behind him. 'This way, Isaac! The best is yet to come.'

'Want to tell your pet gorilla to unhand me then?' Barclay asked, unsuccessfully attempting to shrug Bruno's hand from his shoulder.

Michael gave his bodyguard a nod, at which Bruno grunted and released the doctor.

The four of them descended in single file, Donna bringing up the rear. The tunnel was just under a hundred yards long. A third of the way down the concrete gave way to roughly hewn stone, the notches and grooves of drillbits still visible.

At the far end they reached a curved, polished-chrome door. Moving to block Barclay's view, Michael tapped the code into the keypad by its side. The door slid into its jamb, and they filed through into a corridor lined with brown shag pile carpet. The walls here were papered with a fashionable geometric design that Michael had seen in a magazine, repeating swirls of yellow, orange and a shade of brown that matched the carpet.

At the opposite end of the corridor were two more curved doors, both polished chrome like the first. He strode to the door on the left and punched the code into the keypad beside it, revealing a room with the same brown carpet covering the floor and walls clad in faux brickwork. Against the right wall was a king-sized bed with a gilded headrest, and, against the left, a home cinema system with a screen, projector, tape deck and a range of speakers. The far wall was given over to a long rectangular window overlooking the desert on the other side of the outcrop, five-hundred feet below.

'These are your quarters,' Michael said, stepping to one side. 'Go ahead, Isaac. After you.'

Barclay looked like he was about to object, but Bruno gave a low growl and cracked the knuckles of his good hand, which proved incentive enough for him to step through.

'I hope you find everything to your liking,' Michael said. 'I had the room modelled on my very own in the hotel complex – the presidential suite. Minus the balcony, they're practically identical, although I think your view is a little more dramatic.'

'Lucky me.' Barclay approached the window and peered out, his fingertips pressed to the pane.

'It's reinforced glass. Over eight inches thick, in case you were wondering. I'm informed even a bullet wouldn't make a scratch, although I must admit, I've yet to test the theory. Anyway, the bathroom's through here, and you'll find clean clothes in the wardrobe over there. I had to guess at your size, so I do hope everything fits. If not, just ask and I'll have Donna order some more. What else?' Michael paused and tapped his lips with a fingertip. 'Oh yes! Your meals will be brought down three times a day, but just pick up the phone if you're hungry in between. It's a direct line to Donna, so no external calls, which means no take-out pizza, unfortunately. Otherwise I'm pretty sure the hotel kitchen can cater for anything you want.'

'It's a jail cell,' Barclay stated. 'A high-end one, I'll give you that, but a jail cell all the same.'

'If that's the way you wish to see things, so be it,' Michael said. 'Now, onto the lab.'

He stepped back into the corridor and punched the code into the keypad beside the door on the other side, which opened onto a short flight of steps leading down to a large space filled with metal surfaces. There were four movable workbenches on coasters positioned in a square in the middle, directly below a huge extractor fan set in the ceiling. Against the far wall were an industrial oven and a refrigeration unit, next to a row of glass-panelled cabinets displaying a collection of beakers, flasks, clamps and stands of every size and shape imaginable. Everything gleamed with pristine newness.

Barclay followed Michael in, this time without Bruno's intervention. 'Very impressive,' he said, his reluctance apparently forgotten. 'Where did you find all this stuff? It puts my old lab to shame.'

'The annex was a substantial additional cost in the construction of the resort, but one I insisted on. To avoid drawing any unwelcome attention to our activities, the apparatus was ordered through Bereck & Hertz Pharmaceuticals, then transported to the site with a delivery of kitchen equipment. Sebastian, who you'll be working with closely, placed the order. He's very thorough, but if there's anything he overlooked, just say.'

'Sebastian?'

'Your assistant. Last year I set up the Harrison Foundation, an internship sponsored by Bereck & Hertz cherry-picking the brightest and best young chemists from colleges across the land. I think you'll be impressed when you meet him.'

Barclay shook his head. 'You honestly expect me to give you Tetradyamide after everything that's happened?'

'Despite what you might think, Isaac, I'm a reasonable man, willing to let bygones be bygones. My offer of partnership still stands, you see. Think about it, I've built an empire even though I'm only able to travel a day or two into the past or future. With Tetradyamide there would be no limits on what I could achieve. Together we could rule the world.'

'World domination? That's the plan, is it?'

'It would be a start. You always looked down on me, didn't you, Isaac? Well, the shoe's on the other foot now.'

'I only ever wanted to help you, Michael.'

'And you will. Now, much as I'd love to stay and talk, it's been a long night and I need my beauty sleep. I suggest you get some rest too, we've got a busy day ahead of us.'

6

Isaac woke to the sound of birdsong. The idea briefly crossed his mind that it had all been a bad dream, but then he lifted his head and opened his eyes. The chirping and tweeting were canned, played in a loop over the speakers built in to the walls of his expensively decorated cell. Emitting a groan, he let his head flop back to the pillow.

His gamble had failed and, for the most fleeting of glimpses at Michael's medical records, the game of cat and mouse was at an end, with the mouse – Isaac – trapped between the cat's jaws.

As he lay there, stretched out on the undeniably comfortable bed, staring up at the ugly stucco ceiling, he considered the events of the last twenty-four hours. He had been apprehended immediately after running into Betty Mclean outside the hospital, which meant Michael must have already known where he would be. The only logical conclusion was that Betty had reported their encounter to Michael, and Michael had somehow managed to send that information back to an earlier version of himself in order to have his hired thug waiting in position. Obviously Isaac had catastrophically under-estimated Michael's ability to travel through time in the absence of Tetradyamide.

After several more minutes he climbed out of bed. A beam of slanting light shone in through a gap in the drapes covering the window on the other side of the room. He went over, drew the drapes back and gazed out onto a desert landscape roasting in bright sunlight far below. There didn't appear to be any way of opening the window from inside, but, even if Michael had been lying about the bulletproof glass, the drop on the other side would surely kill anyone foolish enough to try to escape that way.

Turning back, he saw that a tray holding a pot of coffee, a sliced grapefruit and a plate of French toast had been left on the table. For some reason there were two chairs round the table, as though he was expecting company. Tempting as it was to reject anything Michael provided, Isaac hadn't eaten since before boarding the train to San Francisco yesterday, and for the time being his best option was probably to play along and pretend to accept the olive branch Michael had offered until he could figure a way out of this thing. And if he was planning on biding his time, it might be wise to keep his strength up.

After wolfing the whole lot down, Isaac showered and then brushed his teeth for the first time in two weeks. Feeling much refreshed, he returned to the bedroom to find that the door onto the corridor had been opened while he was in the bathroom. His tatty hobo's outfit had mysteriously vanished, so he perused the wardrobe before selecting a cream turtleneck sweater, flared jeans and a pair of brown ankle boots. Aside from his hair and beard, which no amount of shampoo or combing could untangle, the reflection looking back at him in the mirrored door vaguely resembled the man he had once been.

Dressed, Isaac poked his head into the corridor. The sound of voices drifted out from the open door to the lab on the other side. Instead of following it, he crept up the corridor toward the entrance to the tunnel through which they had entered. The door was approximately eight feet tall and six feet wide, and looked like something one might find in a nuclear bunker. There was a keypad on the wall.

He stared at it for a moment. Although he had tried to sneak a glimpse on the other side last night, Michael had deliberately positioned his body in the way while entering the code, making it impossible to make out which buttons he'd pressed. Each button had, however, created a tone, and that had been enough for Isaac to deduce that the number was six digits long. Unfortunately, this meant there were close to a million possible combinations, and, since electronics had never been his strong point, there wasn't much hope of cracking the code that way. But if Isaac were to apply a light adhesive to each button – something that left a faint mark when it came into contact with human skin – he might then be able work out which numbers the code contained. Of course, he still wouldn't know the order in which they needed to be pressed, but it would significantly lower the odds of—

'Isaac, you're up! How did you sleep?'

He turned to see Michael waving him over from the door to the lab and felt his skin crawl. His captor was wearing a checked suit and boots with a slight heel. The neck of his shirt was open halfway to his navel, revealing a patch of chest hair under a gaudy gold chain. In addition to a new glass eye, the crude metal hook of Michael's old prosthetic arm was gone, replaced by a rubber hand so lifelike that, at first glance, you could almost mistake it for the real thing. But the most striking change in Michael's appearance was to the scars on his face, which were so diminished from six years earlier that they were difficult to make out. Obviously he'd had some expensive cosmetic work done – from the looks of things he could easily afford it – but, then again, Isaac remembered Lara using the phrases 'tissue regeneration' and 'extensive healing' in the glimpse of her initial report he'd snatched back at Stribe Lyndhurst.

'I slept surprisingly well,' he said, and forced a smile. 'I've got to say, that bed is something else.'

'The mattress was imported from Italy,' Michael told him. 'I believe we're the only hotel this side of Milan to stock them. Oh, and I wouldn't bother with the keypad. It's the same model used in most high-security military facilities and is, I'm told, completely tamper-proof.'

Isaac glanced at the door one last time and turned back, stretching his smile a little wider. 'Can't blame a guy for trying, can you?'

Michael paused, a faint frown the only indication that this was anything but the good-natured conversation they were acting out. 'No, I guess not,' he conceded. 'But, like

I said, you're wasting your time. Only Donna and I know the code, so I'm afraid your movement about the place will be somewhat restricted when we're not here. Anyway, have you given any more thought to my offer?'

'I have, as it happens,' Isaac said as he followed Michael back down the corridor. 'A good night's sleep can do wonders for a person's sense of perspective and, after careful consideration, I accept.'

'You'll give me the formula for Tetradyamide?'

'It doesn't seem like I've got much choice.'

'So you've finally seen sense. I was beginning to fear we might have to resort to more persuasive methods, if you catch my meaning.'

Isaac caught it all too well. 'I do,' he said, flinching, 'and I can assure you, there'll be no need for that. I'm not so foolish I can't see how the cards are stacked. And besides, Michael, after six years living like a bum, I'd almost forgotten how good a few creature comforts can feel.'

'That's a relief,' Michael said. 'And I think you'll find the rewards for helping me make it most worthwhile. Follow me, Sebastian's dying to meet you.'

Isaac descended the metal steps to the lab. Standing beneath a giant extractor fan in the middle of the room were Donna, who was clutching a stack of paperwork to her chest, and a slight, sandy-haired young man with sideburns and a wispy moustache. Bruno, Michael's bodyguard, was lurking by the door with his arms folded, his right hand strapped with a fresh white bandage.

'Sebastian,' Michael said, striding over, 'allow me to introduce Dr Isaac Barclay.'

The young man stepped forward, clasped Isaac's hand and gave it a vigorous shake. 'It's an absolute honour, Dr Barclay.'

'Yeah, sure,' Isaac said, attempting to prise his hand away. 'Pleased to meet you too.'

Sebastian let out a nervous giggle. 'I've spent the last twelve months studying your work for Bereck & Hertz. Or what was left of it, at least. Some of the advances you made were truly pioneering.'

'Gee, thanks.'

'Sebastian also helped design and equip the lab,' Michael said, gesturing about. 'I was able to dig up the roster of original equipment supplied to your lab at the old the Bereck & Hertz building – fortunately those records remained untouched by your fire – and you should have everything necessary to begin work this afternoon.'

'Seems you've been very thorough,' Isaac said, scratching his chin through the bristles of his beard. 'But not everything in my old lab would've been on the roster. A few bits and pieces were my own and, given the classified nature of the project, it's possible a few items were intentionally left off. Mind if I take a look at the inventory?'

'Of course.' Michael turned to Donna and clicked the fingers of his left hand. 'Find Isaac a copy of the inventory, would you?'

She nodded submissively, laid her stack of paper on a worktop and began flicking through. After several seconds she withdrew a sheet and passed it over.

Isaac plucked it from her fingers and supplied a series of agreeable murmurs and nods as he made a show of scrutinising the list.

'Very good,' he said, looking up at last. 'You've got almost everything, but what about the dissolution apparatus?'

'Dissolution apparatus?' Sebastian repeated.

'You were planning on quality checking the final product, weren't you?'

'I…I…' Sebastian gulped and lowered his head. 'I must have overlooked it, Dr Barclay.'

'No big deal,' Isaac said and passed the sheet to Michael. 'It shouldn't take more than a few days to order in a new set, but I don't really see much point in starting production without it.'

'I'll call the suppliers right away,' Sebastian mumbled.

'Oh, and I also noticed there's no methyl acetoacetate listed?'

'Why, should there be?'

'Definitely. But it's not your fault, it was probably one of the items left off the roster.'

'Right, I'll order some of that too.'

Michael, whose face had grown progressively redder throughout the exchange, turned to Bruno. 'Take Dr Barclay back to his room, would you?' he asked, struggling to keep his voice level.

'Yessir,' Bruno grunted. He grabbed Isaac by the shoulder and steered him up the stairs and out into the corridor.

As the door to the bedroom slid shut behind him, Isaac could make out Michael yelling at Sebastian back in the lab, and allowed himself a genuine smile.

7

Isaac devoted the remainder of the day to searching his room for a means of escape. The window was a nonstarter – he knew that much already – which left finding a way into the corridor and the tunnel beyond as his only option. He tried pulling furniture away from the walls, emptied the wardrobes so he could search behind each, checked the bathroom for vents and even peeled back the carpet in one corner of the bedroom to inspect the floor below, which turned out to be seamless concrete.

Eventually he wilted to the bed and sat there, his elbows propped on knees and his chin in his hands. Although he may have bought some time with his request for new equipment, it was probably no more than a day or two, and before long he would run out of excuses not to begin work. Once that happened he was in no doubt that Michael's talk of partnership would evaporate and his 'persuasive methods' would come into play.

As Isaac sat there, staring despondently at his feet, he became aware of a cool breeze against his skin. Glancing up, he spied a wire gauze about a foot and a half across embedded in the ceiling: an air-conditioning vent.

He slapped his palm against his forehead, jumped up and then dragged one of the dining chairs over from the other side of the room. Standing on the seat, he traced the edge of the gauze with his fingertip and discovered it was fastened around the perimeter with a series of flat-head screws, the kind he should have no trouble removing with a screwdriver or, at a pinch, a knife.

When Donna and Bruno arrived to deliver his dinner that evening, Isaac had already restored the room to its previous state and was sitting with his back against the gilded headrest of his bed, ostensibly watching a rerun of *I Dream of Jeannie* on the home cinema. Despite his attempts to initiate small talk, the duo only supplied one-word answers to his questions before leaving him to his meal: a T-bone steak large enough to feed two. He ate less than half before returning to his bed for another episode of *I Dream of Jeannie*, where he remained until Donna and Bruno returned to collect his tray an hour later.

The moment the door was closed for a second time, he withdrew the steak knife he'd secreted up his sleeve and positioned a dining chair under the air-conditioning vent once again. The knife was just about fit for purpose, and after twenty minutes of scrabbling and an impressive collection of cuts and scratches to his hands, he was able to prise the gauze away.

He poked his head into the cavity above and was greeted with a blast of cold air and darkness on all sides. The duct was only just wider than his body, and creaked under his weight as he pulled himself up. Wriggling forward like a worm, his shoulders brushing either side of the narrow metal tube, he thanked his lucky stars he hadn't eaten the whole steak.

It was slow going, although the pitch-blackness all around made it hard to judge the passage of time, or how far he'd come. Every now and then he twisted his head to look behind and caught a glimpse of the diminishing square of light shining in through the vent in his bedroom.

After a while he reached a section where the duct bent sharply to the left. Rolling onto one side, he squirmed through with only minor scrapes to his knees. The airy darkness on the other side was broken a few yards up ahead by another square of light. Isaac wriggled toward it and found himself looking down through another wire gauze onto the corridor between his bedroom and the lab. The gauze wouldn't budge when he pushed against it with the heels of his hands, and he realised it must be fastened with screws on the other side like the one back in his room.

Another dead-end then. But if Isaac continued in the same direction, at some point he should reach the lab. And if he could squeeze between the giant rotor blades of the extractor fan, he might then be able to drop down and search the place for an adhesive to apply to the keypad in the corridor, should he somehow find himself back there.

The plan was tenuous at best, but it was all he had. He was just about to push on, when, through the gauze, he heard the keypad in the corridor beep. Someone was attempting to enter from the other side.

Without waiting to see who it was, Isaac began wriggling back the way he had come. As he rounded the bend, his body contorting in ways that would make an Olympic gymnast wince, the sound of Michael's voice reached him: 'Isaac? *Iiii-saac*? I hear there was a knife missing from your tray. I do hope for your sake you're not planning anything rash, otherwise there'll be hell to pay!'

Isaac glanced over his shoulder. The vent in his bedroom was only a few yards behind him. If the noise of his hurried retreat hadn't already given him away, there was a chance he could reach it before they had time to punch in the code and enter his room.

Moving like a sea snake in reverse, he squirmed his way back up the duct until he felt his socked feet slide through the gap of the vent. Pushing against the metal walls of the duct, he slid his legs out. He was about to drop down when the buckle of his belt snagged against the lip on the inside edge of the vent, leaving him stuck there, his top half in the air-conditioning duct while his legs and ass dangled from the bedroom ceiling.

Thrashing about, he began rocking his body from side to side, when suddenly the buckle gave and he was sent tumbling. The dining chair broke his fall and splintered under his weight, sending him crashing to the floor in an ungainly heap.

Blinking, he rolled onto his back. Michael, Bruno and Donna were all staring down at him.

'What a shame,' Michael said, tilting his head to one side. 'So my offer of partnership is a no-go then?'

8

'The cutlery will be plastic from now on,' Michael said, examining the buckled steak knife. 'Remind me, Isaac, you right or left handed?'

'Right,' Barclay told him. 'What's it to you?'

Michael turned to Bruno and gave a single nod of his head, at which his bodyguard removed his jacket, rolled up his sleeves and stepped forward, grabbing Barclay by the left wrist.

'Hey, what do you think you're doing! Get your stinking hands off m—'

The doctor's words were cut off by a crunch of breaking bone, followed by a cry that tailed off in a stomach-churning gurgle as his head slumped forward and his body went limp against the rope securing him the remaining dining chair.

Bruno glanced back, a puzzled look on his face. 'Uh, I think he blacked out, boss.'

'Thank you, Bruno,' Michael said. 'That hadn't escaped my notice. Next finger, would you?'

Bruno shrugged and seized Barclay's middle finger, yanking it sharply back like the first. There was another crunch of breaking bone and, with a gasp, Barclay shot upright, his eyes stretched wide as he stared down at his mangled hand, the first two digits of which now stuck out at grossly unnatural angles.

'M-my fingers!' he stammered. 'You've broke my goddam fingers, you bastard!'

'Ten out of ten for diagnosis,' Michael said. 'Glad all those years of medical school weren't wasted. Bruno, next finger, please.'

'Wait, you don't have to do this!' Barclay blurted out. 'Please, give me a chance to explain.'

Michael let out a weary sigh. 'Really, Isaac, there *is* nothing to explain. It's quite obvious you've been leading me on a merry dance here.'

'Okay, okay! From now on I'll cooperate, you have my word.'

'Unfortunately your word no longer holds much weight with me, Isaac. But you're right about one thing – you *will* cooperate. Next finger, Bruno.'

Ignoring Barclay's pleas for mercy, Bruno grabbed him by the wrist again and snapped the third finger of his left hand.

After a minute or two the doctor's wails were replaced by a gentle sobbing.

Michael went over, placed his hand on Barclay's shoulder and eased him back in the chair. 'As I'm sure you're aware, there are over two-hundred bones in the human body, of which the hand contains a mere twenty-seven. Sebastian has ordered the dissolution apparatus you requested, which should arrive tomorrow. After that I'll break another bone for every day you hold out on me, starting with this.' He bent to squeeze the tip of Barclay's left pinkie, then released it and straightened up. 'Donna will be down in a minute to strap your hand. While we wait for the equipment to arrive, I suggest you give your next move some serious consideration.'

9

Isaac gazed down from the steel bars now covering the air-conditioning vent to the mutilated hand in his lap. Without an X-ray it was impossible to decipher the full extent of the damage, but on initial inspection it appeared as though he'd sustained straightforward shaft fractures to the proximal phalanxes of his first and third fingers. The middle finger was a different matter altogether, the swelling around his knuckle indicating a possible dislocation. As well as hurting like hell, the hand would be as good as useless for several weeks, and if his fingers weren't properly aligned he could well suffer limited functionality for the remainder of his life. Which, thinking about it, didn't look like being very long.

At the sound of the keypad on the other side of the door being pressed, he glanced up to see Donna enter the room, a first aid kit under her arm. He narrowed his eyes as she approached and wordlessly perched herself a couple of feet down on the bed. She opened the box, pulled a roll of bandage out and then shuffled closer.

'I don't know why you're bothering,' he said. 'He'll only start all over again unless I give him what he wants.'

'Mr Harrison asked me to take care of your hand, so that's what I'm doing,' she replied, not meeting his eye.

'Humboldt, that's his name. Not Harrison. Michael *Humboldt*.'

She shrugged like it was all the same. 'Hold still, I need to splint your fingers. This is going to hurt.'

Isaac sucked in a breath as Donna straightened his fingers, slid a popsicle stick between each and then wound the bandage around his entire hand, leaving only the unbroken little finger and thumb sticking out. It was only as she drew back that he noticed a long, thin scar running down the palm of her right hand.

'Looks like I'm not the only one having a tough time of it,' he said.

'It's nothing, just a childhood injury.' She stood, adjusted her skirt, returned what was left of the bandage to the box and withdrew a bottle of aspirin. 'Would you like something for the pain?'

Isaac reckoned he had a pretty good handle on the rest of Michael's entourage, but Donna he couldn't work out. Although he'd initially supposed her to be several years older, perhaps in her early forties, he now realised she must be younger than he'd imagined, but did herself no favours with the dowdy outfits and middle-aged hairstyle. As she shook a couple of aspirin from the bottle, he sensed an opportunity and seized her by the wrist. She clenched her fist around the tablets and tried to jerk it away, but he tightened his hold, pulling her closer.

'Listen,' he hissed, 'you seem decent enough, and I know everyone needs a steady paycheck and all, but Michael Humboldt, or Harrison, whatever you want to call him, he's a monster. How can you sleep at night working for someone like that?'

'You're hurting me, Dr Barclay. Please, let go.'

He maintained his grip for a moment longer, then sighed and released her.

She took a step back, massaging her wrist, and looked up to meet his gaze at last. There was a fire to her soft brown eyes that he'd never noticed before, and for a second it was like looking at a different person. 'Mr Harrison has the potential to do so much good,' she said. 'I know it might not always seem that way, but it's there, and I can see it.'

'*Good*?' Isaac spat back. 'Your boss is a killer, a two-bit crook! If you think he's interested in helping anyone other than himself then you need a reality check, Donna.'

She looked away, her shoulders slumping. 'Maybe you're right.'

'Well then help me, for chrissake! You don't honestly think he'll let me walk out of here alive, do you? You could tell me the code for the doors, if you wanted. I'd slip out. No one would ever know.'

'You're asking me to betray him? I…I could never do that.'

'Then I'm a dead man,' Isaac said. 'Not if, only when.'

Donna hesitated as if caught in two minds before eventually sitting beside him again. 'You must stay strong, Dr Barclay,' she said, turning to face him. 'Have faith, both in the powers that be and your own ingenuity. Often it's only in our darkest hour that we truly see the light of day.'

Isaac blinked at her. 'That's what you're telling me, to put my faith in God?'

She opened her mouth, but the keypad in the corridor sounded again before she could respond. The door slid open and Michael swaggered in, accompanied by Bruno.

'How's the patient?' he asked, a toothy grin on his face.

'I've strapped his hand like you asked,' Donna said, her cheeks darkening as she stood. 'I was just about to give him something for the pain.'

'Good, let's leave the man in peace then. I expect he'd like to give some thought to what we've discussed.'

Donna nodded, pressed the aspirins into Isaac's hand and followed Michael and Bruno out through the door.

Isaac paced in circles around his room long into the night, his left hand throbbing and his mouth like a bowl of ash. With the prospect of escape nonexistent, his options essentially boiled down to: 1) taking the easy way and just giving Michael what he wanted; or 2) holding out as long as possible in the hope a solution would mirac-ulously present itself. His inclination was toward the latter, more out of a desire to deny Michael for as long as possible than due to any confidence in what Donna had said about divine intervention or his own resourcefulness, but both paths ultimately led to the same place, and he had little doubt a time would soon come when he would say anything and everything just to make the pain stop. Then, with the formula in his possession and Sebastian on hand to reproduce Tetradyamide, Michael would have no further need for Isaac. In fact, since he was one of the few people who knew the truth behind Michael's success story or his murderous past, Isaac would come to represent a threat.

He stopped pacing, dragged over the remaining dining chair and positioned it under the air-conditioning vent like the first. Climbing onto the seat, he stared up at the steel grate they had fixed over the vent before snapping his fingers. There were five bars in all, each almost an inch in diameter.

Feeling a strange disconnectedness that quietened even the pain of his hand, he tugged his belt from the loops around his pants, slid the end through the buckle, tied it to the central bar and then placed the makeshift noose around his neck.

If he was as good as dead already, Isaac was going to make damn sure he took Tetradyamide to his grave with him.

10

Although not ten in the morning yet, the temperature was already north of seventy degrees and rising as the blazing sun climbed ever higher in the clear blue sky above the Sandstone Springs Resort. Michael lay stretched on his back in a lounger on the Arabian-themed terrace bar by the main pool. Through his gold-plated aviator sun-glasses, he let his gaze settle on several children splashing about on an air mattress, their squeals of excited delight mounting as, one after another, they piled on until the thing capsized.

Feeling an irrational stab of jealousy, he searched his memory for a comparable incident in his own childhood, but the closest he could summon was the time he'd nearly drowned skinny-dipping with Eugene in the creek that ran through the back of the neighbouring farm.

With a sigh, he turned to Lynette, who lay sprawled out in a silver bikini on the lounger beside him, her skin slick with tanning oil.

'I feel like a Margarita,' she said, propping herself up on an elbow. 'You want anything from the bar, Mikey?'

'It's a little early, princess. Even for me.'

Lynette pouted, sat up and slid her feet into her wedge-heeled sandals. 'Suit yourself,' she said, and sauntered off toward the bar, attracting stares from nearly every man in the vicinity.

Michael reached into his shirt pocket for a cigar. Drawing it under his nose, he inhaled the rich, woody aroma and let out another sigh. Really he should have been happy, but instead there was a strange tightness to his chest that he vaguely recognised. He had Barclay exactly where he wanted him, a broken man in every sense of the phrase, and one way or another the formula would soon be his. But still, he didn't have it yet, and perhaps that was what was putting him on edge. Also, while he had half-expected the doctor to try something like his stunt with the air-conditioning vent, truth be told a part of him had hoped the man would be so awestruck by his achievements that he would have finally seen sense and fallen into line, handing over Tetradyamide vol-untarily. But that was probably just wishful thinking on Michael's part, and if he had to break a few bones on the way to getting what he wanted, so much the better.

He bit the end off his cigar and lit up, when a shadow fell across his lounger.

Glancing up, he saw Donna standing before him. 'Mind moving?' he asked, and blew a cloud of smoke in her direction. 'You're blocking my sun.'

'Oh, right. Sorry,' she said, and muffled a cough as she stepped to one side.

'What is it, Donna? I thought my diary was clear this morning.'

'Something's happened, sir. It's Dr Barclay.'

Michael sat upright, pushing his sunglasses back on his head with the hand of his prosthetic. 'Not been at the air-con again, has he?'

'Not exactly.' She gulped and reached up to scratch her ear. In spite of the heat, her face was sickly pale. 'I really think you ought to come and see for yourself, sir.'

Michael nodded, the tightness in his chest cranking up another notch. At that moment Lynette returned, a cock-tail glass in her hand.

'Something's come up,' he said, pulling on his espadrilles.

'Jeez, *again*? You said we'd spend the day together, Mikey. You promised!'

'And we will. But this is business, princess. Why don't you stay here and have another drink or two? I'll be back before you know it.'

Lynette didn't say anything, but turned to smile at a passing lifeguard, a muscled, moustachioed guy who made the mistake of smiling back. Michael made a mental note to fire the man at the next opportunity and then followed Donna around the pool, back into the hotel, through the lobby and out of the revolving doors at the entrance. There was a golf cart parked up under the pillared drive on the other side.

'Mind telling me what's going on?' he asked as he took the passenger seat.

Donna shook her head and climbed behind the wheel, then put her put her foot down hard, causing the cart to lurch forward so suddenly that he had to ditch his cigar in order to grab hold of the roof support. They took off around the fountain and up the drive before cutting onto the maintenance road that looped around the entire site.

The annex was over a mile from the hotel, and she barely let up the whole way, almost throwing him out around the bends. At the electric motor's top speed it only took a few minutes to reach the squat concrete building, at which point she slammed on the brakes so abruptly that the back wheels skidded, spraying the wall with tiny pebbles.

Michael clambered out, his stomach in his mouth. 'Why have I got a bad feeling about this?' he asked, and unlocked the steel door.

Once again Donna said nothing, but followed him into the room that housed the sprinkler control system. After activating the hidden flight of stairs, they hurried down the tunnel before passing through the thick security door at the far end.

The door to Barclay's room remained slid back in its jamb. Instead of offering anything by way of explanation, Donna hung back, her gaze directed down at the shag pile carpet.

Michael entered and then froze. 'Oh,' he said.

Barclay was hanging by his belt from the bars of the grate they had fixed over the air-conditioning vent yesterday evening, the remaining dining chair on its side beneath his feet. His face was a grotesque, puffy mask.

Michael took a tottering step back and turned to Sebastian and Bruno, who were both shuffling their feet on the other side of the room, seemingly unsure where to look. 'Is…is he dead?' he asked, at once realising how pointless the question was.

'Donna and Bruno found him when they brought down his breakfast,' Sebastian said in a quiet voice. 'I've checked for a pulse and couldn't find one.'

'How long, do you think?'

'Obviously I'm not a medical doctor, but his skin was already cold to the touch, so several hours at least, I'm guessing.'

'I see,' Michael said, and stepped back into the corridor.

He had always believed Barclay to be weak and self-serving; the kind of person who would cling to life no matter what, but it appeared he had underestimated the man's resolve. All was not lost, however. It didn't really matter what Barclay did to himself, or how many times he tried to escape. Michael would always be there, a spider poised by its web, ready and waiting to learn from his mistakes.

'What are you going to do?' Donna asked, dabbing her eyes.

Michael stopped and chuckled, the tightness in his chest subsiding. 'What do you think?' he said. 'Put this right, of course!'

11

Six hours earlier

Standing on a chair with his looped belt around his neck, Isaac could make out his reflection through a gap in the drapes covering the blackened window on the far side of the room.

So this was how it all ended, then: no winning Lara back, or his career, and no making Michael Humboldt pay for what he had done. Instead, just this moment – the here and now – followed by a slight shifting of his weight on the chair. After that, a falling sensation, then a snap.

Would there be anything else beyond, or just darkness? And would Lara or his parents ever find out what had become of him? It seemed unlikely, and there would be no search party; to the rest of the world Isaac was already dead, remembered only for the crimes that Michael had pinned on him.

He laughed at the absurdity of it all. Only a few years ago he had been a rising star, the toast of the San Franciscan medical community, but my how that star had faded. Look at him now, a bum with a busted hand, just a few short seconds from taking his own life. This was his darkest hour all right, but at least he could die in the knowledge that Michael would never get hold of Tetradyamide, and compared to that his life seemed a small price to pay.

Taking a final breath, he closed his eyes and, before he could chicken out, began rocking the chair from side to side.

This was it. No turning back now.

Left, right, left, right, left...

...and over it went.

There was a falling sensation but no snap. Instead the belt lassoed tight around his neck, squeezing his airways shut. His feet back-pedalled in thin air, his fingers claw-ing at the noose as every fibre of his being instinctively clung to life.

It was no good; with each passing second the belt tightened. Isaac's vision dimmed, his life ebbing away before him. He remembered childhood vacations with his parents, summers at the beach and Christmases in Aspen; birthdays with grandparents, their faces clear as day despite the years since their deaths; high school, academic success, a sporting achievement thrown in here and there; friends, his first girlfriend, losing his virginity; graduation, his freshman year at college, more girlfriends, more academic success; medical school and the early years of his career, the accomplishments, the accolades, the money; and then Stribe Lyndhurst and his consultancy at Bereck & Hertz. And Lara.

Lara…

Sweet Jesus, he wasn't making a mistake, was he?

But never mind that now; it was too late for such concerns. Darkness encroached on all sides but a bright light beckoned up ahead. He just needed to let go. Nothing on Heaven or Earth could be so easy. Just let go and drift away with that light, to a place where none of it mattered anymore.

Without warning the sensation of falling returned, this time ending with a bump. Isaac's airways were free once more and air flooded into his starving lungs. He coughed and spluttered. The darkness receded from his vision, however the bright light remained.

He blinked and realised he was staring directly into one of the chrome light fittings embedded in the ceiling. A blurry shape moved into his line of sight.

'Well, Isaac, old buddy,' Michael Humboldt said, gazing down at him, 'that was a bit of a close shave, don't you think?'

12

Michael watched Barclay sleeping from a chair beside the doctor's bed. A thick, yellowing bruise had blossomed around the man's neck in the day and a half since his failed suicide attempt, and the skin of his face radiated with burst capillaries. In spite of how close Michael had come to losing Tetradyamide, it was a sight to warm his heart.

'Isaac?' he cajoled, giving Barclay a playful slap. 'Rise and shine, sleeping beauty!'

Barclay's eyelids fluttered open. He blinked drearily, focused on Michael and let out a shuddering groan.

'Welcome back. Bet you never thought you'd see me again, did you?'

'I'm alive,' Barclay croaked. 'But how?'

'A man of your intelligence, I would have thought you might have worked that out for yourself. It's simple, really. Donna and Bruno found you the morning after. When they showed me what you'd done, I brought on one of my seizures and returned to the night before to stop you. We were just in the nick of time, as it happens. A few seconds later and we would've needed to start all over.'

'You mean you brought me back from the dead?'

'Not many folks capable of it, as far as I know. Most have religions started in their name.'

'Is that how you see yourself, some kind of god?'

'With Tetradyamide, I'll be more than a mere mortal.'

'No, Michael, you'll still be capable of dying,' Barclay said. 'Just like the rest of us.'

Michael reclined in his chair and crossed his legs. 'You might not know this, but I tried to kill myself too once. Didn't go through with it, needless to say.'

'Shame.'

'I'll pretend I didn't hear that. But, thinking about it, it was something of a turning point in my life, like what they say about hitting rock bottom and bouncing back. Sadly I don't think the experience will work out that way for you.'

'No?'

'My offer of partnership has now expired, Isaac. Here's my new offer – you give me the formula for Tetradyamide and, in exchange, I'll give you the quick death you seem to want so badly.'

'And if I refuse?'

'Then as before, I'll break a different bone in your body for every day you hold out on me. Once you've healed, we'll start all over again. If you die from your injuries, I'll just bring you back to life. If you try to escape, I'll undo it. And if you kill yourself again? Well, I'm sure you can work out what will happen. You see, Isaac, there really is no way out of this. You have two options – a quick death or a drawn-out, agonising one. It's up to you which you choose, but one way or the other you *will* give me Tetradyamide.'

Barclay stared back, his eyes smouldering.

Michael stood, pulled a rolled exercise book and a pencil from his jacket pocket and tossed them onto the bed. 'From here on out you'll no longer play an active role in production. I'll be back tomorrow morning for the book. If it doesn't contain the complete formula by then, I'll instruct Bruno to go to work on your legs. From what I understand, a broken femur is especially painful.'

13

Isaac pressed the tip of the pencil to the first page of the exercise book, creating a meandering smudge that he didn't seem capable of extending into a recognisable letter. In spite of the numbing effects of whatever cocktail of drugs he'd been pumped full of, the bruising around his neck still burned like a collar of fire; a constant reminder of his failure. Even in death there was no escape, for whatever he did, Michael would always be there, ready to turn the tables before he had the chance to see it through. Either Isaac gave up Tetradyamide in exchange for a quick end to it all, or he held out and was subjected to daily torture until he cracked. The end result was the same both ways: Michael would at long last have the unlimited power he craved, while Isaac himself was done for.

Emitting a sob, Isaac lowered the pencil. As he'd dangled from the looped end of his belt, his life flashing before his eyes, he had believed that he'd reached his lowest point, only to discover there were still further depths to sink to. It might all have been so different if he hadn't run into Betty Mclean outside Stribe Lyndhurst, if he'd somehow managed to cut short his last, lingering gaze at Lara and kept his head down. But, unlike Michael, Isaac didn't have the power to undo his mistakes, even those only a day or two in the past.

And then it came to him in a blinding flash of inspiration, and he suddenly saw that he had been thinking things through back-to-front. What if there was another way out, a way of somehow blocking Michael's ability? Isaac had, after all, already discovered a means of chemically enhancing it, and if that were possible might not the opposite be true? All he really needed, in fact, was to incapacitate Michael for the brief window during which the man could alter the past, and then anything that took place in that time would be set in stone. Provided, of course, that Michael never had access to Tetradyamide again.

Isaac raised the pencil and started to write, a grin on his face. Perhaps Donna had been right and the solution to his predicament really did lie in his own ingenuity.

14

Michael stared glumly at a mounting stack of paperwork on his desk in the office of the presidential suite. The first document awaiting his attention was the contract for a land purchase in Florida: what would soon become the second Sandstone Springs Resort. Although Donna had attached detailed notes from his lawyer, it was hard to concentrate on anything so dull when he was this close to getting Tetradyamide at last.

Pushing his chair back, he lit a cigar, then crossed the room to the door onto the balcony. The sun was going down on another sweltering summer's day, lighting the underside of the wispy cloud cover in a pink glow. From up here on the fifteenth floor he had an uninterrupted view of the entire west side of the site, from the pool and spa complex directly below to the last of the sparkling green fairways in the distance. At the far edge, near the rocky outcrop where his domain met the desert, he could just about make out the unremarkable grey cube of the sprinkler control room, beneath which Sebastian was supposedly hard at work in the annex.

That morning Michael had arrived at Barclay's quarters fully expecting to find the exercise book he'd left there empty, but the doctor had instead handed it over filled cover-to-cover with spidery writing, equations and molecular diagrams. Suspecting a trick of some kind, Michael had locked Barclay in his room and passed the book directly to Sebastian, who had flicked through with growing excitement before looking up with a glint in his eye and saying, 'It's all here, sir, everything I need!'

Leaning against the railings of the balcony, Michael caressed the hand of his prosthetic arm. Once Tetradyamide was within his grasp, his true potential could be unleashed and he would become capable of sending his mind to any moment in time since his injury, no longer shackled to a day or two in the past or future with no degree of accuracy. Who knew what industrial secrets and innovations he might bring back from the 1980s? Flying cars? Portable nuclear reactors? He would find out soon enough, he supposed, but whatever possibilities the future held, their exploitation was only limited by his ambition. Once a few skeletons had been erased from the closet and he could finally drop the 'Harrison' alias, perhaps a foray into politics might be on the cards? Governor Humboldt. That had a ring to it. Or Senator, maybe? Or even – *whisper it* – President Humboldt? Now that *definitely* had a ring to it.

His daydream was disturbed by a ring of a different sort, that of the telephone on his desk. He hurried back inside and picked up the receiver.

'Sebastian, that you? What's happening down there?'

There was a brief pause on the end of the line, then: 'I think I've done it, sir.'

'What, recreated Tetradyamide?'

'I'm testing it as we speak, but provided the results are above a certain purity then, yes, I think so.'

'I'll be down soon,' Michael said. 'If you're as good as your word, Sebastian, then you're about to become richer than you ever believed possible.'

Sebastian gave a nervous laugh. 'Thank you, sir. I'm very much looking forward to it.'

Some fifteen minutes later Michael strode down the steps to the lab in the annex with Donna and Bruno close on his heels. The place was in disarray, with dirty apparatus strewn across almost every surface and a burnt smell that the large fan hadn't quite managed to extract from the air. Sebastian was standing behind a particularly untidy work-bench, his hair tangled and grime smeared across his face and lab coat. Before him was a glass tray containing a white crust that looked like the salt left over from evaporated seawater.

'That it?' Michael asked, unimpressed.

Sebastian beamed with pride. 'I present to you the very first batch of Tetradyamide, Mark II. Obviously I haven't had time to capsulate any yet, but once I'd deciphered Dr Barclay's handwriting, I followed his instructions to the letter.'

'Does it *work*, though?'

'The tests I've just completed indicate a purity of seventy-two percent, which isn't bad for a first attempt.' Sebastian used a small metal measuring spoon to scrape up a portion of the white residue. 'As for whether it works…well, as far as I can tell, there's only one way to find out.'

Michael stepped forward eagerly, then hesitated. 'It is safe, isn't it?'

'Perfectly, sir. It had crossed my mind that Barclay might try to palm us off with the formula for something else, maybe even something toxic, but the process he described in the book closely matches what little information we were able to salvage from the fire at the old Bereck & Hertz building. There's nothing even remotely harmful about it.'

'Okay,' Michael said. 'I'm gonna trust you on this.'

'There's nothing to worry about, sir,' Sebastian said, looking him straight in the eye as he presented a small mound of powder balanced on the end of the spoon. 'You have my word.'

Michael nodded and stepped forward again. Like a kid taking his medicine, he swallowed the powder down and immediately retched, doubling over with his hands on his knees as he fought the urge to puke the dose all over the floor.

'Boss, you okay?' Bruno asked, knotting his brow as he helped Michael upright.

Michael wiped his mouth with the back of his hand. 'I'm fine. I guess I'd forgotten how bad the stuff tastes after all these years.'

'Would you like some water?' Donna asked.

'No,' Michael said. 'You two fetch Barclay. I want him here when it kicks in.'

15

Isaac was sat on his bed, reading a year-old copy of *National Geographic*, when the keypad in the corridor sounded. The door slid open and Donna and Bruno marched in.

'Boss wants you,' Bruno said, glaring at him.

'He does, does he?' Isaac dog-eared the magazine on an article about the indigenous tribes of the Amazon rainforest, swung his feet down and tugged on his boots, then followed the pair out into the corridor and down to the lab.

Michael was standing behind a cluttered workbench, his chest thrust out and his arm around Sebastian's shoulders. 'Isaac!' he exclaimed. 'Good of you to join us. How's the hand?'

'The hand?' Isaac said, gazing down at his bandaged appendage. 'You're *really* asking me how my hand is? Hurts like hell, if you must know, but at least it's a distraction from my impending demise.'

'Glad to hear you're looking on the bright side. You'll be happy to know that your pain will soon be at an end.'

'So your flunky's done it, has he? Been a busy boy, Sebastian?'

The little man gave him a satisfied grin and gestured to a glass drying tray on the workbench. 'Following your instructions, there was really nothing to it,' he said. 'I've got to hand it to you, Dr Barclay, the molecule is quite beautiful in its simplicity.'

Isaac looked back to Michael. 'So what now?'

'Well, the possibilities are endless, aren't they? But here's a thought that's often played on my mind – how about I return to New Year's Eve, 1969, and kill you before you try to cave my head in and set fire to the Bereck & Hertz building? It would give me back six years of lost time and, in addition to the quick death you wanted, erase a whole lot of unpleasantness on your part. What do you say?'

'You've already taken it then?'

'I have,' Michael dropped his arm from Sebastian's shoulders and stepped around the workbench, 'and in a few minutes you'll witness…' He tailed off, pulling up with a frown.

'Feeling all right?' Isaac asked. 'You look like you've seen a ghost.'

Michael blinked and shook his head. The colour had drained from his face and his eyes had taken on a glazed-over appearance. 'What's up with the lighting in here?' he muttered. 'Bruno, take a look at the switch, would you?'

He took another step forward and froze, the features of his face pinched together. His left eye rolled back in his head while the glass one still pointed down, giving him the appearance of a chameleon looking in two directions at once. Then, with a low moan, he keeled over, hitting the floor of the lab face-first.

Isaac fought to keep his expression neutral as his heart thudded against the wall of his chest. The drug he had designed in the space of a single, frenzied, breath-taking day appeared to be working, binding with Michael's neural receptors and inducing a seizure. Its production process and molecular structure were nearly identical to those of Tetradyamide, meaning Sebastian hadn't spotted the difference, however the drug's effects were the opposite, suppressing the regions of the brain associated with time perception instead of stimulating them. A user would, in theory, experience a period without the ability to perceive time: a period of timelessness, in essence.

'Boss!' Bruno rushed over to his master and rolled him onto his back.

'But-but...*what*?' Sebastian said. 'I don't understand.'

Donna turned to Isaac, her fingers over her mouth. 'What have you done?'

'Nothing,' he lied.

She stared angrily at him for a moment and then hurried over to Michael's side.

'Is he dead?' Bruno asked.

Donna lowered her cheek to Michael's lips and held it there for several seconds. 'No, thank goodness,' she said, looking back up. 'He's still breathing. I've seen his seizures before, but they were nothing like this.' She stood and began striding toward the door.

'Wait, where're you going?' Bruno called after her. 'You can't just leave me here with him.'

'To call a doctor,' she answered sharply. 'You keep an eye on Barclay.'

As she passed him, Isaac stepped to block her way. 'I *am* a doctor,' he said. 'Let me take a look.'

'*You*? I'm not letting you anywhere near him, understand?' She narrowed her eyes in disgust and made to sidestep around him. 'I don't know what you did or how you did it, Dr Barclay, but I'm not giving you the chance to finish the job!'

'Listen, Donna, apart from give him the formula he wanted so badly, I haven't done anything. But you're right on one count – he is still breathing. *For now.* By the time another doctor gets here, that might no longer be the case. Hey, Sebastian, how much did you give him anyway?'

Sebastian, who had been glancing between the glass tray on the workbench and Michael's unconscious body, suddenly snapped back to awareness. 'Who, me? One milligram, like *you* specified in *your* notes.'

'I specified point-one milligrams, Sebastian. He's overdosing.'

'*Overdosing*? Is that even possible?'

'Damn right it is if you gave him ten times the specified dose,' Isaac said, unsure whether or not this was true.

Now it was Sebastian's turn to look like he'd seen a ghost. Shaking his head and muttering under his breath, he paced to the back of the lab, then switched tack and doubled back, Isaac's exercise book gripped in one hand. 'Uh-uh, no way!' he yelled. 'You're not pinning this on me. Look here,' he opened the book and thrust it toward Donna, jabbing his finger at a page near the end, '*one* milligram. That's what it says, one milligram!'

Isaac leaned in to get a closer look and cleared his throat. 'That's a point-one,' he said, indicating the place where he had deliberately smudged a zero and dot to make them look like a correction. 'I know my handwriting's bad, but look again. It clearly says point-one.'

Sebastian and Donna bowed their heads and scrunched their brows in tandem. After a moment Sebastian looked up. 'Well how was I supposed to know that? It *looks* like a one, see?'

'If you weren't sure, you could have just asked rather than giving him a lethal dosage.'

'*A lethal dosage*?'

'Potentially.'

Sebastian gulped, swaying like a sapling in the wind. There was a greenish tinge to his skin. 'Oh Jesus,' he muttered. 'That's it, I'm going to jail. We're *all* going to jail!'

'Quit jabbering, you baby!' Donna snapped. Then, turning to Isaac, she lowered her voice: 'Please, Dr Barclay, can you help him?'

Isaac nodded and knelt beside his fallen nemesis. As he reached to check for a pulse, Bruno caught him by the wrist.

'Don't try nothing funny, you hear?'

'Loud and clear,' Isaac said.

Looking Bruno in the eye, he slid his injured left hand into the back pocket of his pants and, trying not to wince at the pressure on his broken fingers, withdrew the sharpened two-inch stub that remained of the pencil Michael had given him. Piercing Michael's jugular vein would take all of his strength, which meant he only had one shot at it. Even if Isaac succeeded, he would, in all probability, be killed immediately afterward, but at least it would be in the knowledge that Michael Humboldt hadn't won their little game.

Bruno maintained eye contact for several more seconds before releasing his wrist, which gave Isaac the chance to make a show of shaking his right hand while secretly switching the pencil into it. He focused on his target – a spot about an inch below Michael's jaw – and visualised the arc of his arm as he raised it and brought it back down. And then he spied the gun hanging in the unclipped holster beneath Bruno's jacket, and a new plan suddenly materialised in his head.

'Help me roll him onto his side, will you?' he asked, dropping the pencil.

Bruno grunted and slid his hands under Michael's back. As he levered him over, Isaac lunged forward and snatched the gun from its holster. Bruno released Michael and shuffled back, his mouth agape.

'Don't do anything you'll regret,' Isaac told him.

Sitting on his haunches, Bruno narrowed his eyes as his slow brain worked through its options and their potential outcomes. Then he nodded, drew himself up and began backing toward the wall.

'A sensible move,' Isaac said, and turned to Sebastian. 'I'm afraid the drug you manufactured, while sharing many similarities with Tetradyamide, in fact has the opposite effect, shutting down the areas of the brain necessary for time travel.'

'You mean like a counteragent?' Sebastian said, his expression an odd combination of shock and curiosity. 'What about the overdose?'

'Yeah, I lied about that. The drug will probably take a few days to fully wear off, by which time it should be too late for your master to return to this moment. He'll be back to his old, rotten self before you know it.'

'So he won't die then?'

Isaac looked down at Michael again. Not only had the man stolen his career, his reputation and his chances of happiness with the woman he loved, but he had also brought Isaac back from beyond the grave only so that he could torture him to death all over again. If anyone deserved to die, it was Michael Humboldt.

Isaac flicked the safety catch, when, out of the corner of his eye, he spied Bruno charging toward him like a linebacker attempting a sack. Before he could fire the bullet Michael so richly deserved, the big man had piled into him. The gun went off as they crumpled to the floor. There was a deafening crack, and the next thing Isaac knew Bruno was slumped over him like a felled tree.

His broken fingers screaming with pain, he heaved Michael's bodyguard up and scrambled out from under him. Bruno sagged lifelessly back to the floor. Miraculously the gun was still in Isaac's hand, and a quick glance down revealed a smudge of smeared blood on the front of his pullover. He looked up again just as Sebastian hit a circular red button on the wall beside the door. Almost immediately the blare of sirens filled the lab.

'What have you done?' Isaac asked, pointing the gun at Sebastian.

Sebastian threw the exercise book down and thrust both hands in the air, his chin quivering. 'Don't shoot, I'll do whatever you say!'

'It's a panic alarm,' Donna explained, calmly stepping forward. 'In a few minutes the place will be swarming with armed guards.'

Isaac gulped and turned back to Michael. A trickle of sweat rolled down his temple and into the bristles of his beard. All he needed to do was pull the trigger and the game of cat and mouse would be over for good. But although he had just shot Bruno, to kill an unconscious man in cold blood was a very different matter.

'Don't do it!' Donna implored, and grabbed him by the sleeve. 'He might have the power to undo his mistakes, Dr Barclay, but you don't. Kill him and you'll always regret it.'

'What choice do I have? You said yourself there'll be guards here any minute. Let him live and I'll only be back at square one.'

'No, it doesn't have to be like that,' she said. 'I know the codes to the doors, remember? There's a way out, but we don't have much time.'

Isaac cast a final glance at Michael Humboldt, his disappointment tinged with a relief. 'All right,' he said, and lowered the gun. 'But you and Sebastian are coming with me until we're long shot of this place. After that, I suggest you find yourselves a new master.'

Chapter II

Harsh Realities

1
November 1916

The man came around to the sensation of cold water lapping against his thighs. He spluttered, expelling a trickle of brine from the corner of his mouth, and opened his eyes. For a moment his vision swam before settling into focus. He was lying on his front, one cheek pressed to the damp sand of a beach that curved away and out of sight under an overcast sky.

Where was he, and what had happened?

He searched his memory for answers and found none. But before he could consider the implications of this alarming fact, another wave broke over his legs, driving the air from his lungs in a silent gasp. He heaved himself up onto all fours and, shivering so violently he could hear his teeth chattering, began crawling away from the water's edge. His body ached all over, and after a few clumsy yards he collapsed exhausted to the sand once more, where he lay flat on his back, sucking in shallow, rasping breaths.

To his left the beach tapered away to the horizon, and ended with a rocky spit of land jutting out into the sea on his right. There were plenty of gulls about, but not another person as far as the eye could see. Glancing down, he noticed that he was wearing a pair of grey oilskin trousers beneath his sodden undershirt and only one boot. What had become of his coat, hat and the other boot, assuming he had ever possessed such things, was a mystery.

He wracked his brain for his name, or even a single recollection upon which he could pin his identity, but again came up empty-handed. Before waking up on this beach a minute ago there was…simply nothing. His knowledge of language aside, he was, to all extents and purposes, newborn: a man with no history. But as this was perplexing as this was, it was equally inconsequential at present, as without warmth and shelter he would soon freeze to death.

Suddenly he felt the disconcerting sensation of being watched, and turned to see a girl, probably no more than six or seven years old, staring down at him from the top of the beach where the sand ran to a light shingle.

'Hello,' he called, and clambered to his feet. 'Are your mother or father with you?'

The girl, who was holding a child's fishing net in her mittened hand, frowned and called back, 'Woher kommst du?'

The question *Where did you come from?* immediately formed in the man's head: she was speaking German.

'I don't know,' he replied. 'Ich weiß es nicht. Kannst du helfen?'

2

Present Day

Christmas Day came and went, and Sam's mum was discharged from hospital on Boxing Day. Still suffering from Post Traumatic Amnesia, she arrived home as angry and bewildered as she was in the timeline Sam had altered at the Tempus Research Facility on Christmas Eve. Her constant questioning about his dad only sharpened Sam's sense of loss, but by now he understood that his ability to manipulate time was a result of the injury he'd sustained in the plane crash that had torn his family apart. There was no way of returning to the time before his coma, which meant there was nothing he could do to bring his dad back or return his mum to the person she had once been.

The new timeline Sam found himself occupying differed in several key respects. By reversing his decision to alert Inspector Hinds to the Thames House bombing, he had replaced his recruitment to the Tempus Project with a reality in which he had no memory of the events since the day of his father's funeral, the crossroads at which the two timelines had split.

It quickly became apparent that he had continued taking his epilepsy medication without Dr McHayden's intervention. There was an alarm on Chrissie's phone that went off twice a day, at which point she would bring him a little triangular pill along with a glass of water to wash it down. On top of the unwelcome side effects, Sam had no intention of taking medicine for a condition he didn't have, but with his sister watching over him like a hawk, he had little choice but to revert to the tactic of hiding the pills under his tongue and then flushing them down the toilet when she wasn't looking.

His relief at seeing Chrissie alive, well and expecting his unborn niece or nephew was tempered by the knowledge that, somewhere out there, the families of the hundred and twenty-nine people killed in the Thames House bombing were passing the holidays without their loved ones. He tried to push the thought to the back of his mind, but the image of Dr McHayden staring out from behind her half-moon spectacles kept resurfacing, a repeated stab of guilt that refused to stay buried for long.

Worse still, by allowing the Thames House bombing to take place, Sam had, in effect, created a reality in which Esteban Haufner, the person who had also sabotaged Flight 0368, was still out there, walking about as a free man. It was almost impossible to get through a day without hearing some mention of Haufner, now labelled 'Britain's most wanted man' by most of the press. The hunt had intensified in the weeks since the atrocity but had so far turned up next to nothing, which led Sam's thoughts back to Michael Humboldt, the man who, according to Lanthorpe and Phelps, had turned Haufner in the first place. Although he could no longer remember the exact coordinates, it occurred to Sam that he knew where Humboldt would be in mid-January – the Atacama Desert, Chile – but this information was as good as useless to him, since if he went to the authorities he could end up alerting them to his ability once again, which he couldn't risk after everything that had happened before Christmas.

And then there was Eva. Sam tried calling Doug's landline on Boxing Day, but the phone just rang and rang. He tried three times the following day and, he estimated, close to twenty the day after, each with the same result.

You just need to come and find me, Eva had said as they'd stood facing one another in the basement laboratory of the Tempus Research Facility, water splashing down from the sprinklers above, so a few days later he visited Doug's flat in person.

The lights were off and the blinds were closed, and when he pressed the intercom button nobody answered. Just as he was about to give up, a man let himself out of the building, giving him enough time to catch the front door before it swung closed. He slipped in and climbed the stairs, finding himself on the third-floor landing outside the door to Doug's flat, just a few metres from where Steele had shot his sister. Except that hadn't really happened, not in this timeline, where Sam had never even set foot in the building before.

Without holding much hope, he knocked and took a step back.

'Can I help you?' a voice behind him asked.

He turned to see a woman standing in the doorway of the flat opposite. She had curlers in her hair and an overweight ginger cat nestled in her arms.

'I'm looking for Doug Bernstein,' he said.

The woman scratched the cat behind the ears, causing it to purr loudly. 'Doug? Sorry, lovie, but I haven't seen him in almost a month. I water his plants while he's in the States, you see, and he usually phones to let me know when he's due back in the country. Would you like me to pass on a message?'

'No,' Sam said, 'thanks anyway.'

He left with McHayden's warning ringing in his ears: *any changes you make in the past could have consequences in the present, and believe me, these might not always work out how you intend.* Esteban Haufner was proof enough of that, but what changes had Sam made that meant Eva was no longer staying with Doug over Christmas?

He shook his head and, feeling more confused than ever, made his way home.

3

If Sam was ever going to see Eva again it looked like he would have to take the words 'come and find me' literally, so the next day he ransacked his room until he tracked down the slip of paper Doug had given him at the funeral. The mobile number had a UK code and was unavailable when he dialled it, but there was also an email address.

He spent most of the afternoon going over what he wanted to say, rejecting several drafts before settling on a fairly neutral message enquiring after the family, providing an update on his mum's condition and asking if Doug wouldn't mind passing Sam's email address on to Eva. It felt excruciatingly indirect, but wherever she was, the Eva in this reality had no memory of what had taken place between them, and although she had insisted that it wouldn't change the way she felt, it definitely complicated the task of approaching her.

As the days ticked by without a reply, Sam's despondency grew, along with his sense of bewilderment. Although this was his life – *his* family, *his* friends, *his* house – it was as if it had all been on loan to someone else for the last month. People kept referring to incidents he couldn't recall, causing him to fluff his lines no matter how hard he tried to play along, and he found himself spending an increasing amount of time alone in his room, reflecting on the events of the December only he could remember.

What had happened to the Tempus Project in this timeline now that Dr McHayden was dead? And who was Isaac, the mysterious stranger who had saved Sam and his friends on Christmas Eve after giving Lewis a vial of that strange, silvery super-Tetradyamide?

They were questions to which he had no answers, and, he supposed, never would.

*****

On New Year's Eve, Lewis rang to ask if Sam wanted to come to a party. It was a nice gesture, but Sam declined and spent the evening watching telly with his grandparents. What with everything on his mind, parties didn't seem all that important anymore, and he didn't think he'd be good company.

He was due to belatedly start at Fraser Golding College on Wednesday the following week (that much about this new timeline had remained the same, it seemed), but his mum had an appointment with Dr Wallis, the family GP, the day before, and despite Chrissie's objection that he didn't need to, Sam insisted on coming as well.

Dr Wallis was middle-aged, with thinning red hair. As Sam, Chrissie and their mum stepped into his office, they found him reclining in a chair with a beaded seat cover.

'So, Rebecca,' Dr Wallis said once they all were seated on the other side of his desk, 'how have you been since returning home?'

'Where *did* you get those curtains?' Sam's mum said, gazing at the window. 'They're atrocious!'

Chrissie watched her for a moment before turning to Dr Wallis. 'She's no better,' she said, her voice low. 'I had hoped we might see some improvement by now, but she barely seems able to process new information, and even when she does, it's gone again five minutes later. And she just seems so *angry* all the time.'

'I see.' Dr Wallis tapped away at his keyboard for a few seconds and then turned back, a stress toy in the shape of Kermit the Frog's head in his hand. 'And how about her memory of the time before her injury?'

Sam and Chrissie exchanged an uneasy glance.

'She remembers most of the older stuff,' Chrissie said, 'but we try not to talk about the move too much. It just confuses her and, every time we bring it up, one way or another it always leads back to Dad.'

Dr Wallis nodded and squeezed his Kermit's head, causing the gel-filled eyes to bulge out and a pink tongue to protrude from its mouth. 'That's concerning, and would seem to indicate your mother's amnesia is severe to very severe.'

'What does that mean?' Sam asked.

'Depending on how long her condition lasts, her rehabilitation may take months or even years, and there may be permanent damage to her memory and cognitive abilities. I'm afraid it's possible she may never fully recover.'

'There must be something we can do,' Chrissie said, leaning forwards.

'Well, there are several new treatments in development, but unfortunately the only thing available on the NHS is cognitive therapy. I'll place Rebecca on the waiting list, of course, and hope something comes up soon, but at the moment that's all I can offer.'

'Right,' Sam said. 'Thanks.'

'Before you go, there was something else.' Dr Wallis gave an awkward chuckle and squeezed Kermit's head again. 'As it happens, Sam, you've saved me from having to call you in separately. The analysis of the blood samples we took last month came back this morning, and has turned up some, um, rather unusual results.'

'Unusual how?'

'We've detected abnormalities in the structure of your blood cells.'

'Abnormalities?' Sam repeated, remembering how Dr McHayden had said something similar in the terrible future he'd prevented. 'You mean like a disease or something?'

'Whatever it is, you've lived your whole life without realising, so I'd try not to worry too much at this stage.' Dr Wallis gave him a smile that was clearly supposed to be reassuring but failed. 'Now, if you'd roll up your sleeve, please, I'd like to take some more blood for testing.'

4

The next morning Lance and Chrissie drove Sam to Fraser Golding College. It was a bitter, drizzly day on which the sun scarcely seemed to have risen. The snowfall of December had by now melted away, replaced by a fine mist that hung in the air, covering everything it touched with a film of moisture.

'Are you sure you want to do this?' Chrissie asked as the ancient Volvo rattled to a stop. 'You could always come back tomorrow if you're not feeling up to it.'

On top of everything else about this new reality, Sam now had to get his head around both the news that his mum might never fully recover and that there might be something wrong with his blood cells. Tempting as the idea of going home was, he'd probably just end up sitting around moping, and he'd done enough of that already.

'I'll be fine,' he said, and unclipped his seatbelt before opening the door. 'Thanks for the lift.'

The main building of Fraser Golding looked grand in a rundown sort of a way, more like a stately home that had been allowed to fall into disrepair than a sixth-form college. There was a set of turnstiles just inside the entrance, where a campus officer gave him a visitor's badge and told him to go to the main reception desk. After having his photo taken, he was issued a permanent ID badge and his timetable.

His first lesson was Politics in Room 116. After meeting Lewis outside the cafeteria, they crossed the courtyard to the modern, glass-fronted Sherman Building where the Humanities Department was situated. Sam had always been able to confide in his friend, and however much he wanted to again, he had to remind himself that this was not the same Lewis who had saved all of their lives on Christmas Eve. The person walking beside him had no memory of that night, just as Sam had no memory of the month before.

'This is me,' Lewis said, stopping outside a door marked 104. 'You're a bit quiet today, Sam. You sure you're feeling all right?'

Sam ran his fingers through his hair, his fingertips briefly resting on the scar behind his ear. 'Yeah,' he said. 'I suppose I'm just a bit nervous after everything that's happened recently.'

'Don't be. This is a fresh start, right?' Lewis angled his head towards a wide spiral staircase. 'Room 116 is on the first floor. Meet you back here after, okay?'

'Okay,' Sam said, and started to climb.

Although feeling fitter than at any time since waking from his coma, he was still breathing heavily by the time he reached the top. Room 116 was at the far end of the corridor. Ignoring his new classmates' stares, he made his way to a chair near the back, lowered himself into it, closed his eyes and began massaging his temples.

In spite of everything he had achieved, the sacrifices he had made in order to escape a reality in which his sister was dead and he was McHayden's prisoner were almost too much to bear. Eva was lost to him, a vague acquaintance with no recollection of anything that had happened between them. And however indirectly, Sam was now responsible for the deaths of those killed in the

Thames House bombing, and through his inaction had brought Esteban Haufner back to life.

He could feel a headache coming on, a slow, intense thumping near the base of his skull. Perhaps Chrissie had been right and it really was too soon. Perhaps he should have stayed at home. Perhaps, if he left now, it wasn't too late to—

A sudden hush spread through the room. Sam opened his eyes and briefly saw stars. A youngish-looking man in a crumpled suit was standing at the front of the class, a pile of exam papers in one hand and a Star Wars mug in the other.

'Welcome back,' he said. 'Did you all have a good break?'

There were a few half-hearted murmurs from around the room.

'Well I didn't.' He placed his mug on a desk and dumped the pile of papers beside it. 'While you lot were off munching mince pies, I was marking your mock exam papers. They were, without exception, dreadful. Julius, yours was particularly awful. Julius? Not here today, is he?' His gaze drifted around the room before settling on Sam. 'Aha! Santa brought us a new student, it appears. Remind me, it's…'

'Sam Rayner.'

'That's right. I'm Mr Paxton, and by virtue of being new, Sam, you're also my star student. Want to introduce yourself?'

Sam hesitated, but it didn't really seem like he could say no. He nodded and rose stiffly from his chair. 'Er, hi. My name's Sam and—'

'Yeah, I think we established that,' a boy with dark, slicked-back hair said.

There was a small titter of laughter.

Sam cleared his throat. 'So, anyway, it's my first day here. I was supposed to start back in September, but I couldn't because of an accident—'

A hand belonging to a short girl with green hair shot up. 'What kind of accident?'

Mr Paxton frowned. 'Well now, Chantelle, I'm not really sure that's pertinent.'

'It's okay,' Sam said. 'It was a plane crash. It was on the news, you probably heard about it.'

'Oh, you're *that* boy!'

A whisper broke out, quickly spreading around the room. As if from nowhere, Sam detected the aroma of burning caramel. He rocked on his heels, the room spinning around him.

'Er, you don't look too well,' Mr Paxton said. 'Maybe you should sit back down?'

Under the influence of Tetradyamide, Sam had been a government asset capable of tracking international criminals across time, and yet here he was, less than two weeks later, an invalid who couldn't even introduce himself in front of class. He clenched his jaw and went to lower himself into his seat again, when the room seemed to pulse around him, ballooning to gigantic proportions and contracting sharply.

As he fell, Sam tried to catch the edge of his desk and missed. He was vaguely aware of the classroom floor rushing up, and then the world shrunk to a point. Just before darkness snapped shut around him, an image popped into his head. It was a man with a smile like a wolf baring its teeth.

5

Sam blinked and the world slotted into focus. He was back home, sitting at the head of the kitchen table. Although he was wearing the same clothes, the section of sky visible through the French doors onto the garden was now dark. Lance and Chrissie were sitting to his left and his grandparents to his right. His mother was staring at him from the opposite end of the table with deep, sunken eyes.

It was happening again. With the epilepsy medication out of his system and Tetradyamide no longer controlling his seizures, Sam was having another fit like the one at his dad's funeral. He tried to let out a groan, but discovered his mouth was full of a biscuit he didn't remember eating and instead coughed, spraying crumbs across the table.

'Dude, take it easy,' Lance said, and gave him an unnecessary slap on the back.

Chrissie, who'd been watching with a pinched expression, let out a tired sigh. 'There has to be something we can do, doesn't there?' she asked. 'A right of appeal or something? I can't seriously believe they'd take all that money for all those years and end up giving us nothing.'

'Bollocks,' their mum said.

In all his life, the strongest curses Sam could remember her using were 'sugar' or 'fiddlesticks', and although he wasn't sure if what she'd just said constituted a swearword, it was the closest she'd come by a long way. Ordinarily he might have laughed, but now it only reminded him of how changed she was from the person who used to smother him with so much affection it was nearly impossible to breathe.

Chrissie's lips had tightened to thin, colourless lines. 'Please, Mum, you don't know that,' she said. 'It's worth looking into, at least.'

'If you think they'll pay us a penny then you're on another planet, Chrissie. It's how these companies work. It's how they make their money.'

'But over *one* missed payment? I just—' Without warning Chrissie's voice cracked and she burst into tears.

'I'll find another job,' Lance said, wrapping his arm around her shoulders. 'Something that pays better than Burger Emporium.'

Sam's mum snorted and folded her arms. 'Oh good, that's settled then! I'm sure there'll be employers queuing up around the block with your extensive qualifications and work experience.'

'Leave it out, Mum,' Chrissie said, and reached up to squeeze Lance's hand. 'At least he's trying to think of something positive we can do.'

'I'll get two jobs if I have to,' Lance muttered.

Sam's mum glared at them, until, out of nowhere, her face changed. 'Is that a new kettle?' she asked, craning her neck. 'What happened to my old one? Matthew? *Matthew*? Where has your father got to?'

Sam covered his face with both hands. 'Guys, stop it,' he said. 'I mean, what are you even arguing about?'

His grandmother reached over and patted him on the arm. 'Oh dear, pet, maybe you should go and have another lie down upstairs? Remember what the doctor said, that stress only will increase the likelihood of another episode.'

'Grandma, this has as much to do with him as it does with any of us,' Chrissie said. 'He's almost seventeen, and it's not like anyone else here is full of ideas.'

'Will someone *please* just tell me what's going on?' Sam asked, raising his voice.

His sister sighed and shook her head. 'A letter arrived from the insurance company today. Apparently Dad missed a payment last summer and they're cancelling his life insurance policy. We could lose the house, Sam.'

6

Sam was lying on his back. His head hummed and fizzed like something in his brain had short-circuited. Directly above him, a black-and-yellow HB pencil hung by its point from a polystyrene ceiling tile.

'Sam, can you hear me?'

He glanced to his side. Mr Paxton was crouched beside him, his face lined with concern. Sam's new classmates were gathered in a circle around them, their expressions ranging from mild amusement to shock.

Gingerly, he propped himself up, then wiped his mouth and looked down to see a smear of blood on the back of his hand.

'Come on, let's get you up,' Mr Paxton said. He slid his hands under Sam's arms and eased him to his feet.

At that moment the classroom door flew open and the girl with green hair came running in with Lewis close behind.

'Mate, what happened?' Lewis asked, stepping through the crowd. 'Chantelle said you collapsed or something.'

'It's happening again,' Sam said.

'What, your epilepsy's come back?'

'Yes. I mean no. I mean…I dunno, I think I saw something that hasn't happened yet.'

'Come on people, back in your seats!' Mr Paxton said, attempting to regain some semblance of order. 'Lewis, Chantelle, take Sam to reception, then come straight back to class. I'm trusting you both here.'

Lewis nodded, lifted Sam's arm over his shoulder and started guiding him to the door, while Chantelle took the other side, which didn't help much given their difference in height.

'Sorry about this,' Sam mumbled as they rode the lift to the ground floor.

Chantelle looked up and grinned. 'Don't worry. If it gets me out of class for a bit, feel free to collapse any time you like.'

The doors opened and they guided him out and across the courtyard before entering the main building. The reception desk was located in a sky-blue room beside the entrance.

'Back so soon?' the receptionist asked, eyeing Sam unsympathetically as Lewis and Chantelle steered him into one of the plastic chairs lined along the wall.

'He passed out,' Chantelle told her, 'right in front of everyone. Bang, crash, and onto the floor! You should've seen it.' She rolled her eyes back so only the whites were visible and started jiggling her body as though she were being electrocuted. Eventually she stopped, lowered her arms and gave Sam an embarrassed smile. 'No offence, but that's what you looked like.'

'Um, none taken, I think.'

'Listen, Sam, I'm going to give your sister a ring,' Lewis said, and headed back into the corridor with his phone pressed to his ear.

'I remember your file now,' the receptionist said. 'It says you suffer from epilepsy.'

'It does?' Sam said.

'Hang on, it's right here.' She span around in her chair, opened a filing cabinet behind her and began rummaging through the top drawer. After a few seconds she turned back with a file and pulled out a sheet of paper. 'See for yourself,' she said, and passed it over.

Although it was the first time Sam had laid eyes on the document, he instantly recognised his own handwriting. Under a section labelled *Existing Medical Conditions* were the words 'I have epilepsy' and then, close to the bottom, his mum's signature in the box marked *Parent/ Carer Consent.*

'I'd better get back to class,' Chantelle said, and slipped out, turning in the opposite direction down the corridor.

'We keep some of your medicine onsite, if I remember correctly,' the receptionist said. 'Would you like me to fetch it for you?'

'No!' Sam blurted out. 'I mean, I think I'd rather just go home, if it's all the same.'

At that moment Lewis returned, providing a timely distraction. 'Chrissie and Lance are on their way,' he said, sliding his phone into his pocket as he took the chair next to Sam. 'So, looks like your medication's stopped working then.'

'Huh?'

'That was your first seizure since your dad's funeral, no?'

'Oh,' Sam said. 'Yeah, suppose it must be.'

'Listen, what you were saying about seeing something that hasn't happened yet—'

'I was just a bit confused,' Sam said, glancing at the receptionist. 'That's all.'

Lewis stared at him intently, then shook his head. 'If you say so. It just reminded me of what happened last time. You know, at your dad's funeral when you started getting all worked up about making a phone call. It always stuck with me because, when I brought it up a few days later, you couldn't even remember it happening.'

Sam swallowed the lump in his throat. Obviously that conversation had taken place with a different version of him. More than anything he wanted to tell Lewis the truth, but it didn't seem right to burden his friend any further, and with the receptionist in earshot now definitely wasn't the time.

Lewis's phone beeped. 'Chrissie and Lance will be here in five minutes,' he said. 'Come on, I'll walk you to the car.'

Sam's seizures had returned, and without Tetradyamide to suppress them he had little reason to believe they wouldn't continue to do so.

'I can't believe this is happening again,' Chrissie said, verbalising his very thoughts as they pulled up outside the house.

'I know,' he said, and climbed out.

'I don't get it, especially after you've been so good about taking your pills.' His sister shook her head and began up the path. 'I suppose I'll just have to make another doctor's appointment and see if they can give you something stronger. And I think you should take the rest of the week off college. At least.'

'I've got to agree with her there,' Lance said.

'Okay,' Sam said. He didn't have the energy to protest, and wanted nothing more than to curl up in bed and pull the covers over his head. Life in this reality felt like one big deception, and his sister being alive was just about the only positive. 'By the way, everything's all right with the house, isn't it?'

Chrissie paused with her key in the lock and frowned before turning it. 'Yeah, why do you ask?'

'So there wasn't a letter from the insurance company this morning?'

'No. Why would there be?'

'No reason,' he said, and followed them in.

As he went to close the door, the postman turned down their path, walked up to him and handed over a stack of letters. The envelope on top had the Imperial Insurance logo in one corner. Sam tore the seal open, his heart sinking as he pulled out the page inside.

7

Chrissie was back in Dr Wallis's office for the second time in as many days. Things had really been looking up over Christmas with her mum coming home from hospital and Sam seeming so much better, but in the last forty-eight hours fate had stuck the knife in and twisted once more. Now, in addition to the increasing discomfort of her pregnancy, she had to contend with the news that her mother might never get better, that her brother's fits had returned and (cherry on top) that the insurance company were cancelling her dad's life insurance policy. If she hadn't felt so much like crying, she might have laughed.

Dr Wallis leaned back in his chair and pressed his fingertips together. 'So, Sam, it appears that your medication is no longer preventing your seizures. It's a shame, really, because Oxcarbazepine is one of the most effective anticonvulsants on the market, but at this stage I think our best option might be to try one of the alternatives. While we wait to see how effective your new medication is, you should try to avoid stressful situations that might increase the chances of another episode, which will mean no school for a few days, I'm afraid.'

Sam looked down and wrung his hands.

'Thank you,' Chrissie said. 'We'll do whatever you recommend, won't we, Sam?

Her brother looked up and gulped. 'I...I...there's something I need to tell you. The reason I had a seizure today is because I haven't been taking my pills.'

'What are you on about?' Chrissie asked. 'I'm the one who's been giving them to you. I've *seen* you taking them.'

Sam shook his head and looked down again. 'No,' he said to his hands. 'I've been spitting them out when you weren't looking.'

Chrissie straightened in her chair, heat flushing through her body. 'I don't understand, why would you do a thing like that?'

Sam shrugged. 'I don't know,' he said eventually. 'They make me feel funny. I don't like taking them.'

'Well now—' Dr Wallis began, but Chrissie was already out of her seat.

'God, how could you?' she yelled, jabbing a finger at Sam. 'As if I didn't have enough on my plate already with Mum and the whole Imperial Insurance thing!'

Before he could respond, she turned away and strode from Dr Wallis's office, slamming the door behind her. Sam caught up just as she'd stepped through the automatic doors.

'Leave me alone,' she said. 'I'm so angry I can't even look at you.'

'Please, Chrissie, I'm sorry. I wasn't thinking.'

'To be honest, Sam, I'm not interested in your apologies or your excuses. I've been so worried about you, but you treat your epilepsy like it's a big joke.' She pulled his pills from her handbag, shook the packet under his nose and then held it over the bin by the door. 'I mean, is there even any point me even carrying these about anymore?'

He stared back, his shoulders trembling.

'Didn't think so,' she said, and dropped the packet in.

8

Sam was at the desk in his room, staring down at the packet of epilepsy pills he'd fished from the bin at the doctor's surgery after Chrissie had stormed off. It seemed he faced a simple choice: either continue as he had been and keep lying to his sister and everyone he cared about, or take one of the little triangular pills in the hope that his medication would suppress his fits again and allow him to return to something close to an ordinary way of life.

An ordinary life.

But what would that be like? Eva was gone, his mum had amnesia and his dad was still dead. Imperial Insurance were about to leave the family penniless and, in all probability, homeless. And, just to top it all off, he had the Thames House bombing on his conscience, while Esteban Haufner was somewhere out there, walking about scot-free. But after watching Chrissie die on Christmas Eve, Sam couldn't bring himself to let her down again. Saving her was the reason he had decided to alter the timelines in the first place, and there were no guarantees he could fix his problems even if he didn't start taking his medication.

He bit his lip, opened his desk drawer and placed the packet inside, if only to remove it from his line of sight. What he needed was a distraction, something to temporarily take his mind off the decision he couldn't make, so he switched his computer on and logged in to his email account.

There was a reply from Doug waiting at the top of his inbox:

> *Hi Sam,*
> *Good to hear from you. The girls are well and send their love. I was supposed to be in London for a few*

*months, but following the bombing the
bank instructed all non-British employees to remain out of the region until
things settle down.*

*Please pass on our best wishes to your
mom. I can't tell you what a relief it is
to hear that she's woken up and is back
home with you. I hope you don't mind,
but I discussed her condition with a
doctor friend of mine, who mentioned a
groundbreaking new treatment for Post
Traumatic Amnesia. I've pasted a link
below.*

*Let me know if there's anything I can
do,*

Doug

So that explained why the flat in Mulberry Crescent
was unoccupied then.

Sam clicked the link at bottom of the email and was
redirected to a page on the website of the New York
Centre of Psychoanalytic Studies. It described recent
advances made by a Dr Rosen in the field of optogentics,
which, as far as he could work out, involved using light to
stimulate a person's neurons. He scrolled down a bit, his
jaw dropping when he saw that the treatment was priced
at almost fifty thousand dollars. There was no way the
family could afford such a cost, especially when they
couldn't even manage the monthly mortgage repayments.

After bookmarking the page, he shut his computer
down and then leaned back with his hands behind his
head. Things could be so different if only he had access to
Tetradyamide again. With it, not only was he able to
control his seizures but could turn them into something
useful. He'd been capable of almost anything under its

influence, even bringing his sister back from the dead. Compared to that, raising the funds for his mum's treatment and keeping a roof over their heads should be a doddle. But in this timeline Lara McHayden was dead, and his only connection to Tetradyamide lost.

He shook his head, reached for his drawer again and then pulled up sharply. Perhaps there was another connection he hadn't thought of before.

9

Lewis sat shivering in the back seat of Lance's Volvo, his hood up and his coat pulled tightly around his body. The heating control was on the blink, leaving them with the choice between slowly freezing or a blast of hot air so loud it was impossible to hear anyone speak, and they had alternated between the two extremes at ten-minute intervals throughout the journey.

In all honesty, he felt more than a little uncomfortable about the venture. Obviously it was good that Sam had opened up at last, but the garbled phone call Lewis had received a few hours ago had filled him with dread and contained phrases such as 'parallel timeline', 'government research facility' and 'top-secret drug'. So when he'd reluctantly agreed to tag along, it was more to keep an eye on Sam than because he believed anything his friend had told him.

'Can we switch the heating on again?' he asked, leaning forwards. 'I'm turning into an icicle back here.'

Lance grunted and reached for the switch, when Sam (in the passenger seat) suddenly grabbed his arm. He jerked the steering wheel to one side, causing the car to veer into the middle of the road.

'That's it!' Sam yelled.

'Dude, are you sure?' Lance arched his eyebrows at Lewis in the rear-view mirror. 'You've said that, like, three times already.'

'This time I'm positive,' Sam said, and pointed to an approaching side road that led into a thick wood of pine trees. 'Look, if I'm wrong again we can turn round and go home, and you have my apologies for wasting your time.'

'That's good enough for me,' Lance said. He slowed and turned onto the road, which was really no more than a heavily furrowed track. Lewis could hear various nuts and bolts rattling in the car's bodywork as the rickety suspension failed to absorb the uneven ground.

'This is it,' Sam muttered, grinning to himself. 'This is *definitely* it!'

Lewis couldn't remember the last time he had seen his friend smile. Since collapsing at Matthew's funeral the month before, Sam had seemed so different – distant and quiet, like all of the joy had been sucked out of him – and while it was good that he appeared to be in better spirits, there was something vaguely disturbing about that grin.

'Listen,' Sam said, 'would you believe me if I told you that the answer to all our problems might be at the end of this path?'

'No,' Lewis said, catching Lance's eye in the mirror again. 'Not really.'

'How about riches beyond your wildest dreams?'

'Riches beyond my wildest dreams?' Lewis scratched his chin. 'You've got me interested there. Go on.'

Sam opened his mouth, but before he could say anything the headlights revealed a metal fence topped with razor wire up ahead. Lance stopped the car.

'Kill the lights,' Sam hissed.

'Why are you whispering?' Lance asked.

'Just do it!'

Lance rolled his eyes. By the time he had turned off the engine and pulled his keys from the ignition, Sam was already out of the car and hurrying towards a wooden hut set next to a gate in the fence. Lewis climbed out too and stepped straight in a puddle. Mud splattered over his trouser leg and his new trainers, and, for the umpteenth time that evening, he found himself wishing he'd stayed at home.

'I've got a bad feeling about this,' he said, stepping over another puddle to join Lance.

'Why? Not scared, are you?'

'Me?' Lewis huffed. 'No chance, it's just…well, uh, it doesn't really look like we should be here, does it?'

Lance only shrugged and began following Sam.

By the time they'd caught up with him, Sam was tugging at a padlock securing a thick chain around the middle of the gate. Lewis stood on tiptoes and peered through one of the hut's broken windows, wincing at the whiff of stale urine. The interior had been stripped bare and the walls were covered with graffiti.

'Doesn't look like anyone's home,' he said, settling back on his heels. 'Can we go now?'

Sam shook his head. 'We need to get to the other side of that fence. Somehow.'

'Unless you remembered bolt cutters, I don't see how we're going to do that.'

'Look,' Lance said, pointing to a section about ten metres down from where they were standing.

At first Lewis couldn't tell what he was supposed to be seeing, but then a gust of wind shook the fence, exposing a small gap about two feet high in the bottom of the metal links.

'Good work,' Sam said, and set off towards it. He ducked his head, scrambled through on his hands and knees and then straightened up on the other side. 'See, nothing to it!'

Lance tied his hair back before ducking through too.

'Guys, wait!' Lewis called, his throat strangely dry. 'Is this even legal?'

'We're not doing anything wrong,' Sam said, and helped Lance up on the other side.

'What about trespassing?'

'We're just having a look around. Come on, there's no one here. Stop being a wuss.'

Lewis stayed where he was for a few seconds, watching Sam and Lance slowly disappear into the darkness on the other side of the fence. Something had changed about his friend, a new reckless streak that he didn't recognise, but short of waiting on his own, he didn't have much choice but to follow them, so, with a heavy heart, he dropped to all fours and crawled through the gap in the fence, muttering curses as strand of loose wire pierced the material of his coat and tore a hole in the shoulder.

After another hundred metres or so they reached a low concrete building with metal shutters drawn over the windows and doors. A sign with the words *KPP&R Logistics* lay flat on the ground, covered with muddy footprints.

'What *is* this place?' Lewis asked. He kicked the sign with his toe, breaking off a chunk of rotten wood.

'It's the place I told you about earlier,' Sam said, 'the government research facility.'

'Doesn't look like much of a government anything anymore.'

Sam frowned, squatted on his haunches and began tugging at the bottom of the shutter covering the main door. 'Give me a hand, will you?'

Lewis joined him but it made no difference: the thing wouldn't budge.

'Dudes, you're wasting your time,' Lance said eventually. 'It's locked. And anyway, like Lewis said, whatever it used to be, this place is, like, totally abandoned.'

'Thank you, Lance! At least I'm not the only one seeing sense,' Lewis said.

Sam shook his head, his lips pressed together. 'No. I didn't come all this way just to give up the minute things got difficult. Come on, let's check around the back. If it's locked, what I'm looking for might still be here.'

Lewis traipsed behind the others as they circled the building, his relief growing with each shuttered window they came across, until, on the opposite side, he let out a groan; there were no windows back here, only a single, narrow door. In the moonlight he could see that the shutter was bent and buckled, and had been forced halfway up its track.

Sam let out a whoop and scurried over. He crouched to reach under the shutter and then looked back with a grin before pushing the door open and ducking into the pitch-blackness behind it.

'I'm pretty sure breaking and entering *is* illegal,' Lewis called after him.

'Technically we haven't broken anything,' Lance said and followed Sam in. 'The shutter was like that when we found it.'

'Great, just wonderful!' Lewis said, throwing his hands in the air. 'In that case I stand corrected. Please, carry on.'

'A-ha!' he heard Sam say, and yellow light suddenly poured out from under the shutter.

Lewis stooped to peer inside. Sam and Lance were standing in what looked like a cleaning cupboard, with a mop and bucket in one corner and an industrial-sized pack of loo roll on the floor. Set in the far wall was another door, which Sam was about to open.

'Sam, wait!' Lewis said. But it was too late; his friend had already disappeared into the next room, followed by Lance. 'Fine then, I'll just stay here, shall I?'

His question was answered by a loud howl in the distance behind him. Glancing back, he could just about make out the wire fence, and, beyond it, the tops of pine trees silhouetted against the night sky. Whatever was making the noise sounded large and hungry, but Lewis had no intention of sticking around to find out what it was, so he scrambled under the shutter too.

On the other side of the cleaning cupboard he entered a small room that looked like it had once been a kitchen, although all of the appliances had been ripped from the walls and the sink was full of broken glass and cigarette butts. Sam and Lance were standing on the other side of a third door, on the edge of a dark expanse that reeked of stale smoke. As Lewis stepped through to join them, Sam hit a switch on the wall and a row of fluorescent tubes flickered on overhead.

The place looked like the venue of a party that had got seriously out of hand. A large, overturned desk lay just in front of them and, to their right, several metal-framed chairs had been wrenched from the floor and stacked in a heap. There was an empty vending machine with a broken glass panel against the wall to their left, and, in the far corner, the burn marks of a fire that had reached high enough to scorch the ceiling.

'What *is* this place?' Lewis asked again.

Sam ignored him, approached the vending machine and started trying to prise it away from the wall, which seemed pretty pointless given its size. Eventually he gave up, walked back and began examining the underside of the desk.

'There used to be a button that activated a lift behind that vending machine,' he said, 'but it's gone now, only a bunch of snapped wires.'

Lewis stepped forwards, his palms up. 'Okay, Sam, you know I want to help, and until now I think I've been pretty patient, but spending the night poking around in a derelict industrial unit isn't my idea of a laugh. Please, can we go now?'

For a moment it looked like Sam was about to object again, but then he sighed and shook his head. 'I've made a mistake,' he said. 'It was a long shot, I suppose, but it doesn't look like we're going to find anything here.'

'At last!' Lewis said. 'I thought you were never going to—'

He was interrupted by the hiss of a hydraulic piston. With a grinding noise the vending machine slid to one side, revealing the interior of a lift, just as Sam had said. A stocky man with eczema on his face was standing inside, a cardboard box under one arm. He stepped out, looked up and then froze, his hand over his heart.

'Malcolm,' Sam said, 'it's me.'

The man dropped his box and broke into a run, headed straight for the door to the kitchen through which Lewis, Sam and Lance had just entered.

'Stop him!' Sam yelled.

Lance vaulted the desk like a hurdler, tackled the man around the waist and knocked him to the floor in a tangle of flailing limbs.

Lewis stepped around the desk to see Lance sitting on the man's chest, pinning his arms to the floor. 'Trespassing, breaking and entering, *now* assault?' he said. 'Thanks a lot, guys, this is going to look great on my university application next year.'

10

'Er, sorry about that,' Sam said, watching as Malcolm Fairview dabbed his bloody lip with a handkerchief.

Lance tugged at his collar, his cheeks reddening. 'Yeah, sorry. I don't know what came over me there.'

Sam remembered a reality in which his sister's boyfriend had launched himself at a pistol-wielding Agent Steele in a similar manner to the way in which he'd just taken Fairview down. It seemed there was more to Lance than first met the eye.

Fairview loosened his tie and pulled a strip of tablets from his jacket pocket. 'You almost gave me a heart attack,' he said, and popped one under his tongue. 'Now, correct me if I leave anything out here, but you expect me to believe that you were recruited by Dr McHayden back in December, after which I trained you for the best part of a month, at this very facility no less, and now I don't remember any of it?'

'That's because I altered the timelines on Christmas Eve,' Sam explained. 'In the original timeline – the one I remember but no one else does – I prevented the Thames House bombing by tipping off the police. That's what got me noticed by Dr McHayden.'

'But why would you then go and undo such a thing?' Fairview asked. 'More than a hundred people were killed that day, including Dr McHayden herself. What are you, Sam, some kind of a monster?'

Sam took a deep breath as a familiar ball of self-loathing spread through his gut; it was a question he had asked himself many times over since Christmas. 'I don't want to speak ill of the dead, but Dr McHayden wasn't what she seemed,' he said eventually. 'She had plans for the Tempus Project that went far beyond exploring time travel, and when I tried to leave she threatened my family. Reversing my discovery was the only option I had at the time. Believe me, I'm trying to put things right.'

Lewis, who had been standing by quietly until that point, suddenly sprang forward and started scooping up the papers and personal effects that had spilled from Fairview's cardboard box. 'You'll have to excuse my friend,' he said, handing the scientist back his wedding photo. 'I know how bonkers this all sounds, but Sam's been under a lot of stress. He was injured in a plane crash in September last year. He lost his dad and—'

'A plane crash?'

'British Airways Flight 0368,' Sam said. He turned his head to the side and parted his hair to reveal the scar behind his ear. 'It's how I got this.'

Fairview took a step closer, squinting at the scar. 'September, you say? But that looks years old, not months.'

'The doctors tell me it's healing really well,' Sam said and let his hair fall back. 'A piece of metal pieced my skull and got stuck in my brain. They had to operate to remove it. According to Dr McHayden, it's the reason I'm able to manipulate time.'

'Excuse me, but *time travel*?' Lewis cut in. 'I mean, how is that even possible?'

Fairview let out a nervous giggle and scratched the side of his neck, showering his shirt with flecks of dead skin. 'According to certain theories, time is not a linear, continuous thing, but a series of eternal "nows", each separate but connected. Our sequencing of those nows is what we humans perceive as the passage of time. The work of the Tempus Project was based around the hypothesis that, were a person to suffer an injury that affected the regions of the brain associated with time perception, this might alter the way they perceive these nows, enabling him or her to move around in time much the way you or I might physically move about in the other three dimensions. With chemical enhancement, it was speculated that a person might be able to make conscious decisions about *when* in time they experience, much like you might choose where to stand in three-dimensional space. The problem being, of course, that brain injuries have a tendency to kill people, or at very least incapacitate them to such an extent as to render such questions moot.'

'Not me,' Sam said.

'No,' Fairview conceded, 'not you. Honestly, this is what I've spent the best part of the last decade researching. I can't tell you how thrilling it is to meet you, Sam.'

Lance exhaled loudly, loosened his ponytail and swept his hair back with his hands. 'Dudes, this is totally making my head hurt.'

'The thing I don't get,' Lewis said, 'is why the rest of us don't have any memory of this other timeline you're talking about.'

'Parallel universes,' Fairview told him. 'According to quantum theory, any time you make a decision a new, separate universe is created. Say you're walking down a path with a fork in it. You've got two options – turn left or turn right. If you chose the fork on the right, the universe will branch in two separate directions, just like the path. A parallel universe will be created in which a version of you took the left fork instead. In theory, there's a universe out there where you made a different choice in every decision you've taken in your entire life.'

'But that must mean there's an infinite number of universes,' Lewis said.

'Not quite infinite, but a number so large it might as well be. The point I'm trying to make is that if someone were able to alter the decisions they've made, they might conceivably be able to switch their consciousness from one universe to another.' He shot Sam a glance and let slip another giggle. 'It would appear that your friend here is from a parallel universe.'

'Woah, trippy!' Lance said.

'So you believe me?' Sam asked Fairview.

The scientist cocked his head to one side and stroked his chin. 'Given the nature of my former employment, I'm inclined to. But funding was withdrawn after Dr McHayden's death. There *is* no Tempus Project anymore, Sam, and I'm out of a job. Which begs the question of what exactly you're doing here.'

'That's the thing,' Sam said. 'I'm looking for Tetra-dyamide.'

'So, another interested party then?' Fairview muttered. 'And what makes you think you'll find it here?'

'There's a metal cabinet full of the stuff in the basement. Or there used to be, at least.'

Fairview shook his head. 'Not in this timeline. I produced a couple of trial batches last year, but in the absence of a subject to test it on we had no way of establishing whether or not the stuff worked, meaning production was never stepped up.'

'Oh,' Sam said, his shoulders dropping as he realised this was yet another unintended consequence of his decision to alter the timelines on Christmas Eve.

'That's not to say I didn't keep a little back, however.'

'Excuse me?'

'Purely for research purposes, you understand.' Fairview smiled mischievously. 'Why don't you come over to my place tomorrow morning and we can discuss things in more detail?'

11

Sam emerged from Notting Hill Gate underground station to pavements still busy with people making their way to work. A group of nuns near the exit were collecting for the construction of a new animal hospice. After dropping a couple of pounds in their bucket and accepting a leaflet, Sam asked for directions and then stepped back as they bickered over the shortest route to the address Malcolm Fairview had given him. He thanked them and, as he turned away, pulled out his phone, opened the maps app, typed in the postcode and followed that instead.

Although he hated lying to her again, he had told Chrissie that he didn't want to fall any further behind with his studies and was visiting the library, and had then left the house and rode the rush-hour tube across London. He hadn't really known what to expect in returning to the Tempus Research Facility yesterday evening, but the best he had hoped for was some clue as to where he might find Fairview: a payslip or a list of employees' addresses or something along those lines. That he would actually run into the man himself went far beyond anything he had imagined, and a fluttery, nauseous sensation now bubbled in his stomach as he made his way down roads lined with tall, flat-fronted houses. After believing his only connection to Tetradyamide had died along with McHayden, he was, according to the app on his phone, only ten minutes from the prospect of gaining more.

Going slowly to avoid the slippery patches where the sun had yet to melt the frost on the paving slabs, he told himself that things would be different this time. Without the Tempus Project guiding his actions, he could use his ability to fix his own problems. He would find Eva again and win her love for a second time, make enough money to keep a roof over his family's heads and pay for his mum's treatment in America and, somehow, undo the

Thames House bombing and bring Esteban Haufner to justice. At the moment he wasn't quite sure how he was going to manage all that, but once he had Tetradyamide again pretty much anything was possible.

Eventually he reached a crescent that curved around and out of sight to the left. He followed it until he came to number 47, another flat-fronted house with an unruly, bare-branched tree that was beginning to crack the bricks in the wall of the front garden. After stepping through the gate, he trotted down the steps that led to the basement flat: 47C.

The blinds behind the front window were closed, but there was muffled classical music coming from somewhere inside. Sam raised his finger to the doorbell, took a deep breath and pressed it. There was a thump that sounded like someone knocking over a chair in one of the rooms. He waited a minute, but the door remained unanswered. Judging by the size of the house, the basement flat couldn't have been particularly big, so perhaps the bell wasn't working.

He gave it a few more seconds and then rapped on the door with his knuckles. Again, there was no answer.

He glanced at his watch: it was still a few minutes before ten o'clock. He was early, so it was possible Fairview had popped out and forgotten to switch his music off.

After climbing the steps to pavement again, he glanced up and down the road. Apart from an elderly lady peering at him through the window of the house next door, there was no sign of Fairview or, for that matter, anyone else, so he stomped down the steps again, took a pen from his backpack and wrote a short note on the back of the leaflet the nuns had given him, which he then folded in half and dropped through the letterbox.

He was about to leave when he realised he had nothing to go home to. Chrissie had already told the college that he wouldn't be returning until next week, and the prospect of sitting around empty-handed in his room was too disheartening to even contemplate. No, he decided; having already come this far, he was going to wait.

He sat on the bottom step, propped his elbows on his knees and rested his chin in his hands. After a while he noticed there was a gravel path leading beyond a set of wheelie bins, so he stood up again, slung his bag over his shoulder and followed it around the side of the building until he found himself in a large back garden. Winter had worn the lawn into a muddy sheet covered by a thread-bare layer of grass. A trellis fence supporting several flowerless rose bushes topped the wall at the far end, but the middle panel had become dislodged and lay broken on the ground. Behind him, a short flight of steps led down to a patio, where, on the other side of a bird-feeder and a picnic table, he could see the back door to Fairview's flat.

Sam climbed down and, cupping his hands around his eyes, peered through the glass panel in the door. He found himself looking into the kitchen, where two mugs of tea sat on the worktop, teabags bobbing near the surface of the water.

When he tried the handle, to his surprise the door opened. 'Hello?' he called, stepping in. 'Anyone home? Malcolm? Mr Fairview?'

There was no reply, only silence interrupted by an intermittent scratching noise.

He walked under an archway and into the sitting room. Matching striped sofas were positioned at opposite ends of a frayed Persian carpet that stretched almost to the skirting boards. Against the far wall stood an old oak bookcase, the shelves of which sagged under an extensive collection of books, scientific journals and vinyl records.

The scratching noise was coming from an old-fashioned turntable on a dresser behind one of the sofas. He walked over and lifted the needle from the central groove of the record, which was still spinning on the plate.

It appeared as though his first guess had been spot-on and Fairview must have popped out and forgotten to switch his music off, probably to get milk for the cups of tea stewing in the kitchen, come to think of it. Which meant the scientist could be back at any minute and perhaps might not be best pleased to find Sam lurking inside his flat rather than waiting out front like a normal person.

Shaking his head at his own thoughtlessness, Sam hurried to collect the note he'd just posted through the door. A couple of months ago the idea of letting himself into someone else's home would have never occurred to him, but now he'd just done it without thinking twice. It seemed as though his experiences with the Tempus Project in the December-only-he-could-remember had changed him, and he wasn't all that sure it was for the better.

He lifted the folded leaflet from the doormat, stuffed it in his pocket and turned back. As he made his way down the hall again, he cast a quick glance through the open door of what looked like a bedroom. A pair of worn brown brogues protruded from behind the bed, soles out as if attached to the feet of someone lying on the floor.

Sam did a double-take and stepped in, then skirted around the bed before stopping and letting out a gasp. Fairview was flat on his back, perfectly still, his blank eyes staring up at the ceiling.

'Malcolm, are you all right?'

Fairview didn't move.

Sam rushed over, dropped to his knees and took the man's hand in his own. The skin was warm to the touch, but when he pressed his fingers to the inside of Fairview's wrist he couldn't feel a pulse.

Another dead body, then. The first was Chrissie, killed by Agent Steele's stray bullet, then the guard McHayden had shot later that evening, followed by Doug, stabbed in the neck by Clarke a few seconds after. Although Sam had always liked Malcolm Fairview, he felt strangely numb inside, as though so much bloodshed in a single night had hardened him to the sight of death.

He let go of the scientist's arm, which dropped limply to the floor, and clambered to his feet. His head was beginning to throb and he could detect a hint of burning caramel in the air. There was a telephone on top of the chest of drawers by the door. Hoping to reach it before another seizure came on, he staggered over, snatched up the handset and dialled 999.

After a couple of rings a woman's voice said, 'Emergency services, which service do you require?'

'Ambulance,' Sam said. 'I need an ambulance.'

'One moment please.' There was a pause and a click before the operator spoke again. 'And your location?'

'Er, 47C Beaumont Crescent, Notting Hill. I just stopped by to see someone and...and...I think he's dead.'

'Okay, a unit has been dispatched. And your name is?'

Sam lowered the phone. On the chest of drawers were several packets of the tablets Fairview had pulled from his pocket at the Tempus Research Facility yesterday evening. He picked one up and turned it over. The label read *Isosorbide Mononitrate: use for the treatment of angina and related heart conditions. Keep out of reach of children.*

So, a heart attack, it appeared.

Sam returned the packet to its place and lifted the handset again, when all of a sudden he spotted a small brown pill bottle in amongst the collection of cough syrup, eau de toilette and eczema cream amassed around the base of a mirror on the chest of drawers. There was a chip in the glass near the lid and the label was beginning to peel away in one corner. He picked it up, popped the lid open and gazed down at the yellow pills it contained. The smell of burning caramel immediately receded.

'Sir, are you still there?' the voice on the end of the phone asked. 'I need a name.'

Without another word, Sam hung up, dropped the bottle of Tetradyamide into his backpack and walked out.

Chapter III

Easy Money

1

April 1919

Spring arrived late in 1919, winter stretching its icy fingers well into the month of April. It was almost two and a half years since Stephen Rutherford had woken in a hospital bed to find his head strapped in bandages and his body numb below the waist. In addition to a cranial injury, he had broken his back on that fateful night on the North Sea and been carried to a lifeboat by another sailor as their ship, the *Northern Star*, went down, making him one of only forty-two survivors from a crew originally twelve-hundred strong. Joseph, the brother he had sworn to protect, had been lost at sea.

The initial prognosis on Stephen's injuries was not encouraging; he would likely spend the rest of his days a cripple, and a month later had returned to the family home in Lower Blinkhorn confined to a wheelchair. As he continued his rehabilitation, the first of his funny turns had reared its ugly head. To begin with these were terrifying and perplexing in equal measure. His mother, who witnessed the third such incident, afterwards described how Stephen had suddenly gone limp in his chair before being seized by a bout of violent tremors. She had run from the cottage screaming, uncertain whether to summon the doctor or the parish vicar.

Stephen's own experience of the incident had been decidedly different; one minute he was sitting in the kitchen, watching his mother prepare cheese sandwiches for lunch, and the next he was lying in his bed, surrounded by pitch-blackness. After a bewildering five minutes trapped in the night either before or after, he had come to in the kitchen once again, back in his wheelchair with a huddle of concerned neighbours looking on.

Each of his turns after that had only served to strengthen his conviction that God was in some way testing him, and he began to document them in a journal. But since they rarely took him more than a few hours into the immediate past or future and with no obvious purpose, he failed to comprehend their significance. They appeared to be connected to feelings of anger, fear or regret, so much so that he had hidden the photograph taken of him and Joseph on the day they had joined the merchant navy, since it brought on a turn nearly every time he looked at the thing.

By avoiding situations that might provoke such emotions and adhering to a strict regime of prayer and silent contemplation, he had been able to limit the occurrence of his turns to such an extent that, at times, it was almost possible to forget the ominous shadow they cast over his existence, and as the months wore on he was pleasantly surprised by the return of some sensation to his legs. At first this was no more than a vague, intermittent tingling in his toes, but by the turn of 1918 he had begun to take his first tentative steps, and a year later, with the ink still wet on the Armistice of Compiègne, he had finally felt strong enough to begin searching for employment again.

His return to health sadly coincided with his mother's fall from it. What started as a cough, innocuous enough at first that he barely questioned her assertions that it was just a passing cold, had become progressively hacking and violent as the fever and night sweats took hold, and when he secured a job as a junior porter at the train station in nearby Upper Blinkhorn shortly after his eighteenth birthday, she was an emaciated shadow of herself.

On the Friday of his second week at the station, Stephen cycled home with the late afternoon sun on his face. The countryside had at last roused from its slumber in a single, glorious outpouring of colour, and the air was filled with birdsong and the scent of freshly mown grass.

Upon reaching the cottage, he leaned his bicycle against the low stone wall, latched the gate behind him and began up the path, the jacket of his Lancashire and Yorkshire Railway uniform slung over his shoulder. As he stepped through the door, he was greeted by an eerie silence.

'Mam?' he called. 'Where are you, Mam?'

He opened the door to the drawing room and found her seated in her favourite armchair, her head lolling to one side and her fingers, scrawny as twigs, clenched around a blood-soaked handkerchief. When she did not stir, he rushed over, crouched beside her and shook her gently by the shoulders. Without a sound, his mother slumped lifelessly into his arms.

Letting out a cry that seemed to emanate from the very base of his stomach, he eased her body back and went to stand. His head suddenly throbbed and his vision became spotted by stars. He felt his knees tremble beneath him as his memory flitted back to the moment he had spotted Joseph's oilskin hat bobbing up and down on the surface of the fiery sea. The impotent frustration was too much to bear.

As he took a step back, Stephen felt himself falling. He blinked, but instead of hitting the floor was, without warning, back in the saddle of his bicycle, the wind in his face as he sped along the road in the direction of Upper Blinkhorn.

The shock of the transition sent him snaking into a ditch, where the front wheel caught, catapulting him over the handlebars and into the bordering hedgerow. Dazed, he disentangled himself, clambered out and, after brushing a few of the larger items of foliage from the folds of his uniform, assessed the damage. The bicycle appeared miraculously unscathed, as was Stephen, aside from a few scratches to his face and hands.

As he straightened the handlebars, a thought occurred. He pulled out his father's gold fob watch and flipped it open. It was just after half past seven and, in light of the fact he had the weekend off, this could only mean one thing: he had been transported back to that morning, less than fifteen minutes after he had left the cottage, in fact, at which time his mother had been very much alive.

Without a moment's hesitation, he jumped in the saddle and turned towards home again, pumping the peddles with all his might. By the time he reached the house of Dr Shuttleworth, the village doctor, his face was streaming with perspiration. He ditched his bicycle by the roadside and hammered on the door with his fist.

Shuttleworth opened wearing his undershirt, his braces hanging by his knees and a cup of tea in his hand. 'Stephen?' he said, blinking through the lenses of his spectacles. 'It's not eight o'clock yet, son. What can I do for you?'

'It's my mam,' Stephen said. 'Please, sir, it's urgent. She needs your help.'

With a nod, Shuttleworth went to fetch his case and then followed Stephen on foot, wheezing as he struggled to keep up.

'Mam?' Stephen called as he burst through the door of their cottage.

There was a hacking from the direction of the drawing room. He followed the sound and found her in her armchair again.

'Stevie?' she said, and slid her handkerchief into her sleeve in an attempt to conceal the bloodstains. 'What are you doing back so soon, flower?'

'I—'

At that moment Shuttleworth arrived. He took one look at Stephen's mother and placed a hand on the young man's shoulder. 'Why don't you give us a minute, eh? I'll wager she could do with a cup of tea.'

Stephen nodded, returned to the kitchen and filled the kettle. It had yet to boil when the doctor stepped out of the drawing room, shaking his head.

'Well?' Stephen demanded.

'She's badly, son. It's consumption, and quite advanced by my reckoning.'

'Please, there must be something you can do.'

Shuttleworth dipped his head. 'Not at this stage, my boy. I'm sorry, but she'll likely not make it through the weekend.'

Stephen nodded and returned to the drawing room, a hollow sensation gnawing at his insides. 'Why didn't you tell me it was so serious?' he asked, kneeling by his mother's chair.

'Didn't want you fretting, flower,' she said. 'If it's my time to meet my maker then so be it. I'll be with your brother and father soon enough.'

Stephen had never felt so alone in all his life and, despite his best efforts to stay strong for her, let out a sob. 'Please, Mam,' he said. 'I can't lose you too.'

'Hush now,' she said, and stroked his hair. 'God has a plan for you, Stephen. You have a good heart, my love. Follow it and everything will work out in the end, of that I have no doubt.'

'I will, Mam,' he said. Hugging her, he closed his eyes. 'I love you.'

'And I love you,' she said.

All of a sudden there was a lurch like the sensation of falling just before one drifts off to sleep. Stephen opened his eyes and saw that he was flat on his back on the rug. The light shining in through the windows had dimmed and changed direction, and his mother's body sat slumped in the armchair, her head to one side and a blood-soaked handkerchief in her hand.

He shivered at the sudden drop in temperature and clambered to his feet. Although he had not been able to save his mother, he had at least been given a chance to say goodbye, and the purpose of his funny turns was, perhaps, a little clearer.

2

Present Day

Sam slid his shoes off the second he was through the front door and raced upstairs before anyone could intercept him. Once his bedroom door was closed, he wedged a chair under the handle, which was the closest thing he had to a lock, then sat on the corner of his bed and pulled the bottle of Tetradyamide out of his backpack. He could feel another headache coming on and, staring down, realised his hands were shaking at the enormity of what had happened.

Malcolm Fairview was dead…

…and Sam had found him and done nothing.

Well, not entirely nothing: he'd called an ambulance and taken the bottle of Tetradyamide before running away.

He shoved the bottle back in his bag, burrowed under the duvet and hugged his knees to his chest. Almost immediately an image popped into his mind: Fairview on his back, dead eyes staring blankly at the ceiling. Feeling the sting of bile at the back of his throat, Sam let out a shudder. In hindsight he obviously should have waited until the ambulance arrived, and it was difficult to escape the conclusion that the things he had seen and done in that alternative December had changed him so drastically he couldn't tell right from wrong anymore.

All of a sudden there was a knock at the door. He poked his head out from under his covers to see the handle move half an inch before striking the back of the chair.

'Sam?' Chrissie called from the landing. 'That you?'

'Er, yeah,' he called back. 'Who else would it be?'

There was a pause, then: 'Why are you back from the library so early? I wasn't expecting you till after lunch. And why won't your door open?'

'I'm in bed. I didn't feel well and—'

'Not another seizure, was it?'

'No no, nothing like that. I felt a bit gippy, that's all. Probably just my epilepsy medication. It gives me a funny tummy sometimes.' He bit his lip, hoping his voice hadn't wavered as his lies stacked up on one another like a house of cards. 'I'm going to try and go back to sleep for a bit, all right?'

'Okay,' Chrissie said. There was a moment of silence, followed by the sound of her footsteps retreating down the stairs.

Sam waited for a while before taking the Tetra-dyamide out again. Resting back against his pillows, he turned the chipped brown bottle around and around in his hands. Eventually he opened the lid, shook a sticky little pill out and dropped it into his mouth. Grimacing at the taste, he washed it down with a gulp of water from the glass beside his bed, and within a few seconds the throbbing at the back of his head had receded.

Once the drug took effect he should probably return to the night before and warn Fairview. But then what would he say, *Oh, by the way, you might want to be careful because you're going to drop dead tomorrow morning*? Apart from convincing Fairview that Sam was a crackpot, the only thing that was likely to achieve would be to ruin the man's last night alive.

Malcolm Fairview had been in his mid-to-late forties – perfect heart attack age, really – and, judging by his build, hadn't exercised much. The only things that could have saved him were a low-cholesterol diet and years of gym sessions, and while Tetradyamide made Sam powerful, there were limits to what even he could do. Besides, warning Fairview could well prevent the scientist from inviting Sam over that morning, which would in turn remove the bottle of pills from Sam's possession and create a new timeline in which he would be unable to put things right.

So, then, although sad, Fairview's death was probably unavoidable, and at the moment there were bigger fish to fry. Although Esteban Haufner had since vanished, Sam knew exactly where he would be on the day of his dad's funeral, which also happened to be the day of the Thames House bombing. It seemed feasible that, if he could return to that point and prevent the bombing once again, he might then be able to save the lives of those killed while simultaneously gaining revenge for his father. In doing so, however, there remained a distinct possibility that he might create a new timeline identical to the one he had altered on Christmas Eve. Even if he tipped off the police anonymously this time around, McHayden and the Tempus Project would still be out there, and finding himself back in a reality in which Chrissie was dead and he was a prisoner wasn a risk Sam couldn't take. In fact, so much seemed to hinge on the day of the bombing that it was starting to feel like a sort of temporal crossroads, and he was too afraid to return there in case he made a mistake that he couldn't later correct.

He let out a sigh and looked inside the bottle. It was difficult to estimate how many pills it contained, but it seem to be more or less a hundred, which meant more or less a hundred opportunities to see into the future or alter the past. There had to be some other way to stop Haufner, one that didn't involve such disastrous consequences. Unfortunately Sam couldn't see what that was at the moment, but he had plenty of other problems that should be far simpler to solve.

A warm shiver suddenly danced up his spine, and the walls of his bedroom became tinged with colour. Letting out a deep breath, he closed his eyes. Finding a way to pay for his mum's treatment in America and keep a roof over his family's heads might be a start, as would finding Eva again. He would just have to work his way up to the Haufner problem and then, once that was solved, perhaps travel back a couple months and advise Fairview to book a check-up with his cardiologist.

3

Frances lifted the line of police tape for Campbell to duck under and then trotted down the steps to the basement flat after him. Once inside, a forensics officer handed them each a set of white overalls. After pulling these on over their clothes and sliding on vinyl booties and latex gloves, they followed the man to a darkened bedroom off the main hall.

As they entered, Bikram Kaur, Lead Scenes of Crime Officer, turned and lowered his camera. Instead of a hood, he wore a blue turban and a hair net over his thick beard.

'Ah, Detective Campbell, Sergeant Hinds! What took you?'

Frances flinched internally, as she did whenever addressed by her lowly new rank. In the aftermath of the Thames House bombing, SO15 – otherwise known as Counter Terrorism Command – had been subjected to an independent investigation as Whitehall sought a scapegoat on whom to direct the finger of blame. The investigation was a whitewash and SO15 had been officially disbanded the week before Christmas, with a new cross-departmental Counter Terrorism Force set up in its place. With the exception of those with friends in the right places, most senior officers had been stripped of their posts. Due to her perceived failures in the Flight 0368 case, a crime for which Esteban Haufner was also believed to be responsible, Frances had been one of the first in the firing line, and was offered the choice of handing in her resignation or accepting a demotion. After devoting most of her adult life to policing, she'd had no intention of resigning, so had accepted the latter option through gritted teeth, effectively negating the decade of hard graft it had taken to her rise to the rank of Inspector.

'We've been busy,' Campbell replied gruffly. 'No rest for the wicked. Or those trying to catch them.'

'What've we got?' Frances asked, trying to focus on the job in hand as she stepped around the bed.

Kaur nodded towards the body of a middle-aged man lying spread-eagled on the floor. 'Malcolm Fairview. Forty-six years old. Divorced. No children. A former government scientist, recently made redundant. History of angina.'

'The cause of death?'

'A cardiac arrest, it appears.'

'Then why are we here?'

Kaur crouched and, with a knowing smile, gestured to a small dot on the side of Fairview's neck. 'A puncture wound,' he explained. 'The absence of scabbing indicates it was delivered immediately prior to death. Looks like a toxin was administered by injection, possibly cyanide in light of the cardiac arrest. The toxicology report will tell us one way or the other.' He stood again, peeled off his latex gloves, took a packet of mints from his pocket and popped one in his mouth. 'There are no visible defence wounds and the initial inspection of the flat shows no evidence of forced entry, all of which points towards the likelihood that the killer was known to his victim.'

'What about the time of death?' Campbell asked.

'The body temperature is still relatively high, and rigor mortis and lividity are only just setting in, which rules out anything longer than a few hours. Best guess, I'd say somewhere around ten this morning.'

'That's right about the time the call to emergency services was clocked.' Campbell pulled his notepad out, opened it and tapped a page with his finger. 'Yep, logged at 10:11, lasting twenty-eight seconds.'

'Can you get us a recording?' Frances asked.

'They're already sending one over.'

'Good.' She turned back to Kaur. 'Anything else you can tell us?'

'Plenty.' He crunched his mint between his teeth and swallowed the broken fragments. 'This way.'

They followed him out of the bedroom, down the hall and into a living room where two members of his team were still dusting for prints. At the far end was a window overlooking the back garden and, off to one side, an archway leading to a kitchen, where two mugs of cold, dark tea sat stewing on the worktop.

Kaur knelt next to a large black crate in the middle of the Persian carpet and pulled out the handset of a telephone sealed in a plastic evidence bag. 'We've found two sets of prints in the flat, the majority belonging to the victim and the other an unknown.' He turned the bagged telephone over, handed it to Campbell and pointed to a strip of clear plastic covering the impression of a hand. 'The unknown. There's another handset in the kitchen, but this was in the same room as the body. We've lifted a complete thumbprint and the first three fingers of the right hand. We also found more prints on the handle of the back door, which was left unlocked.'

'Probably how the killer made his way out,' Campbell said, and passed the phone to Frances.

After studying the prints for a moment, she handed it back to Kaur.

'There's more,' he said, and reached into the box again, pulling out a larger bag containing a laptop. 'Julie found this in a flowerbed at the bottom of the garden, next to a broken trellis fence. It's password protected, meaning we'll have to pass it over to Cybercrimes to get it unlocked. Normally takes a few days.'

'Good work,' Campbell said. 'Let us know when you get the toxicology report back, or if anything else turns up, will you?'

'Naturally,' Kaur said, and popped another mint in his mouth. 'We do all the leg work and you lot take the credit, as per usual.'

After changing out of their overalls, Frances and Campbell left the flat and climbed back in the car. In addition to the affront to her self-esteem, one of the principle drawbacks of Frances's demotion was that it had brought her into close contact with Mark Campbell again. The pair had been classmates as cadets. In those days she had been the star of the class, often helping him with assignments, but now, as if to add insult to injury, he was her boss.

'So,' he said, starting the engine, 'any ideas?'

Frances buckled her seatbelt and drummed her fingers against her chin. 'Did you notice the teas on the kitchen counter?'

'What, you think the victim was expecting someone?'

'Given what Kaur told us, I think it's quite possible that the victim let his killer into the flat willingly. Then at some point our man catches Fairview unawares, injects him with a toxin and calls emergency services. Perhaps he was disturbed, because he leaves in a hurry, fleeing the scene via the back door and dropping the laptop as he escapes over the wall at the end of the garden.'

'Sounds plausible enough,' he said and performed a U-turn. 'The thing I don't get is, why call emergency services?'

'A good question,' she said. 'And I suspect answering it will go a long way to finding our killer. In the meantime we could begin canvassing neighbours to see if anyone saw or heard anything. My gut feeling is that this may have something to do with Fairview's former employment. After all, why else would anyone take his laptop?'

'Burglary?' he suggested. 'Believe me, I've seen people killed for less.'

Frances thought it unlikely, but decided to keep her own counsel. 'I'd call the ex-wife in for questioning, too,' she said. 'Nine times out of ten a bitter spouse is involved.'

'Good idea.'

At that moment Campbell's phone chimed. He pulled over, tapped the screen and held it to his ear.

After a minute he looked up. 'It's the recording of the call to emergency services,' he said, and passed the phone over.

Frances heard the operator say, 'Emergency services, which service do you require?'

'Ambulance,' the voice of a young man said. 'I need an ambulance.'

'One moment please. And your location?'

'Er, 47C Beaumont Crescent, Notting Hill. I just stopped by to see someone and…and I think he's dead.'

'Okay, a unit has been dispatched. And your name is?' A stretch of silence, then: 'Sir, are you still there? I need a name.'

The recording ended with a rustle and a click as the caller hung up.

'What's the matter?' Campbell asked as Frances passed his phone back.

'I could be wrong,' she said, 'but I think I recognise that voice from somewhere.'

4

'That was never a red card,' Lewis said, flinging the TV remote across the settee in disgust. 'He barely even touched the guy.'

'Red card,' Conner, his little brother, repeated from the armchair beside him. 'Red-card-red-card-red-card...'

The doorbell rang. Lewis heaved himself up and went to answer it. Sam was standing on the front step, grinning like a madman. Even though it was chucking it down outside, he didn't have his hood up and his hair was drenched and flat to his forehead.

'All right, mate,' Lewis said. 'You want a towel or something?'

'Hmmm?'

'For your hair. It is raining, you realise.'

Sam rubbed his hand over his hair, lowered it for inspection and looked genuinely surprised to find water there. He looked up again and laughed. 'No, I'm fine.'

'If you say so.' Lewis stepped to one side and ushered him in. 'How'd it go on Thursday then? That Fairview bloke give you what you wanted?'

Sam rubbed his nose and looked away, then unzipped his coat and pulled a brown bottle and a small, wire-bound notepad from the inside pocket.

'That's it? That's what all the fuss was about?'

'Tetradyamide,' Sam said, shaking the bottle to make a rattling sound.

'And he just gave it to you, no questions asked?'

'Er, you could say that.'

'And he's definitely not going to press charges over what happened with Lance?'

'I can categorically promise you he won't be pressing charges.' Sam put the bottle and notepad in his trouser pockets, then took his coat off and hung it on the end of the banister. 'So, are you watching the football?'

'Wish I wasn't,' Lewis said. 'West Ham are two nil down and just had a man sent off. It isn't even half time yet and the game's as good as over.'

'I wouldn't be so sure.'

Lewis paused in the doorway to the lounge and gave his friend a scathing look. 'To be honest, that just shows how little you know about football, Sam.'

As they entered, Conner looked up from the settee, gave them a gap-toothed smile and waved the remote. Instead of the lunchtime derby between West Ham United and Arsenal, the television now showed a bunch of people dressed in dinosaur costumes dancing around a papier-mâché volcano to sickeningly upbeat music.

Lewis lunged for the remote, but Conner ducked, rolled across the cushions, drew himself up and then jumped the gap between the settee and armchair.

'Lewis, Lewis, you can't catch me! Lewis, Lewis, you smell like wee!'

'That's it, you've had it!' Lewis hurled himself at his brother, but again Conner was too fast and dived onto the floor, somersaulting across the carpet before leaping to his feet again by the door.

Sam pulled a pound coin from his pocket. 'This is for you, Conner. *If* we can have the remote back.'

Conner tilted his head to one side, weighing the offer.

'And there'll be another pound after the match is over,' Sam said, 'if you go upstairs and play with your toys and leave me and Lewis to watch it in peace.'

'*Two pounds*? To go and play with my toys?'

'That's right – one now, one later.'

Conner dropped the remote and snatched the coin from Sam's hand. As he disappeared up the stairs, Lewis heard him shout, 'Muppets!'

Sam scooped up the remote from the floor and passed it over. 'Conner's growing fast,' he said.

'Tell me about it.' Lewis flopped onto the settee and changed the channel back. 'Anyway, why the sudden interest in football? I thought you always said it was boring.'

'It is,' Sam said. He sat next to Lewis and pulled the notepad out again. 'Unless, of course, you happen to know the result already.'

'Even I can tell you that. Away win.'

'No.' Sam squinted down at the page. 'Arsenal have their goalkeeper sent off and give away a penalty on 43 minutes, which Taylor scores, making it 1-2 at halftime. Taylor scores two more goals in the second half, on 65 and 86 minutes, and West Ham go on to win 3-2.'

Lewis snorted and glanced at the clock in the corner of the screen, which read forty-one minutes and fifty-six seconds. 'Yeah, right,' he said. 'A Taylor hat trick? He hasn't even scored this season. I'd love to see the odds on *that* happening!'

'Why don't we check then?' Sam dipped his head towards the family PC in the corner of the room. 'You know, on your dad's online betting account.'

'You've got to be joking! He'll skin me alive if he finds out I've been at that again. Remember what I told you about the last time?'

'It won't be like the last time, Lewis. This is a sure thing.'

'Now you're beginning to sound like my old man. Trust me, Sam, gambling is a mug's game. There's only one sure thing, and that's that there's no such thing as a "sure thing".'

They were interrupted by a whistle on the TV, followed by a loud cheer. Lewis turned to the screen to see the referee point to the penalty spot and then, brandishing a red card, march over to the Arsenal keeper. The time on the clock read forty-three minutes and twelve seconds.

'See, what did I tell you?' Sam said

Lewis continued to stare, his mouth open as Taylor stepped up, slotted the penalty into the bottom-left corner and then wheeled away, punching the air.

'That's impossible,' he said, and with immense effort closed his mouth.

'Not impossible,' Sam said, 'just highly unlikely.'

'But *how*? How could you know that?'

Sam patted the trouser pocket containing the bottle. 'After I got the pills on Thursday, I travelled forward to this evening, saw *Match of the Day* – which was like watching paint dry, by the way – and then returned to the present after each match and wrote down the result, times of the goals and names of the scorers. Apparently they give you better odds for stuff like that. It was pretty straightforward, really.'

The referee's whistle sounded again for halftime. Lewis watched as the West Ham players trotted into the tunnel with newfound energy, whilst most of the Arsenal team stayed on the pitch to berate the referee.

'Fair enough,' he said. 'I'll go switch the computer on.'

An hour later, Lewis and Sam were shoulder-to-shoulder at the computer desk, looking at an overview of his dad's online betting account. The section that had previously displayed an amount of £238.14 now listed a balance of £7,858.62. Behind them, the muted TV showed the West Ham players celebrating the most improbable of comebacks.

'So, do you believe me now?' Sam asked.

Lewis pressed a finger to the monitor, causing the image to ripple. The thing felt too solid to be a figment of his imagination. 'My eyes say yes, but my brain says no.'

Sam leaned back and grinned. 'I know the feeling.'

'But I don't get it. You say you've been able to do all this since waking up from your coma, so why only tell me last week?'

'Remember, I'm the Sam from a parallel universe, right? What you're talking about, that was a different me, at least between my dad's funeral and Christmas Eve. In this timeline all that stuff with the Tempus Project never happened and, technically speaking, Thursday would have been the first time I'd ever taken Tetradyamide. The reason the other Sam didn't tell you about it was…well, because there wasn't anything to tell.'

'I see, I think,' Lewis said, wondering which version of his friend he preferred. 'You do seem a bit, um, different.'

'What I'm trying to say, Lewis, is that in the timeline only I remember – *my* timeline – you knew pretty much everything all along. And, believe it or not, when things went wrong, you sort of saved the day. If it wasn't for you, Chrissie would still be dead and I'd be strapped to a trolley in a cell.'

'Me? Save the day? Well now, that I can believe.' Lewis puffed out his chest. Perhaps new-Sam wasn't so bad after all, and he certainly knew some useful tricks.

Sam began to laugh, then stopped abruptly. 'To be honest, it's a bit of a relief having someone to talk to again. Listen, about Malcolm Fairview, he didn't exactly *give* me the Tetradyamide.'

'What, you nicked it?'

'No! It's just, when I got to his flat, he was, well, sort of dead.'

'*Dead?*'

Sam nodded. 'He was lying on the floor, like he'd just collapsed. He suffered from angina, so it was a heart attack, I think. I tried calling an ambulance and then, when I saw the Tetradyamide, I…just sort of took it and left. I know it was wrong, and I was thinking about what I could do to save him, but…' He trailed off, his gaze flicking back to the monitor.

Lewis glanced across too, blinking as he took in the balance of his dad's account again. 'A heart attack, you say?'

'I think so.'

'Probably not much you could have done about it then.'

'That's what I thought.'

'But you've got the Tetradyamide, at least.'

'Yeah, there's that.'

Lewis rubbed his chin. 'There are six more games kicking off at three o'clock. You have the results, yes?'

'Right here,' Sam said, and gave his notebook a little wave.

'Which means we can place bets on them all, if we're quick about it,' Lewis said. 'That seven thousand is just the beginning. The bigger the bets we place, the bigger the—'

He was interrupted by the sound of someone belching and turned to see his father in the doorway.

'What're you two plonkers looking so guilty for?' his father asked, scratching the hairy underside of his belly beneath his work shirt.

'Um, nothing,' Lewis said and hit the standby button on the monitor. 'Sam was just leaving, weren't you, Sam?'

Sam made a show of checking his watch. 'Is that the time? Wow, I really should be—'

'Oh no you don't!' Lewis's father stepped around them and pressed the button on the monitor again, causing it to flicker back into life. 'Thought as much, you little so-and-sos. How much of my hard-earned cash have you squandered this time? I can promise you one thing, you'll be paying back every last...' He fell silent as he registered the balance of his account. 'Well I'll be a monkey's uncle,' he said, turning back. 'How the bloody hell did you manage that?'

5

Sam jumped to his feet and stuffed his notepad into his back pocket. 'Sorry, it was all my idea. Please, Justin, don't be angry with Lewis, I can explain.'

'*You can*?' Lewis asked, blinking at him.

Justin scratched his beer gut again, lowered his backside onto the armrest of the sofa and folded his arms. 'Go ahead, sonny Jim. I'd absolutely love to know how there's nearly eight grand in my account. I've been placing bets for nearly twenty-five years, and this is by far my biggest win. And all without me actually doing anything.'

Sam stared back for a few seconds and then shook his head and sighed. 'The thing is, Justin, we recently found out the insurance company are cancelling my dad's life insurance policy over a missed payment. The direct debit for the mortgage goes out next week, and unless I find a way to pay, it's going to bounce. There's also this new treatment in America which I think might help my mum, but it's expensive. I got this hot tip about the West Ham match from someone at college, so I asked Lewis to help me place a bet. He only logged into your account because I made him do it. Please, if anyone's going to get in trouble here, it should be me.'

Lewis's dad held a hand up to silence him. 'All right, enough of the sob story,' he said. 'I know you've been through a lot recently, Sam, but if you needed money, you should've just asked. What you've done is technically theft—'

'Hang on,' Lewis said. 'How can it be theft if there's more money in your account than to begin with?'

Justin turned a death-stare on him. 'All right, smart-arse, not theft exactly, but it's…it's not right, is it? For starters neither of you is old enough to gamble. And what if you'd lost, what then? If you'd cleaned me out there'd be plenty of trouble to go round for everyone, believe you me.'

'But that didn't happen,' Sam said.

'But you didn't know for sure it wouldn't, did you?'

Sam open and closed his mouth, realising there was nothing he could say without giving the game away. After a while he shook his head. 'No, I suppose not.'

'Anyway, be that as it may, none of it answers the question of what I should do with the seven-and-a-half grand's worth of winnings sitting in my account that aren't mine. How much did you say Rebecca's treatment cost?'

'Fifty thousand,' Sam said. 'That's dollars, not pounds.'

Justin baulked. 'Well, I'll transfer it into your bank account this afternoon, but I think you're going to need a few more of them "hot tips".'

'You'll let me keep it?'

'I can't very well go lecturing the two of you on doing the right thing and then keep it myself, now can I?' Justin stood and tucked his shirt into his belt. 'It might not be fifty thousand, Sam, but it's a start, and it should at least cover your mortgage for a few months. Lewis, go and get a pen and paper from the kitchen and I'll take his bank details.'

'Okay,' Lewis said, and disappeared into the hall.

'Thanks, Justin, I appreciate it,' Sam said. 'If there's anything I can do, just say.'

Lewis's dad raised one corner of his mouth in a lopsided smile. 'Now that you mention it, there might be something. This hot tip of yours, I'd like to know a bit more about it.'

Sam hooked his finger and tugged at the collar of his jumper. 'I...er...there's not much to tell, really. He's just this kid at college. Josh...or Jake, I think. I hardly know him, really. The other day I overheard him talking with someone else, saying that his uncle had this tip about the West Ham game, that it would finish 3-2, so I thought I'd give it a shot. Like I said, I was desperate.'

'The thing about betting on football, Sam, is that you can have a good idea about who's going to win based on form, or even hazard a guess that there might be a lot of goals, but unless a game's rigged, I can't for the life of me think of a way of knowing for sure what the final score will be.' The smile on Justin's face had grown into something closer to a smirk. 'Is that what happened?' he asked. 'You somehow found out a Premier League game was rigged and decided to cash in? It would take some pretty powerful people to pull off something like that.'

'I...I wouldn't know anything about that,' Sam said, suddenly desperate to get out of there. 'Like I said, I just overheard some kid at college. It was probably dumb luck that I didn't lose your money. I'm sorry, it won't happen again.'

'If you say so,' Justin said, although his tone made Sam suspect the matter was far from over.

At that moment Lewis returned, clutching a pen and paper. Justin blinked for the first time in what felt like ages, the smirk vanishing from his face.

Sam scribbled his account number and sort code, then passed the sheet over. 'Thanks again,' he said. 'I should probably get going now.'

'No problem.' Justin folded the piece of paper, slid it into his shirt pocket and winked. 'Remember to let me know if you get any other hot tips, okay?'

'Er, yeah, sure thing,' Sam said and followed his friend into the hall.

'What was all that about?' Lewis asked as he opened the front door onto a day that hadn't improved a bit since Sam had arrived.

'I think he suspects something,' Sam said, and slid his arms into the damp sleeves of his coat. 'He wanted to know where I got the tip.'

'Yeah, good thinking back there, by the way. I was wondering how you were going to explain that.'

'I'm getting pretty good at improvising,' Sam said. *And lying.*

'Doesn't look like we'll be able to use his account again, though.'

'He already thinks I'm involved in rigging Premier League matches. I don't think I'll be able to improvise my way out of that one.'

'What about the three o'clock games? They'll be starting any minute.'

Sam shrugged. At least he now knew his plan worked, and his family were in no immediate danger of losing their house. There might even be enough money left over for a ticket to Montclair, assuming he'd ever have the nerve to set foot on a plane again.

'There'll be other games,' he said. 'I counted the pills yesterday and there are ninety-seven in the bottle, not including the one I took on Thursday. From what I understand, there are fixtures pretty much every weekend.'

'And weekdays too, sometimes,' Lewis said. 'It doesn't just have to be football either, there are loads of sports we could bet on.'

'Except we can't use your dad's account anymore.'

'No.'

'And neither of us is old enough to gamble.'

'No.'

Sam sighed. 'What we need is someone who's older than eighteen. Someone we can trust.'

They stood in silence for a few seconds until Lewis clicked his fingers. 'I think I know just the person!'

6

One week later

It was Friday evening, over a week since Malcolm Fairview's death, and Frances was sat hunched at her desk at New Scotland Yard. So far little about the case made any sense. They had called in Cynthia Fairview, the victim's ex-wife, for questioning on the day of the murder, but the woman had appeared convincingly distraught and, in any case, had a watertight alibi. The second set of fingerprints found at the crime scene had drawn a blank when put through the database, however an elderly neighbour reported seeing a young man loitering at the scene close to the time of death. And then, a few days ago, the toxicology reports from the autopsy had come back, indicating a level of potassium cyanide in the victim's blood consistent with the cardiac arrest that had killed him.

In Frances's view it had all the hallmarks of a professional hit, adding further weight to her theory that the murder was in some way connected to Fairview's past employment, but when she'd contacted the Security Service for further information, her requests were flatly rebuffed with the words 'classified' and 'top secret'.

Most perplexing of all was the call to emergency services. She had listened to the recording so many times she could recite it from memory, and on each occasion had been unable to shake the feeling that she recognised the caller's voice from somewhere. Unfortunately, no matter how hard she wracked her brain, she could neither work out where from, nor construct a plausible explanation as to why the killer would call for an ambulance before fleeing the scene.

Leaning back in her chair, she linked her hands behind her head. It was getting late and she was due at her brother's house for a dinner party in less than an hour. She strongly suspected it was another of her sister-in-law's attempts to fix her up, the latest being the time Debbie had introduced her to Colin, a History professor at the university where she worked. On top of his rampant halitosis, Colin was well into his fifties and had spent most of the evening talking about his research into British warships of the colonial era. Needless to say, they hadn't hit it off and, bored out of her mind, Frances had drunk too much white wine and done little to hide her displeasure at the potential match.

Resolved to give the next blind date more of a chance, she shut her computer down and had just pulled her coat on when the phone on her desk started ringing.

'Hinds?' the voice on the other end of the line asked. 'It's Kaur. I have some news.'

'You do?'

'Cybercrimes have unlocked Fairview's laptop. There were several dozen encrypted files, mostly chemical formulas that go way over my head, if I'm honest. I've just emailed copies over, and I'll have the laptop couriered to your office this evening.'

'I'll be here,' Frances said, and booted up her computer before returning to her chair.

'There was one more thing.' He made a slurping noise that sounded a lot like he was sucking on a mint. 'Not sure how relevant it is, but seeing as how you used to work at CT Command, I thought you might be interested. According to his browsing history, Fairview accessed several websites the evening before he was killed, all relating to the sabotage of British Airways Flight 0368 last year. You were involved in the investigation, weren't you?'

'I was,' she said, a sudden chill sweeping through her. 'And I think you might be on to something, Bikram. Can you send me a list of the sites?'

'Will do,' he said and hung up.

As Frances lowered the phone, Campbell strode past, an oversized teddy bear under his arm. 'You still here?' he asked. 'It's Georgia's fifth birthday, so we're taking the kids out for pizza and ice-cream.'

'Ring and tell them you're going be late,' she said. 'I know who made the call to emergency services.'

7

The three partners and co-conspirators sat facing one another in a triangle; Sam on the corner of his bed, Lewis on a stool at the computer desk and Lance cross-legged on the carpet. Last weekend Lance had agreed to join their scheme and set up an online betting account, after which Sam had travelled forward to Wednesday night and found out the result of the midweek match between Liverpool and West Bromwich Albion (a 1-0 home win). With that bet they had more than trebled the £7,600 that Justin had transferred into Sam's bank account, which, mortgage payments aside, left him almost halfway to paying for his mum's treatment.

The following day Lance had handed in his resig-nation at the fast food restaurant where he worked, spent his final wage packet on a diamond ring and then proposed to Chrissie, which, it turned out, had proved to be the ultimate distraction in preventing her from asking awkward questions.

'There are six games tomorrow and four more on Sunday,' Lewis said, scrolling through a webpage that listed the coming weekend's fixtures. 'That gives us ten chances to multiply our money.' He turned in his seat and grinned. 'If everything goes to plan, by this time next week we'll be millionaires!'

'You mean Lance will be a millionaire,' Sam corrected.

'Yeah, about that,' Lewis said. 'I've been looking into setting up a private limited company, with Lance as the Director and you and me listed as employees. We covered it all in Business Studies last term. With Lance as the figurehead and you predicting the future, Sam, we could diversify our interests, moving into currency trading and the stock market. It's still gambling, really, but with the prospect of better returns.'

'And what's your role in all this?' Lance asked.

'*Me*? I'm the brains of the operation, obviously! I was thinking it might even be sensible to make a loss on some ventures so as not to attract interest.'

Sam stood, crossed the room and opened the bottom drawer of his wardrobe, where his bottle of Tetradyamide was hidden in a balled pair of socks. There were now ninety-six pills, which, while it might seem like a lot, was hardly an unlimited supply. Appealing as Lewis's plan was, once Sam's financial problems were solved, his mum was better and he had Eva back, there were probably better uses for it than simply lining their own pockets. For one thing Esteban Haufner was still out there and might be preparing to strike again. Sam was, in fact, counting on it. McHayden had once described him as 'the ultimate defence against threats to the nation', and with

Tetradyamide in his possession he would be ready and waiting should Haufner stick his neck out.

'So that's it then?' Lance asked, springing dexterously to his feet and eyeing the bottle in Sam's hand. 'The drug that makes all this possible?'

'Yeah,' Sam said, and tightened his grip around it.

'Let's have a look then.'

Sam licked his lips and gazed down at Lance's outstretched hand. The bottle of Tetradyamide was *his*, and the thought of anyone else touching it gave him an odd, twitchy feeling. But then he was probably being irrational; if he couldn't trust Lance then whom could he trust? He nodded and slowly, almost reluctantly, passed the bottle over.

'Tarter...tetra...tetradynamo...' Lance mumbled, squinting at the faded label.

'Tetradyamide.'

'And what happens when you take it?'

Sam scratched his head. 'Well, normally it takes a few minutes to kick in, then I start to feel, I don't know, sort of funny. It's like time gets disjointed, frozen moments instead of a continuous flow, sort of like the pages in a book. When that happens I can choose when and where to send my mind, same way as you'd flick back and forwards through a book.'

'Like an out of body experience?' Lance twisted the cap off the bottle and shook a pill into his hand. 'Sounds way cool. Apart from the smell, I'm almost tempted to take one.'

'Don't!' Sam yelled, surprised at the volume of his own voice. 'Sorry, it's just that's all I've got. They're too valuable to waste, Lance. On you it would only slow down your perception of time and make it look like Lewis and I were moving really, really slowly, but to us it would look like you were moving really fast, if you see what I

Damian Knight

mean. It's only because of *this*,' he tapped the scar behind his ear, 'that I can do what I can do.'

'What happens to your body when your mind is, you know, *away*?' Lewis asked. 'Is it like when you collapsed at your dad's funeral?'

Sam frowned. He had been sitting down on every occasion he'd taken Tetradyamide and had always come around in the same place. 'I'm not sure,' he said. 'Could be, although I don't remember biting my tongue or anything like that, so maybe my body just goes limp. Why don't you stick around for a bit and see for yourself? I'd be interested to know, now you mention it.'

'Sounds kind of vulnerable,' Lewis said. 'You know, to tied shoelaces and marker-pen moustaches.'

'That's not funny,' Sam said. 'Lance, can I have the bottle back now? I'm getting nervous you might drop it or something.'

With a sigh, Lance returned the cap and handed the bottle back. 'You know, I quite like the idea of making time slow down. Maybe I can give it a try when you see that scientist dude again and get some more.'

'There won't be any more,' Sam said, shooting Lewis a nervous glance. 'Listen, Lance, before we go any further, there's something I should probably tell—'

He was interrupted by the doorbell.

'Expecting anyone?' Lewis asked.

Sam shook his head, wrapped the socks around the bottle once again and returned it to the drawer in his wardrobe. After removing the chair from under the door handle, he poked his head out. The shapes of several people were moving about on the other side of the frosted glass panel in the front door. The bell sounded again, and his grandmother came scurrying out of the kitchen to answer it.

134

Sam stepped out onto the landing. Standing on the other side of the door was a person he had last spoken to on the day of his father's funeral, or, more actually, in this timeline hadn't.

'Inspector Hinds,' he said. 'I haven't seen you since...'

'The day you completed the facial composite. And it's Sergeant now.' She stepped over the threshold, pulled a folded sheet of paper from her pocket and handed it to Sam's grandmother. 'This is a search warrant, madam. It's a criminal offence to obstruct us in the line of our duties.'

'What's going on?' Sam asked. He glanced over his shoulder to see Lewis and Lance emerge from his bedroom.

Hinds cleared her throat. 'Samuel Rayner, I'm arresting you for the murder of Malcolm Fairview. You do not have to say anything, but it may harm your defence if you fail to mention anything while questioned that you later rely on in court.'

Chapter IV

Rough Justice

1

August 1927

It was a warm, late-summer's morning and the country-side around Upper Blinkhorn station baked in the rising sun. Not long after arriving at work, Stephen was called into Phillip Deacon's office and found him scraping out the blackened contents of his pipe.

'Have a seat, lad,' the stationmaster said, angling the mouthpiece at a chair on the other side of his desk. 'There's summat I wish to discuss.'

During eight years under Deacon's tutelage, Stephen had risen from the rank of junior porter to that of assistant stationmaster, second in command only to the man himself. Deacon had taken Stephen under his wing (no doubt as a pet project at first) and over the years a friendship of sorts had developed, with the older man providing some of the support and guidance so absent in Stephen's life. If not quite the father figure Stephen longed for, Deacon had become more like the friendly uncle he never had, all of which made the formal nature of the meeting a little unsettling to say the least.

'Nowt to fret about,' Deacon said, obviously sensing Stephen's apprehension. He withdrew a tobacco pouch and began refilling his pipe. 'Just wanted a word concerning arrangements for next year. I haven't told the others yet, but I'm coming up for retirement this December.'

'Oh,' Stephen said, struggling to make sense of the idea of the place without Deacon in charge. 'I had no idea, Phil.'

'No reason you should, lad. The thing is, I want you to take over the reins when I leave.'

'As stationmaster?'

'Aye.' Deacon struck a match, dipped the flame into the bowl of his pipe and puffed smoke from the corner of his mouth. 'The other men respect you, Stephen, and you've proved time and again that you're up to task.'

'Don't you think I'm a little young still?'

'Not much younger than I was when I first stepped into the job. It would mean an increase in salary, too – more than a hundred pounds a year.'

Stephen smiled, wishing his mother were alive to see him. 'It'd be an honour, Phil.'

'Grand, that's settled then.' Deacon rose from his chair and led Stephen to the door. 'It's a relief to know the place will be in capable hands once I'm gone. Andrew's had his beady eye on the job for a while now. Just between the two of us, it gives me the collywobbles to think what might happen with him running the place.'

Deacon's nephew, Andrew Potts, was a signalman at the station. He was a little too fond of the drink and used

his familial connections to flaunt company rules, fre-
quently turning up for work late and dishevelled.

'One last thing,' Deacon said as they stepped out into
the warm sunshine falling on the platform. 'Since we're
on the topic of not getting any younger, have you given
any thought to settling down yet?'

Stephen felt beads of perspiration spring out across his
forehead and wiped them away with the back of his hand.
Potential wives were hardly ten to the dozen in the
village, and since his mother's death his attentions had
been divided between his job at the station and the task of
exploring his gift from above, which was how he had
finally come to regard his funny turns.

The turning point had come three years ago, when, in
the summer of 1924, he had taken a week's holiday in
London. Aside from the occasional trip to Sheffield or
Leeds, Stephen was unaccustomed to city living and had
been immediately intoxicated by the hustle and bustle of
the nation's capital. On his second-to-last day, he'd
visited the library of the British Museum, where he
discovered a dusty, yellow-paged tome entitled *The
Principles and Practices of Buddhist Monks* tucked away
on one of the more secluded shelves. After reading it
cover-to-cover in a single sitting, he had sequestered the
book under his jacket (an act of which he still felt
ashamed) and soon began practising what it referred to as
'meditation'.

Over the following months and years he had
incorporated the techniques into his daily prayer routine,
honing his concentration and mental fortitude to the point
where he was able to summon one of his funny turns
almost at will, and extending the distance that he could
propel his mind to several days into the past or future.
Disappointingly, though, opportunities to do God's work
in and around the village had so far been as thin on the

ground as eligible young ladies, and over the past year or so Stephen had grown increasingly frustrated, not to mention lonely.

'It's something I've been giving some thought to,' he admitted.

Deacon chuckled and hiked up his belt. 'Glad to hear it, lad. Good for keeping up appearances, too. I don't mean to pry, but a young fellow like yourself living alone…people start to talk.'

Stephen wiped his forehead again and squinted against the sun. There was another reason behind his reluctance to start courting: his mother aside, he had never told a living soul about his funny turns, and there was no knowing how another person might react.

'There's this niece I have,' Deacon went on, 'other side of the family from Andrew, of course. She's a nice lass, pretty as a picture too, and—'

He was cut off by a boom loud enough to rattle the waiting room windows in their frames, and stepped back, his pipe dangling from his lips.

Stephen spun around. A thin curl of smoke was rising from the direction of the signal box a mile down the line. Without a thought he took off towards it, scarcely breaking stride as he vaulted from the end of the platform.

After a hundred yards along the side of the track, a quick look behind showed several of his colleagues following after, Deacon close to the back. The smoke mushroomed into a cloud as Stephen approached, soon blotting out the sun. A stitch began to throb in his side but he pushed on through the pain.

Eventually he rounded the embankment where the track cut into a hill and skidded to a stop as his mind struggled to comprehend the scene of utter devastation that greeted him two-hundred yards farther down the line. It seemed as though there had been a collision between the 0836 Wakefield express and a freight train that should have been shunted to a siding while it overtook. The front three carriages of the Wakefield train had become derailed and lay toppled on the slope of the embankment like a child's scattered building blocks. Dazed survivors were slowly gathering on a field of wildflowers at the bottom of the slope, where some were attending to the others' wounds among the buttercups, poppies and daisies. By the foot of the steps leading up to the signal box, Andrew Potts staggered about with a look of abject bewilderment on his face.

Stephen shook himself into action and made straight for the first carriage. Comprised almost entirely of wood, it had crumpled like a squashed matchbox. A fire had broken out, presumably fuelled by gas for the on-board lamps. After tearing off his jacket and hat, he wrapped his shirt around his face to cover his airways, climbed on top of the carriage and slid in through the frame of a shattered window, dropping to the opposite wall with a crunch of broken glass.

Flames danced high all around him, hungrily devouring the wooden structure. Crouched, he peered through thick, stinging smoke. The majority of the seating had become detached from the floor, which now stood like a wall to his left, and lay in a jumbled heap among the bodies of between ten and twenty passengers.

'Hello?' Stephen called out, scanning the hellish sight for any sign of life.

He saw none and was about to turn back when a faint groan, only just audible above the crackle of burning wood, caught his attention. Scrambling forwards on hands and knees, he homed in on the source: the sound was coming from the far end of the carriage, where a loose wall panel had fallen across an upturned bench.

He yanked the panel back. Lying beneath it was a beautiful young woman with a fringe of soft brown curls. A golden locket hung on a chain around her neck.

'Miss, can you hear me?'

Her eyelids fluttered open, her gaze briefly resting on his face before they drifted closed again.

Stephen heaved the wall panel up and flung it away. Only then did he notice the blood soaking through the material of her dress: protruding from her abdomen was a splinter of wood roughly the size and length of his forearm.

He gripped the semi-conscious woman under the arms and dragged her back towards the window through which he had entered. The carriage was approximately ten feet wide, and he would have struggled to reach the upper wall even without the additional weight. He laid the woman down and pulled an unattached bench over, then lifted her onto his shoulder and, standing on top of the bench, heaved her up and out of the window before clambering through himself.

A small crowd had by now amassed on the side of the embankment, Deacon among their number. Stephen unwrapped his shirt from his face, took a breath of fresh air and scooped the woman up once more.

'Help!' he cried. 'I've got a survivor here!'

Deacon came hurrying to meet him, but froze when he saw the spear of wood skewering the woman's stomach.

Stephen lowered her gently to the grass. 'She needs a doctor, Phil. Do you think I should pull it out?'

Deacon shook his head and crouched beside them. After several seconds he looked up. 'It won't do any good, lad. She's already gone.'

'Can't be,' Stephen said, his knees suddenly weak. 'She was alive when I found her. She opened her eyes and looked right at me.'

Deacon drew himself up and placed a hand on Stephen's shoulder. 'You did your best, lad. Nowt anyone else could've done. She's with the Lord now.' Suddenly he spied Potts still meandering about by the signal box and released Stephen. 'You!' he bellowed, and charged towards his nephew. 'This is your fault!'

'U-uncle Phillip?' Potts stammered.

Deacon grabbed him by the collar and lifted him clean off his feet, shaking the man like a rag doll. 'What happened, you imbecile? You were supposed to divert the damn freight train!'

'I'm sorry, Uncle, I…I must have dozed off.'

'*Dozed off?*' Deacon yelled, and cuffed him around the head. 'There's people lost their lives on account of your negligence, and you're telling me you dozed off?'

Stephen turned back to the beautiful, dead stranger by his feet. 'Don't worry,' he said, and bent to stroke her hair. 'I know exactly what to do. It's what I've been waiting for.'

He planted a kiss on her forehead, stood and walked down the embankment, past Deacon and the whimpering Potts and around the side of the signal box. Once out of sight, he slumped against the wall and closed his eyes, clearing his mind of all external sensations and focusing on no more than the air passing in and out of his lungs, each breath a little deeper than the last.

Anger and loss flowed over him, swallowing him up, drowning him in their hollow ache. He felt his body begin to tingle and shake as one of his funny turns took hold. The world beyond his eyelids darkened as though the sun had gone down, and then suddenly Stephen saw himself back at the handrail of the *Northern Star*, his brother's oilskin hat bobbing up and down on the waves below.

He blinked and was outside the signal box again. With no volition of his own, he saw himself stand and walk stutteringly back up the embankment, where he stopped and crouched by the young woman's body. He scooped her up and carried her back to the burning carriage, then slid through the empty window and deposited her under a fallen wall panel at the far end before crawling back out on his hands and knees.

After pulling on his shirt, hat and jacket, he watched himself sprint towards the station, the cloud of smoke shrinking before him with each long, backward stride. Eventually he reached the platform and rejoined Deacon. They entered the stationmaster's office, where they silently discussed Deacon's plans for retirement before Stephen rose from his chair and strolled back towards the ticket office.

He blinked again and, with a slight lurch, found himself standing beside James Cardwell, one of the porters at the station.

'Deacon wants you in his office,' Cardwell said, and bit into an apple.

'Tell him it'll have to wait,' Stephen replied. He turned away and tore down the platform towards the signal box once more. On this occasion nobody followed.

He maintained his pace, ignoring the stitch in his side and pushing himself even harder than before. On rounding the embankment, he found the track up ahead empty, a few puffs of steam visible around the bend the only sign of the impending disaster. Without slowing, he bounded down the embankment and then up the stairs to the signal box.

On bursting through the door, he discovered Potts asleep in his chair, the man's chin on his chest and a near-empty bottle of whisky in his hand.

'Wake up, you drunken fool!'

Potts stirred, peering at him with bloodshot eyes. 'Rutherford? What the bloody hell do *you* want?'

Through the window of the cabin, Stephen glimpsed the engine of the freight train appear around the bend. 'That train!' he roared. 'You need to divert it before the Wakefield express arrives!'

Potts glared and heaved himself up. 'You might have my uncle wrapped around yer little finger, Rutherford, but don't for a minute think you can take that tone with me!'

'Just do your damn job and divert the train!'

'Gerrout!' Potts yelled, staggering slightly.

By now all twelve cars of the freight train had pulled into view. With a hiss of braking pistons, it slowed before coming to a stop outside the signal box. In the distance, puffs of steam from the advancing Wakefield express rose ominously from behind the hill

'Out of my way!' Stephen demanded, realising his only hope rested in diverting the second train instead.

As he stepped towards the lever frame beneath the window, Potts moved to block him, whisky sloshing from the neck of his bottle. There was no time to argue about it. Stephen clenched his fist and landed a firm blow on Potts's chin. The signalman's head snapped to one side, the bottle slipping from his hand as he crashed to the floor in an inelegant heap.

Stephen stepped over him. The machine consisted of approximately thirty interlocking levers that needed to be applied in specific combinations to control the various signals and points along the approach to Upper Blinkhorn. Although he had been given a rudimentary demonstration on his promotion to assistant stationmaster two years ago, for the life of him he could not remember which lever controlled the points for the siding.

The Wakefield train suddenly appeared around the bend, sunlight reflecting off its chimney. There were less than two-hundred yards of track separating its front buffers from the last car of the stationary freight train, and that was closing fast.

Stephen let out a silent gasp and began haphazardly pulling levers.

One hundred yards…

A whistle sounded from the Wakefield express, followed by another screech of braking pistons as the driver realised too late what was about to happen. Stephen kept tugging levers, hoping to somehow stumble upon the correct combination.

Fifty yards…

The train began to decelerate, not enough to avert the collision but enough to buy him a precious second or two. He pulled another lever, then released it and tried another. There seemed something familiar about the configuration in front of him, but he couldn't be certain. Perhaps it was the lever to his left?

The fate of the train and all onboard rested in the decision he was about to take. There was no time to think, just to act, one way or the other, for better or worse. He reached for the first lever, ready to return it to the vertical position, when suddenly the engine of the Wakefield train veered to the right. It continued to brake, its carriages following until they came to a rest on the tracks of the siding, side by side with the stationary freight train on the main line.

He let out a breath and stumbled backwards, his hand over his chest. His heel caught on Potts's outstretched leg, and he was sent tumbling onto his backside beside the unconscious man. He dragged himself to his feet again, lurched to the door and, gripping the handrail, staggered down the stairs. In the distance he could see several of his colleagues approaching from the station, Deacon close to the back.

'What the devil are you playing at?' the driver of the freight train shouted as he descended the rungs of the engine.

Stephen ignored him, circled around the signal box and, closing his eyes, slumped in the same position as before. He had done it, but a second later and he would have released the lever controlling the points for the siding, thereby condemning those onboard to death.

'What's the meaning of this?'

Stephen opened his eyes, and found that he was back in the signal box. Deacon was in one of the chairs and Potts in the other, his nose bloody and a bruise that would soon deepen to a black eye smouldering on the side of his face.

'Ah,' Stephen said, 'I can explain.'

'Grand.' Deacon lifted his pipe, placed it between his teeth and leaned back with his hands over his belly. 'Let's hear it then.'

'He was drinking on the job, Phil,' Stephen said, glancing about for the incriminating bottle, which had inconveniently disappeared. 'I had to do something otherwise there would have been a collision.'

'He's lying,' Potts stated, sounding as though the blow to the head had sobered him up somewhat.

'Then why wasn't the freight train shunted to siding as it should have been? Answer me that!'

'Because you stormed in and attacked me before I could do it. There nearly *was* a collision, Uncle Phillip. Honestly, it's a miracle I was able to push him off and switch the tracks in time.'

Stephen stared at the man, struggling against the urge to pick up where they had left off.

'Besides,' Potts went on with a shrug, 'how could he *possibly* have known there'd be a collision? It doesn't make any sense, at least not to me.'

'Well?' Deacon asked, arching his eyebrows at Stephen.

'Call it a sixth sense.'

Potts chuckled and shook his head. 'See, his mind's completely addled! Away with the fairies, by my reckoning.'

'Thank you, Andrew,' Deacon said. 'That'll be all.'

Potts rose from his seat, smirking as he barged past Stephen on his way out.

'This is most disappointing, lad,' Deacon said. 'I had such high hopes for you.'

'I'm telling the truth,' Stephen protested. 'Come on, Phil, you know what he's like.'

'Aye, that I do. But all the same, it's hard to fault in his reasoning. *A sixth sense*? What are you saying, lad, that you read it in the tea leaves?'

'Something like that,' Stephen said, for want of anything better. 'Now and then I get a feeling just before something bad is about to happen and…and…'

'You're putting me in one heck of a position here. Leaving your post without permission, then striking a workmate? And now all this sixth-sense mumbo-jumbo?' He let out a sigh, stood and hiked his trousers up. 'It pains me to say this, but I'm going to have to ask you to take the rest of the day off while I consider your future.'

'But—'

'That'll be all.'

Stephen turned to leave, hanging his head at the memory of his fleeting pride upon being offered the stationmaster's job. His disappointment was short-lived, however; on opening the signal box door he saw a crowd of disgruntled passengers gathered on the field of wildflowers. He approached, recognising several familiar faces, at least one of whom he had clambered over in the burning carriage.

'…an absolute bloody disgrace,' one man said.

'Tell me about it,' said another. 'My boss is going to have my guts when I show up late again.'

Stephen allowed himself a smile. It may yet cost him his job, but the opportunity to do God's work had at long last presented itself and he had not let it slip by.

There was a sudden gust of wind and a woman's cloche hat blew against the toes of his boots. He stooped to retrieve it, straightened up and found himself face to face with a beautiful young woman. She had a fringe of soft brown curls and a gold locket around her neck. He stared at her, momentarily lost for words.

'I think that's mine,' she said, nodding towards the hat.

'Oh,' he said and handed it back.

'Thank you.' The woman pulled the hat over her curls and looked up again, smiling. 'You know, you look awfully familiar. Have we met?'

Stephen remembered the sight of a splinter of wood protruding from her stomach and shook his head to dispel it. 'Not that I recall,' he said. 'I'm Stephen Rutherford.'

'It's a pleasure to make your acquaintance,' she said. 'I'm Nell.'

2

Present Day

The time following Sam's arrest passed in a dreamlike daze, although what took place felt more like the stuff of nightmares. After being escorted into the back of a waiting police car with his family staring on in disbelief, he was driven to New Scotland Yard. Once his finger-prints and mugshot had been taken and his personal possessions removed (including his belt and the laces from his shoes), he was led to a cell and left to stew in his own juices for several hours. Then, about twenty minutes ago, a pair of uniformed officers had arrived to take him to a narrow room where he was made to line up alongside six other boys, all roughly his age and with a similar build and hair colour to his own. They'd stood there facing a mirrored window, each holding a numbered card and nobody saying a word until Hinds had eventually opened the door. She'd shown the others out and then led him to a dingy interview room where his sister was sitting on one of the chairs around the table. The clock on the wall said it was almost four in the morning.

Chrissie half-stood as they entered, then faltered and sat back down. Sam rushed over and threw his arms around her, blubbing into the collar of her coat. Hinds stood watching them for a moment, then shook her head and closed the door, leaving them alone.

'You didn't do what they're saying, did you?' Chrissie asked, pushing Sam back and holding him at arm's length. There were dark circles beneath her eyes and her fingernails were chewed down to stumps.

'Chrissie, how can you even think that?'

'Sorry. I know you'd never hurt anyone, it's just…' She looked down, pinched the bridge of nose and then looked back up. 'I know there has to be a reasonable explanation for all this, I just don't get why the police would think you've got anything to do with that poor man's death. But whatever happened, we'll get through it together. As a family. Like we always do.'

He sat beside her and let out a sob, tears blurring his vision. Reasonable explanations were in alarmingly short supply. He'd been at the crime scene. He'd called an ambulance on Fairview's house phone. In fact, he'd even *touched* the dead body when checking for a pulse. Given the remarkably thorough job he'd done of implicating himself, the police had every reason to suspect he was involved. The worst part was Sam only had himself to blame. He had been so blinded by the prospect of getting what he wanted that he'd allowed himself to think Fairview's death was the result of natural causes. And with the bottle of Tetradyamide in his possession for over a week (more than enough time to go back and change what had happened), he'd instead used it for his own selfish purposes. Had the events of December changed him so much that he was willing to put his desires above the life of an innocent man? And, if so, what kind of person did that make him?

There was a rattle of keys on the other side of the thick metal door, followed by the clunk of a lock sliding back. He looked up to see a man wearing a crumpled suit and a green tie stained with what looked suspiciously like tomato ketchup enter the room.

'Good evening,' the man said, and adjusted his comb-over. 'I'm Gordon Levine, the criminal defence lawyer assigned to your case.' He joined them at the table, opened his briefcase and pulled out a handheld tape recorder, which he placed between them. 'Excuse the outdated technology, but I've been using a Dictaphone for over twenty years and if it ain't broke. Anyway, Mr Rayner. Sam. You don't mind if I call you Sam, do you?'

'No, that's fine,' Sam said and sniffed.

'Good.' Levine tweaked the knot of his tie and forced an awkward smile. 'At the moment, Sam, things don't look very promising. From what I can tell the police have the foundations of a strong case against you.'

'But he didn't do it,' Chrissie said.

The lawyer gave another smile that was even more awkward than the first. 'And rest assured I'll do everything in my power to help your brother, Miss Rayner. What I need from you, Sam, is to tell me exactly what happened last Thursday, starting at the very beginning.'

Sam shifted his weight in his chair and glanced at Chrissie. He really didn't know where to start, or how much he should say.

'Go on,' she whispered, reaching over to take his hand. 'Whatever happened last week, now's your chance to explain.'

He took a deep breath. 'Okay, I was there but, like my sister told you, I didn't do it. Until this evening I didn't even realise anything had been *done*. When I found Malcolm Fairview, he was already dead. I thought it must be a heart attack or something, so I called an ambulance from his house phone.'

'And then left the scene, correct?'

'Right.'

'Very well,' Levine said. 'And what exactly was the nature of your relationship with Mr Fairview?'

'I—' Sam stopped and looked down at his hands. What was he supposed to say, that he'd met Malcolm Fairview in an alternative reality that no longer existed? His lawyer would think he was a raving lunatic.

Levine cleared his throat. 'Sam, I really cannot overstate the seriousness of your predicament. The police have placed you at the scene of the crime beyond reasonable doubt. You yourself freely admit you were there. Unless you can explain what you were doing there and why you left before the ambulance arrived, there really is very little I can do to prevent you being charged with Mr Fairview's murder.'

Sam bit his lip and wrung his hands. In this timeline there was absolutely nothing linking him to the Tempus Project or the dead scientist. He was, to all extents and purposes, a stranger who had blundered into a crime scene, left incriminating evidence all over the place and then walked out again.

Levine switched the Dictaphone off and returned it to his briefcase. 'Very well,' he said, rising from his chair. 'I can see we're not getting anywhere here. I'm on your side, Sam, but unless you can give me a reasonable explanation for what you were doing at the crime scene, I'm afraid there's not a lot I can do. The arresting officers will be here to interview you shortly. I suggest you take the time available to think things over.'

3

Sam watched his defence lawyer bang twice on the door and step out the moment it was opened. Once they were alone again, he turned to face his sister. Chrissie stared at him for a long, agonising moment before raising a shaking hand to her forehead.

'God, Sam, what *have* you got yourself into?'

'Nothing good,' he said.

'Then tell me! Please, I want to believe you had nothing to do with this but I'm struggling to make sense of anything that's going on.'

He met her gaze, his jaw clenched. 'All right,' he said eventually, 'but I need you to promise to hear me out before you say anything. Can you do that?'

She folded her arms and gave him a light-lipped nod.

'Okay, here goes then,' he said, and exhaled a loud breath. 'The reason I stopped taking my epilepsy medication is that I don't have epilepsy.'

'But—'

'You agreed to hear me out, didn't you?'

'Fine, go on then.'

'Okay, so…I suppose it all started at the end of last year when I came out of my coma. The brain injury did something weird to me, something that messed up the way I process time. My fits are actually these episodes where I come round in a different time and place, often several hours in the past or future.'

'That's the most ridiculous thing I've ever heard!'

'I know how it sounds, Chrissie, but it's the truth. That's what happened the other day when I collapsed at college. Remember the family meeting we had about Dad's life insurance?'

'It's kind of hard to forget.'

'That was me from earlier that morning. It was how I knew about the letter from Imperial Insurance before it was even delivered.'

She pressed her fist to her mouth and puffed her cheeks out. 'I remember now,' she said, 'just before the postman arrived...'

'Right.'

'But that's not possible. It's just *not* possible.'

'I'd probably say the same if I were in your shoes, but if you want to help me then you're going to reconsider what you think is and isn't possible.'

She frowned in a way that did little to fill him with confidence, but didn't otherwise object.

'So,' he went on, 'during the seizure I had at Dad's funeral, I suddenly found myself back home, later that evening. We were all watching telly and there was this news report about the Thames House bombing. They showed CCTV footage of Esteban Haufner. I recognised him from the day of the plane crash, and when I came round again I rang Sergeant Hinds – or Inspector, as she was then – and told her what was about to happen.'

'You mean that woman who arrested you?'

'I know. What are the chances, right?' he said, wondering if Hinds wasn't somehow stalking him across multiple timelines. 'But what I'm trying to tell you is that the police managed to stop Haufner before he could set off the bomb. I prevented the Thames House bombing, Chrissie.'

'You're not making any sense, Sam. The bomb *did* go off. Loads of people were killed, and the police are still searching for Haufner.'

'Tell me about it,' he said. 'And I'm coming to that. But what happened next is that I created a separate time-line, one in which I'd prevented the Thames House bombing from happening. In *that* timeline I was recruited to a secret organisation called the Tempus Project who were researching people with time-travelling capabilities. They told me I'd become a government asset, a sort of early-warning system to help prevent anything like the Thames House bombing from happening again, and I spent pretty much the whole of December training at their research facility, which is how I ended up meeting Malcolm Fairview.'

'*So you do know him!*'

'Yeah, but in a different timeline. Fairview had recreated this drug called Tetradyamide which helped control and focus my episodes, allowing me to choose when they happened and where they sent me. But the Tempus Project wasn't what it seemed, not by a long shot. It was run by someone called Lara McHayden, and what she really wanted was to turn me into a weapon, using my ability to help track down and eliminate government targets. When I tried to leave, she wouldn't let me. She'd bugged our house and then, when I tried to run, sent someone to bring me in. This all happened on Christmas Eve, and you...you were...' He glanced away, his voice catching in his throat. 'Let's just say things got messy. In the end I had to use my ability to go back to the day of Dad's funeral and undo my decision to call Hinds, which created a new reality where the Thames House bombing still took place – *this* reality. In this timeline I've got no memory of anything that took place between the funeral and Christmas Day.'

Chrissie unfolded her arms and rubbed the back of her neck. 'This takes some getting your head around, but assuming I accept what you're telling me, none of it explains what you were doing at Malcolm Fairview's flat on the day he was murdered.'

'Tetradyamide,' Sam said. 'After I found out about Imperial Insurance cancelling Dad's life insurance policy and the potential treatment for Mum's amnesia, I knew I had to do something. I thought Tetradyamide might be the answer, so I asked Lance to drive Lewis and me to the Tempus Research Facility last week. The place was abandoned, but Malcolm Fairview was there collecting some of his stuff. Once I told him who I was and what I could do, he invited me to his flat the next day. He was already dead when I got there, Chrissie. He had a heart condition, so I thought there was nothing I could do. I called an ambulance, but then I saw a bottle of Tetra-dyamide and I...I just sort of hung up and took it.' He paused to steady himself and laid both hands flat on the table. 'Like I told Levine, the first thing I knew about Fairview being murdered was when the police turned up at our house a few hours ago.'

His sister was watching him with her lips pursed. 'I don't honestly know what you expect me to say.'

'That you believe me? That you'll try and help?'

'I'll try and help, at least.'

Sam nodded. It wasn't exactly the answer he'd wanted, but at least it was something.

'In that case there's something I need you to do,' he said.

4

Dawn was still several hours away when Chrissie's taxi pulled up outside her house. If she'd thought the night after the plane crash had been the longest of her life then the one drawing to an end was running it a close second. What her brother had told her was so far-fetched, so totally beyond the scope of anything she'd previously thought possible, that she could now see only two options: either Sam had suffered some sort of massive psychological breakdown and concocted the whole thing while somehow getting involved in the murder of a government scientist or he was telling the truth, and frankly she wasn't sure which prospect terrified her more.

She paid the driver and climbed out of the taxi, noting the two white vans parked on the other side of the road. Such had been her haste to follow Sam to the police station yesterday evening that she had forgotten her phone, so had no clue as to developments back at the house, but in spite of the hour all of the downstairs curtains were open and the lights were on, filling her with foreboding as she trudged down the path.

As she pulled her keys from her handbag, the diamond in her engagement ring sparkled. She paused to gaze at it before letting herself in, wondering how something that only a few hours ago had given her butterflies every time she looked at it could now provoke no emotion whatsoever. Sam had told her that Lance had driven him and Lewis to some sort of research facility the night before the murder, and she recalled swallowing some cockeyed excuse about the three of them going to the cinema together. Was Lance also involved in whatever Sam had managed to get himself caught up in? She'd confront him soon enough, she supposed, but first she had her brother's strange request to complete.

On stepping through the door, she found the hallway in utter disarray. A row of black plastic crates had been stacked against the near wall, and unfamiliar voices could be heard in the kitchen and living room. Trying to make as little noise as possible, she crept up the stairs, when all of a sudden the door to her brother's bedroom swung open and a man in white overalls stepped onto the first-floor landing with Sam's computer under his arm.

'Hey, that's private property!' she said. 'Where do you think you're going with that?'

The man gave a weary sigh that suggested he'd met such a reaction more than once. 'Young lady,' he said, even though he wasn't much older than her, 'I'm a Scenes of Crime Officer, and this is evidence in an active police investigation. You can't be here while we work.'

'Where are my family then?'

'Booked in to a hotel for the night. They left the address over there.' He gestured to the notepad beside the phone on the hall table. When Chrissie made no attempt to retrieve it, he sighed again and shifted the computer to his other arm. 'Look, I understand this must be upsetting as well as inconvenient for you, but I'm going to have to ask you to leave.'

'Fine, I'll just grab a few things together and be out of you hair.'

'I'm afraid I can't allow that.'

Chrissie willed her bottom lip to wobble, which wasn't too difficult given the circumstances, then burst into tears and sagged theatrically onto the stairs.

The man laid the computer onto the landing floor and trotted down to her. 'There there,' he said, patting her awkwardly on the back with a hand covered by a latex glove. 'There's no need to cry. We're almost done here and then you can have your house back.'

'It's not that,' she said, dabbing her eyes and nudging her coat back to display her baby bump. 'I know you've got a job to do, but I'm pregnant and have a vitamin deficiency which could be harmful to the baby. After everything that happened last night, I missed my supplement and…and…'

'A vitamin deficiency?'

'That's right. I just want to get my supplement from the attic room. I'll be two minutes.'

He hesitated and pressed a finger to the spot between his eyebrows. 'All right, but be quick and don't touch anything. And don't tell anyone I said you could, otherwise it's my neck on the block.'

'You're a life saver,' she said and clambered to her feet, flashing him the warmest smile she could muster. 'Thank you, you won't even know I was here.'

'Sure, just be quick about it.'

Chrissie nodded, hurried past him and onto the landing and then up the first few stairs leading to her bedroom. She stopped halfway and turned to peer through a gap in the banisters. The Scenes of Crime Officer had his back to her and was busy packing Sam's computer into one of the crates in the hall. Holding her breath, she slid her shoes off, scooped them up in one hand and then crept down to the first-floor landing again before slipping into Sam's room unnoticed.

The place had been well and truly ransacked, with the mattress lying upturned on the bed, the contents of the shelves stacked on the floor and a pile of clothes heaped next to the wardrobe. She crossed the room and opened the wardrobe doors to find a clothes rail lined with empty hangers. Crouching, she checked the bottom drawer, where her brother had told her she would find a brown pill bottle hidden in a balled pair of socks.

Whether it had ever been there or not, the drawer was now empty.

5

Frances gazed across the table at Rayner. Her suspect was sitting beside his lawyer with his head bowed. His hair had grown back and his face had filled out in the weeks since she'd interviewed him with Agent Steele, but the haunted look in his eyes was as the same as ever, if not worse. So far he'd hardly said a word apart from to protest his innocence, and in a few hours they would be faced with the choice of either charging him or releasing him.

Placing her elbows on the table, she tented her fingers and leaned forwards. 'So, Sam, here's the situation. An eyewitness has picked you out from an identity parade, placing you at the crime scene around the estimated time of death. We've also found your fingerprints in several locations within the flat, and your voice pattern has been matched to the recording of a phone call made from the victim's landline. You can see how this all looks, can't you?'

Rayner stared down at his hands and mumbled something too quietly to make it out.

'We've also accessed the victim's laptop,' she went on. 'His browsing history shows that he was researching the crash of Flight 0368 the night before you, one of only two survivors, apparently wander into his house and discover him dead. Talk to me, Sam. The truth, that's all I want. If you're covering for someone then you need to tell us. How is Flight 0368 connected to Malcolm Fairview's death? Is it anything to do with the seven-thousand-five-hundred pounds paid into your bank account last week?'

Rayner jerked his head up, his posture stiffening. 'No, that's got nothing to do with it! The money was a payment from my friend's dad, you can check.'

Levine raised a hand, stopping Rayner before he could go on. 'That's conjecture, Sergeant,' he said. 'It proves nothing, as well you know.'

Frances nodded to concede the point, but Campbell, in the chair beside her, banged both fists on the table.

'You think this is all a game, do you?' he yelled, wagging a finger at Rayner. 'There's a man lying dead in the morgue, and you won't even tell us why!'

'Detective Campbell,' Levine said, 'might I remind you that my client has stated his innocence of the alleged offence on several occasions.'

Campbell's face was a deepening shade of red. 'He's up to his neck in it. C'mon, you little bastard, admit it! Where'd you get the cyanide?'

'No!' Rayner pleaded. 'Please, you've got it all wrong!'

Campbell growled, looking like he might burst a blood vessel, but Frances placed a hand on his arm to still him.

'Sam,' she said, her voice level and calm, 'no one wants this to go any further than it has to, but at the moment everything points to you. You need to give us something to work with here. If you didn't kill Malcolm Fairview then what were you doing at his flat that day?'

'It's hard to explain,' Rayner said and gave a slight shake of his head. 'I was walking down the road and must have heard a noise or something. I followed it around the back of the house and—'

'What sort of noise?' Campbell demanded.

'I don't know. A bang or a crash, I think. It sounded like someone was hurt.'

'So,' Frances said, 'you followed this noise around the back and…'

Rayner glanced to Levine, who spread his hands for his client to continue.

'I looked through the window,' he said. 'I couldn't see anyone, but when I tried the back door it was unlocked. I let myself in and had a look around, and that's when I saw him – Mr Fairview, I mean – lying on his back. When I realised he was dead I thought it must be a heart attack, not that he'd been murdered or anything, so I called an ambulance on his house phone and then, I don't know, sort of freaked out and ran.'

'Are you in the habit of letting yourself into other people's property?' Campbell asked.

'Like I said, I heard a noise.'

'So you'd never met Malcolm Fairview before finding him dead?'

Rayner paused for a moment and blinked. 'No.'

Frances pulled out an evidence bag containing a note written on the back of a leaflet about a proposed animal hospice in Notting Hill and slid it across the table:

Malcolm,
I came over on Thursday morning like we arranged
but there was no one home.
Please call me - 07263 212 851
Sam

'Your house was searched immediately after you were brought in,' she told him. 'This was in the waste-paper basket in your bedroom. A handwriting analyst has already matched it to samples from your schoolwork. So, I'll ask you again, Sam, do you still maintain that you'd never met Malcolm Fairview?'

Rayner's face sagged. He linked his hands around the back of his neck and stared silently at the table.

Levine raised the note and, jiggling his leg, read it.

'That wasn't the only thing we found,' Frances said, and placed a second evidence bag on the table. 'This was in a pair of socks in your wardrobe. They're not cocaine or ecstasy, as far as I can tell. We're having a sample analysed as we speak, so we'll know what they are soon enough. Care to shed any light on the matter?'

Rayner gaped at the pill bottle and raised a hand to his mouth. What little colour was left in his face slowly drained away.

'Okay,' he said after a moment. 'The truth.'

'That might be a good place to start.'

'The truth is I first met Malcolm Fairview over a month ago. He was a scientist at the Tempus Project, a secret government organisation researching time-travel abilities in people with traumatic brain injuries,' he turned his head and tapped his now-covered scar, 'people like me. Mr Fairview taught me how to control my ability using a drug called Tetradyamide. That's what the pills are. Things with the Tempus Project got…complicated, let's say. My family were in danger, so I altered the timelines and created a new reality in which the Tempus Project was shut down after the Thames House bombing. Even though we'd technically never met before, I tracked down Mr Fairview at the Tempus Research Facility, the place where he trained me, and he invited me to his flat the next day, the day he was killed.' He took a deep breath, held it for a couple of seconds and then released it. 'That's what I was doing there, Sergeant Hinds. Everything else I told you about finding Fairview dead and thinking it was a heart attack is the truth. Apart from calling an ambulance, I didn't think there was anything I could do for him, and when I saw the bottle of Tetradyamide on his chest of drawers I just took it and ran. I know it was the wrong thing to do, but I wasn't thinking straight at the time.'

'Enough!' Levine slapped the note down on the table. 'I need to speak with my client. *Alone.*'

'Of course,' Frances said. She gathered up the evidence bags and stood. 'You have one hour, Mr Levine.'

6

Things were far worse than Sam had allowed himself to believe. In addition to the other evidence stacked up against him, the police had found the note and bottle of Tetradyamide in his bedroom, and while the former proved Sam had lied about not knowing Fairview, the latter meant he had sent Chrissie on a wild-goose chase.

'What's going on here?' Levine asked. 'You don't actually believe a word of what you just said there, do you?'

'It's the truth,' Sam said.

'I see.' The lawyer pinched the loose flap of skin beneath his chin, his lips pressed together. 'In that case my honest advice is that you consider changing your plea.'

'How do you mean?'

'I have to be blunt with you, Sam, but it's my honest opinion that you're suffering from some form of delusional schizophrenia, no doubt a result of your brain injury last autumn. If you admit to killing Malcolm Fairview, I may be able to get you a reduced sentence of the grounds of diminished responsibility. A thorough psychological assessment would be necessary, of course.'

Sam stared back, wondering whether he'd misheard. 'You expect me to admit to something I didn't do?'

'But did you, though?' Levine asked, meeting his gaze.

'No!'

'Very well then.' The lawyer switched his Dictaphone off, rose from his seat and flattened his ketchup-stained tie. 'I'm sorry, Sam, but under the circumstances I really don't see how I can defend you.'

7

After dropping the pill bottle and note off at the evidence room, Frances returned to the Homicide and Serious Crimes office and made her way directly to the kitchen for a much-needed caffeine fix. Her ploy with the note had worked a treat, proving that Rayner had been lying to their faces, and they now had more than enough evidence to charge him. What he had told them about time travel and secret government organisations was deeply concerning, however, and did little to ease Frances's fears that the murder was in some way connected to the sabotage of Flight 0368, an event to which she herself was inextricably linked.

As she stirred milk and sugar into her coffee, Campbell strode in with a wide grin on his face. 'Nice work back there, Sergeant,' he said. 'Looks like we've got him.'

'Yes,' Frances said. 'I suppose it does.'

He stopped smiling. 'What's got your goat? Not my bad-cop routine, I hope. It worked, didn't it?'

'No, it's not that, just…' She shook her head.

'That nonsense he was spouting about time travel?' Campbell shrugged and poured himself a mug of coffee from the pot. 'The kid's obviously got a few screws loose. Sad, really. It sounds like he doesn't even remember doing it and invented this fantasy as a coping mechanism. That or he knows exactly what he's doing and made the whole thing up in the hope of getting off the hook.'

'Perhaps,' she said. 'But I can't help thinking there's more to this than meets the eye. Like where a sixteen-year-old boy gets his hands on cyanide, for starters.'

'You can get almost anything on the dark net these days if you know what you're doing. The main thing is we've got our killer, Frances. The rest is just details.'

'Hmmm,' she said noncommittally.

'This is because you've met him before, isn't it? If that's what you're worrying about, relax. It's a strange coincidence, nothing more. We need to look at the facts in front of us and Rayner's in it up to his eyeballs. The note proves he was already known to Fairview.'

'You're right, I suppose.'

'Better believe it,' Campbell said and took a sip of his coffee.

Mug in hand, Frances made her way to her desk, flopped into her chair and closed her eyes. She'd been on the go for nearly thirty-six hours straight, and there was only so much caffeine could do against the mounting sleep deprivation. Maybe she really was letting her prior association with Rayner affect her judgement. After all, it was only natural to search for patterns that weren't there, to seek meaning in coincidence. It was how people made sense of the world, a thing as naturally engrained in the human psyche as a healthy fear of heights or loud noises. The hard part, of course, and an essential requirement of her job, was to put such feelings aside and analyse the evidence with cold, hard objectivity. Which wasn't easy when you were dead on your feet. With any luck Levine would be convincing Rayner to change his plea to guilty at this very moment, and in a couple of hours' time she'd be curled up in bed with a good book and Hercule, her cat, beside her.

She opened her eyes to see Campbell approaching.

'You weren't asleep, were you?' he asked.

'No, just resting my eyes.'

'Good,' he said, bouncing from foot to foot, 'because you're not going to believe what's just happened!'

'Rayner's changed his plea?'

'Not exactly. I bumped into Gordon Levine on my way back from the gents. He says he's withdrawing representation, Frances. He's dropped the case, citing professional embarrassment.'

8

Sam sat alone in the interview room, his back arched over the table and his head in his hands. In a last, desperate roll of the dice he had tried telling the truth, but his lawyer (or, more accurately, *ex*-lawyer) hadn't believed a word of it. Now he was out of ideas, with no way of proving his innocence or reversing what had happened without his bottle of Tetradyamide, which the police had found in his room.

His miserable thoughts were disturbed by the sound of the door being unlocked. He lifted his head to see a uniformed police officer show Chrissie in. She hurried over and took the chair beside him.

'There was nothing there,' she said as soon as they were alone. 'Forensics were already searching the house.'

'I know,' he told her. 'Sergeant Hinds interviewed me an hour ago. She's got the pills, Chrissie. And they found a note I wrote to Malcolm Fairview in the bin in my room.'

'Oh,' she said. 'Where's Levine got to?'

'He's gone. I tried telling him the truth and he didn't buy it. Said he could get me diminished responsibility if I plead guilty and claim I'm mentally unstable because of my injury. When I refused, he said he was dropping the case. Said he didn't think he could win based on the evidence.'

Chrissie bit her lip.

'I didn't do the wrong thing, did I?' he asked.

'No, of course not.' She wrapped an arm around his shoulders and leaned her head against his. 'I was serious when I said we'd get through this as a family. Don't worry, little brother, if you didn't kill Malcolm Fairview then that means someone else *did*. There are other lawyers out there, you just leave it with me.'

He sniffed and gave her a weak smile. 'Thanks,' he said. 'You always know the right thing to say.'

'It's a rare natural gift,' she said, and hugged him a little closer.

The door opened and Hinds stepped in, once again accompanied by the bad-tempered Detective Campbell.

'This is a charge sheet,' Campbell said, handing Sam a sheet of paper.

'A what?'

'Due to the weight of evidence against you, Mr Rayner, I have no choice but to charge you with the murder of Malcolm Fairview.'

'But he doesn't even have a lawyer!' Chrissie protested. 'That arsehole just walked out on him.'

'Your brother will be allocated a new defence lawyer once someone willing to represent him can be found,' Hinds said. 'In the meantime, Sam, you'll be placed on remand at an Institute for Young Offenders until a date can be scheduled for your court hearing.'

9

Frances stifled a yawn as she stood beside Campbell under the rotating prism of the New Scotland Yard sign.

'Ready?' the news reporter, a woman with a botched face-lift that gave her a permanently shocked expression, asked.

'Born ready,' Campbell said and glanced to Frances, who nodded in response.

'Good, let's go then.' The reporter turned to the television camera directed towards them and raised her microphone. 'Good afternoon, you join me live with Detective Mark Campbell and Sergeant Frances Hinds of the Metropolitan Police, who inform me that they've made a breakthrough in the investigation into the murder of Malcolm Fairview, a former government scientist found dead at his west-London flat nine days ago.' She thrust the microphone towards Campbell, nearly bumping him on the nose. 'Detective, what more can you tell us about the case?'

Campbell cleared his throat and, obviously relishing the limelight, flashed a toothy smile. 'Thank you, Amanda, that's correct. We made an arrest yesterday evening and have since charged a suspect.'

'And do you believe, as several of my colleagues in the press are speculating, that the killing was connected to Mr Fairview's former employment?'

'No, that's not an avenue we're currently exploring. While we can't rule anything out in terms of motive yet, what I will say is that the suspect is a minor, believed to be a survivor of the British Airways Flight 0368 tragedy last year.'

A murmur spread through the crowd amassed just out of shot.

'So there's no truth to the rumours that the murder was, in fact, a professional hit carried out by a foreign government agency?'

Campbell glanced at Frances again, his eyes wide.

'There's no evidence to support that whatsoever,' she said, stepping in. 'Romantic as the notion sounds, it appears we're dealing with a lone killer, a deeply troubled young man who has seemingly slipped through the mental health services' net. Now, I'm afraid that's all we're prepared to say at this stage. We'll bring you more information as and when we have it.'

'Thank you, Sergeant,' the reporter said, withdrawing the microphone and turning to the camera again. 'Back to you in the studio, Colin.'

'Vultures,' Frances muttered as they made their way through the Homicide and Serious Crimes office. 'They'll twist a story any which way they think will get highest viewer figures, and the truth be damned!'

'That's a bit harsh, don't you think?' Campbell said.

'Not in my experience,' she said, recalling her treatment in press in the aftermath of the Thames House bombing.

'Never mind, it's done now.' He stopped by his desk and turned to her. 'I'm going to wrap up and get out of here while there's still something of the weekend left. I suggest you do the same.'

'Sounds like a good idea,' she said, imagining herself on the sofa with the tall glass of white wine and the leftover Chinese takeaway she had in the fridge.

After topping up her coffee, she returned to her own desk and hammered out her report. No sooner had she hit the print button than the phone on her desk rang. With an exhausted sigh, she picked up.

'Hinds? It's Kaur here. I have news, of sorts. The chemical analysis of the pills found in Rayner's bedroom is back from the lab.'

'And?'

'That's the thing, we don't exactly know what they are.'

'What do you mean you don't know what they are?'

He gave an uncomfortable laugh. 'I've got the report right in front of me. It states that the sample pill contains a new molecule, previously unheard of.'

'It can't do,' Frances said. 'That's impossible.'

'That's what I thought, so I rang the technician at the lab. She told me that she'd never seen anything like it in her whole career, and she's six months off retirement. I'll email a copy over so you can take a look for yourself.'

'Okay, thanks,' Frances said, and hung up.

With each new fact that emerged, the case seemed to grow stranger still. What was Sam Rayner doing in possession of a previously unheard-of molecule? Suddenly the idea of a professional hit didn't seem so unlikely, but who in their right mind would hire a brain-damaged teenager as an assassin?

She shut down her computer and pulled on her coat; it looked like her sofa was going to have to wait a while longer.

10

Sam let out a whimper and stared down at the shackles around his ankles and wrists. The unthinkable had happened: he had been charged with Malcolm Fairview's murder and, having been refused bail due to the serious nature of the crime, was in the process of being transferred to Her Majesty's Young Offenders Institution

Knotsbridge, where he was supposed to remain until his hearing.

No matter how much he protested his innocence, nobody would ever believe the true circumstances by which he had blundered into a crime scene nine days ago. All of the evidence pointed towards Sam as Fairview's killer, and unless he could find a way out of his predicament (which didn't seem very likely without Tetradyamide) he was now stuck, trapped in a dead-end timeline with no way of reversing the events that had led him to this point. The opportunity to cure his mum's amnesia and keep a roof over his family's heads was lost. He would never see Eva again, and if Esteban Haufner ever stuck his neck out there would be nothing Sam could do while rotting away in a cell.

Feeling a strange numbness in his chest, he glanced through the window to see the prison transfer van turn off the duel carriageway and onto a pot-holed side road. In the fading light he could make out a sprawling Victorian building ringed by a high brick wall about half a mile up ahead.

He sniffed, trying his best to hold back the tears. What if there was another way out, one he hadn't thought of before? Although he didn't have his bottle of Tetradyamide any longer, if he could somehow bring on one of his seizures he might conceivably end up back in the past. It was only a day since his arrest, and if he could return to a time before Hinds had shown up at his house last night then he might be able to take Tetradyamide and undo implicating himself in Fairview's murder, or, better yet, prevent it from happening in the first place. If there was a common theme to all of his unintended seizures, from the first few he'd experienced in hospital last year to the day he'd collapsed at college a week and a half ago, it was that he had been distressed beforehand every time, and his current state of mind was even worse than on any of those occasions.

As the van pulled up outside a gate in the wall, he closed his eyes and, hoping against hope, willed himself to smell burning caramel. A few seconds passed, but nothing happened; all he could smell was the lingering aroma of bleach in the back of the van, and when he opened his eyes the only thing to have changed was that the gate now stood open before them.

It hadn't worked, but then again Fairview had once told Sam that Tetradyamide would stop his seizures, and although it was several days since Sam had last taken any, perhaps there was still trace of the drug in his system.

The driver released the handbrake, allowing the van to crawl forwards. Sam turned back and caught a final glimpse of freedom through the rear window before the gate swung shut. They crossed a courtyard where, apart for a circle of cloudy, darkening sky directly above, all view of the outside world was obscured by the walls. The van stopped outside a building that might once have been grand but was now weatherworn and grimy, the bricks caked in competing splodges of moss and lichen. A ring of gargoyles with nightmarish, eroded faces circled the roof. One of the police officers in the front cabin climbed out and opened the rear doors, letting a gust of cold air sweep into the van. He unlocked the padlock connecting Sam's shackles to a metal ring on the floor and then barked, 'Out!'

Sam did as instructed, gravel crunching beneath his feet as he clambered from the van. A smaller door set in the huge, metal-studded wooden doors of the entrance opened, and a short man in a grey suit emerged, flanked on either side by a uniformed prison guard. He stopped a few feet from Sam, looked him up and down and then raised the clipboard in his hand.

'Name?' he asked indifferently.

'Sam Rayner,' Sam said, struggling to keep his voice from cracking.

The man made a mark on his clipboard and then lowered it, his thin moustache twitching. 'I'm Warden Jenkins,' he said in a flat, monotone voice. 'Welcome to Knotbridge, son.'

11

Frances passed through the revolving doors of the Security Service's temporary headquarters and found herself in the waiting area of a rather unremarkable office block. Apart from the armed police stationed outside there was little to differentiate it from any of the media and tech firms based along the road.

'Can I help you?' a bored-looking receptionist asked, glancing up from filing her nails as Frances approached.

'I hope so.' Frances loosened her scarf, opened her coat and displayed her credentials. 'I'm investigating the murder of Malcolm Fairview.'

The woman narrowed her eyes. 'One moment please,' she said, and pressed a button on her phone before speaking into the microphone of her headset. 'Someone will be down shortly. Why don't you take a seat, Sergeant?'

Frances nodded and lowered herself onto one of the sofas in the waiting area. Rubbing her clammy palms against her skirt, she wished she had something to drink, if only to settle her stomach, but there didn't appear to be a water fountain nearby.

After a few minutes the doors to one of the lifts opened and a bespectacled man with curly, greying hair stepped out.

'Sergeant Hinds?' he asked, sitting on the sofa across from her. 'Benjamin Vaughn, Secretary to the Director General. I understand you're investigating Malcolm Fairview's death?'

'That's right,' Frances said. 'He was on your payroll, I believe.'

Vaughn nodded. 'He was, although the nature of Mr Fairview's work remains classified. Besides, you've already charged someone, haven't you?'

'We have,' she admitted, 'however a new piece of evidence has come to light. The suspect was in possession of a bottle of pills containing a previously unheard-of molecule.' She hesitated, fearing that she was about to embarrass herself. 'I'm looking for information about the Tempus Project.'

'Beg your pardon?'

'The Tempus Project. It's a research group investigating people with time-travelling capabilities.'

'*Time-travelling capabilities*?' Vaughn repeated. 'Is this some sort of a wind-up? '

'I only wish it were.'

'Well I've never heard of anything so outlandish,' he said brusquely, 'and even if I had, I'm hardly likely to discuss it with *you*.' He leaned in closer, locking her in a gaze that had nothing friendly about it. 'Listen, Sergeant Hinds – *or should that be Inspector*? – I know all about you and your role in what happened at Thames House. If you think your name will open any doors around here, you're sorely mistaken.'

'I see,' she said, rising to her feet. 'In that case I won't take up any more of your time.'

Frances stepped out onto the icy pavement, her face flushed with heat against the chill night air. If she was ever going to get to the bottom of what the mysterious pills found in Rayner's bedroom were, it did not appear the answer would be forthcoming from the Security Service. With a dejected sigh, she turned towards the tube station again and suddenly found herself facing a tall and strikingly handsome young man.

She froze and sucked in a sharp breath. 'Agent Steele?'

'Inspector Hinds, I thought it was you! What brings you to our not-so-illustrious new headquarters?'

'Following up a lead in a case I'm working,' she told him. 'I just met with Benjamin Vaughn.'

'Oh? And how did you find him?'

'Not particularly helpful.'

Steele chuckled. 'The man's a pompous arse, Inspector. Don't take it to heart.'

'Thank you,' she said. 'And actually it's just plain old Sergeant now. I was demoted and transferred to Homicide and Serious Crimes after CT Command was disbanded.'

'I'm sorry to hear that,' he said. 'And since we're on the topic of new terms of address, I suppose I'm just "Mr Steele" following my retirement.'

'You're no longer with the Security Service?'

'I was at Thames House on the day of the bombing.' He raised the walking stick in his hand. 'My injuries mean I'm no longer fit for active service, or so I'm told.'

Here we go again, Frances thought, and lifted her chin as she prepared for the inevitable onslaught. 'Look, I'm sorry about what happened that day,' she said, perhaps a little too forcefully. 'Believe me, if I could go back there's plenty I'd do differently.'

Steele lowered his stick and batted the comment away with a leather-gloved hand. 'Hogwash. What happened to CT Command is an absolute disgrace, if you ask me. You were doing your best under difficult circumstances. If there's blame to go around, it lies firmly at the feet of those responsible for the political brinkmanship that's been going on since the attack.'

'Oh,' she said. 'I must admit, it's a relief to hear you say that.'

'Don't forget, I was also involved in the investigation into Flight 0368.'

'Yes, of course,' she said, a dark, sickening sensation bubbling through her as she realised that she had last seen him on the day they had interviewed Sam Rayner together.

'Ironic how being injured in the line of duty can transform one from a scapegoat to a hero, don't you think?'

'I should be going,' she said. 'It was good to see you again, Mr Steele.'

'Likewise. And, please, call me George.'

'All right then, George. In that case I'm Frances.'

'You know, Frances, I've often wondered if our paths would cross again,' he said, leaning on his stick and smiling broadly. 'Since I'm no longer technically a government employee, I don't suppose there'd be any conflict of interests if we took a spot of dinner together. What do you say? My treat, of course.'

Chapter V

Dead End

1

October 1940

Ignoring the policeman directing the search from the pavement, Stephen rolled up his shirtsleeves and clambered onto the treacherous pile of rubble that had once been the greengrocers at the corner of Belmont Road, Stepney. Floral-print wallpaper lined what was left of a first-storey bedroom, where a fireplace and basin now hung suspended above his head, snapped planks of wood and loose clumps of mortar all that remained of the ripped-away floor. With a shudder he recalled what the place had looked like yesterday afternoon, when he had called by to warn the owner, a Mr Haverstock, of the coming night's air raid.

It was now over a year since Neville Chamberlain, the then Prime Minister, had declared war on Germany, which had prompted Stephen and Nell to move south to

London. Aside from the rationing and the daily reports of Hitler's armies sweeping through the continent, the immediate impact on their lives had been minimal, but when the first Luftwaffe attacks on the city began last month a clear opportunity to do God's work had presented itself.

Applying the same techniques used to avert the Upper Blinkhorn rail crash, each day Stephen would send his awareness forwards to the following morning, where he would then embark on the task of recording and memorising the location of new bombsites before returning to the present and encouraging the victims to move on. In this manner he had saved countless lives over the last few weeks, but as the bombing had intensified, both in frequency and ferocity, there became limits to what a single person could do, forcing him to focus on those explosions resulting in the highest number of casualties, or those involving children, which were mercifully rare thanks to the mass evacuations the year before.

Sadly, there were also those who would not heed his warnings, the greengrocers on Belmont Road proving exactly such an instance. Mr Haverstock housed three generations of his family above the shop, including his eleven-year-old son, Oscar. Yesterday, in the face of Stephen's pleas to abandon the building, Haverstock had become increasingly hostile in his rebuttals, stating that he had spent twenty years building the business and would not be cowed into leaving it to the whims of looters. There had been plenty of others to save that day, and after a heated ten-minute exchange Stephen conceded defeat. That night, however, he had been unable to sleep what with thinking about the dead child, and had returned directly the next morning to see what help he could lend.

Bricks cascading with every step, he picked his way over the rubble to the spot at the rear of the site where

Haverstock and his son would later be found, both asphyxiated, and then held himself still and listened. Nothing could be heard above the hubbub on the road, but if he were somehow able to direct the search this way then perchance some good might still come of the situation.

After waiting another minute he turned back to the pavement and called out, 'Over here, I think I hear something!'

The policeman at the head of the search party peered up at him. 'Sir, we don't know how stable the site is yet. Two men were killed in Leyton last week when a wall collapsed and—'

'Shh.' Stephen raised a finger to his lips and cupped his other hand behind his ear. 'There it is again!'

Shaking his head, the policeman clambered up and over the mound of shattered masonry to join him.

'Can't hear nothing,' he said eventually. 'What sort of sound did you say it was?'

'A tapping, like metal on metal.'

'You sure about that, sir?'

'Certain,' Stephen said.

The policeman turned back towards the pavement and waved over the group of waiting men, and in less than a minute they had organised themselves into a production line, shifting debris away from the rear of the site.

By midday they had cleared a depression that reached almost to ground level. Stephen's hands were calloused and cracked and his shirt dripping with sweat. He bent to shift another lump of brickwork, when all of a sudden he found himself looking down on a twisted bed frame and, beneath it, the startled, dust-caked face of young Oscar Haverstock, who apart from a few cuts and bruises appeared in perfect health.

Immediately the production line broke up as the other men rushed to help free the boy.

'My dad's still down there!' Oscar cried out as he was carried away. 'I could hear him the whole time.'

'Don't worry, sonny,' the policeman said. 'We'll have him out in a jiffy, too.'

Although buried only a couple of yards from his son, it took them a further fifteen minutes to uncover Haverstock. A portly fellow with a dimpled chin scrambled down to the foot of the depression to help Stephen wrench him free, but Haverstock let out such a shriek that they had no choice but to release him.

'My leg,' the greengrocer moaned. 'I can't feel my leg!'

Stephen continued to clear rubble until the source of the Haverstock's discomfort became apparent: a wooden beam several yards in length had fallen across his legs, leaving his left foot protruding at a grossly unnatural angle.

'Water,' Stephen said to the man with the dimpled chin. 'Fetch him something to drink.'

The man nodded and clambered out, returning a moment later with a dented canteen. He unfastened the stopper and, with trembling hands, offered it to Haverstock, who took a long swig that ended with a splutter.

'Let's get about shifting this thing, shall we?' Stephen said, turning to the half-dozen men now standing about aimlessly.

With a barrage of shouted instructions he divided them into two groups, keeping half at the bottom of the depression with him and sending the other to half to the top, where the end of the beam jutted out. The second group began to lift, grunting with the effort as they raised the beam inch by inch to create a gap into which the first group were able to slide loose debris, forming a wedge that prevented it from dropping back down. As Haverstock let out another frightful cry, Stephen seized him by the shoulders and dragged him free at long last. The greengrocer's left foot hung limply beneath his trouser leg.

'Come on,' Stephen said, draping Haverstock's arm around his shoulder while the man with the dimpled chin took the other side. 'Let's find someone to take a look at that leg.'

Haverstock's eyes suddenly flashed with rage. 'It's you!' he gasped, and yanked his arm away. 'You was here yesterday, warning me about all this. It's all I could think about while I was down there!'

'What's he talking about?' the other man asked.

'Same bloke was here yesterday,' Haverstock told him. 'Said I needed to move my family on 'cos the Bosh was going to bomb Stepney that night. Thought he was off his nut at the time, but now…' He directed a mournful stare at the wreckage of his former home and livelihood. 'Dear God, Margret! Please, tell me you've found my wife.'

'Your son's waiting just over there,' their companion said. 'Don't worry, we'll keep looking until we find her.'

Haverstock reluctantly tore his gaze away from the wreckage and allowed himself to be led down to the pavement.

Once they had settled him onto a stretcher, the other man turned to Stephen. 'Clifford Whitman,' he said, holding out his hand.

'Stephen Rutherford,' Stephen said, shaking it.

'Tell me, Mr Rutherford, is that true what he said about you warning him?'

'The poor fellow's been down there all night with a broken leg and no food or water. He's obviously delirious.'

Whitman studied Stephen's face through narrowed eyes. 'You know, old chap, there's been talk of a man matching your description warning people their houses are going to be hit, and the next day they come home to a pile of rubble. Some have been calling him the Angel of the Blitz.'

'I...wouldn't know anything about that,' Stephen said.

'Well, those are the rumours, in any case. Personally I have to ask myself how a man might come to possess prior knowledge of where a German bomb is going to hit. I'd be interested to know your thoughts on the matter.'

Stephen tottered, feeling as though the exertion of the search must be catching up with him. 'It was interesting to meet you, Mr Whitman,' he said, and wiped his brow. 'I really must be going.'

Stephen spent the remainder of the afternoon warning victims of the coming night's raid. Dusk was approaching by the time he arrived home and the blackout curtains were already drawn. He opened the door to find Nell at the kitchen table, needlework in her lap and one of her rationing stews bubbling over the stove.

After bringing her back to life thirteen years earlier, Stephen had fallen for the girl he had originally pulled from a burning train carriage, and had revealed the true circumstances of their meeting only a few weeks into their courtship. Once her initial shock had died down, Nell hadn't run a mile as he was expecting, but instead challenged him to prove his gift from above. He had recited the headlines from the following day's *Yorkshire Evening Post* word for word, and the next day, his powers confirmed, had proposed.

'Smells good,' he said, lifting the lid on the pot. No matter how limited the ingredients, his wife had a talent for combining them in ways that made it nigh on impossible to tell. 'When's it ready?'

'An hour ago,' she said, and set down the stocking she was darning. 'How was your day?'

'Disconcerting.' He fetched a pair of bowls and began dishing out. 'The owner of one of the properties I visited yesterday refused to move on. A greengrocer, name of Haverstock.'

'Wouldn't be the first.'

'True, but there was a child in the building, an eleven-year-old boy.'

'Why wasn't he evacuated?'

'Apparently his father kept him behind to help out in the shop,' Stephen said. He served her a bowl of stew and sat beside her with his own. 'I went back this morning and was able to direct the search party to the boy and his father before they suffocated.'

'Why so glum then?'

'I think I was recognised, Nell. It seems word of my work is spreading. There's talk of an "Angel of the Blitz".'

She sniggered, then stopped and frowned, a fingertip delicately rested on her lips. 'Really, dearest, it just goes to show what a difference you're making. That's a good thing, don't you think?'

'I'm not so sure. For one thing it caused me to leave Haverstock's early. The rest of his family were still down there and weren't so lucky, I'd wager.'

'Stephen,' Nell said, and reached over the table to squeeze his hand, 'you mustn't torment yourself so. If you were only able to save two lives instead of three, that's still two that would have otherwise been lost. As I keep telling you, you can only do so much.'

'You're right, as always.'

'It's why you married me,' she said breezily. 'I have some news of my own, as it happens. I paid a visit to the doctor today and—'

'Not poorly are you, my love?'

She paused for a moment and then smiled. 'No, Stephen. He says I'm with child.'

He leapt to his feet, lifted Nell up and spun her around before setting her down and showering her face with kisses. The couple had been trying for a baby for over a decade without success, and had arrived at the conclusion that it was not in God's plan to bless them. That had all changed in an instant, but before Stephen could express his delight there came a loud rap at the door.

'At this hour?' Nell said. 'Who can that be?'

He shrugged, wondering the same, released her and went to the door. Standing on the other side were three policemen, their faces grim.

'What's this about?' Stephen demanded.

'You're under arrest, sir,' the policeman in the middle said. 'On suspicion of treason.'

Stephen could hear the distant wails of air raid sirens beyond the walls of his cell. According to his father's fob watch it was nearly three hours since his arrest, and although he had yet to be officially charged, he knew well enough the punishment for treason: death by hanging. They had no evidence against him aside from hearsay and coincidence, but in times such as these, when fear and mistrust ran almost as high as public outcry, people had been convicted for less.

But that would only happen if Stephen allowed it, and he had no intention of proceedings going any further. Such had been his desire to save as many lives as possible that he had become careless. Soon, however, he would have a family to protect – *a bloodline* – and he could no longer operate with such impunity.

He slid his boots off, lowered himself to the cold, hard floor and tucked each foot onto the opposing thigh in what *The Principles and Practices of Buddhist Monks* referred to as the 'lotus position'. Then, resting his hands in his lap, he closed his eyes and drew a deep breath.

After a minute or two of concentrating on no more than the air passing in and out of his lungs, a warm shiver danced over him. He was about to send his awareness back to that morning when he heard footsteps approaching along the corridor. They stopped outside his cell. There was a brief jangling of keys and, as he opened his eyes and rose to his feet, the door swung open before him.

'Hello again,' Clifford Whitman said, stepping in.

'*Whitman!*' Stephen gawked at the man he had met earlier that day. 'What the devil are *you* doing here?'

'I can only apologise for what must have been a distressing few hours, but I thought it best we speak in private.' Whitman transferred a thin cardboard file from his right hand to his left and produced a packet of cigarettes. He offered one, which Stephen declined, and then lit up himself. 'It seems you've been a busy bee, old chap.'

'I haven't the foggiest what you're suggesting,' Stephen lied.

Whitman shook his head, trails of smoke drifting from his nostrils. 'Come now, let's dispense with the charade, shall we? It may surprise you to know, but our meeting today wasn't entirely coincidental.' He opened the file and gazed down at the topmost page. 'In the last month there have been more than thirty recorded sightings of this so-called Angel of the Blitz. The Prime Minister is extremely interested in your activities.'

'*The Prime Minister*?'

'He tasked me with looking into the matter. There was some speculation among the Chiefs of Staff that you may be a German spy, however Mr Churchill believes your actions to be at odds with that theory.'

Stephen felt his cheeks burn. 'I'm quite certain there must have been some mistake.'

Whitman unclipped a page from the back of the file and passed it over. On it was a pencil sketch of a slender-faced man bearing a striking resemblance to Stephen.

The mention of the Prime Minister had piqued Stephen's interest, and since he planned to reverse his discovery the moment he was alone again there seemed little harm in satisfying his curiosity. 'What do you want?' he asked, handing the sketch back.

'Why, to know how it is that you do what you do, of course!'

'I suffered a cranial injury and a broken back in 1916,' Stephen said. He sat on the edge of the bench and began pulling his boots on. 'As well as gifting me the use of my legs again, God gave me the ability to see into the future. I use it to do His work, finding out where bombs will drop and then warning the victims beforehand.'

Whitman stared at him silently for a moment before dropping the end of his cigarette and grinding it under his heel. 'Remarkable,' he said.

'What do intend to do with me? Am I still under arrest?'

'The charges will be dropped immediately, Mr Rutherford. The Prime Minister would like to meet with you in person.'

'*Me*? But why?'

'There's a war going on, old chap, and, in case you hadn't noticed, our side isn't winning.' Whitman smiled and lit another cigarette. 'Provided you can learn to keep a lower profile, I suspect we may have use for a man of your talents.'

2

Present Day

Ordinarily Lewis avoided the news like the plague, but since Lance hadn't returned any of his texts he was starved of information. He stared at the television as the end credits rolled by, unable to move until his father pressed standby on the remote.

'Doesn't look like we'll be getting any more of them hot tips from your friend then.'

'What's wrong with you, Dad?' Lewis asked, appalled at the man's insensitivity. 'It's Sam they were talking about. You know, he's been coming round here since we were, like, six years old? He's even been on holiday with us. You don't *really* think he'd do something like that, do you?'

'Sounds like the police have already made up their minds, so it doesn't really matter what I think.' Lewis's father sat upright, his eyes suddenly widening. 'Hang on, you don't think this has got something to do with all that match-fixing business from last weekend, do you? I warned him about that, you know.'

Lewis shook his head and was about to take himself up to his room when his phone beeped. It was a reply from Lance at last:

SERIOUSLY need 2 talk. Meet end of ur road in 5?

He typed a quick reply and then stood up. 'Um, I might nip out for a bit, okay?'

'On a school night? Does your mother know?'

'It's Saturday, Dad. And I'm only going to the shops.'

'Fair enough.' His father drained his beer, scrunched the can and belched. 'In that case pick me up another couple of tins.'

Lewis didn't bother replying and hurried to the front door, snatching his coat from the end of the banister on his way out. It was a clear, cold night with the temperature already below freezing. Apart from a man walking a dog in the opposite direction, the road was deserted. Lewis buried his hands in his pockets and paced in the direction of Sam's house. He was almost at the end of the road when he saw Lance coming the other way and called out to him.

Lance glanced about anxiously and scurried over, his face haggard beneath the rim of his Peruvian beanie. 'Dude, keep your voice down!' he hissed.

'Why?'

Lance sighed and rubbed his chin. 'I don't know, maybe I'm just being paranoid. I didn't get much sleep last night.'

'Me neither,' Lewis said. 'How're things back at the Rayners'?'

'Not good,' Lance said, and glanced over his shoulder again. 'We stayed in a hotel while they searched the place overnight, and Chrissie's spent all night and most of today with Sam at the police station. They've charged him, Lewis.'

'I know, it was on the news,' Lewis said. 'Come on, let's walk.'

They turned onto the road next to the park, taking slow, shuffling steps under the glow of the streetlights.

'They're placing him on remand in a young offenders institute,' Lance said, staring straight ahead. 'Those places are almost as bad as adult prisons, Lewis. Chrissie's going out of her mind.'

'I bet.'

'Apparently he told them the whole shebang – time travel, the Tempus Project, *everything*. You can guess what the police thought.'

'That he's bonkers?'

'His lawyer even walked out on him. Chrissie's trying to find a new one.'

Lewis stopped and ground his teeth. 'Listen, I was thinking maybe we should go to the police and tell them about meeting Malcolm Fairview at that research facility place and gambling and everything. You never know, it might help. The money we made last week proves that Sam's telling the truth.'

'Dude, think about it, the money doesn't prove a thing except that we won a few bets. One lucky week, that's it! Remember, in this timeline Sam was never recruited to the Tempus Project. There won't be any record of him, and if we tell the police he took us to meet Malcolm Fairview the day before the murder it's only going to make Sam look even guiltier, *see*?'

'Well we've got to do something.'

Lance took a step closer and gripped Lewis's arm, squeezing it a little too hard. 'That's why I wanted to talk to you,' he said, his voice low. 'Remember when Sam showed us the bottle of pills right before the police arrived yesterday? He was being all tetchy and weird about it.'

'Yeah, course.' Lewis hesitated as he realised what Lance was getting at. 'Wait, you don't think it might still be there, do you?'

'No, Chrissie checked already. The police must have found it. *But...*' Lance released Lewis's arm, dipped his hand into the pocket of his duffel coat and pulled out a folded piece of paper, which he unwrapped to reveal a small yellow pill.

'*You took one*?'

'Slowing down time perception?' Lance said, a sheepish look on his face. 'It sounded fun and…well, Sam had the whole bottle. I didn't think he'd miss one pill.'

'You do realise what this means, don't you?' Lewis asked.

'I know,' Lance said. 'First we have to find a way to get it to Sam, though.'

3

Frances gazed at George across their table in a secluded corner of Chez Henri, the upmarket French bistro he'd chosen. The place was lavishly decorated, if a little overdone, with an elaborate water feature at the centre and a pianist tickling the ivories on the far side.

'Anything whet your appetite?' George asked, lowering his menu.

'I'm not really sure,' she said. 'French was never my strong point at school.'

'Then perhaps you'll allow me the liberty of ordering for us both?'

She let slip an involuntary giggle, then clapped her hand over her mouth. The thought of romance had never really entered her mind on their previous encounter, when if anything George had seemed a little standoffish. But perhaps that was just his professional persona.

He smiled and turned in his chair to wave the waiter over, revealing a Union Jack patterned cufflink beneath the sleeve of his jacket.

'Ah, Mr Steele, nice to see you again!' the waiter said, beaming as he approached. 'We usually see you every week. I was beginning to worry.'

George paused for a fraction of a second, his lip quivering. 'I'm afraid that was somewhat unavoidable, Richard. I suffered an impairment last month.'

'Nothing serious, I hope?'

'My right leg was amputated below the knee.'

Richard gulped and took a step back.

'An occupational hazard,' George went on, seemingly unfazed. 'And I escaped the incident with my life, so one can be thankful for small mercies, I suppose.'

'It's good to hear you're looking on the bright side, Mr Steele. So, are you ready to order?'

'We'll start with the terrine, followed by the pan-fried Dover sole.' George snapped his menu closed and handed it over. 'And to drink, a bottle of sparkling water and the 2011 Pouilly-fumé, I think.'

'An excellent choice.' Richard jotted the order in his notepad, collected the menus and departed with a bow.

'I like the cufflinks,' Frances said. 'Very patriotic.'

George glanced at his wrists. 'These? A small memento from my time at the Security Service, something they reserve for those injured in the line of duty. A parting gift, you might say.'

'They couldn't have kept you on in some capacity?'

'I was offered a desk job, but...well, let's just say I'm not cut out for shuffling paper. Rest assured though, there are plenty of opportunities out there for someone with my experience. I had a job offer only this afternoon, believe it or not!'

At that moment the waiter arrived back with an ice bucket. 'Your *entrées* won't be a moment,' he said, and topped up their glasses.

Once they were alone again, George held Frances in his gaze for a long moment. His eyes were the brightest shade of blue she'd ever seen.

'I managed to catch your television appearance,' he said, breaking the silence eventually.

'Oh, that,' she said. 'I can't stand that sort of thing, but it's part and parcel of the job, I suppose.'

'I thought you came across very well. A natural in front of the camera, you might say. You mentioned that you've charged a suspect?'

Strictly speaking, discussing the case was off bounds, but George was hardly Joe Public and, after the brick wall she'd met with back at the Security Service, there was a chance he might be more forthcoming than his former colleague.

She took a sip of wine and, lowering her voice, said, 'Just between us, it's Sam Rayner.'

He spluttered on his mineral water. 'Surely not the boy we interviewed together last year?'

'The very same.'

'Well I never, what a strange coincidence!' He dabbed his chin with a napkin. 'Any idea why he did it?'

'That's actually what I was doing when I bumped into you. In spite of the evidence, Rayner denies the charges and claims he discovered the body by chance. He claims he met the victim after being recruited to something called the Tempus Project, a government-funded organisation researching people with time-travelling capabilities. Don't suppose you've ever heard of anything like it?'

'Can't say that I have. And although plenty of things go on in the corridors of power that a foot soldier with my level of clearance wouldn't know about, I suspect time travel isn't among them.'

'No, of course not.' She cleared her throat. 'We found a bottle of pills containing a new molecule at Rayner's house, so if he's experimenting with mind-altering drugs a more likely explanation would be that he suffered a psychotic episode and has no recollection of killing Fairview. Of course, the brain injury he suffered last year may also have contributed.'

George blinked and took another sip of his water. 'How very tragic,' he said. 'It sounds like, even months after, Esteban Haufner's crimes have claimed another two victims.'

Frances felt a sudden chill sweep over her. 'You knew him, didn't you?' she asked.

'Esteban?' He nodded and stared down at his hands. 'We met in Northern Ireland the year after I completed my training. We were friends, for a while.'

'Your friend ruined my career.'

'I said we *were* friends, Frances. Past tense.' He twisted in his chair and hiked up his right trouser leg, revealing the alloy shaft of a prosthetic limb. 'Trust me, it's the sort of thing that can put a dampener on even the closest of friendships. After what Esteban's done, what I wouldn't give for ten minutes alone with him and no witnesses.'

'I suppose we'll just have to form an orderly queue then,' she said, pleased to have found some common ground, no matter how macabre.

George gazed at her for a moment, a faint smile on his lips. 'Tell me, Frances, do you enjoy the opera?'

'Opera?' she said, recalling a school trip to *The Magic Flute* during which she had fallen asleep. 'It's not something I know much about, but I've always liked the music.'

'Good. It's the last week of *Madam Butterfly* at the Royal Opera House. It's almost sold out, but I managed to get tickets to Tuesday's performance.' He lifted the dripping wine bottle from the bucket and topped up her glass. 'I'd be delighted if you'd join me.'

4

That first, awful night at Knotsbridge felt like it would never end. Sam lay curled under an itchy blanket, crying for his mother and willing himself to smell burned caramel again. It didn't work, and the long, sleepless hours stretched on and on. Regret, self-loathing and the image of Fairview's lifeless face circled one another in an endless loop around his head, until at long last a light bulb behind a wire mesh in the ceiling flickered on.

His cell was approximately eight feet by ten, just big enough to take three strides down the middle before having to turn back. Damp from a roof with a thousand leaks had bubbled the paintwork and gave the place a dank, funky, cave-like smell. At one end were a basin and a lavatory beneath a narrow, barred window, and, at the other, a thick metal door through which he could now hear the assorted murmurs and yells of Unit B stirring into life.

With a groan, he pushed his blanket back, swung his bare feet from the bed and rubbed his eyes. The clock on the wall said it was seven in the morning. Being a Sunday, the rest of his family would still be tucked up in bed, with the possible exception of Grandpa, who always got up early. Sam would have given anything to be back home with them, but at the moment it didn't seem very likely he'd ever set foot in his house again. Or, for that matter, return his mum to the person she had once been, bring Esteban Haufner to justice or win Eva back.

He pulled on the grey jogging bottoms, blue t-shirt and white plimsolls he'd been issued the evening before. After another minute or so he heard the door to his cell being unlocked and went to peer out. Her Majesty's Young Offenders Institution Knotsbridge was situated in a crumbling Victorian building that had once been an adult prison and now housed close to a hundred inmates between the ages of 15 and 18, with cells spread over four units (A, B, C and D), all fanning out like the spokes of a bicycle wheel from a central hub where a canteen, IT suite, library and other communal areas were situated. The other inmates on Unit B were gradually emerging from their cells and lining up against the railings of the walkway, so Sam did the same and turned to face his empty cell with the handrail against the small of his back. A guard holding a clipboard paced down the central aisle on the floor below, reeling off a string of prisoner numbers.

Once the roll was complete, they formed a line and traipsed through to the gloomy canteen in the central hub, where a breakfast of cold, lumpy porridge was served. Sam sat at a table in the far corner and was thankfully left alone. In spite of how awful the porridge tasted, he cleaned his scuffed plastic bowl and went back for seconds.

At seven-thirty they were instructed to shelve their trays and form another line. Instead of returning to their cells, the twenty or so boys were handed a blue windbreaker each and then led to the door onto an exercise yard enclosed by a tall chain-link fence. Sam's windbreaker was several sizes too big and hung almost to his knees.

As he rolled the sleeves up, the guard with the clipboard approached.

'Rayner?'

'Er, yeah, that's me.'

'This way,' the guard said, and waved him out of line.

'Where're we going?' Sam asked as he left the other boys to file out into the breaking of a grizzly, grey-skied day.

'Medical room.'

'Why?'

'You ask a lot of questions, matey,' the guard said, leading him back through the cafeteria. He pointed at his clipboard. 'Says here you need your medication. For your epilepsy, right?'

Sam stopped in his tracks. In this timeline his medication had prevented his seizures throughout December, and since he was pinning all of his hopes on their return, there was no way he could start taking his pills.

The guard took another couple of steps before turning back. 'Come on, we ain't got all day. Things to do, places to be and all that.'

Sam followed him up a creaking metal staircase, desperately searching for an excuse. At the top they turned down a dimly lit corridor. Halfway along was a door with a windowed counter. The guard pressed a button on the frame, and the frosted panel slid back to reveal a shaggy-haired man in a white coat. The guard passed him a sheet from his clipboard. The man studied it for a moment and turned away, returning a few seconds later with a small plastic cup, which he handed to Sam.

Sam stared down at the triangular pill at the bottom, his muscles tensing.

'Come on,' the guard said. 'Down the hatch.'

'No.'

'What's that? I don't think I heard you right.'

'I'm not taking it.'

The guard let out a deep sigh and massaged his forehead. 'Listen, matey, I'll let that slide seeing as it's your first day here, but my instructions are to make sure you take your medicine. We can do it the easy way or the hard way, your choice.'

Sam stared at him for a moment, then tipped the pill onto the floor and crushed it under his foot.

'Hard way it is then.' The guard unclipped a walkie-talkie, held it to his mouth and pressed a button on the side. 'Leroy, it's Pete,' he said. 'Reckon we might have a problem here – the new boy on Unit B is refusing to take his meds.'

There was a fizzle of static and then a crackly voice replied, 'Right you are, Pete. Take him back to his cell and I'll meet you there.'

'Roger that.' Pete lowered his walkie-talkie and clipped it onto his belt again. 'You,' he said, turning to the pharmacist, 'grab some of them pills and follow me.'

He gripped Sam by the elbow and, with the pharmacist scurrying along behind, propelled him back along the corridor, down the metal staircase and through the cafeteria once more.

On reaching Unit B, Sam looked up to see another guard waiting by his cell: Leroy, he supposed. The man must have been at least 6'5", and his frame was wide enough to fully obscure the doorway.

As they approached, he stepped to one side and pulled his nightstick out. 'In!' he barked, pointing it through the door.

Sam hesitated, then thought better of it, walked to the middle of his cell, stopped and turned around.

Leroy narrowed his eyes and shot him a dirty look. 'So, won't take your meds, will you?'

'Little sod stamped it under his foot,' Pete said. 'Right in front of me, too.'

'Oh, he'll take 'em all right,' Leroy said. 'All he needs is a bit of motivation. Where are they then?'

The pharmacist scuttled forward like a crab, a strip of Sam's epilepsy medication extended in his hand. 'Can I go now?' he asked feebly. 'I'm only supposed to dispense the inmates' medication. There's nothing in my duties about administering it.'

Leroy snatched the pills from him. 'Fine, get lost then.'

The pharmacist nodded and, looking very much relieved, bolted through the door.

'Last chance,' Leroy said, turning back to Sam. 'You going to take the damn things or not?'

'Um…' Sam raised his chin and squinted at the ceiling, '…not, I think.'

'Right, that's it!' Pete yelled, his eyelid twitching. 'I've had just about enough of your—'

'Hold his arms,' Leroy said, his voice disturbingly calm, and popped a pill from the strip.

'Huh?'

'You hold his arms, I'll make sure he takes it.'

Pete nodded, stepped behind Sam and seized his wrists, pinning them behind his back.

'No, wait—' Sam began, but Leroy reached over and squeezed his nose shut. He spluttered, panic exploding in his chest, but as he tried to take a breath, Leroy shoved the pill into his mouth and clamped his jaw shut.

Although Sam swallowed the pill almost immediately, they held him like that for a further thirty seconds before releasing him. With a whimper he dropped to his knees, his chest burning and his eyes stinging with tears.

Leroy crouched beside him. Squeezing Sam's cheeks, he forced his mouth open and tilted his head from side to side as he peered inside.

'Good,' he said at last. He released Sam's face, wiped his hand on his trouser leg and stood. 'It's done.'

'Cheers, mate,' Pete said quietly, and glanced at Sam in an almost apologetic way. 'Appreciate your help.'

'No worries,' Leroy said. 'Maybe next time he'll think twice about refusing his meds.'

5

It didn't take long for the dull fog brought on by Sam's epilepsy medication to settle over him, and he spent the rest of his first morning at Knotsbridge locked in his cell, sobbing uncontrollably. Any hope of an escape route through his seizures had been snuffed out, and it occurred to him that, after everything he had done to escape a terrible future at the hands of Dr McHayden, all he'd really achieved was to swap one prison for another. As he sat on the corner of his bed, watching the hands of the clock circle with glacial slowness, the idea began to form in his head that perhaps this was his destiny, a thing he could no more outrun than his shadow.

After that he kept his head down, and as the days of his first week at Knotsbridge slowly passed and the prospect of his seizures ever returning faded, he settled into a routine of sorts.

Lights on was at seven a.m., followed by breakfast in the canteen and a trip to the windowed counter of the medical room, where he now took his epilepsy pill willingly. Then it was thirty minutes of compulsory exercise in the yard with the other boys from Unit B.

While inside, inmates were expected to enrol on one of the educational or vocational courses available, and the rest of the mornings were given over to what were known as 'activities'. Although there wasn't much chance of being accepted to university if convicted, Sam decided he might as well continue his A-levels through a distance-learning programme instead of signing up for one of the over-subscribed construction or mechanics courses. Perhaps he was clinging to a remnant of his old life, but there was something reassuring about the familiarity of schoolwork, plus he got to spend most of his time in the empty library, which suited him down to the ground.

Lunch was at 11:30, and then he was back in his cell for another hour and a half. Afternoon activities ran until 4 p.m., followed by two more hours in his cell before an hour's 'association'. Along with exercise in the yard, this was by far the worst part of the day, as he was forced to mix with the other inmates. Most were serving time for gang-related crimes, with some already on their third or fourth convictions. Luckily word seemed to have spread that Sam was awaiting trial for murder, and apart from a few menacing stares thrown in his direction, he was pretty much left to himself.

After dinner in the canteen at 7 p.m., he was taken to the medical room for his evening pill and then locked in his cell again. Lights out was at eleven, and that was it until the following morning, when the whole process started afresh.

All of that time in his cell gave him plenty of chance for reflection. There could be no hiding from the fact that Sam had made a total mess of the second chance granted to him in this timeline, and, barring the sort of inter-vention that had saved him on Christmas Eve, he would probably wind up serving a prison sentence for a crime he didn't commit.

He often found himself contemplating what Eva was doing in this timeline, and what she would make of the news of his arrest. The things they had shared in Decem-ber had been erased from her memory, leaving only the faltering friendship briefly established in Montclair late last summer. The Eva who only he could remember had told Sam that he just needed to come and find her, but if he was convicted they would both be well into their twenties by the time he was released, by which time she could already be married with children. If she'd even speak to him, that was.

Things might have been so different if only he had used Tetradyamide to go back to save Fairview's life, but with no way of correcting his mistakes the future looked unavoidably bleak. In his darkest hours he even found himself wondering if the charges against him might be true, and whether he had lost his mind after his brain injury and imagined everything that he thought had taken place since.

There was, however, one small crumb of comfort. Assuming he hadn't really killed Malcolm Fairview, someone else must have, and if that person could be found then it might exonerate Sam. Unfortunately there wasn't much he could do about it without a lawyer. Chrissie had told him that she was looking for a new one, so it appeared he would just have to wait for visitors' day and hope for better news.

On the Friday at the end of his first week, a welcome break appeared in his routine. Instead of association at 6 p.m., Sam was escorted to the central hub. He was led to a room on the top floor, where he found a small, bearded man sitting on a foldout chair.

'Ah, good evening,' the man said, looking up from a folder spread open in his lap. 'It's Sam, yes? I'm Neal, the institute psychologist. Please, take a weight off.'

Sam nodded and sat on a second foldout chair that had been positioned to face Neal's. Like pretty much everywhere else in Knotsbridge, the room smelled strongly of damp and, judging by the industrial floor polisher leaning against the far wall, doubled as a storage cupboard.

'I think I can take it from here, thank you Pete,' Neal said, and crossed his legs at the knee, leaving one socked and sandalled foot dangling a few inches above the lino floor.

The guard, who was hanging back by the door, frowned. 'You sure? He's a slippery little so-and-so, this one.'

Neal removed a small plastic box from the pocket of his jacket and waved it in the air. 'I have my panic button, see? Have no fear, my good man, I shan't hesitate to use it if needs must. But I don't think that will be necessary, will it, Sam?'

Sam shook his head.

'Don't say I didn't warn you,' Pete said, and stepped out, closing the door behind him.

Neal smiled at Sam for an uncomfortably long moment, then licked his thumb and turned a page in his folder. 'Hmm, it says here that you were placed on remand last week, awaiting trial for murder. Is that correct?'

'I didn't do it!' Sam blurted out, almost instinctively.

'Um-hum.' Neal clicked the push button on his ballpoint pen and made a quick note. 'I beg your pardon, awaiting trial for an *alleged* murder.'

'Yeah, that's right, I suppose.'

'What I have here is a transcript of the interview conducted after your arrest. It says, and I quote, "The truth is I first met Malcolm Fairview just over a month ago. He was a scientist at the Tempus Project, a secret government organisation researching time-travel abilities in people with traumatic brain injuries, people like me." Sound familiar?'

'If that's what it says.'

Neal made another note and began twirling his pen between his fingers. 'You do realise that time travel isn't possible, don't you?'

'But—'

'And the Security Service have no record of a "Tempus Project" or anything remotely like it under their network of operations.'

'That's a lie!' Sam protested, leaning forward in his chair. 'All right, in this reality the Tempus Project was shut down after Thames House bombing, but it still existed before that. There *must* be records somewhere.'

'This reality?' Neal said. 'You make it sound as if there were any other.' He jotted yet another note in his folder, then clicked the nib of his pen away. 'The thing you need to realise, Sam, is that these are no more than delusions, a fantasy world you've constructed to help you cope with what by any stretch must have been a difficult few months. Like I said, time travel doesn't exist, and the notion that the Security Service would condone such pseudoscience, let alone fund it, is frankly inconceivable. I'm here to help you, Sam. I only want the truth.'

Sam wrung his hands in his lap. He was all too aware of where telling the truth had got him so far, and what Neal had just said struck a chord with his own worst fears.

'You expect me to tell you I made the whole thing up?' he said eventually. 'What I told the police *is* the truth.'

Neal gave a weary nod, closed his folder and stood. 'In that case I think we're done for today. Unless you're able to see your delusions for what they really are, Sam, then I think treating you may be beyond the scope of my skills. The best place for you might be a secure psychiatric hospital.'

'Can't be any worse than this place,' Sam muttered.

'I wouldn't be so sure of that. We'll discuss the matter further in our next session, but in the meantime I'd like you to have a long, hard think about what really happened.'

6

George was flat on his back, staring up at the ceiling. Hinds snored lightly beside him with her arm flopped across his chest. Reaching over, he covered her nostrils with his thumb and forefinger. After a couple of seconds she spluttered, withdrew her arm and rolled over to face the other way.

Although their affair was only a few days old, he was beginning to tire of the whole sham. Hinds was eager to please and, he supposed, the sex was enjoyable enough, providing a necessary outlet for his bodily urges, but it had taken only a couple of dates for her true colours to come to the fore as she'd begun constantly wheedling for compliments and assurances which he was forced to supply in order to maintain his guise. Ho-hum. If he was ever to win the prize he so craved, sacrifices would need to be made along the way, however it was becoming increasingly clear that the sooner he could complete his task and be rid of the irritating woman the better.

Moving slowly so as to prevent the springs of the mattress creaking, he slid from under the sheets, climbed out and reattached his prosthetic leg. A streetlamp on the other side of the curtains filled the small bedroom of Hinds's ex-council flat with a faint glow. He picked his way over the mounds of discarded clothing littering the floor to the dressing table chair, where his own attire lay neatly folded. One of his cufflinks had become loose again and lay glinting on the floor. He scooped it up, popped it in his shirt pocket and then slid his good leg into his trousers. His prosthetic proved more problematic. As he twisted and turned to free the carbon-fibre foot from a fold of material, he wobbled, lost his balance and had to grab hold of the dressing table to stop from crashing to the floor. A perfume bottle toppled over and rolled towards the edge. As it dropped, he reached up and caught it.

Holding his breath, he glanced over his shoulder. Hinds was still facing the other way, her long, dark hair spread across the pillow and her body rising and falling in time with her muffled snores. One of the manifold problems of one-leggedness was that it did not exactly lend itself to stealth, but at least he'd had the foresight to ply her with alcohol the previous evening (not that she needed much encouragement) and with any luck she wouldn't wake for several hours.

He returned the perfume bottle to its previous position, let himself out of the bedroom and gently eased the door closed. The open plan living-room-cum-kitchen was in a similar state of disarray, with an empty wine bottle and the remnants of last night's takeaway festering on the table. He crossed the room, his skin tightening as he passed a sofa plastered with cat hair. The culprit, a mangy, flea-bitten tabby named Hercule, lay curled in a basket on the other side of the room.

Upon reaching Hinds's desk, George switched on the computer and then stretched to retrieve the miniature camera he'd hidden on the top shelf of the bookcase two days earlier. The monitor flickered into life, displaying a blue screen. He placed the camera in his pocket, pulled out a flash drive, plugged it into the USB port and entered the password he'd filmed her using before they met for drinks last night. The screen cut to a desktop background of Hinds and her three brothers grinning like idiots, all in muddy rugby shirts. Shaking his head, George clicked on a folder titled *Work Stuff* and scrolled down until he located another marked *Fairview Case*. He dragged and dropped the contents to his flash drive and then, as it loaded across, limped to the coat stand by the front door.

Hinds's coat was hanging beneath his own. He rifled through the pockets until he located her set of keys. Aside from the two she had used to unlock the front door, there was no way of knowing which was which, so he pressed each of the remaining seven keys into a putty mold disguised as a business card holder.

He was on the last key when something brushed against the ankle of his left leg. Glancing down, he saw Hercule circling his feet.

'Piss off!' he muttered, flapping at the cat.

In response, Hercule purred and nuzzled the shin of his prosthetic.

George muttered a few choice insults, then drove his toe into the filthy animal's ribcage, launching it into the air. Hercule mewed, twisted in midflight and, as cats have a way of doing, somehow righted itself before landing on all fours. With a hiss, it scurried back to the kitchen, ears pressed flat to its head.

'George?' Hinds called from the bedroom. 'What you doing, hun?'

He spun around, wincing as his false leg failed to follow. Which pocket had he found her keys in? With no time to think, he shoved them into the nearest one and hobbled back to the computer. The download window indicated there were ten seconds remaining.

'Come on, come on,' he growled, one hand on the flash drive.

Out of the corner of his eye, he spied the handle of the bedroom door turn. There was a gentle ping and the download window disappeared. He yanked the flash drive out, dropped it in his pocket, hit the power button and turned around.

Hinds stepped into the room, rubbing her sleep-encrusted eyes. 'What are you doing out of bed?' she asked. 'It's four in the morning.'

'I thought I heard a noise.'

Hercule slunk from the kitchen, glared at George and hurried over to its mistress.

'Probably just the cat.' She scooped the vile beast up and, scratching it behind the ears, carried it over to the kitchen, where she opened a sachet of cat food and emptied the contents into a bowl. 'You were just hungry, weren't you, my little French detective?'

'There's been a spate of burglaries in the area,' George said, resisting the urge to inform her that Agatha Christie's famous creation was, in fact, a Belgian. 'You can never be too careful in this day and age.'

Hinds stepped towards him, hooking the fallen strap of her nightdress over her shoulder. 'My knight in shining armour,' she said, and linked her arms around his waist. 'Trying to protect me, were you?'

He did his best to disguise his gag reflex at her stale breath and somehow turned it into a bashful smile. 'Guilty as charged, my lady.'

'We're perfectly safe. Listen, hun, I was thinking of inviting my brother and his wife over for dinner tomorrow evening. They can't wait to meet you.'

'Can't,' he said, perhaps a little too hurriedly, and cleared his throat. 'Remember that job interview I told you about? I'll be out of town for a couple of days at least.'

She pouted exaggeratedly.

'How about next weekend?' he asked, knowing full well that if everything went to plan he'd be long gone by then. 'I think my diary's pretty clear.'

Hinds smiled again and stood on tiptoes to kiss him on the lips. 'Sounds good,' she said. 'Sooo…now the flat's clear of burglars and Hercule has a full stomach, what do you say we go back to bed? If I'm not going to see you for a couple of days, we'll just have to make the most of this morning.'

'With pleasure,' George said, and let her lead him back to the bedroom.

7

It was Saturday afternoon, and Chrissie and her mum had taken a taxi to visit Sam for what would be the first (and hopefully the last) time since he had been charged with murder. From a distance Knotsbridge Young Offenders Institution looked almost grand, but as they passed through a gate in the wall she noticed the crumbling brickwork and cracked tiles in the roof.

The driver dropped them outside the visitors' entrance, where there was already a queue forming. They joined the back, Chrissie's mother glancing about with eager anticipation as though they were waiting to enter an art gallery or museum. Chrissie's stomach churned when she spotted the guards searching each person at the door, and as they edged closer she hoped her anxiety wasn't obvious for all to see. She needn't have worried, though; there was only a single female guard on duty and, already dealing with a backlog, the flustered woman only gave Chrissie a half-hearted pat down and a cursory rummage through her handbag before waving her through.

They filed into a wide, damp-smelling hall filled with tables and chairs. Chrissie led her mum to a table near the middle, as far as possible from the prying eyes of the guards stationed around the edge.

After a couple of minutes Sam was escorted through a set of double doors at the other end. He craned his neck and glanced about before spotting them, then hurried over and threw his arms around Chrissie and their mum before breaking down in a fit of tears. It took him a minute or two to pull himself together, after which he took a seat at the opposite side of the table and dabbed his face with his sleeve. There were dark circles beneath his eyes and it looked as though he'd lost weight.

Their mother, who'd been staring about with a vacant expression, suddenly perked up. 'I must say, sweetie, I don't think much of your new school. The least they could do is offer us a cup of tea. Wouldn't you rather sit your A-levels somewhere else?'

Sam gulped and looked down.

'This isn't a school, Mum,' Chrissie said, resting a hand on her arm, 'it's a young offenders institute. Sam was arrested last week, remember?'

'Well, it could still do with a lick of paint.'

No one said anything for a while, and then Sam looked up again. 'I can't handle it in here,' he said. 'I've been seeing this psychologist, Neal. He thinks I'm delusional and imagined the whole thing. He says they'll move me to a secure psychiatric hospital unless I can see my delusions for what they are. What if he's right, Chrissie? What if I really did imagine the whole thing?'

'You didn't,' she said.

'Really? You seemed pretty unconvinced the last time I saw you.'

'Lance told me everything.' As casually as she could manage, she bent to unzip her boot and withdrew the folded piece of paper tucked into her sock. 'He also gave me this.'

'I don't understand,' he said, frowning as she slid it across the table.

'It's one of those pills you asked me to find.'

He opened and closed his mouth, looking like he might fall out of his seat. Slowly he unwrapped the paper and let out a gasp as he stared down at the yellow pill inside.

'But...*how*? The police searched the house, didn't they? I thought they found the whole lot.'

'Not quite,' she told him. 'Apparently Lance took it from the bottle just before you were arrested. Normally I'd have given him an earful, but on this occasion...'

With shaking hands, Sam folded the paper around the pill again and placed it in his pocket. 'This changes everything,' he said, a smile lifting the corners of his mouth.

'Good,' Chrissie said. 'That's what I was hoping you might say.'

8

'The first visitors' day usually shakes most boys up,' Pete said as he unlocked the door to Sam's cell. 'I reckon it's when reality finally kicks in and they realise they ain't got mummy to tuck 'em in no more. You look like your bleedin' lottery numbers just came up.'

'Lottery?' Sam said, realising that he, Lewis and Lance had probably missed a trick concentrating on football scores. He coughed into his fist and tried to keep from bouncing on his heels. 'Just pleased to see my family, that's all.'

Pete ushered him in and shook his head. 'Bleedin' nutter,' he muttered as he closed the door.

Once the clanking of footsteps had faded along the metal walkway, Sam performed a couple of victory laps around his cell and then collapsed onto his bed, for once shedding tears of joy. Yet again his friends and family had come through for him, and soon the last, horrible week would be just another memory of something that hadn't happened.

Sitting up, he pulled the pill out of his pocket, unwrapped it and raised it between his thumb and finger.

It looked real enough, and when he touched it to the tip of his tongue it tasted just as awful as ever. Wonderfully awful. Delicious, even.

He was about to swallow it down when a worrying thought occurred to him: it was only a few hours since he'd last taken his medication, and he only had the single dose of Tetradyamide, which meant only one chance to get out of the mess he was in. When he had used Tetradyamide the week before his arrest, he hadn't taken his epilepsy medication since Christmas, and back in the December-only-he-could-remember McHayden had supplied him with placebo pills. Thinking about it, there was no way of knowing whether or not his medication might suppress the effects of Tetradyamide as well as his involuntary seizures.

It was too big a risk, he decided. If things went wrong he would be stuck in this dead-end timeline, possibly for the rest of his life. With a sigh, he folded the sheet of paper around the pill again and returned it to his pocket.

Following his evening trip to the medical room, the first thing Sam did on being locked in his cell again was to rush to the lavatory and stick his fingers down his throat, emptying his stomach of the Spaghetti Bolognese served in the canteen for dinner and, he hoped, the epilepsy pill he'd swallowed five minutes ago.

Wiping his mouth with the back of his hand, he straightened up, then filled his plastic cup at the tap and drained it in a single gulp. It was now almost eight in the evening, and if he stayed up all night drinking water and then took his dose of Tetradyamide just before by lights on the next day, it would give him approximately eleven hours to flush what remained of his medication out of his system, which might just be enough.

After refilling his cup, he carried it over to his bed and opened his sketchpad. To pass the time he had been working on a drawing of Eva's face, and the prospect of seeing her again suddenly didn't seem so improbable. If everything went to plan, in a few hours he would finally have a chance to put things right.

Perhaps the most obvious place to start was the first day of December: the temporal crossroads at which both his father's funeral and the Thames House bombing had taken place. But he had already decided that returning to that point was too dangerous, because Lara McHadyen and the Tempus Project would still be out there, lurking in the shadows. With only a single chance at fixing things he needed something more certain. A safer bet was, perhaps, to return to the day everything had gone wrong in this timeline: the day of Malcolm Fairview's murder. If Sam could save Fairview's life then the bottle of Tetradyamide he had taken from the flat would still be there, and provided he could then persuade Fairview to help him again (which the man had seemed eager enough to do the first time around), there would potentially be plenty more chances to prevent the Thames House bombing.

His thoughts were disturbed by muffled shouts outside his cell. He closed his sketchpad, drained the last of his water and went to the door. Peering through the reinforced glass of the window, he saw Leroy rush past in the direction of the central hub, followed by Pete and the remaining two guards on Unit B, all with their nightsticks drawn.

Sam frowned and stepped back. Although he'd only been at Knotsbridge a week, this was highly irregular. Obviously there must have been a disturbance of some sort in one of the other units.

He pulled his pill out again and unwrapped it. All of a sudden there were more shouts from the direction of the central hub, and then, to his shock, two gunshots rang out in quick succession.

Without hesitating, Sam stuffed the pill in his mouth and swallowed it down. There was a brief pause followed by a third gunshot before the cell and the corridor outside were plunged into darkness.

9

Sam cowered in the corner of his cell, the blackness around him echoing with the yells of the other inmates in Unit B. There was another distant smatter of gunfire and then the shouting from the central hub fell silent.

Dropping to his hands and knees, he crawled blindly forwards until his shoulder connected with the leg of his bed and then rolled over and dragged himself under. He could only guess at what was going on out there, but it sounded like another prisoner had somehow got hold of a gun and was trying to shoot his way out, and one of the guards had probably cut the power in an attempt to disorientate him. Yesterday, or even a few hours ago, Sam might have considered this an opportunity, but now it only represented a threat to his plans.

After a few minutes under his bed he became aware of a vague tingling in his limbs. His eyes were now accustomed enough to the dark that he could make out the bottom of the mattress a couple of inches above his nose, but none of the swirling colours that normally tinged his vision as Tetradyamide took hold were present.

He gave it another minute and then poked his head out. At the same instant a torch beam sliced through the darkness on the other side of the window in his door. There was someone out there, but Sam had no idea whether it was one of the guards or the person responsible for the shooting.

Unable to wait any longer, he drew his head back and closed his eyes, trying to turn the pages of time. At first nothing happened, and his breath caught in his chest as he realised that his epilepsy medication, no matter how weakened, might be interfering with the Tetradyamide.

But then the yells from the adjoining cells were suddenly cut off, as was the draught blowing across the floor. He briefly saw the underside of the mattress before rolling out and crawling back to the corner of his cell, where he stood and, as the lights flickered on, spat a small yellow pill into the palm of his hand.

Channelling his concentration, he focused on his destination: a Thursday morning two weeks gone. With an almost resistant lurch, the pages jerked back faster.

While the Tetradyamide appeared to be working, his control had never felt so tenuous. He saw himself re-gurgitate a cupful of water and open his sketchbook. As he stepped to the basin, the water in his cup flowed upwards into the tap, and then the turning of the pages grew so fast that all detail was lost. He was vaguely aware of standing next to the windowed counter of the medical room before the backwards-playing images became no more than flashes of light and colour.

After a while these were spliced with intermittent periods of darkness, each signifying an earlier night at Knotsbridge. He counted them off one by one, reaching the day of his arrest and passing into the week before. It took all of his willpower to maintain his control, but eventually the jarring bursts of light and dark slowed, giving way to the view of a road lined with tall, flat-fronted houses: Malcolm Fairview's road.

Judging from the direction he was facing, Sam still hadn't reached the flat yet, but if he was going to prevent

Fairview's murder he needed more time. He flicked the pages slowly back, seeing himself reverse down the pavement, weaving in between occasional patches of frost.

Eventually he reached the tube station, where he stopped at the entrance for a silent conversation with a group of nuns before two shiny pound coins leapt from their collection bucket and into his outstretched hand. Then he saw himself back through the barriers and onto a lift, which carried him down to a queue at the bottom.

Two more lifts arrived as he edged down a short flight of steps and backwards onto the crowded platform. Finally he stepped aboard a waiting train and lowered himself into a seat. It was only as the doors slid closed that he mouthed the word, 'Play.'

The rewinding images ground to a halt and Sam was suddenly aware of tinny, too-loud music seeping from the headphones of the girl in the next seat. Someone nearby was wearing too much cologne. And then, with a beeping noise, the doors slid open.

He flew out of his seat, elbowing his way past the other passengers waiting to get off.

'Oi, learn some manners!' someone shouted as he dived past.

Sam didn't look back but raced up the stairs two at a time. Sucking in a breath, he squeezed his way around the patiently waiting crowd at the bottom of the lifts and managed to wedge his foot between the closing doors of a departing one before forcing his way on. To an array of muttered complaints and insults, he pushed to the front and was first out when the doors opened at ground level. Barely slowing, he raced through the barriers and, after dodging a collection-bucket-wielding nun, hit the pavement at full sprint.

It didn't take long before a stitch began to throb in his side, but he put his head down and powered through it, at one point skidding on a patch of icy ground but somehow regaining his footing.

By the time he turned onto Beaumont Crescent his heart was hammering and the pain in his side had become almost unbearable, however he kept going until he reached the tree by the cracked wall outside number 47.

Hands on knees, he stopped to catch his breath. Then, crouching, he eased the gate open and crept down the steps to the basement flat. Everything was exactly as he remembered, right down to the muffled classical music coming from somewhere inside. He was about to press the doorbell when it dawned on him that the killer might already be there. Up until then Sam had been so pre-occupied with the question of whether or not he could get back to this point that he hadn't given any thought to how he'd prevent Fairview's murder if he actually managed it. Not knowing what else to do, he followed the gravel path around the side of the building again. As he sneaked down the steps to the patio, he glanced up and through the living room window just as Malcolm Fairview walked into sight.

Sam felt his legs go weak, and ducked behind a potted bush for cover. Fairview was still alive, and now all Sam had to do was to warn him and together get the hell out of there, thereby altering the timelines and creating a new present in which Fairview had never been killed and Sam was never arrested.

Craning his neck, Sam peered out to see the scientist enter the kitchen, fill his kettle at the sink and then place it on its stand. He took a deep breath and drew himself up. Just as he was about to step out, Fairview suddenly turned around and strode through the living room door and into the hall.

Sam ducked behind the bush again and unzipped his coat. In spite of the chill to the air, his hands felt clammy.

Less than a minute had passed before Fairview returned, glancing over his shoulder as if talking to someone out of sight. He went back into the kitchen, took two mugs from the cupboard above the sink and dropped a teabag into each. After topping them up with boiling water, he stepped into the living room again.

Sam realised Fairview must have just let his killer into the flat, and scanned the patio for something to use as a weapon. Sticking from the soil in the raised flowerbed behind him was a three-pronged gardening fork. He snatched it up and turned back to the living room window just as a man with a shaved head and a beard stepped through the door from the hall.

Although his appearance was drastically different, there could be no mistaking those bulging eyes and the smile that looked like a wolf bearing its teeth: it was Esteban Haufner, the man who had killed Sam's dad.

10

From his position behind a potted bush, Sam gaped through the rear window of Fairview's flat. In sabotaging Flight 0368 and planting the bomb at Thames House, Esteban Haufner had ruined Sam's life across multiple timelines. And now he was about to do it all over again by killing Malcolm Fairview.

Deep tremors shook Sam's body, rocking him back and forth. The question as to why Haufner had done (or would do) these things barely registered; all that mattered was stopping him. But what was a skinny, brain-damaged kid with a blunt gardening fork going to do against a trained killer who'd evaded capture for almost two months? If he went in there alone, he'd probably get himself killed too.

Realising what a laughable weapon it was, he went to drop the gardening fork, only to discover that he couldn't move. The world around fell oddly silent, the background rustle of the wind through the trees snapped out. Less than twenty feet away, Haufner and Fairview stood as still as mannequins.

Sam was frozen, trapped in a single moment, just like his first few seizures in hospital last year. But before he could make sense of what was happening, time seemed to skip forwards as though he were missing a page in the book. As if from nowhere a robin redbreast materialised on the patio before him, its head cocked to one side. Haufner and Fairview vanished, teleporting halfway across the room and reappearing by the door to the hall.

Stutteringly, the pages began to turn again and the scene sprang into life. As Fairview stepped into the hall, Haufner paused to pull on a pair of leather gloves, reached into his pocket and then followed him out. Finally able to move, Sam clambered to his feet, startling the robin into flight. He dropped the gardening fork and raced around the side of the house and up the front steps.

Scanning the road, he found it deserted. There was no way of knowing how much time he'd bought in which to prevent the murder, but it could only have been a few minutes at most. With no other option, he pulled out his phone and dialled 999.

'Emergency services,' a woman's voice said. 'Which service do you require?'

'I need a police car. *Now!*'

'What's your location?'

'47C Beaumont Crescent, Notting Hill,' Sam said, and took a breath. 'Please hurry, there's going to be a murder.'

There was a pause followed by a click. 'Okay, a unit has been dispatched. Just stay calm and tell me what's happened. Let's start with your name.'

Sam looked up to see the curtains in the neighbouring house twitch and caught a glimpse of an elderly lady at the window, probably the same person who would pick him out from an identity parade on the night of his arrest.

'Are you still there?' the operator asked. 'I need a name.'

Feeling a horrible sense of déjà vu, Sam hung up. Short of letting himself into the flat, he had just re-established the conditions by which he'd originally implicated himself in Fairview's murder.

Time was running out...

...*or was it*?

With Tetradyamide in his blood, Sam could still correct his mistake. Come to think of it, all he really needed to do was travel back a few more hours and make sure he left home early, giving himself plenty of time to warn Fairview before Haufner arrived.

He threw his hands in the air at not thinking of it sooner, closed his eyes and formed the word 'Back' in his head.

The scene before him ground to a halt, but instead of rewinding, he was left standing in a frozen snapshot of the moment once again. He tried to sweep the pages back, putting every last ounce of his mental strength into the task, but nothing happened and he was left staring at the still image of an unruly, bare-branched tree that was beginning to crack the bricks of the wall in the front garden.

'Back!' he repeated, now screaming the word in his head. 'Back, damn you!'

So slowly that it was almost imperceptible at first, the scene began to lighten like a gap in the clouds had appeared overhead. As he watched, the colour washed from the image of the tree until, like a pencil sketch, only the dark outlines of the trunk and branches remained. After a while these vanished too, leaving Sam floating in a sea of white light.

Chapter VI

A Wanted Man

1

June 1954

It was the twins' thirteenth birthday, a day of monumental importance in the Rutherford household. Once the cake had been cut and the presents opened, Nell made herself scarce while Stephen sat with the children at the table he had built from mountain ash the summer before.

'Me first,' Nora said, and presented her bandaged right hand.

'No, me!' Marcus objected, elbowing his sister in the ribs and laying his hand next to hers.

Stephen gave an exasperated sigh. Perhaps it was the isolation of their upbringing and the consequent lack of playmates, but it seemed as though the twins had been at each other's throats from the moment they were old enough to walk and talk. When Marcus had shown an interest in shooting, Nora had insisted that she wanted to too, practising day in and day out until she was twice the marksman of her brother. And when Nora had taken up the piano, Marcus had soon after spotted a fiddle for sale at the market in Ilulissat and begged Stephen to buy it for him. Both children had become skilled musicians in the years since, but instead of playing together practised at opposite ends of the farmhouse, creating a cacophony of competing sounds that left Stephen and Nell wincing.

'Does it really matter who goes first?' he asked.

'Yes,' Nora said matter-of-factly. ' I go first 'cos I'm the oldest.'

'By all of five minutes,' Marcus grumbled. He rolled his eyes but withdrew his hand all the same.

An anxious silence settled over the table as Stephen began peeling back his daughter's bandage. She bit her lip as he reached the gauze covering her palm, then let out a quiet gasp as he prised it away to expose a long, puffy scab, still red around the edges.

'It didn't work,' she said, lowering her head.

Stephen rested a hand on her shoulder and gave it a squeeze. 'It doesn't matter.'

'Yes,' she said and looked up him with tear-rimmed eyes, 'it does.'

'Me next,' Marcus chimed in, showing no concern for his sister's dismay.

Stephen nodded and slowly unwrapped the boy's bandage. The gauze over Marcus's palm came away with almost no resistance. On this occasion there was no scab, only a faint white line in place of the cut Stephen had delivered with a scalpel the week before.

'It's healed!' Marcus exclaimed.

'Yes, that it has,' Stephen said, tracing the line with his finger.

Nora let out a sob, pushed her chair back and ran from the farmhouse, slamming the door behind her.

* * * * *

Stephen gave his daughter thirty minutes to cool off before going after her. It was a beautiful summer's day, barely necessitating the sheepskin coat he wore, and the never-setting sun of the summer months had long since melted away the snows around the farmhouse to reveal a lush scrub dotted with wildflowers.

After meeting Clifford Whitman in the autumn of 1940, Stephen had used his gift from above to subtly influence the direction of the war. The Normandy landings had originally been repelled after the location of the landing sites was leaked to the Germans, allowing them to secretly strengthen their defences in key positions along the coast, but when the source of the leak had been identified a few days after the failed assault, Stephen was able to relay the news back to Whitman weeks beforehand, after which the mole was fed a constant stream of misinformation that ultimately led to the enemy fortifying positions hundreds of miles to the east.

Once Hitler was defeated and peace returned, Stephen and Nell had purchased a remote plot on the west coast of Greenland. Although the family still lived modestly, Stephen had used his gift to predict the rise of several emergent post-war industries, making a series of profitable investments, not least shares in a combine harvester firm that continued to bring in a significant income. In the face of the looming threat of a new conflict between East and West, he had channelled this newfound wealth into expanding his network of operations, acquiring high-ranking contacts in both the American and the Soviet governments.

And now, with the discovery that Marcus shared the healing ability that made travel through time possible, there was the prospect not only of an apprentice to join Stephen's work but also a successor to continue it.

It didn't take long to find Nora; she had taken herself off to the stream that ran through the edge of their land, and was sitting on a rocky outcrop, tossing pebbles into the freezing water that flowed from the snow-capped hills on one horizon down to the head of the murky fjord that lead into Baffin Bay on the other. Although she must have heard her father's approach, she didn't look up as he sat beside her, but selected another pebble, assessed its weight and then pitched it into the stream, resulting in a sizeable splash.

'I'm sorry,' Stephen said. 'I know how much you wanted this.'

Nora remained staring steadfastly ahead.

He picked a pebble from the ground by his feet and sent it after hers, missing the stream and striking the slope of the opposite bank.

'It's not fair,' she said eventually.

'I know,' he said, 'but it is what it is.'

She turned to face him at last. Although her eyes were dry, her cheeks remained blotchy and red and streaked by recent tears. 'Why him and not me?' she asked.

'Because that is God's will, poppet. It isn't our place to question it.'

'But isn't that what you do every time you alter the past, Father? Question God's will?'

He chuckled; it was a theological dilemma to which he had devoted much contemplation. 'God gave me my gift for a reason,' he explained, 'therefore to *not* use it would be against His will.'

She paused to consider this before looking away again. 'It's still not fair.'

'Often that's the way of life.'

'So what happens now?'

'Now?' Stephen ran his fingers through his hair, which these days contained more silver than it did black.

'In a few days' time I'll perform surgery on Marcus to recreate the cranial injury I sustained in 1916. Afterwards – God willing – he should develop powers similar to my own.'

Nora sniffed and tossed another pebble into the stream. 'You knew I wouldn't heal, didn't you?'

'I had my suspicions. When you broke your arm so badly two winters back…'

'I know,' she said. 'Me too.'

'Then why go through with it?'

'Do you really have to ask?' She paused to stare angrily down at the scab on her right palm, managing to look a great deal like her mother while she did so. 'Ever since I can remember, all I've ever heard is how important your work is. If I can't heal like you and Marcus then what am I supposed to do? What's my role?'

Stephen tucked a curl behind her ear and smiled. 'My child,' he said, 'you are a Rutherford, and there will always be a role for you in this family.'

2
Present Day

On Sunday morning Chrissie jolted awake to the view of dull dawn light slipping in through a gap in her curtains. She sat up, her chest tightening. Lance groaned, rolled onto his side and tugged the covers over his head.

Was this a new timeline? And, if so, why could she still remember the old one? Surely if Sam had used the Tetradyamide she'd given him to prevent himself from ever getting involved in Malcolm Fairview's murder then her memories should have been replaced by those of a timeline in which her brother had never been arrested.

It appeared there was only one way to know for certain, so she climbed out of bed and tiptoed to the door.

As she crept down the stairs, the sound of Grandpa's radio drifted out from the kitchen.

She paused outside Sam's room to collect herself before knocking. There was no answer, so she opened the door and peered inside. Her brother's bed was empty and the floor was still strewn with the mess left by the forensics team the week before, confirming her fears. The logical conclusion was that something must have gone wrong at Knotsbridge and the guards had found the pill before Sam could take it.

Shaking her head, she turned back to see a shadow move across the other side of the frosted panel in the front door. Suddenly there was a colossal thud. The wood around the lock splintered and the door flew open on its hinges.

Standing on the other side was a policeman in full body armour with a red battering ram in his hands. Several armed officers poured past him and into the house. They split up, two racing up the stairs towards her and the remainder sweeping through rooms on the ground floor.

She stepped to one side as they bustled past, her hand over her belly. Several calls of 'Clear!' echoed around the house and then, one by one, the armed officers re-emerged with their weapons lowered.

The policeman with the battering ram stepped through the demolished door frame and raised his goggles. 'Your brother, where is he?'

'His cell at Knotsbridge, I assume,' Chrissie said.

'No,' the man said. 'Someone broke him out yesterday evening.'

3

It was as though Sam's consciousness had been severed from his body and left stuck in the space between time-lines. With emptiness stretching out in every direction and nothing on which to orient himself, he had no idea how long he'd floated there; it could have been minutes, days, weeks or even months.

As if from nowhere a force exerted itself. It felt like his disembodied mind was being sucked through the nozzle of a vacuum cleaner. He experienced the sensation of falling but without the awareness of movement, nor up or down. Dark scratches began to etch themselves in the whiteness, carving the outline of an image. Gradually objects took shape around him. At first everything looked blurred and faded, but as new scratches added definition and detail, colour slowly bled into the picture.

He blinked and found that he was lying in a grand four-poster bed made with plain white sheets. His head ached like his brain had been torn apart and then crudely stitched together again. It sounded a lot like a storm was raging outside, but his only view was through the parted white drapes at the foot of the bed, where he could make out the interior of a dimly lit room with a fireplace directly opposite. A log crackled in the hearth, throwing out a soft orange orb that illuminated a stuffed stag's head on a placard above the mantelpiece. Glancing down, he saw that he was wearing brown-and-cream-striped py-jamas that weren't his.

Groggily, he propped himself up, his stomach churning as though he hadn't eaten in days. He had the vague impression that something bad had happened, but thinking about it only made his headache worse. Suddenly he heard a faint plop like a droplet of water landing in a half-full bucket, and a memory of his cell at

Knotsbridge and the roof with a thousand leaks came rushing back.

What had happened, and where was he? Wherever it was, it definitely wasn't Knotsbridge. At least he didn't seem to be in any immediate danger, and in the comforting warmth of the fire he let his head flop back to the pillow and massaged his eyelids to the sound of rain lashing outside.

Little by little fragments of his memory returned. He recalled the single dose of Tetradyamide that Chrissie had given him. He had planned to reverse Fairview's murder, but something had gone wrong and...

...*Esteban Haufner had been at the crime scene.*

Sam threw back the sheets and leaped from the bed, his pulse racing. He had failed to prevent Fairview's murder once again, and in the process had re-established many of the conditions that had led to his arrest.

There was a window set in the wall to his right. Barefooted, he staggered over, pulled the curtains back and found himself looking down onto a dark, wet and windswept country garden. The landscape beyond its hedge borders was empty and barren in all directions, without so much as the light of another house as far as the eye could see.

It didn't make sense, because any changes he might have made on the day of Fairview's murder should have created a new timeline in which he was either still in Knotsbridge or was going about his old life at home with his family. What could he have possibly done to end up here, wherever here was?

'Good evening,' a voice with an American accent said from the other side of the room.

Sam spun around, his heart in his mouth. At that moment a fork of lightning tore through the sky behind him. The flash of pale light through the window briefly lit up a figure on a sofa on the far side of the bed.

'Who's there?' Sam called out.

As darkness returned to the room, the figure heaved itself up and, using a walking stick for support, hobbled towards him. It was an elderly man, hunched and frail, and as the rumble of thunder reached them, the glow of the fire revealed a round, egg-shaped head devoid of hair, the right side of which was covered by a faint burn mark.

'It's a pleasure to meet you at last,' the man said. 'My name is Michael Humboldt.'

4

It felt as though an elephant was standing on Sam's chest, squashing the air from his lungs, and his knees wobbled beneath him. He floundered backwards and had to grab hold of one of the curtains in order to prevent himself crashing to the floor. Michael Humboldt, the man who had turned Esteban Haufner, was standing less than ten feet away.

'Y-*you*!'

'Ah, you already know who I am,' Humboldt said, leaning on his walking stick and nodding with understanding. 'So our paths have crossed in another timeline then?'

Sam closed his mouth before he could give anything else away. Humboldt was right, of course; in this reality Sam had never met Lanthorpe and Phelps at the Tempus Research Facility and had never been tasked with tracking down Humboldt's location prior to a missile strike. In theory, he should have no idea who Michael Humboldt was.

'I don't know what you're talking about,' he said, playing for time.

Humboldt gave a tired sigh. There were dark shadows beneath his eyes and a pale, sickly complexion to his skin. 'Drop the games, would you? I know exactly who you are, Sam, and what you're capable of.'

Sam hesitated, unsure how to respond. Somehow Humboldt already knew about his ability, which, come to think about it, was probably the very reason he was here. And if that were true it might mean Sam had something to bargain with.

'Where are we?' he asked. 'How did I get here? And what do you want with me?'

Humboldt blew air through his lips. 'Phew, that's a lot of questions. But let's deal with them each in turn. Firstly, we're in south Wales, not far from the Brecon Beacons. I purchased the property almost thirty years ago as part of an investment portfolio. Sadly it hasn't worked out as much of an investment, but I've never had the heart to sell the place. As for your second question, since you managed to get yourself arrested and charged with murder, the only way I could speak with you was to break you out.'

'That was you?' Sam asked, remembering the sound of gunfire at Knotsbridge.

'An associate of mine,' Humboldt said. 'Sometimes extreme circumstances call for extreme measures. Anyway, I believe that answers your first two questions. As to what I want with you,' he turned and pointed to the sofa he'd been sitting on with the handle of his walking stick, which, Sam now noticed, was shaped like a dragon's head, 'the answer to that is a little more complicated. Please, let's sit and I'll do my best to explain.'

'I think I'd rather stand,' Sam said, trying not to teeter.

'Suit yourself.' Humboldt hobbled to the sofa and lowered himself on one side, the ancient leather cushions creaking under his weight. 'Age and ill health mean I no longer have the luxury of that choice.'

'Get on with it,' Sam snapped, frustration getting the better of his fear. 'Why am I here?'

Humboldt smiled, shadows from the fire playing across his face. 'You're here because we're two of a kind, Sam.'

5

Sam's vision wavered and he suddenly found himself reeling again. Unable to remain upright, he stumbled to the sofa and slumped beside Humboldt. '*Two of a kind?* I…I don't get it.'

'Why, did you think you were the first time traveller?'

Sam swallowed the lump in his throat and cast his mind back to the day last autumn when he'd been recruited to the Tempus Project. Lara McHayden had told him the story of an injured American soldier who claimed to have become unstuck in time. She'd also told him the soldier had killed himself, which couldn't possibly have been true because, in that instant, Sam knew beyond any doubt that he was talking to the same person.

'Dr McHayden told me about you,' he said. 'You're the soldier, the one she worked with in the 60s.'

'The very same.' Humboldt cracked a smile, turned his head and pointed to the base of his skull, indicating a scar of a different texture to his faded burns. 'The source of my powers,' he said, turning back. 'You have something similar, I presume?'

Without his noticing, Sam's fingers had strayed beneath his hair, feeling out the ridge of his own scar. He quickly lowered his hand.

'Such an injury would kill an ordinary person,' Humboldt went on, 'but you and I are different. We share a unique genetic trait, Sam, one that enables our cells to heal at a vastly accelerated rate. That trait is the only reason you survived and recovered from the damage to your brain. The resulting scar tissue is what gives us our ability to travel through time.'

Sam blinked at him, momentarily lost for words. Back at St Benedict's they had described his recovery as extraordinarily rapid, and suddenly his entire life seemed to unravel into a succession of rapidly fading bruises and too-soon-healed scabs. Was this all somehow connected to what Dr Wallis had told him about the abnormalities in his cells? He glanced down at the thin white scar on his knuckle from the time Chrissie had put his little finger between the teeth of a pair of pliers when they were kids. Back then the doctors had said he might lose the finger, but now you could hardly tell.

He looked up again. After months of nothing but questions, he was finally closer to getting some answers. Of course he still didn't trust Humboldt one bit, but if McHayden had lied about the man taking his own life then what other mistruths might she have spun?

'I don't know why you expect me to believe anything you say,' he said, as much for his own benefit as Humboldt's. 'You're a criminal, a terrorist. *You* turned Esteban Haufner and that makes you just as responsible for my father's death as he is!'

'I can only apologise about Esteban,' Humboldt said, staring down at the floor. 'For a time he was a highly valuable asset to my organisation. Then, last year, it became apparent he'd stopped following orders and was operating under his own agenda. I made the decision to have him eliminated, which, it turns out, was a monumental misjudgement on my part. Esteban set about exacting his revenge and, since he knew he would never be able to get to me directly, targeted my research instead. I hate to disappoint you, Sam, but the sabotage of Flight 0368, the Thames House bombing and Malcolm Fairview's assassination were not acts of my doing, but acts of retaliation intended to cause me harm.'

'Cause *you* harm?'

'If it's any consolation, he'll be getting his come-uppance soon enough.'

Sam shook his head. 'But what have any of those things got to do with you? It was *my* dad who died in the crash and *me* who got blamed for Fairview's death. How does any of that affect you?'

'That's what I've been trying to explain,' Humboldt said, glancing back up. 'The healing gene is a trait unique to the men of our family. We are of the same bloodline, you and I, and the sabotage of Flight 0368 was intended to stop me finding *you*.'

6

Sam recoiled against the armrest of the sofa. '*Family*?' he repeated, spitting the word back. 'Have you completely lost the plot? I've never even met you before, in this timeline or any other!'

'Maybe, maybe not,' Humboldt said with a dismissive shrug. 'We only have the memories of what we experience, so who's to say what may or may not have taken place in other timelines? Either way, it doesn't change the fact that we're related.'

Sam's stomach churned again, bile stinging the back of his throat. 'You're lying,' he croaked. 'You have to be.'

'In recent months researching my family tree has become something of a hobby of mine,' Humboldt said. He raised his walking stick and began inspecting the handle with great interest. 'Tell me, Sam, how much do you know about your ancestry?'

Sam stared back across the sofa, his jaw clenched. Although it pained him to admit, he didn't know much beyond his immediate family. His mum was estranged from her parents over some ancient quarrel that had never been resolved, and the only relatives she even loosely kept in touch with were her cousins from Cardiff. On his dad's side there were Grandma and Grandpa, of course, and Auntie Laura, his dad's childless sister. But apart from that…

Humboldt lowered his stick and gazed at Sam with eyes that pointed in slightly different directions. 'Allow me to give a little of my own background, if I may. I was born in Missouri in the spring of 1950. My father was Kurt Humboldt, a violent drunk who told me next to nothing of his own upbringing, meaning that what little I learned of my paternal lineage came from my mother, rest her soul. My paternal grandfather, Gerhardt von Humboldt, was a German immigrant who, along with his wife and sons, fled to the United States in the 1930s during the Nazis' rise to power, dropping the 'von' part of the name along the way.' He reached into his shirt pocket, pulled out a photograph and passed it to Sam. It showed a couple posing with two young boys in matching sailor outfits. Although printed on glossy modern paper, it was black and white and looked like it had been taken at some point in the early twentieth century. 'Last year, as part of my research, I even visited Ottendorf, the fishing village Gerhardt hailed from. Apart from my grandfather there was no record of anyone by the name of Humboldt ever having lived in the area, and while Pa was alive he never so much as hinted at the fact he had a brother.'

Sam handed the photograph back. 'Fascinating as this is, I don't see what any of it's got to do with me.'

'I'm coming to that,' Humboldt said. 'So, after a bit of digging, I discovered that my father's brother, Bernard Humboldt – or Uncle Bernie as I like to think of him – joined the army shortly after the outbreak of World War II. Military records show that, after a brief stint in North Africa, he was posted to England in the build-up to D-Day. It was here he met Beatrice Rayner, your great-grandmother. Although their relationship lasted only a few days, Beatrice fell pregnant. Uncle Bernie was killed on Omaha Beach less than a month later. There's no way of knowing whether she ever told him she was expecting their baby, but Beatrice listed his name on the birth certificate of her son, Alfred Rayner.'

'Grandpa?' Sam said, everything slotting into place.

'My first cousin,' Humboldt said. 'Which makes you and me first cousins twice removed, if I'm not mistaken.'

Sam drooped forwards, his head in his hands. The tightness in his chest felt like the early stages of a heart attack, but try as he might he couldn't help but be drawn in by what he was hearing.

'However indirectly, I suppose that does make me responsible for what Esteban did to you,' Humboldt said. 'You see, I trusted him to lead the search for my relatives. Obviously he discovered more than he let on and, when he turned on me, tried to kill you and your family before I could reach you. In fact, Sam, it was only the news of your arrest that alerted me to your existence. Had I known sooner, all of this would have been unnecessary.'

Sam raised his head. 'But if you're like me, why not just travel back and find me sooner? And what about Thames House and Malcolm Fairview? How did any of that stop you finding me?'

'Again with the questions?' Humboldt gave a rueful smile. 'I expect, however, that this time the answers all boil down to the same thing – Tetradyamide.'

'*Tetradyamide*?'

'That's right,' Humboldt said, gently massaging his scalp. 'I've spent nearly five decades trying to recreate the stuff. Even without it and only my limited ability to work with, I've built a business empire simply by learning to take advantage of my seizures whenever they come on.'

'A *business empire*? Is that what they're calling drugs and arms trafficking these days?'

Humboldt's eyes twitched, his brow creasing. 'I see you already know something of my history then. Like you, Sam, I never asked for my ability, but it seemed a waste not to use my talents for my own benefit. I take it the idea's never crossed your mind then?'

'I...er...' Sam mumbled, remembering his brief business venture with Lewis and Lance.

'Hmm, as I thought,' Humboldt said. 'Anyway, in the absence of Tetradyamide I've only ever been able to travel a day or two into the immediate past or future. For a while this was enough to evade capture. When the coastguard intercepted one of my shipments, I would simply bring on a seizure, travel back to the day before and redirect it. Unfortunately the accumulation of wealth tends to leave a paper trail and, while the authorities were never able to catch me in the act, during the 1980s the IRS built a tax evasion case against me. I've been on the run ever since.

'Esteban was well aware of my attempts to recreate Tetradyamide, and knew that I'd recently found out about Dr McHayden's work for the Tempus Project. I can only assume that both the Thames House bombing and Malcolm Fairview's assassination were attempts to cut off a new supply of the drug before I could find it.'

'Okay,' Sam said, 'even if I accept what you're telling me, it still doesn't explain what I'm doing here.'

The night sky through the window was lit by another flash of lightning, brighter and closer than the first. 'You're here because I need your help,' Humboldt said, raising his voice to be heard over the rumble of thunder. 'I'm dying, Sam, and you're the only person who can save me.'

7

'You want *me* to save *you*?' Sam said, hardly able believe his ears. 'You're not actually serious, are you?'

Humboldt let out a sigh and stared down at his walking stick again. There was something sad, almost vulnerable about his expression. 'Without warning my seizures dried up on me last summer,' he said, 'and with them my ability to travel through time. I began suffering headaches – blinding, excruciating headaches during which I could hardly move. My doctor performed a series of tests and scans that revealed a tumour around the size of a dime pressing against my basal ganglia,' he turned his head and tapped the scar at the base of his skull again, 'the region of the brain where that build up of scar tissue gives me – I mean *us* – our powers. The tumour was deemed inoperable under any existing medical procedure, so naturally I did the only thing available to me and diverted the entire resources of my business operations to finding a cure. I even tried a few alternative therapies, everything from acupuncture to visiting a faith healer in Chile.'

'Chile?' Sam said, remembering the missile strike he had averted in the December-only-he-could-remember. 'You don't mean the Atacama Desert, do you?'

'I was there until a few days ago,' Humboldt said. 'How did you know?'

'Just a lucky guess,' Sam lied, and bit his lip. 'We did a project about it at school last year. It's one of the driest places on Earth, I think.'

Humboldt frowned and then shrugged. 'I'll take your word for it. Regrettably the healer turned out to be a fraud. There are plenty of people out there willing to make a quick buck out of others' misfortune, it would appear. And despite the increased funding, my research team's progress on a cure was initially slow after a number of false starts. In recent weeks, however, they've reported promising results in the development of several potential treatments, including chemotherapy, radio- therapy, proton beam therapy, carmustine implants, stereotactic radiosurgery and several tumour-shrinking drugs intended to reduce my tumour to an operable size. But with so many potential treatments in the pipeline, I've had to spread my bets, channelling equal funding into each. At the moment I have no way of knowing which projects, if any, will prove effective.

'It's late January now, and my doctor says I won't live to see April.' He paused, his miserable expression replaced by one of steely determination. 'But with you here, Sam, I wouldn't need to spread my bets anymore. Instead, I could focus funding into a single project and begin that treatment immediately. With Tetradyamide, you could then travel forward to the summer and find out if it's worked. If not and I've punched my ticket by then, you could simply return to the present, report back to me and I'll drop that line of treatment and focus on a different one instead. We could repeat the process until we find a cure that works.'

'Is kidnapping people how you normally go about asking for their help?'

'I've resorted to it before,' Humboldt said. 'However you're not a prisoner here, Sam. You're free to leave any time you choose.'

'*Really*?' Sam asked, rising unsteadily to his feet. 'You mean I can just walk out of here and you won't stop me?'

'By all means,' Humboldt said, and spread his hands, one of which, Sam realised, was a prosthetic so realistic that it was almost impossible to tell it apart from the real thing. 'If you don't want to help me, I can't force you. Just say the word and I'll have Donna, my assistant, arrange to drop you off at the nearest town in the morning. But before you make a decision, remember that the police are still looking for you and your escape from Knotsbridge isn't going to reflect too well.'

'But I didn't escape – *you* broke me out. And Haufner killed Malcolm Fairview. I haven't actually done anything.'

'I know that and you know that,' Humboldt said nonchalantly. 'The police might see things differently, however.'

'You could always try telling them the truth,' Sam said.

'Help you when you won't help me? That's not very fair, is it? Besides, they're hardly likely to believe the word of a wanted man, and you haven't even heard what I'm willing to offer you in exchange yet.'

Sam eyed Humboldt up. It was hard to fault the man's logic, and if Sam walked out now then the only thing waiting for him was probably another prison cell.

'All right, let's hear it,' he said, sitting back down. 'What are you offering?'

'The very thing you want most of all,' Humboldt said. 'I can bring your father back.'

8

Sam's muscles all seemed to go loose in the same instant, and he briefly felt himself sliding down the cushions of the sofa before grabbing the armrest to halt his descent to the floor. Ever since that fateful day at the end of last summer, he had wanted nothing more than to undo the plane crash that had torn his family apart. Reversing that event had been his primary motive for joining the Tempus Project, but after discovering he couldn't pass back to a time before his injury he had reluctantly arrived at the conclusion that it wasn't something he'd ever achieve.

Humboldt was watching him intently. 'I sustained my injury way back in 1969,' he said, a faint smile on his lips. 'Once my tumour is successfully removed and my ability to travel through time returns, I could theoretically use Tetradyamide to return to any point after that date, including last September, if I so wish. With prior knowledge of what Esteban's planning, it shouldn't be too difficult to intervene *before* he brings down Flight 0368, creating a new timeline in which your father was never killed.'

Sam stared back, again at a loss for words.

Humboldt's smile had grown into a broad grin. 'Do what I ask of you, Sam, and this will be your reward. It's a straight swap – you save my life and I'll save your father's.'

Tears of joy clouded Sam's vision, but then he saw an obvious flaw in Humboldt's plan. 'Tetradyamide,' he said. 'You told me Haufner bombed Thames House and killed Malcolm Fairview to stop you getting it. I, er, may have sort of found a bottle at Fairview's flat, but the police confiscated it when they arrested me. How am I supposed to travel all the way to next summer without Tetradyamide? I can't even decide when one of my seizures comes on, let alone where it takes me.'

'There's a knack to it. I could show you some time, if you like. But for now, suffice it to say I've finally managed to acquire a small quantity.'

'Of *Tetradyamide*? But how?'

'I have my ways.' Humboldt chuckled and, using his stick for support, heaved himself up. 'But it's getting late and you must be hungry. Why don't you freshen up and we can discuss the finer details over dinner?'

9

George took a sip of lukewarm mineral water and surveyed the stuffy, low-ceilinged interior of the country pub in which he'd spent the last half hour waiting. On the far side, sitting below a mediocre watercolour depicting a fox-hunting scene, Esteban Haufner faced the other way, a newspaper spread out on the table before him. He had drastically altered his appearance in the two months since the CCTV cameras at Thames House had captured his grainy image, but in spite of the shaven head, beard and thick-framed spectacles, George would have recognised his old friend anywhere.

A bell rang behind the bar and the burly landlady called, 'Time, ladies and gents! Last orders please!'

George glanced at his wristwatch. When he looked up again, Esteban's table had been vacated, a crumpled newspaper and an empty glass with froth settling at the bottom all that remained.

Muttering under his breath, he snatched his coat from the back of his chair. Monday night was quiz night and the place was busy, costing him valuable seconds as he elbowed a path to the door. He stepped outside to find that the wind had picked up, blowing in clouds that cloaked the starlight. There was a dense quality to the air that hinted at a coming storm. As he peered up and down the dark, deserted lane, panic briefly flared within him until he caught sight of a figure disappearing into the shadows to his left. He tugged his tweed flat cap low over his face, pulled his gloves on and, swinging his arms, strode after.

Throughout their training at the Security Service, George and Esteban had been closely matched, with George holding the upper hand over the obstacle course. Now, on his unfamiliar prosthetic leg, he struggled to keep up. After a few hundred yards the residual noise of the pub had dwindled behind them, lost to whistling of the wind, and his stump began to ache. He gritted his teeth and picked up the pace, desperate not to let Esteban out of his sight a second time.

Before long Esteban turned onto a narrow path that ran beside a row of thatched cottages on the edge of the village. George followed, sidestepping puddle-filled pot-holes. At the gate to the last cottage in the row, Esteban glanced over his shoulder, forcing George to duck into a gap in the hedgerow, where he paused for a moment to savour the rush of adrenalin.

He peered out again just as the door of the cottage swung shut. A few seconds passed and then the light behind a first-floor window came on, throwing a rectangle of illumination onto the front garden. He stepped out from his hiding place and crept up the path. The weather-worn door sported a lock that looked almost as old as the cottage itself. Stooping, he withdrew his trusty lock pick and then, on a hunch, tried the handle first, and was mildly surprised when the door opened unimpeded.

The interior of the cottage was dark apart from a dim glow emanating from the top of a staircase towards the back of the building, from which the patter of running water could be heard. An undercurrent of stale cigarette smoke lurked beneath the prevailing aroma of cleaning fluid.

George stepped inside, a smirk on his lips, but no sooner had his foot hit the mat than a bright light snapped on, aimed directly in his face. Blinking, he raised an arm to shield his eyes. The source of the light was several metres to his left, where he could now make out the shape of a man in an armchair, a double-barrelled shotgun cradled in his lap.

He gulped and lowered his arm, realising too late that he had walked into a trap.

'George, what a pleasant surprise!' Esteban said jovially, and angled the lamp on the side table next to him towards the floor. 'Please, do come in. There's a light switch on the wall to your right. And, if you'd be so kind, close the door behind you. You're letting the warm air escape.'

George did as instructed, noticing how sparsely furnished the cottage was, with an overflowing ashtray on the kitchen counter the only break in the otherwise fastidious level of cleanliness.

Esteban gestured to a second armchair across from his own and tracked George with the barrel of the shotgun every step of the way as he went to sit. 'You look as though you are recovering well,' he said. 'I do apologise about the leg – nothing personal, I hope you understand.' He lifted a hand from the shotgun, reached for a bottle of scotch and poured a healthy measure into a waiting tumbler. 'I would offer you a drink, but as I recall you do not enjoy the loss of control. Well, never mind. To old friends!'

'Old friends,' George echoed, his pistol a tempting weight in his shoulder holster. There was little doubt that if he went for it, Esteban would empty both barrels into him before he had it out of his coat.

'Emotional as the reunion is, am I to assume you're here on business?'

'I'm afraid so.'

Esteban took a swig of scotch and rolled it over his tongue before swallowing. 'In that case I really must insist on your gun. No sudden movements, please.'

George nodded, withdrew his Glock and held it up, the barrel between his thumb and forefinger. 'Only a precaution, I assure you.'

'Naturally. Never leave home without it, eh? Now, be a good chap and pass it over.'

George dropped the pistol onto the carpet and, using his good foot, toe-poked it towards Esteban's chair.

Keeping the shotgun trained on him, Esteban stooped to retrieve the pistol, then leaned back and placed it on the table beside him. 'Still have a penchant for the leather gloves, I see.'

'It's cold outside,' George said.

'Very true. Nothing to do with unsatisfactory sanitation levels in the wider world then?'

'Would it be unwise of me to remind you that I'm not the only one to suffer from such a disposition?'

Esteban laughed. 'Touché! Still, it's nice and toasty in here, and my own standards of hygiene are exemplary, as you rightly point out. Please, there really is no need for the gloves. Take them off. I insist.'

George forced a shrug of indifference, removed his gloves, folded them and slid them into his coat pocket. 'There, better?'

'Much,' Esteban said. 'So, Michael Humboldt sent you to kill me, did he?'

'Quite the opposite,' George said. 'All is forgiven, Esteban. He wants you to come back in.'

Esteban spluttered on another mouthful of scotch. 'Please, George, the man has already sent his assassins after me on *three* occasions. As you can plainly see, I am still here and they are not. You can tell him where to stick his forgiveness, if you'll forgive the expression.'

George sighed. 'Anything I can do or say to change your mind?'

'No, too much water under the bridge for that. But Flight 0368, Thames House, Malcolm Fairview...have you stopped to consider why I did these things?'

'Revenge, I assumed.'

'In part, yes. But what did Humboldt offer you in exchange for your allegiance? Wealth? Power? The chance to change the world?'

'Amongst other things.'

'Or your missing leg back, perhaps?'

George lowered his gaze, his chest tightening.

'You do realise he is no longer capable of such feats?' Esteban said. '*That* is why I did what I did, to stop him finding what he searches for.'

'The drug, you mean?'

'And the blood relative he so craves. Without these things, Humboldt is powerless and the empire he has built is there for anyone with the courage to take it.' Esteban leaned forwards, his eyes bulging. 'Help me, George, and together we can share the spoils.'

'Help you? What could you possibly want from me?'

'You know where he is, I think, otherwise you would not be here. You could get close enough to strike the blow that I cannot.'

George hesitated and adjusted his cuffs. 'The idea has some merit,' he said at last. 'You know, maybe I will join you for that drink and you can explain what you want me to do.'

'I never thought I'd see the day!' Esteban exclaimed. 'The glasses are in the unit next to the sink. Please, help yourself.'

'Would you mind?' George asked, and hiked up his trouser leg to afford Esteban a glimpse of his prosthetic. 'Getting about isn't as easy these days, and after the walk from the pub I could do with the rest.'

Esteban hesitated, his expression hardening in tandem with his grip around the shotgun.

'What, not afraid of an unarmed, one-legged man, are you?'

'No, of course not.' Esteban stood, slid George's pistol into his pocket and, with the shotgun balanced in the crook of his arm, retrieved another tumbler from the kitchen. 'Forgive me, but it would appear my recent experiences have left me mistrustful,' he said, and filled it from the bottle beside his armchair. 'But mark my words, George, Humboldt is a snake. He cannot give you the things he promised, and will turn on you the moment he thinks you have outlived your usefulness.'

'You may be right,' George said. He reached forward to take the tumbler, but instead grabbed Esteban by the wrist, drawing him to his chest and simultaneously raising his knee to knock the barrel of the shotgun away. Esteban's eyes widened in bewilderment as George withdrew a syringe from his pocket and plunged the needle into his old friend's neck. 'However Michael Humboldt also promised me your life, and on that point it seems he was true to his word.'

Esteban's eyes drifted closed and his body went limp. The tumbler slipped from his hand, spilling its contents as it rolled across the carpet.

10

Sam swallowed his last mouthful of leek and potato soup and placed his spoon in the empty bowl. The dining room on the ground floor of Michael Humboldt's sprawling, rickety old house was several times larger than the bedroom in which he'd woken but had the same smell of dry rot, plus a matching fireplace at the far side, this time with a mangy zebra's head mounted above the mantelpiece. A grandfather clock was gathering dust in one corner, the cobweb-tangled pendulum unmoving behind the glass panel and the hands perpetually stuck on ten minutes to three.

Back in the bedroom, Sam had been shown to a wardrobe and then left to change, granting him a few minutes alone to gather his thoughts before dinner. Although he was still struggling to get his head around the implications of everything Humboldt had told him, the main thing was he'd been offered the chance to save his dad, and that was something he could never turn down.

After browsing the contents of the wardrobe, he'd selected a pair of canvas trainers, jeans and a navy blue zip-up hoodie, all with the labels still attached. As he'd finished dressing there had been a knock on the door and a grey-haired old lady had entered, introducing herself as Donna, Humboldt's assistant. She had shown him along a hallway and down a creaking staircase that looked like something out of a haunted house. Sam had tried asking questions as he'd followed, but she didn't even glance back, making him suspect that she was probably hard of hearing. At the bottom of the staircase they'd turned down another hallway before entering the dining room. Waiting at a long table with a line of three-pronged candlestick holders down its middle were Humboldt and a little man with sideburns and a handlebar moustache, who was introduced as Sebastian, Humboldt's lead researcher.

'How was the soup?' Humboldt asked, looking up from the opposite end of the table.

'Er, not bad thanks,' Sam said. 'I must have been hungrier than I realised.'

'That's hardly surprising,' Sebastian said. 'You haven't eaten in two days.'

'*What*?'

Humboldt dabbed the corner of his mouth with a napkin. 'I'm afraid he's right, Sam. In order to safely extract you from Knotsbridge, I instructed my associate to administer a drug that an old friend of mine developed several decades back – a counteragent, if you will. Obviously I didn't want you slipping into a seizure and doing anything that might interfere with our plans. Its effects are the polar opposite of Tetradyamide, essentially preventing a person like you or me from travelling through time. On me it lasted for forty-eight hours, give or take, but you started coming around after only a single day. We kept you sedated for another twenty-four hours, just to be sure the counteragent had left your system and you'd be ready to use Tetradyamide again. You were nourished through a drip the whole time, of course.'

Sam gawped back, but it actually explained a lot, such as why he had lost control of the pages of time and then whited out when he'd tried to undo Fairview's murder. But considering that all he had really achieved was to incriminate himself again, perhaps Humboldt had actually done him a favour.

He took a sip from the glass of water next to his placemat and cleared his throat. 'So, you said you have Tetradyamide?'

'That I do,' Humboldt said and grinned. 'Donna, would you mind?'

Humboldt's elderly assistant nodded, pushed her chair back and left through a door at the end of the room, returning a moment later with a silver platter covered by a domed lid.

'Much appreciated,' Humboldt said as she set it before him. 'How're our main courses coming along?'

'Shouldn't be long now, sir,' she said, then collected their empty bowls and exited through the same door, which Sam realised must lead on to the kitchen.

Dispensing with the walking stick, Humboldt carried the platter over to Sam's end of the table. 'Funny how you can spend your whole life looking for something and then, once you find it, not be able to use it,' he said, lifting the lid. 'Fate has a twisted sense of humour, it would seem.'

In the middle of the platter was a brown pill bottle. The label was beginning to peel away in one corner and there was a chip in the glass near the lid. Sam stared at it in disbelief; it was so like the one confiscated from his house as to be almost identical. Scratch that, it *was* identical.

'That's the bottle the police took when they searched my house!' he blurted out. 'How did *you* get it?'

Humboldt chuckled. 'It wasn't easy, but with enough money and the right people in the right places, almost anything can be arranged. So what do you say, Sam? My life in exchange for your father's, do we have a deal?'

It briefly occurred to Sam that he might be alone in the house with only Humboldt, Donna and Sebastian, and that if he made a break for it there would be little the ancient trio could do to stop him. But with the prospect of saving his father dangling before him, he immediately dismissed the idea.

'Okay,' he said. 'I'll do it.'

'Excellent!' Humboldt said, and passed the bottle over.

Sam flipped the lid open and shook out a sticky little pill. After rolling it between his thumb and finger, he washed it down with a sip of water.

At that moment Donna backed through the door with a tray supporting four steaming plates.

'Ah, our mains!' Humboldt returned the pill bottle to the platter and lifted it away to make space for her to lay a plate in front of Sam. 'I hope you like lamb cutlets. They're one of Donna's specialities.'

Sam felt his stomach growl. The cutlets looked mouth-wateringly good, but the soup had only whetted his appetite and he would have eaten pretty much anything put in front of him.

Humboldt deposited the platter on a serving table and returned to his seat, draping his napkin over his lap. 'Please, go ahead. I'm not one for formalities.'

Sam didn't need a second invitation and tucked in, while Donna served the others and then took her own seat again.

'You know,' Humboldt said after a while, 'it's a real treat to be able to share a meal with family. Not something I've done in years, in fact. My mother died when I was a child, and I lost my brother and father the same year as my injury. Since then Donna and Sebastian are pretty much the closest thing to a family I've had. It may be just the prospect of my own death, but often I've found myself wondering what it would have been like to have had children of my own. Maybe even an heir to inherit everything I've built.' He shook his head, his smile fading. 'But I suspect we now have a few minutes before the Tetradyamide takes effect. What do you say we discuss the details of our arrangement?'

'All right,' Sam said through a mouthful of cutlet.

Sebastian lowered his knife and fork. 'Mr Humboldt has recently made several alterations to his will stipulating that you, Sam, are to be accommodated and provided for in the event of his death. A meeting has been scheduled with Dr Claybourne, Mr Humboldt's private physician, for noon on the first day of August, during which I've instructed her to feed back the results of the first course of treatment we plan to proceed with.'

'That's all you have to do, Sam,' Humboldt said. 'When the Tetradyamide kicks in, I want you to travel forward to that meeting, listen to what Dr Claybourne tells you and then report her findings back to us in the present. Once cured, my ability to travel through time should return and I'll be in a position to prevent the incident in which your father was killed.' He spread his hands. 'That's the deal – you scratch my back and I'll scratch yours.'

'Hang on,' Sam said. 'What if none of the treatments work? If you can't be cured, my dad will still be dead, won't he?'

'In which case you've lost nothing,' Sebastian stated, his voice high and reedy.

'But that's a worst-case scenario,' Humboldt cut in. 'And at least you can rest assured in the knowledge that you've done everything in your power to bring you father back. But if the plan fails the first time, we'll just repeat the process, bringing back information from August over and over, refining the lines of enquiry until we have a working cure.'

'I see,' Sam said. Suddenly a warm tingle climbed his spine. The edges of his vision had become tinted with colour, and the grain of the wooden tabletop seemed to ripple and swirl before his eyes. 'It's starting to take effect, I think.'

'Good,' Humboldt said. 'Ready when you are.'

Sam closed his eyes. After a moment the first stabs of coloured light appeared. As he watched on, they swam and swirled, multiplying and merging to form the image of the table before him, stripped bones and a circle of grease all that remained of his plate of food.

He focused on his destination: noon, the first day of August. With a jolt the scene skipped ahead. He briefly saw Donna collect his plate and then the turning of the pages grew so fast that all detail was lost.

Unlike back at Knotsbridge, there was clearly nothing wrong with Sam's control this time around; however he now had over six months to cross. Steeling his mind, he ploughed forward, and soon the passing days and nights became discernible only as intervals of light and dark. One by one he counted them off, until somewhere around the two-hundred mark the pages began to slow.

Sam had tried to travel this far into the future once before, when he had come around as McHayden's prisoner, drugged up and strapped to a trolley in the Tempus Research Facility. He braced himself as the scene slowly ground to a halt before him, wary of where he might end up, but gradually the image of a white-sanded beach leading down to a clear turquoise ocean took shape. The leaves of a palm tree encroached on his view. A sleek white yacht was anchored about a hundred metres out and, far in the distance, he could make out the cone of a volcanic island poking just above the line of the horizon where the ocean met a bright blue sky flecked with wispy tendrils of cloud.

He blinked and the murmur of gently breaking waves filled his ears. Before him the ocean sparkled and glistened as it rolled in the bright sunlight. He was sitting on a lounger in the shade of a large umbrella. The intense heat was alleviated by a gentle inland breeze. Glancing down, he saw that he was wearing a white t-shirt, swimming shorts and flip-flops. The exposed skin of his arms and legs was coated in a thick layer of oily sunblock.

'Well now, by my watch it's just gone midday, the time of our so-called meeting,' a female voice said. 'Has your alter-ego arrived yet?'

Sam looked up to see a young, dark-skinned woman on a sun lounger to the right of his own. She was wearing an orange bikini and sarong, and was so breathtakingly beautiful that she would have made most catwalk models seem drab and unspectacular by comparison.

'Dr Claybourne?'

The woman peered over the top of her sunshades, her mouth dropping open. For a second she struggled to close it, then grinned at him with perfectly straight, perfectly white teeth.

'Ha, that's a good one!' she said. 'Next you're going to tell me you're the Sam Rayner from January, here to collect my results for Mr Humboldt.'

'Er, that's right. I think.'

She swung her legs from her lounger, pushed her shades to the top of her head and sat staring at him as though transfixed. 'You're serious, aren't you?' she said at last. 'I can see it in your eyes, there's something different.'

'A few minutes ago I was eating lamb cutlets in the dining room of Michael Humboldt's house in south Wales,' he told her. 'I've got to say, I prefer it here.'

She threw her head back and laughed, pounding the sun lounger with her fist. Eventually she managed to pull herself together and stood up. Wiping tears from her eyes, she slid her feet into a pair of flip-flops lying in the sand. 'Sorry, but I was rather expecting the whole thing not to work. Since it has, I suppose I should introduce myself. Dr Clarrisa Claybourne, at your service.'

'Sam Rayner,' he said, standing as well. 'From January. And where is *here*, by the way?'

'Why, that's easy, Sam-Rayner-from-January.' She spread her arms wide and spun in a slow circle. 'This is Swordfish Island. We're in the Pacific Ocean, a couple of thousand kilometres south of Hawaii.' She stopped spinning, lowered her arms and turned that dazzling smile on him again. 'It's one of the most remote places in the world, and part of the estate Mr Humboldt left you in his will.'

11

'Oh, right,' Sam said. Then: 'Hang on, *what*?'

Instead of answering him, Claybourne turned and made towards a flight of rough stone stairs carved into the face of a low cliff at the back of the beach. The peak of another volcano towered high above them, its sides lined with a dense covering of vegetation.

'Wait!' Sam called, and hurried after, the soles of his flip-flops slapping against his bare heels. 'What did you just say?'

'Mr Humboldt passed away in March,' she replied, glancing over her shoulder without slowing her pace. 'Let's get out of the sun and I'll explain.'

As Sam began to climb, a tiny lizard with blue streaks down its sides scurried out from a crack and darted across the step beneath his falling foot. He pulled back, stumbled and had to grab hold of a thick, weathered rope hanging from a series of brass loops to steady himself. Up ahead, Claybourne turned a corner in the stairs and disappeared out of sight.

Sam followed, hauling himself up by the rope balustrade before emerging onto the terrace of a huge, colonial-style mansion. It was dominated by a vast swimming pool in the shape of an oasis, complete with a central island where several palm trees grew. The mural of a dragon's head like the one on Humboldt's walking stick was visible at the bottom through the clear, shimmering water. In the distance, a pair of armed guards patrolled the edge of a garden bursting with bright tropical plants Sam couldn't even begin to guess the name of.

He stopped and stared, awestruck. It was the sort of place he imagined was used to shoot adverts for sports cars, or aftershave or expensive wristwatches, the sort of purchases that were as much lifestyle statements as functional items.

On the other side of the pool was a wide balcony, where a table stood in the shade of an awning. Claybourne strode over to it, her long braids swinging behind her back.

'Okay,' Sam said, jogging to catch up. 'You did just say that Humboldt left me the island in his will, didn't you?'

'Absolutely.'

'You mean this place is *mine*? As in, I own it?'

'And everything in it.' She took a chair at the table and fanned herself with her hand. 'Apart from the funds earmarked for medical research, Mr Humboldt left you, his sole living relative, everything he owned. In addition to his business empire, he bequeathed you an estate of approximately two dozen properties scattered across the globe, including Swordfish Island, several hotels and the house in Wales you just mentioned.'

Even though he'd only been in the sun a few minutes, Sam was beginning to feel light-headed and flopped into the chair beside her. It appeared as though Humboldt had been telling the truth about his terminal brain tumour, which probably meant he'd also been telling the truth about saving Sam's dad, and in spite of the old man's reputation, Sam felt a pang of sadness at the passing of his first cousin twice removed.

Carrying a pitcher of iced tea, a sweltering-looking man in a full butler's uniform (coattails, white gloves and all) emerged from a door in the wall of glass where the mansion met the balcony. He filled a tall glass, ice cubes clunking as he poured, then passed it to Claybourne and filled another.

'Iced tea, sir?' he asked, passing the second glass to Sam.

'Thanks,' Sam said, and took a long swig, savouring the sensation of cold liquid sliding down his throat. Although it sounded strange to be addressed as 'sir', he supposed that, if he owned the island and everything in it, he was technically the man's boss.

'So I take it Mr Humboldt's treatment didn't work then,' he said, turning to Claybourne.

She shook her head and linked her hands in her lap. 'He died March twenty-seventh, I'm sorry to say. The last few days of his life were spent in excruciating agony, but he declined the morphine I offered him, saying he wanted to stay lucid to the very end. A brave decision, but not one I would have taken myself.'

Sam took another swig of iced tea. Tempting as it was to stay in this future timeline a little longer, he already had the information he needed. The first of Humboldt's treatments had failed, and the sooner he relayed the news back, the sooner they could get on with the process of saving his dad.

'I should be going,' he said. 'Thank you, Dr Claybourne.'

'Don't mention it, Sam-Rayner-from-January. I'm only doing my job, and one I'm paid very well for at that.' She displayed her dazzling smile again and raised her glass in a toast. 'Until we meet again. Or, since we're already acquainted, maybe that should be until we meet for the first time. I don't know, what do you think?'

'Your guess is as good as mine,' Sam said. He clinked his glass against hers and silently mouthed the word, 'Now.'

The scene before him froze and then rippled backwards, gathering pace until all he could make out were the flashes of light that signalled the passing days. Once again he counted them off, and around about the two-hundred mark the turning of the pages began to slow until he could make out the dining room of the house in Wales, with Humboldt watching him from the opposite end of the table.

He blinked and then shivered as the temperature plummeted.

'Welcome back!' Humboldt said. 'What news from August?'

'I met Dr Claybourne like you asked,' Sam told him.

'Enchanting, isn't she? And what did you think of Swordfish Island?'

'Very nice. I like the mural in the swimming pool.' Sam shifted his weight in his chair as he pondered the best way to break the bad news. 'The first treatment didn't work,' he said, deciding there was no best way. 'I'm sorry, Mr Humboldt, but you're going to die on 27th March.'

Humboldt stared back with cold, flat eyes, his lips curled into a grimace. 'That so?' he said, and let out a sigh. 'Well, I guess it was too much to hope for that we'd strike it lucky on our first attempt.'

'Never mind,' Sebastian chimed in, 'we chalk off one line of enquiry and move on to the next. Option A has failed, so we move on to Option B. Are you ready to try again, Sam?'

Much as Sam would have liked a few minutes' rest, it wasn't going to bring his dad back, so he nodded and closed his eyes, concentrating on his destination again: noon, the first day of August.

This time he didn't bother counting off the days as he traversed the months separating him from that date, but waited patiently until the turning of the pages slowed and he was once again presented with the image of a white-sanded beach leading down to the pristine ocean surrounding Swordfish Island. Everything was exactly the same as before, right down to the palm leaves at the edge of his view.

He blinked and the temperature soared to what felt like somewhere in the low thirties.

'Well now, by my watch it's just gone midday, the time of our—'

'Yeah yeah, I know,' he said, turning to the sun lounger beside him, 'the time of our so-called meeting. And yes, my alter-ego has arrived already.'

Claybourne pushed her shades to the top of her head. 'What, you mean it actually *worked*?'

'Yep, a few minutes ago I was sitting at a table in Humboldt's house in Wales. It's much nicer here, etcetera, etcetera.'

She laughed and banged her fist against her lounger, then stood and slid her feet into her flip-flops. 'Sorry, but I was rather expecting the whole thing to fail miserably. Since it hasn't, I suppose I should introduce myself. Dr Clarrisa Claybourne, at your service.'

'Sam-Rayner-from-January,' he said, standing too. 'Believe it or not, Dr Claybourne, we've actually done this before. Next you're going to tell me we're on Sword-fish Island, part of the estate Mr Humboldt left me in his will, and then you're going to suggest we get out of the sun so you can explain. I like iced tea as much as the next person, but I think I'd rather just cut to the chase. Mr Humboldt died on 27th March in excruciating agony after declining the morphine you offered him. That about right?'

Claybourne gulped and shook her head. 'Almost. He died March nineteenth.'

'The nineteenth?' Sam said. 'Are you sure? That's over a week earlier.'

'I was Mr Humboldt's private physician,' she said, a touch defensively. 'I'm hardly likely to forget when he died. You are right about declining morphine, though.'

Out of the corner of his eye, Sam spotted a small green lizard with blue stripes scurry across the first of the stone steps leading up to the swimming pool and mansion. Everything else about this reality seemed the same, and he was certain he hadn't misheard Claybourne the first time they'd met. Only one thing made sense: Option B had been even less successful than Option A, shortening Humboldt's life by a full eight days.

'Okay,' he said. 'Thank you, Dr Claybourne.'

'Don't mention it, Sam-Rayner-from-January. I'm only doing my job, and one I'm paid very well for at that.' She smiled and dipped her head. 'Until we meet again. Or, since we're already acquainted, maybe that should be until we meet for the first time. I don't know, what do you think?'

'Still haven't a clue,' Sam said, 'but since I've got a feeling we'll be doing this again in a minute, I'll try to think of a better answer for next time. See you soon.' He closed his eyes and mouthed the word, 'Now.'

The scene froze, framing Claybourne's perplexed face, and then shot backwards. Sam watched the days and nights whizz by before his eyes. The sensation was beginning to give him motion sickness, and he wondered how much more he could take before he could no longer go on. It was therefore something of a relief when the pages finally slowed and he found himself sitting across the dining table from Humboldt again.

He blinked and the scene shuddered into life. Donna's seat was empty and, glancing down, he saw that his empty plate had been cleared away.

'So,' Humboldt said, watching him expectantly, 'Option B then. How'd that work out?'

'Not well,' Sam told him. 'This time you die on 19th March.'

Humboldt scrunched his napkin into a ball and flung it onto the table. 'Even earlier than before? Oh well, I never expected this to be easy. Onto Option C, I guess.'

'Right,' Sam said, massaging his eyes. 'I'll do my best, but all this backwards and forwards takes it out of me after a while. How many potential treatments did you say there were?'

'Seventeen in total,' Sebastian said.

'*Seventeen*!'

Humboldt chuckled. 'Don't worry, Sam. Let's give it one more try. If it doesn't work, we can call it a night and try again in the morning. What do you say, maybe third time's the charm?'

'Maybe,' Sam said without holding much hope.

He closed his eyes and focused on the date of the meeting once more. As the intervening months flashed by a day at a time, he wondered what would happen when all seventeen treatments ran out. Obviously he would never get his dad back, but would Humboldt still write Sam into his will?

As the pages finally began to slow, the scene changed, the beach and ocean replaced by the view of a large mahogany desk. Sam blinked and felt a cool gust of air-conditioning against his skin. He was in what appeared to be a home office, with soft classical music playing in the background. On the other side of the desk, Michael Humboldt was sitting in a high-backed, almost throne-like chair beneath a portrait of himself on horseback.

'Welcome, Sam,' he said. 'I've been expecting you.'

12

'You're alive,' Sam said, immediately realising this was somewhat stating the obvious.

'Yes, thanks to you.' Humboldt leaned back in his oversized chair and spread his hands, one real and the other artificial. The signs of approaching death had been erased from his body in the space of what felt like just a few minutes; a powerful reminder that it was, in fact, more than half a year since Sam had laid eyes on the man. Gone were the frail, huddled posture, the shadows be-neath the eyes and the pale, withered skin. In their place Humboldt now sported a deep tan and, truth be told, could have done with shedding a few pounds.

'So the treatment worked then?' Sam asked.

'Third time lucky, didn't I say something like that?'

'I think it was third time's the charm.'

'Ah, that it was!' Humboldt pointed his left index finger at Sam like a gun and fired off an imaginary round. 'Option C, a breakthrough new tumour-shrinking drug, turned out to be more effective than Sebastian or any of his team had envisaged, reducing my tumour to an operable size after only a few weeks' use. I had the tumour removed in April, and Dr Claybourne assures me the surgery couldn't have gone better.'

'That's…great.'

'Of course, I'm not out of the woods yet. There're biopsies every other week, but I've been in remission for over three months now. And the icing on the cake is I also own the patent on a new drug that could potentially save thousands of lives every year while earning me a tidy income in the process. Not bad for a night's work!'

'What about my dad?'

'Straight to the point as ever, Sam.' Humboldt laughed and rose nimbly from his chair. 'Follow me, I have something to show you.'

Hardly placing any weight on his walking stick, he led Sam out of the office and down a long, whitewashed corridor with terracotta floor tiles. More portraits hung along the walls, depicting Humboldt in a variety of improbable poses, such as fly-fishing, at the seat of a concert piano and planting a flag at the peak of a mountain. His appearance had been touched up to varying degrees, with a chiselled jaw line and an athletic physique that he probably hadn't possessed even as a young man. Without exception, his scars and disabilities had been completely overlooked.

'Where are we?' Sam asked as they reached the bottom of a spiral staircase.

'My place on Swordfish Island,' Humboldt said, taking the stairs like a man half his age. 'It's pretty much our permanent residence these days. Your room's this way.'

'My room?'

'You've lived here with me since the end of January.' Humboldt stepped out onto the second-floor landing. 'With Tetradyamide in full-scale production and you by my side, Sam, the last few months have been by far and away the most productive of my career.'

He opened a rustic-looking door onto a large room with a king-size bed on one side. Sam stepped through and glanced about. At the far end a set of sliding doors opened onto a balcony overlooking the ocean. Mounted on the near wall was a huge telly with an array of top-of-the-range gaming hardware that would have made Lewis weep with jealousy. There were also a surfboard and a wakeboard leaning in one corner and, through the door to the en suite bathroom, the curve of an enormous Jacuzzi bathtub.

'I don't get it,' Sam said, turning back. 'Why are you showing me this?'

From his position by the door, Humboldt raised his walking stick and directed the tip at the bedside table, where a picture frame was positioned facing the other way.

Frowning, Sam walked over and picked it up. The photo behind the glass showed Chrissie and Lance outside a church with confetti scattered around their feet. Chrissie was wearing a strapless wedding gown and Lance a grey morning suit with a white carnation in the lapel. Although Sam had no memory of any such event, he was standing to the left of the photo next to his grandparents. On the right side of the shot were his mum, a baby cradled in her arms, and his dad, grinning like an idiot and very much alive.

13

Sam spun around, the picture frame gripped in both hands. 'When was this taken?'

'Last month at your sister and Lance Asquith's wedding,' Humboldt replied. 'Unfortunately I couldn't make it myself. The baby your mother is holding is their son. From what I understand, the three of them are currently enjoying an all-expenses-paid honeymoon in Barbados. A most generous wedding gift on your part, I must say.'

'But my dad,' Sam said. 'He's standing right there.'

Humboldt drew his shoulders back and chuckled. 'You scratch my back and I'll scratch yours, remember that?'

'You mean he's *alive*?'

'Of course. In this timeline Esteban Haufner was apprehended the day before Flight 0368, meaning the crash never took place.'

'So the Thames House bombing…'

'Likewise never happened.'

Sam glanced down at the photo, his eyes welling with tears. Apart from finding Eva again, this was everything he could have wished for. 'I want to see him,' he said, looking back up. 'I want to see my dad.'

'Of course you do,' Humboldt said. 'All that's required is for you to return to January, keep your end of our bargain and this is the future that awaits you.'

Sam's hands had begun to tremble. 'Okay,' he said, returning the picture frame to the bedside table. 'Thank you, Mr Humboldt. I don't know how I can ever repay you.'

Humboldt crossed the room and rested his left hand (the real one) on Sam's shoulder. 'I think saving my life is repayment enough. It's what we agreed on, Sam, and my word is my bond. And we're family, right? You can call me Michael, if you like. Or…how about Uncle Michael?'

Sam nodded and sniffed. 'Okay, Uncle Michael. See you back in January,' he said, and closed his eyes, mouthing the word, 'Now.'

The scene before him froze, then shot backwards. He briefly saw himself looking down on the photo of Chrissie's wedding again before everything became a blur, leaving only the flashing strobe effect that signified the passing days and nights.

Eventually the turning of the pages slowed and he found himself sitting across from Humboldt at the dining table in the house in south Wales once again. The man's sickly complexion had returned, supplanting his previous healthy tan.

Sam blinked and the scene gained motion. On the table before him was a bowl of ice cream.

'When do I cash in my chips this time around?' Humboldt asked, eyeing him cautiously.

'You don't,' Sam said. 'You were alive in August. Or at least, you will be. I saw you with my own eyes.'

'Option C worked then?'

'Apparently you have the tumour surgically removed in April. We were on Swordfish Island together. You said I'd been living there and working with you. You even asked me to call you "Uncle Michael".'

Humboldt grinned. 'That's got kind of a ring to it, you know. I've never been an uncle before. Donna, fetch a bottle of champagne, would you? This calls for a cele-bration!'

'Yessir,' she said, and retreated to the kitchen.

Sam spooned chocolate ice cream into his mouth. After everything he'd been through he was finally within touching distance of putting things right.

'I've kept my end of the bargain,' he said after a moment. 'Now it's your turn, Uncle Michael. What about my dad?'

'All in good time,' Humboldt said. 'Remember, I'll only be able to save your father once my tumour is re-moved and my ability to travel through time returns. First we need to contact my research team and instruct them to drop everything and focus on fast-tracking Option C. Sebastian?'

'I'll get right on it,' the little man said. He dabbed his moustache with his napkin, pushed his chair back and headed out into the hall just as Donna bustled in through the other door with a bottle of champagne.

Humboldt popped the cork, topped up four glasses, passed one to Donna and then held another out to Sam.

Sam heaved himself up and went to take it. For some reason he'd expected everything to be resolved that evening, and the prospect of having to wait another three months to save his dad felt like the ultimate anti-climax.

'Don't be so downbeat,' Humboldt said. 'I know it might seem like a long time, but you've already set in motion the events that will bring your father back. Have a little patience, won't you?'

'Okay,' Sam said, and took a sip of champagne. It tasted slightly bitter, as though the bottle had been kept in the cellar a few years too long. 'It's just, what are we going to do until April?'

'Given that we're both wanted men, I think it might be sensible to keep our heads down. But take it from me, if you're planning on laying low for a while, Swordfish Island is an excellent place to do it.'

'What about my family?'

'What, you want to bring them along too?'

Sam laughed, imagining what his grandparents would make of the place. 'No, but they're probably worrying about what's happened to me,' he said. 'The last thing they knew I was still at Knotsbridge.'

Humboldt nodded slowly. 'I expect the police will have already alerted them to your "escape". No doubt they're watching your house in case you show up there. They've probably got the phones tapped too, come to think of it. I'm sorry, Sam, but contacting them at this stage is an unacceptable risk.'

'My sister will be going out of her mind. *Literally*. I've got to let them know I'm okay.'

'I understand. Perhaps the safest thing might be to write a letter and post it on our way to the airfield tomorrow.'

It seemed the true cost of helping Humboldt was the life of a fugitive, but if that was what it took to save Sam's dad then it was a small price to pay.

'It's done, sir,' Sebastian said, walking back in. 'My team will drop everything and begin work on Option C immediately.'

'Good, that's settled then.' Humboldt passed Sebastian the final glass of champagne and raised his own in the air. 'I propose a toast – to family, and a long and prosperous future!'

'To family,' Sam mumbled. He raised his glass and took another, longer sip. Once again there was an unpleasant aftertaste that lingered in his mouth. He grimaced but, whatever it was, the others were all happily draining their glasses and didn't seem to have noticed.

'Something wrong?' Humboldt asked, arching his eyebrows.

'Can't you taste that?' Sam tried to say, but his words came out slurred, sounding more like, 'Gank goo gaysk gak?'

'No,' Humboldt replied. 'Mine's fine.'

Sam blinked. White light was beginning to seep into his vision. He felt his knees give, but before he fell, the scene froze, leaving him staring into Michael Humboldt's smirking face. The colour began to drain away from the image until all that was left was a vague outline. And then the white light overpowered that too.

14

George's mobile phone had been unavailable since he'd departed for his mysterious job interview on Saturday morning. It was possible he'd lost it, Frances supposed, or that the battery had run flat and he'd forgotten to pack a charger, but the ongoing lack of contact was enough to make her question the foundations of their whirlwind romance.

When she was woken by her own phone ringing in the small hours of Tuesday morning, she had fully expected it to be George finally replying to one of her numerous messages or texts, so her initial reaction on hearing Campbell's voice on the end of the line was one of disappointment. That feeling had lasted only as long as it took Campbell to break the news that Esteban Haufner was dead, and less than five minutes later she was behind the wheel of her car, on her way to the address in rural Berkshire that Campbell had given her.

'It's really him,' she said, looking up from Haufner's mutilated, one-legged body.

Kaur lowered his camera. 'We found a packed bag containing several passports, all under different aliases. Of course, I'll have to run his prints and dental records through the database for official confirmation. We were lucky to find the body so soon, really. A gas leak was reported in the cottage two doors up just before one a.m. and the landlady, a Mrs Granger, took it upon herself to alert her tenants. When Haufner – or Jones, as he's been calling himself – didn't open the door, she let herself in and found him like this.'

'How long's he been dead?' Campbell asked, rubbing the stubble on his chin.

'The pool of blood around the body is still damp towards the middle,' Kaur said. 'Coupled with the relatively high body temperature that would place the time of death somewhere between eleven and twelve yesterday evening. Probably no more than an hour or two before Granger found him.'

Campbell clicked his tongue against the roof of his mouth. 'I can't get my head around what the bastard's doing this close to London. I know he looks different, but that takes some serious nerve in my book.'

'Hiding in plain sight,' Frances muttered.

'Indeed,' Kaur said, unwrapping a mint. 'The sheer volume of blood indicates that the victim was still alive when his leg was amputated. Apart from the shotgun over there – which is loaded, by the way – there's no sign of a struggle or defence wounds of any kind, so he was probably sedated at the time. Again, I'd have to run a toxicology report for confirmation one way or the other.'

'*Victim*?' Campbell repeated. 'Hard to think of him as that! If we ever catch up with Rayner again, I might be tempted to shake his hand before bringing him in.'

'You think Rayner did this?' Frances asked.

'Or whoever he's working with. Come on, think about it, first he escapes Knotsbridge in one of the most audacious prison breaks this country has ever scene – "a military-style operation" some of the papers are calling it – and then, two days later, this?'

Frances nodded. The theory had some appeal, but maybe that was because, since first laying eyes on Haufner's missing leg, she had been desperately seeking an alternative to the possibility that George was somehow responsible. 'Why would Rayner want Haufner dead though?' she asked. 'And why cut off his leg?'

'Don't forget, his father was killed in the crash of Flight 0368,' Campbell said. 'He's got as much reason to want Haufner dead as anybody. As for the leg, perhaps he just wanted the bastard to suffer. I know I would.' He turned to Kaur. 'Any sign of a murder weapon yet? Or the missing limb?'

'No, Detective, although judging from the cut marks I'd say we're looking for a hacksaw or something similar. I've come across a few killers taking trophies in my time, but what anyone would want with a severed human leg is beyond me.' Kaur gestured to a member of his team who was shining a light source over a pair of matching armchairs positioned on either side of the fireplace. 'Julie's been dusting for prints. So far the only ones we've lifted have been from the shotgun, whisky bottle and a pair of tumblers, all of which are consistent with the victim.'

'Anything else you can tell us?' Frances asked.

'Very little. Apart from the mess down here, we've turned up barely a shred of evidence in the entire cottage. The bedroom upstairs doesn't appear slept in, and there's not so much as a toothbrush or bar of soap in the bathroom. It's almost as if Haufner was preparing to run when he was killed.'

'Right,' Campbell said, and tucked his notepad into his jacket pocket. 'I suppose we should have a word with the landlady then. Any idea where we can find her?'

'She lives in the first cottage in the row,' Kaur told him, 'but I expect you'll find her with the crowd outside still. It's not often something like this happens in these parts. It's caused quite a com—'

'There's something here!' Julie suddenly exclaimed.

Frances turned to see Kaur's colleague straighten up with a metal object clasped between a pair of tweezers. 'What is it?' she asked.

'Looks like a cufflink,' Julie said. She dropped the object into a plastic evidence bag and handed it over.

Frances felt an ice-cold chill strike her very core: the cufflink had a Union Jack emblazoned on one side, exactly like the 'parting gift' George had worn on their first date.

Chapter VII

Fight and Flight

1

Following what was the best night's sleep he had enjoyed since before his injury, George awoke on Tuesday morning feeling every inch a new man. Exacting his revenge had been like sampling the sweetest elixir ever tasted, and he remained in bed for several more minutes, smiling up at the ceiling of his Fitzrovia flat and mentally replaying the look of wide-eyed astonishment as he had plunged a hypodermic needle into his old friend's neck.

After leaving the village in Berkshire late last night, he had driven back to London, Esteban's right foreleg in a plastic bag on the passenger seat of his stolen car. He had stopped near Embankment and then strolled across one of the Golden Jubilee Bridges, pausing halfway to drop the severed limb into the dark, swirling waters of the Thames. It would probably wash up somewhere further down-stream (bodies and their constituent parts almost always did), but by then he would be thousands of miles away and far beyond the jurisdiction of anyone who might be able to connect the dots.

In taking Esteban's life, in addition to those of the guards who had stood in his way at Knotsbridge, George had transitioned from custodian of the law to outlaw, thereby crossing a line from which there could be no return. In truth, however, that line had already been crossed when he had removed the pill bottle from the evidence room at Scotland Yard using the key he had copied from Hinds, or, come to think of it, on the very day he had accepted Michael Humboldt's proposal. Still, at this stage it made little difference; if the Security Service no longer had any use for his services then it was only logical to sell them to the highest bidder, and moral qualms had never been something to hold him back.

After a while he climbed from his bed and hopped his way to the shower, where he remained for his customary six minutes and thirty seconds before returning to the bedroom to attach his prosthetic leg and dress. He selected a sharp Savile Row three-piece from his wardrobe (handcrafted by artisan carpenters in Catalonia) and began filling his suitcase. There would be no need for winter clothing where he was going, which was a shame, really, since it meant leaving behind some of his favourite attire. Although there would be plenty in the way of financial compensation, what bothered him the most was the loss of the home and possessions he had spent the last five years refining into the pinnacle of minimalist sophistication. *Auf wiedersehen* to the light fittings from Liechtenstein, *heippa* flooring from Finland and *annyeong* kitchen cabinets from Korea. All gone but not forgotten.

With his suitcase filled, George went to close the wardrobe door when a glint of metal near the back of the top shelf caught his eye. He pulled the object out, a thin smile of reminiscence raising the corners of his mouth. It was a bronze trophy shaped like a man striking a football: the Academy Player of the Year award George had won as a fifteen-year-old at Newcastle United, the highlight of his brief and ultimately doomed sporting career. The thing must have been up there since he'd purchased the wardrobe shortly after moving in. Quite why he had hung on to it all these years, he couldn't say.

With a wistful shake of his head, he returned the trophy to its place, then zipped his case up and checked the mobile phone Humboldt had provided him.

There was a single text message from the only number on the contacts list:

The package is secured. Pilot informs me weather conditions are now favourable.
We eagerly await your arrival.

George replied that he would be there in a few hours, traffic permitting, and hastened to the door of his flat.

Halfway down the hall he pulled up, doubled back and retrieved his football trophy before cramming it into his case. Shaking his head at such an uncharacteristic bout of sentimentality, he stepped out of his flat and, after a mournful glance behind, closed the door for the final time.

2

Sam came around to the sensation of movement. His headache had returned, only worse. Once again he had the impression that something bad had happened, but the details were strangely missing.

He forced his sticky eyelids open and took a moment to absorb his surroundings. It seemed that he was strapped to the back seat of a people carrier. The view through the windows was of fields rushing by on a clear winter's day. His hands, secured at the wrists by a cable tie, rested limply in his lap. Beside him was an old woman who was knitting what looked like a half-finished scarf. Two men, also around retirement age, were sitting on the backwards-facing chairs across from them. One was short with sideburns and a handlebar moustache, the other taller with a bald head and a sickly complexion. A third man was behind the wheel up front, but Sam couldn't make out his face from this angle.

'Ah, welcome back!' the bald man said. He had a faint mark down one side of his face and was holding a walking stick with a handle shaped like a dragon's head.

'Where am I?' Sam asked.

'In transit to an airfield near the Dorset coast. Shouldn't be long now.'

'Oh,' Sam said. And then his memory returned, crashing through his muddled mind like a car with the brakes cut. The man was Michael Humboldt – *or was that Uncle Michael?* – an internationally wanted criminal who had broken Sam out of Knotsbridge. They had struck a deal, the two of them, Humboldt's life in exchange for that of Sam's dad. Sam had kept his end, using Tetradyamide to travel through time to find a cure for the old man's brain tumour. He'd succeeded, meeting Humboldt alive and well in August, and then...then...

'What happened?' he yelled. 'What did you put in my champagne?'

'Remember the counteragent I told you about?' Humboldt gave a what-can-you-do sort of a shrug. 'You've actually come round even faster than before. I make it a shade under fifteen hours.' He turned to the little man beside him. 'Hey, Sebastian, you sure you got the formula right this time?'

'Of course!' Sebastian whined. 'It's an *exact* re-production of the drug Dr Barclay created in 1976. Unlike Tetradyamide, I actually had a sample to analyse on this occasion. Perhaps – I don't know, I'm just putting this out there – his tolerance might be higher than yours? Either way, he shouldn't be able to use his ability for several hours yet.'

'Whatever you say,' Humboldt said. 'We'll give him another dose as soon as we're in the air.'

'But why?' Sam asked. 'I did what you wanted, didn't I? What about your end of our deal?'

'Yes, I'm afraid that will never happen,' Humboldt said, twirling the shaft of his walking stick. 'You see, Sam, what we have here is something of a paradox. Consider this, if you will – your father was killed in the same event in which you yourself were injured, thereby gaining your ability to travel through time. If I alter the timelines to prevent said event from taking place, I would, in effect, be creating a new timeline in which you'd never developed your powers and would therefore be unable to save my life. Obviously I could never allow such a thing to happen.'

Sam stared back, dumbfounded. He'd been so eager to believe there was a chance he might get his dad back, so blinded by the prospect of becoming Humboldt's heir, that he hadn't even considered the consequences such an alteration to the past might create in the present. Now that he really thought about it, however, Humboldt's logic was impeccable; if the plane crash that had killed Sam's dad were ever reversed, Sam would also lose his ability to turn the pages of time.

But there was one thing that still didn't make sense. 'My sister's wedding,' he said. 'When I met you on

Swordfish Island, you showed me a photo. My dad was there. *Alive*. How can that be if you don't undo the plane crash?'

Humboldt chuckled, pulled a photograph from his jacket pocket, leaned over and slid it between Sam's bound hands. 'This what you're talking about, by any chance?'

Sam looked down. It was the same photo that had been (or would be) sitting on his bedside table on Swordfish Island half a year in the future, right down to the baby in his mum's arms and the cheesy grin on his dad's face.

'B-but how?' he asked, looking back up. 'I don't get it.'

'Come on, Sam, don't tell me you've never heard of Photoshop? I acquired the original picture from a company specialising in stock photography – it was first used in a wedding brochure, I believe – and had someone to digitally insert the faces of your family over those of the models.' He shook his head in exaggerated dis-appointment. 'And here I was thinking your generation were all supposed to be technological whiz kids!'

Sam felt his stomach turn. He looked across to the woman beside him (Donna, her name was), hoping against hope she'd wink or give him some sign that it was all a joke. Instead she continued knitting, a faraway look on her face as if the whole shakedown was of no more interest than a conversation overheard on the bus.

He squinted down at the photo again. On closer in-spection he realised that the shadows on his family's faces didn't quite match up with those their bodies cast on the ground. His dad's hair was a little less salt and a little more pepper than Sam remembered, and he and Sam were also the same height, whereas in reality Sam had been a couple of inches shorter.

With a groan, he let the photo slip from his fingers and drift to the floor of the car. How had he not spotted the inconsistencies earlier? Perhaps, in his desire to believe Humboldt's promises, he hadn't really wanted to.

'So what happens now?' he asked, his voice barely more than a whimper.

'We fly back to Swordfish Island where I can begin the course of tumour-shrinking drugs you identified,' Humboldt said. 'As for you, Sam, we need to set up the conditions for your consciousness from last night to enter your body and keep its appointment with Dr Claybourne. Until August, that'll mean keeping you on a continuous supply of counteragent, but needs must. I wouldn't want you bailing out on me, now would I?'

'And then what?'

'The answer to that is a little more complicated.' Humboldt ran his hand over his head and smiled, leaving little doubt that he was enjoying every moment. 'With you in captivity, a cure for my tumour in development and a working formulae for Tetradyamide in my possession at long last, I already have everything I need. I guess I could spin some yarn about setting you free after your meeting with Dr Claybourne, but I think we both know that's not going to happen. Here's the problem, Sam – once your body has fulfilled its task, I'll no longer have any need for it. Or, for that matter, you.'

3

Sam now saw that Humboldt's promises had been nothing but lies, and like a gullible fool he'd gobbled them up. Once he had kept his appointment with Dr Claybourne in August, Humboldt would kill him. He would never see family and friends again, never find Eva and never bring his dad back to life or return his mum to the person she had once been.

In that instant he wanted nothing so much as to throttle his first cousin twice removed with his bare hands. He began thrashing against his seatbelt, kicking his feet and swaying from side to side in a desperate bid to free himself. It was useless, though; the seatbelt held firm and, if anything, the cable tie cinched tighter around his wrists.

'I could have you sedated, if you'd prefer,' Humboldt said. 'Only it might make the whole experience less distressing on your part.'

Sam slumped back against his seat, the pulse behind his ears thumping. Suddenly the car crested a hill and he could make out the control tower and single hanger of a small airfield in the distance, the sort of place where people learned to fly in single-engine planes or took skydiving lessons at the weekend. Today, however, a small private jet stood waiting on the strip of runway beside the hanger.

'So that's it then,' he said. 'You're going to keep me until you don't need me anymore and then kill me? What about all that crap about family you spouted back at the house? I suppose that was all lies too, was it?'

'Not in the slightest,' Humboldt said. 'It's the fact we're family that makes you such a threat, Sam. You don't honestly believe I'd let someone who has the ability to undo all of my good work in an instant live, do you? And besides, I had to gain your trust somehow, otherwise you would have only used the Tetradyamide I gave you to fix your own problems instead of saving my life.'

Sam could do nothing but glare back. While at one time he might have caved in, the events of the last few months had hardened him, and he wouldn't give Humboldt the satisfaction. He realised that he was pretty much done for once they boarded the plane, but until then he still had time on his side and a lingering glimmer of hope. At some point they would have to undo his seatbelt in order to get him out of the car, and even with his hands tied, his head humming from the counteragent and his ability to turn the pages of time blocked, making a break for it might be the best and only opportunity he was going to get.

As the gates to the airfield loomed into view, the car slowed before turning off the road and coming to a stop.

'We're here,' the driver said and twisted round in his seat.

Sam's breath caught in his chest: it was Agent Steele, the man who had shot his sister in the timeline he had altered on Christmas Eve. 'Y-you!' he spluttered.

'Hello, Sam,' Steele said, fixing him with a cold blue gaze. 'It's good to see you again.'

4

As the people carrier stopped at the gates of a rundown airfield, Frances pulled over and climbed out of her car. It was now late afternoon with less than an hour of daylight remaining, but the moment she had laid eyes on the cufflink found at the scene of Esteban Haufner's murder that morning felt like a lifetime ago, and she barely remembered the garbled excuse she had given Campbell before driving back to London.

Dawn was breaking as she'd parked across the road from George's grand apartment building in Fitzrovia. She had sat there for half an hour, her fingernails digging indentations into the steering wheel as theories fizzed through her head like electric sparks. All of a sudden a light had switched on behind the drawn curtains of George's fifth-floor flat. Another twenty minutes had passed before it went dark again, and then a short while

later a white hatchback had emerged from the underground car park with George behind the wheel. Frances
had briefly considered pulling him over and arresting him
on the spot, but it was unlikely she'd ever get to the
bottom of what he was up to that way, so she'd begun
tailing him instead.

Rush hour had made it easy to hide amongst the traffic
as she followed him out of the city. When they'd reached
the greenbelt, the roads grew quieter and she was forced
to pull back to a safer distance. George had kept away
from motorways, sticking mainly to back roads and
country lanes as he wove his way in a north-westerly
direction, crossing into south Wales by mid-morning.

Another hour had passed before his car finally slowed
and turned through the moss-and-lichen-spotted gateposts
of a country estate. Frances had parked a couple of
hundred metres down the road, located the pair of
binoculars she kept in the boot and then skirted around
the property until she came to a slight rise that gave her
an uninterrupted view over the wall. From the cover of a
rain-dampened bush, she had observed the hatchback
parked next to a black people carrier in the weed-knotted
drive of an apparently derelict house.

After a few minutes George had emerged through the
front door with an unconscious young man slung over his
shoulder in a fireman's lift. Frances had turned the dial on
her binoculars, sharpening the focus and catching a
glimpse of Sam Rayner's face as George bundled him
through the rear door of the people carrier. After everything else that day she was hardly surprised, but whatever
Rayner's role in the whole game was, it didn't appear to
be a willing one.

Before she could swallow the lump in her throat,
George had doubled back to the house, returning a minute
later with a suitcase in either hand, an old woman and two

old men in tow. Frances had turned the dial on her binoculars once again, adjusting the focus. One of the men had been immediately recognisable: a face she had seen in countless photographs during her time at CT Command. It was Michael Humboldt, otherwise known as Michael Harrison, the man who had turned Esteban Haufner. And also, it appeared, George.

It was then that Frances had finally come to her senses. George had obviously been manipulating her all along, winning her affections in order to get to Rayner. Over the last week she had allowed her emotions to get the better of her judgement, making mistake after mistake, but here was a chance to put things right, not to mention restore her damaged reputation. She had raced back to her car, her phone pressed to her ear as she filled Campbell in on everything she had seen.

5

George fought to keep a straight face at the sight of Rayner's stunned expression. The boy had, of course, been in the midst of one of his seizures when George had snatched him from a prison cell three days earlier, so this was technically the first time they had met since George and Hinds had interviewed him in connection with Flight 0368 at the end of last year.

Feeling goosebumps prickle his neck at the strange twist of fate that had conspired to bring them all together again, George left the vehicle idling in neutral (his injury regrettably made operating a manual gearstick impossible), clambered out and went to open the gate. After climbing back in, he guided them through and followed the muddy, pot-holed path up to the airfield's two buildings: a rusting, corrugated-iron hanger and a low, 70s-built concrete tower.

During the drive a new plan had begun to take shape in his head, in part seeded by what Esteban had told him the night before. The offer of permanent employment at ten times the salary of what he made at the Security Service was tempting, but once they were out of harm's way, George's role would be fulfilled and Humboldt would hold all of the cards. The way in which the man had just played Rayner for a fool was ample proof there were no guarantees he would make good on his promise to undo the Thames House bombing and return George's leg. But Humboldt was still weak and, as Esteban had correctly surmised, his empire there for the taking. Once they reached Swordfish Island there was nothing Humboldt could offer that Rayner couldn't be forced to provide and, now that he had a taste for criminality, nothing to stop George taking the man's throne.

Doing his best not to outwardly grin, George parked by the hanger, climbed out again and opened the sliding rear door. Humboldt stepped onto the age-cracked tarmac and, using his stick for support, straightened up before taking a deep breath of the crisp winter's air. He was followed by his scientist, Sebastian, and the old dear employed as his assistant, Donna.

'Thank you, George,' he said, raising his voice to be heard over the drone of the aircraft's engines. 'Do me a favour and get the kid out too, would you?'

'Certainly.' George bowed his head in suitably deferential manner and climbed into the rear compartment, where he found Rayner staring up at him, his face ashen.

'I suppose you're wondering what I'm doing working for a man like Humboldt,' he said, leaning forward to unclip the boy's seatbelt. 'Rest assured, my motives are entirely honourable. I'm driven purely by self-interest, you see. That and a little financial remuneration.'

The buckle clicked open. As he attempted to haul Rayner up, the boy sprang from his seat, swinging his bound fists into George's chin with such unexpected speed and ferocity that he was knocked off balance and sent sprawling onto the seat opposite.

6

In the second it took Steele to topple onto the rear-facing seats on the other side of the compartment, Sam was up and out of the people carrier. Humboldt and his entourage were standing a few feet to one side, but they barely had time to look up as he shot past them in a blur.

The airfield was set on a desolate strip of coastline with the sea just about visible as a grey smudge on the horizon. Turning away from the private jet near the hanger, Sam began bounding down the path towards the gate onto the road.

The counteragent was still clouding his senses, leaving him unbalanced on his feet. He managed a total of six lumbering strides, his cable-tied hands swinging loosely from side to side, when a deafening crack rang out behind him, stopping him in his tracks.

He turned back to see Steele leaning against the side of the people carrier, one hand rubbing his chin and the other holding a pistol pointed straight at him.

'Don't try anything stupid,' Steele said, and took a step closer.

Sam froze, paralysed by indecision as a cold wind tugged at his clothing. If he was in that plane when it took off, he was as good as dead, but there didn't seem much chance of Steele missing again, if that was actually what had happened the first time. Shakily, he raised his hands over his head.

Steele lowered the gun, strode over, grabbed Sam by the neck of his hoodie and began dragging him back towards the people carrier so roughly that the toes of his shoes scraped over the ground. Humboldt was standing with both hands on the handle of his walking sick, shaking his head like a teacher who'd just caught Sam cheating in a test.

'Do you want me to tie his legs?' Steele asked.

'No,' Humboldt said. 'No need. How long does a bullet wound to the leg take to heal?'

'A few weeks,' Sebastian said.

'Good, plenty of time till August then. George, feel free to shoot him in the leg if he tries to run again.'

'Gladly,' Steele said, eyeing Sam in a way that left him no doubt that this was true.

A hatch on the side of the plane opened, swinging down to reveal a flight of retractable steps on the other side, and a man in a pilot's uniform poked his head out.

'Good afternoon, Captain Litchfield,' Humboldt shouted. 'How go the preparations?'

'What was that noise?' the pilot called back, glancing about nervously. 'It sounded like a gunshot.'

'Nothing to worry about, my good man. How soon can we leave?'

Litchfield pushed his cap back and rubbed his forehead. 'Just completing the final checks, sir. Another five minutes or so, I estimate.'

'Excellent!' Humboldt turned back. 'George, help our young friend on board, would you? Then give me a hand with the cases. In a few hours' time we'll be sipping cocktails in the sun. Or you and I will, at least.'

Sam let out a groan, when all of a sudden a blue car sped up the path from the road, veered around the side of the people carrier and screeched to a stop, blocking the way to the plane.

7

Frances threw open the door of her car and jumped out. Apparently Campbell and his reinforcements were only minutes away, but the question of whether she should wait for backup had been rendered irrelevant by the shot George had fired, and she'd realised that if she didn't act immediately the chance would be lost. Thankfully, the jet's engines had masked the sound of her approach, letting her gatecrash the party unannounced.

An eerie calmness settled over her as she faced George over the bonnet, her muscles taut in readiness. There was something liberating about the feeling, as though with fear and uncertainty stripped away she could at last think clearly. This was her moment, her chance to turn the tables on the man who had tricked her, and nothing would stand in her way.

'*Frances*?' George said, his features contorting into an ugly snarl.

She stared back, her jaw set; she needed to stall for time. 'It's over, George,' she said. 'I know you killed Esteban Haufner.'

'Who *is* this annoying person?' Humboldt demanded.

'One of the police officers investigating the Malcolm Fairview murder,' George said. 'I had to, um, befriend her in order to get you your pills.'

'I see. So she's no longer of any use to us then?'

'None whatsoever.'

'Good,' Humboldt said. 'In that case she's in our way. Eliminate her.'

George released the collar of Rayner's hooded top and shoved him in the back, sending him stumbling. As he raised his gun and took aim, Frances realised that the few seconds by which she'd delayed their escape were about to cost her life. She lowered her gaze, but before George could open fire, Campbell's car raced up the path and skidded to a halt beside her own. The door flew open and he clambered out, his hands raised.

George frowned and swung the sights of his pistol from Frances to Campbell.

'Mark, what the hell are you doing?' she asked out of the corner of her mouth.

'Saving your bacon, I think,' he said, edging towards her.

'Where's the cavalry?'

'Right behind. They'll be here any minute.'

Humboldt glared at George. 'What are you waiting for, imbecile? Shoot them already! Shoot them both!'

George hesitated, visibly bristling at the insult, then directed his gun back at Frances.

Instinct took over, banishing all rational thought from her mind. Without really knowing what she was doing, she dived onto the bonnet of her car and slid across towards him. He got a shot off and, as she hit the ground on the other side, the window of the passenger seat exploded in a shower of broken glass.

If she was cut, she didn't feel it. Springing nimbly to her feet, she charged at George as he took aim again. There were still several feet between them when he squeezed the trigger, the gun levelled directly at her.

She was too late.

She wasn't going to reach him in time.

Twisting her head to one side, she raised her hands in self-defence, as if that would make a blind bit of difference. And then Campbell tackled her around the waist, knocking her clean off her feet and slamming her to the ground.

8

After everything that had happened over the last couple of weeks, Sergeant Hinds wasn't high on Sam's list of favourite people, but that had changed the moment he saw her climb out of the car blocking their way to the plane. At some point Steele must have released him, because out of nowhere he had found himself staggering. Unable to balance with his hands tied, he'd stumbled to one knee just as a second car arrived and Detective Campbell had jumped out.

What happened next took place too quickly for Sam to fully comprehend, but sensing a window of opportunity open before him, he had heaved himself up and run for it again. In the confusion no one seemed to be paying him any attention, and with each stride towards freedom his spirits rose.

Ten metres became twenty, then thirty. Still no one stopped him. It was going to happen; he was going to make it.

Suddenly another gunshot rang out.

Without breaking stride, Sam stole a glance over his shoulder. He saw Steele pointing his gun at Hinds while Campbell threw himself at her from one side. What he didn't see was the pothole into which his front foot was about to land, sending him face-planting onto the runway.

9

Never for a moment had George believed that he would see Frances Hinds again. But somehow, inexplicable as it seemed, here she was, charging towards him with a crazed, animalistic look on her face. As he pulled the trigger a second time, she recoiled, her arms raised to shield her face. From this distance it was nearly impossible to miss. His gun barked and the muzzle flared, but at that precise moment the new arrival on the scene rugby tackled her to the ground, an angry red slash opening in the side of the man's neck.

George lowered his pistol. After his sweet revenge the night before, the gifts seemed to just keep on coming. And then he heard the wail of sirens over the rumble of jet engines. Glancing towards the gates of the airfield, he saw a police car blaze up the road on the other side of the hedgerow, followed by another and another.

'Quick!' Humboldt bellowed, pointing to where Rayner was lying face down on the runway. 'Help me with the kid!'

George ignored him and stalked towards his stricken prey, bloodlust thrumming through him like a drug. Hinds lay on her side, trapped under the body of her gallant protector. Blood flowed freely onto the runway; the bullet had passed straight through the man's neck and out the other side, severing an artery and leaving a wound that gaped like the mouth of a grisly Halloween pumpkin. Death must have been disappointingly quick.

Crouching, George rolled him off. Hinds appeared to be unconscious. There was a deep cut on her forehead where it had connected with the tarmac, but it was impossible to tell how much of the blood pouring down her face was her own and how much belonged to the dead man beside her.

As the first of the police cars sped through the gate to the airfield, Sebastian grabbed George by the sleeve, one of Humboldt's suitcases in his other hand. 'Hurry!' he urged. 'Leave them, we don't have time!'

George stood and shrugged the small man away. Sebastian blinked at him for a moment and then scurried off.

Two police cars had by now come to a stop fifty yards down the runway, forming a rudimentary blockade. The doors flew open in the same instant and the officers of an armed response unit poured out.

George glanced to Hinds again and saw her staring straight back at him, her eyes burning with fiery hatred.

10

George stood over Hinds, wondering how on earth she had ever found him.

'You bastard!' she said, glancing at her friend's lifeless body. 'He had a family, you know. A wife, kids.'

'Rest assured, the bullet was meant for you,' George told her.

She glared up at him, her teeth bared. Blood from the cut to her head was running into her eyes but she didn't so much as blink. 'So you were working for Humboldt all along then?'

'Not all along, just since you arrested Rayner.'

'And you and me? The fancy restaurants, the nights at the opera...'

'An act, I'm afraid. I needed you to fulfil a task.'

'You've sold your soul, George. And for what? Look around, you're surrounded.'

George glanced up. He could make out an officer with a sniper rifle crouched behind the car on the right side of the blockade.

'How did you find me?' he asked, looking back down.

'Haufner's body was discovered late last night,' she told him. 'I had my suspicions after seeing what you'd done to his leg, but then your cufflink turned up at the scene. I was waiting outside your flat when you left this morning and followed you here.'

'I see,' he said, and shook his head.

'Put the gun down, George. The game's up.'

She was right, of course. He should never have returned to his flat, but overconfidence and sentimentality had been his downfall.

Hinds was now smiling beneath her mask of blood. 'You're going to spend the rest of your life behind bars,' she said.

'No, I think not.' George raised his pistol again and pointed it at her head. He would rather die than turn himself in, but at least he would have the satisfaction of killing her first. This was their destiny, he realised. Had been since the moment he'd first walked back into her life.

'Put the weapon down!' a voice over a loudspeaker boomed. 'I won't ask again!'

'Goodbye, Frances,' George said.

As he placed his finger over the trigger, a loud crack rang out and a white-hot searing sensation materialised in the centre of his chest. The gun slipped from his hand as he staggered back, his prosthetic leg giving way beneath him. Slowly his view flickered upwards, shifting from Hinds to the shattered window of her car to a bank of cloud to an unbroken segment of the clear blue sky. Darkness began to encroach on all sides, and the last thing George saw was a dirty seagull hanging in the air above him.

11

Sam's head swam, his vision filled by stars. He blinked and discovered that he was lying face-down on the runway. The skin from his right cheek to his shoulder blade felt like one long graze, and one of his back teeth was loose.

Spitting flecks of gravel from his mouth, he rolled over and propped himself up on his elbow. Suddenly another gunshot sounded, somehow louder and sharper than before, as if amplified. He looked up to see the Agent Steele standing over Sergeant Hinds and the body of Detective Campbell. The man who had killed Chrissie in an alternate timeline dropped his pistol and keeled over backwards, a dark red circle spreading out from the middle of his shirt.

Sam scrambled to his feet. While he had been knocked out, several police cars had arrived on the scene, forming a line across the runway. An officer with a long-barrelled sniper rifle was crouched behind the car on the right.

In spite of the murder charges still hanging over Sam's head, it was a sight to fill him with joy. Wincing at a dull ache in his ribs, he raised his tied hands over his head and took a step forward.

Before he could take another, he felt the touch of a cold blade against his neck.

12

Sam turned to see Humboldt standing by his shoulder. The old man had separated the dragon's-head handle from the shaft of his walking stick, revealing the ten-inch blade of the dagger which was now pressed to Sam's Adam's apple.

'Oh no you don't,' Humboldt whispered, his lips millimetres from Sam's ear.

Sam gulped and glanced longingly towards the line of police cars blocking the runway. A helmeted officer in a bulletproof vest straightened up behind the middle car and raised a loudspeaker to her lips.

'Put the weapon down!' she said. 'I repeat, put the weapon down!'

The sniper lifted his rifle again and took aim through the telescopic sights.

'Take the shot!' Sam yelled. 'Go on, do it!'

'He won't,' Humboldt said, dragging him back like a human shield. 'Not if there's a chance he might hit you. That's the problem with cops, too afraid of civilian casualties to do what's necessary. Not something I've ever suffered from, as luck would have it.'

Out of the corner of his eye, Sam glimpsed the pilot leaning out of the hatch in the side of the plane again.

'Captain Litchfield,' Humboldt called out, 'are we ready for take-off yet?'

Litchfield blinked and drew a shaking hand down his face as he took in the scene of carnage before him. 'Yes, but...but...'

'Excellent! Donna, remind me to double the captain's fee in the light of his outstanding contribution this afternoon.'

'This wasn't part of the deal!' Litchfield said.

'On second thoughts, treble it. Now, Captain, if you'd kindly take your seat in the cockpit, we'll be joining you shortly.'

Litchfield blinked again, then nodded and disappeared back inside the plane.

Humboldt had continued edging back the whole while, keeping Sam positioned in front of his body with the blade of the dagger. They were now almost level with Donna, who was clutching a plaid holdall bag to her chest as she rocked on her heels and gaped down at the blood-spattered runway where Hinds sat hunched between the bodies of Campbell and Steele.

'Put down the knife!' the police officer with the loud-speaker demanded. 'Release the hostage and nobody else need get hurt.'

'No chance! Try anything and I'll slit his goddam throat!' Humboldt yelled back. Turning to Sebastian, he tilted his head towards Hinds and lowered his voice. 'The woman, might as well bring her along too.'

'But—' Sebastian began.

'You know, you're beginning to sound a lot like Captain Litchfield. We need the kid alive, remember? The cop on the other hand...well, she might prove useful.'

Sebastian's face dropped, but he scooped up the pistol lying next to Steele's limp, outstretched hand. Hinds was bleeding heavily from a cut to her head and looked like she might pass out at any moment. He lifted her to her feet and, gripping the pistol as though it were contaminated, shepherded her over to the foot of the steps leading up to the plane.

As Humboldt manoeuvred Sam alongside them, Hinds glanced over with wide, pleading eyes. Sam met her gaze for a moment and then looked away, knowing there was nothing he could do for her.

There appeared to be some uncertainty over at the line of police cars, where the single sniper now had two targets to cover. The officer with the loudspeaker turned away and began gesticulating as she frantically dished out instructions. A few seconds passed and then two armed officers broke out from cover and started skirting around the plane.

'Trying to flank us,' Humboldt muttered, digging the blade a little deeper into the soft skin of Sam's neck. 'Fat lot of good it will do them.'

He began mounting the steps, towing Sam along with him. Donna followed, still clutching the bag like it was an abandoned baby, and then Sebastian and the semi-conscious Hinds. Sam glanced back and caught a glimpse of the cream-leather and polished-wood interior of the jet.

Suddenly two more police cars tore through the gates of the airfield. One stopped, blocking the path to the road, while the other joined the line of cars on the runway. A second sniper jumped out and took up a position behind the bonnet.

With a strength that belied his tumour-ridden body, Humboldt shoved Sam through the hatch, sending him skidding across the carpeted floor of the cabin. Donna, Sebastian and Hinds bundled through, and then Humboldt slammed the door shut, cutting off Sam's last remaining chance of escape.

13

Sam rolled onto his back and heaved himself up into a seated position. There was now a carpet burn down his left cheek to match the gravel-specked graze on the right one. During the face-off on the runway and their retreat to the plane, the cable tie had cinched so tight that trickles of blood ran from his wrists to the tips of his fingers. He wiped his hands on the cabin floor, leaving streaks of red over the previously spotless carpet.

They were in the aisle that ran down the length of the plane between two rows of rotating leather armchairs. At the front of the cabin was a door onto the cockpit, and at the rear, beyond a section with a sofa and TV screen, a door to what looked like a kitchen area. Sebastian eased Detective Hinds into one of the armchairs. She looked in a state of shock, her eyes wide and vacant in her blood-streaked face as her body swayed gently from side to side.

Captain Litchfield emerged from the cockpit, his face dripping with sweat beneath the peak of his up-tilted hat.

'What the hell are you doing?' Humboldt screeched. 'Get back in there and prepare for take-off this instant!'

Litchfield rubbed the back of his neck. 'Sir, there's a police negotiator on the radio. They want you to release the hostages.'

'You're kidding, right? Tell them they've got sixty seconds to move their blockade, otherwise one of their precious hostages gets it.'

'But—'

Humboldt flung the empty shaft of his walking stick onto a chair and strode down the aisle. He stopped just before Litchfield and raised the blade of his dagger under the pilot's chin. 'Say "but" again, I double dare you.'

A bead of sweat rolled down the bridge of the Litchfield's nose and dangled from the tip. He shook his head, dislodging it.

'That's better,' Humboldt said, and lowered the dagger. 'Listen, Captain, I appreciate your concern but the whole thing's a bluff. A collision would endanger everyone on board, including the hostages. They won't risk harming them, you'll see. They'll move the blockade as soon as you start taxiing. Now, pretty please with a cherry on top, go tell the negotiator they've got sixty seconds to get out of the way, then prepare for take-off, okay?'

Litchfield opened his mouth as if he was about to object, then glanced nervously at the dagger in Humboldt's hand and backed into the cockpit. After a moment the pitch of the engines cranked up a notch.

Humboldt turned back with a satisfied smile. 'Donna, Sebastian, get the kid up off the floor, would you? He's making a mess of the carpet. And find something to secure the woman's hands with while you're at it.'

Donna nodded, finally releasing her grip on the holdall bag and setting it on the floor. After helping Sam to his feet, she steered him into the chair across from Hinds and fastened the seatbelt around his waist, while Sebastian surveyed the cabin with a blank look on his face, Steele's pistol gripped loosely by his side.

'Like what, sir?' he asked eventually.

Humboldt sighed, glanced about and then hacked the seatbelt from another chair before handing it over and reattaching the shaft of his walking stick.

'Good idea,' Sebastian said.

He passed the pistol to Donna, who deposited in the pocket of her cardigan, and then set about binding Hinds's wrists with the length of seatbelt.

All of a sudden there was a lurch. Sam had a direct line of sight through the cockpit's open door and out through the windscreen. The ground outside started to move, slowly at first but gradually picking up speed. Just as Humboldt had predicted, the police blockade scattered as they approached, leaving only clear runway ahead.

The airfield shot past, the acceleration pushing Sam back like a shove to the chest. The cabin tilted as the front wheel lifted. He experienced the brief sensation of weightlessness and then the runway and police cars were shrinking away through the circular window next to his chair.

His mind flitted back to the moment Flight 0368 had taken off at Newark Airport. It was the last time he had seen his father alive, a day that would set in motion the events that would ultimately lead him to this point. Out of nowhere he felt his chest spasm, his breathing reduced to shallow, rasping gasps as he mentally replayed the events of that fateful morning last September. Black spots appeared before his eyes, swimming and swirling. He blinked, trying to clear them, and then everything went dark

14

Sam opened his eyes and realised he must have fainted during takeoff. The plane had levelled out and, through the window to his side, he could see the setting sun filling a blanket of cloud on the western horizon with orange light. A pair of sleek, grey fighter jets hung in the sky a few hundred metres away, but as he looked on they both dipped their wings and peeled off before dropping out of sight.

A ball of dread materialised in his chest like a dead weight: in a few hours' time they would reach Swordfish Island, where he would spend the next six months pumped full of Humboldt's counteragent while they waited for his consciousness from the night before to enter his body. He was defeated, but would resist to the bitter end, doing everything in his power to derail Humboldt's plans.

Looking about the cabin, he saw that the door to the cockpit was now closed. Humboldt was dozing in one of the seats a few rows ahead with his walking stick across his lap, while Donna and Sebastian were talking in hushed voices by the door to the kitchen.

Sam glanced over to Hinds and found her staring straight back, her face and hair crusted with dried blood. She arched her eyebrows and angled her head in the direction of the gently snoring Humboldt. Sam frowned and shrugged his shoulders to show that he didn't know what she was getting at, but she wriggled her right arm and slowly withdrew her hand from the knotted length of seatbelt Sebastian had used to bind her wrists together. She nodded towards Humboldt again, this time silently mouthing the words, 'His walking stick.'

The penny dropped: if Hinds could reach Humboldt without waking him, she might then be able to lift the weapon from his lap. Of course, that still left Donna,

Sebastian and Captain Litchfield to contend with, but if Sam and Hinds could take Humboldt hostage then it was conceivable they might be able to turn the tables and force the others to land the plane. It was insanely dangerous and probably wouldn't work, but it wasn't as if they had much to lose. And if they were as good as dead anyway, they might as well go down fighting.

Sam raised his hands, gave Hinds the thumbs up and made a snipping action with his fingers to indicate that she should slice the cable tie around his wrists once she had the dagger. She hesitated for a moment and then nodded. After a final glance towards the rear of the cabin, she removed her hand from the knot and noiselessly unclipped her seatbelt. Then, with painstaking care, she began inching herself up from her seat.

'We've just left British airspace, sir.'

Sam jerked his head around to see Litchfield standing by the cockpit door.

Humboldt stirred in his chair and sat up, rubbing his eyes. 'We have? Who's steering the plane then?'

'The autopilot.'

'Ah, okay. And what about our escort?'

'They left a minute ago. They can't follow us from here.'

'See?' Humboldt chuckled. 'Told you they wouldn't try anything with hostages on board. Donna? Sebastian? Where have you gotten to?'

As Litchfield closed the cockpit door behind him, Sam risked another glance at Hinds. She was back in her seat with her hand through the knot again and her eyes closed as if passed out, but the strap of her unbuckled seatbelt now dangled conspicuously by the side of her chair.

'Are you hungry, sir?' Donna asked. 'I was just checking the food situation. There are several servings of duck a l'orange and vegetable moussaka—'

'Sure, whatever,' Humboldt said, waving her away. 'Sebastian, how long since the kid had his last dose of counteragent?'

'He should be good for several hours yet,' Sebastian replied.

Humboldt shook his head. 'No, I'm not taking any chances, not when we're almost there. Prepare another dose, would you?'

'Right away,' Sebastian said. He fetched the holdall bag Donna had carried onboard and followed her into the kitchen.

Sam turned back to Hinds, desperate to somehow alert her to the unfastened seatbelt hanging by her side, but her eyes remained closed as she faked unconsciousness.

Humboldt stood and stretched, then sauntered down the aisle towards them. He stopped by Hinds's chair without seeming to notice her unbuckled seatbelt. Then, gripping the shaft of his stick with his artificial hand, he twisted the handle and unsheathed the dagger once more.

'Wakey wakey, sweetheart,' he said, waving the blade an inch from the tip of her nose.

Hinds opened her eyes and glared at him.

'It's been a blast,' he said, 'but it looks like you've outlived your usefulness. The question remains, however, of what to do with you. Any suggestions?'

She muttered something too quiet to be heard.

'What's that?' Humboldt asked, and stooped to bring his ear closer.

As he did so, she yanked her free hand out of the knot, reached up and grabbed the wrist of his knife hand. He staggered back, his mouth open, and bumped into the chair behind him. In that split second she was up and out of her chair. Still gripping Humboldt's wrist, she raised her knee into his groin. He doubled over with a grunt. The dagger wavered back and forth between them. For a moment it looked like she might wrench it from his grip, but as the surprise of her unexpected attack subsided, he began to regain the upper hand, using his superior weight to twist the blade back towards her.

Sam had to do something, but with his hands tied he couldn't reach the buckle of his seatbelt. Instead he tried using his elbow to gain a purchase. The buckle opened halfway and then snapped shut with a metallic clunk. Gritting his teeth, he tried again. Inch by inch the clip scraped down the sleeve of his hoodie towards his elbow. It was about to slip again and then, at the very last moment, the catch released and the buckle clicked opened.

He shot out of his chair and charged across the aisle, piling into Humboldt's side. Both Humboldt and Hinds slammed against the curved wall of the cabin. Hinds's head connected heavily with the rim of the window and she slumped to the floor. As Humboldt dragged Sam down with him, the dagger tumbled from his hand and went bouncing across the floor before disappearing under a chair on the other side of the aisle.

Sam thrashed his arms and legs to disentangle himself from Humboldt's flailing grip and began slithering across the carpet on his elbows and knees. He could just make out the glint of the blade in the shadows beneath the chair when a voice from the rear of the cabin shouted, 'Stop!'

Rolling onto his side, he looked up to see Sebastian step through the door to the kitchen, followed by Donna with Steele's pistol in her hand.

15

Sam lay stretched across the floor of the cabin, Humboldt's dagger tantalisingly out of reach.

'That's enough,' Donna said, and tightened her grip around the handle of the pistol. Her posture was rigid and there was a new edge to her voice that he had never detected before.

Humboldt grinned and drew himself up. Adjusting his prosthetic arm, which had become twisted during the scuffle, he stepped over the unconscious body of Sergeant Hinds, into the aisle and around Sam.

'Good work, Donna,' he said, and bent to retrieve the dagger from under the chair. 'Just in the nick of time.'

'Put it down, Michael,' she said.

Humboldt's grin faltered. 'Say what?'

'Put it down. It's over.'

'Damn right it's over! I've won, Donna. *We've* won. Sebastian, tie the cop up properly this time, then give the kid his counteragent, would you?'

The small man didn't budge but stared back blankly, his face ghostly pale.

'No, Michael, you haven't won,' Donna said, digging the barrel of the gun into Sebastian's ribs. 'I can't let you go through with this. What you're doing ends here.'

Humboldt blinked several times in rapid succession. 'What are you talking about, Donna?'

'My name isn't Donna,' she said. 'It's Nora Rutherford.'

He lowered the dagger, his eyebrows bunched in confusion. 'Am I missing the punch line or something? Your name is Donna Buxton. You've been on my payroll since 1970. I probably know you better than I know any living soul.'

'I'm sorry to tell you this, Michael, but the person you think you know is a fabrication, a character I assumed on my father's orders. After the press coverage of your winning streak in 1969 alerted the family to your existence, he sent me to keep an eye on you. My role was initially to gain your trust in order to ascertain whether or not you could be transformed into a useful asset.' She sighed and shook her head. 'You had the potential to do so much good, but instead you devoted your life to greed and the pursuit of power.'

Although Sam couldn't make sense of what he was hearing, it sounded a lot like the direction of proceedings had just swung in his favour. He rolled onto his backside and, taking advantage of the distraction, shuffled away down the carpet.

Humboldt was studying the dragon's-head handle of his dagger with a dazed look on his face. Several seconds passed before he looked up again. 'So what, you're a spy?'

'I suppose that would be an accurate description,' Donna (or Nora) said. 'After I realised you possessed neither the personality nor the moral compass to make a viable ally, we decided it was best that I maintain a watch over you, subtly manipulating your activities in order to limit the damage you could do.'

'And the family you speak of?'

'*Our* family, Michael. Yours, Rayner's and mine. The man you think of as Gerhardt von Humboldt was in fact my long-lost uncle, Joseph Rutherford.'

'*Rutherford*? Garbage, I've never even heard of the name!' Humboldt took a step towards her, his knuckles white around the handle of his dagger, but she levelled the pistol at his chest. He pulled up and forced an uneasy chuckle. 'C'mon, you've seen the documents, Donna or Nora or whatever-you-say-your-name-is. You know as well as I do that my grandfather was a German immigrant.'

'He was born Joseph Rutherford, brother to Stephen Rutherford, my father. Both men were sailors on the *Northern Star*, a British merchant vessel sunk by a German submarine attack in 1916. While my father suffered a cranial injury and developed powers similar to those of young Mr Rayner and yourself, Joseph was presumed lost at sea. It was only years later when you first showed me your grandfather's photograph that I realised you were descended from a previously unknown branch of the family.'

'I don't believe you,' Humboldt said, although his shoulders had sagged and his fingers gone limp around the handle of the dagger. 'You're making this up. Must be.'

'Think about it, Michael – the reason we never found any of your grandfather's relatives during our search last year is because he never *had* any. It appears Joseph must have lost his memory and been washed up in northern Germany. Due to his fluency in the language, he was probably taken for a local sailor fallen overboard. It seems he made his home in Ottendorf and began a new life under the name von Humboldt, later marrying your grandmother. We have no reason to believe he ever learned his true identity, even after moving to America in the 1930s.'

Humboldt scowled, his face darkening. 'You betrayed me,' he said flatly. 'I trusted you like family, and you betrayed me.'

'We *are* family, Michael. You, me and the boy.'

Humboldt glanced back, halting the progress of Sam's slow bum-shuffle towards the cockpit door.

'You aside, he's the last living male that we know of in Joseph's bloodline,' she went on. 'Rayner's importance to the family is therefore paramount, and once I'd learned of his existence I needed you to lead me to him. I had hoped that your plan to find a cure would fail and you would pass away as nature intended without me having to break cover. There was even still some hope of that when the police showed up at the airfield, but it seems you now leave me no choice but to intervene.'

'All these years I trusted you. We ran my operations side by side. You had your finger in every pie and…and you were actually my *enemy*? I don't get it, why not just kill me years ago and be done with it?'

'That was my suggestion,' she said, a gleam in her eye. 'Fortunately for you, my father was a man of faith and adhered to a strict moral code. It is not our way to take life, Michael, even one as corrupted as yours. Besides, it was through you that we first learned of Dr Barclay and his work on Tetradyamide.'

'*Barclay*!' Humboldt yelled, the veins in his forehead popping. 'What the hell's *he* got to do with any of this?'

'His work on Tetradyamide helped revolutionise what we do, allowing my brother, Marcus, to massively upscale the project our father started. In that respect, I suppose you could call him an honorary member of the family.'

Humboldt looked fit to burst. 'I…I've spent my life searching for Tetradyamide,' he spluttered, 'and you're telling me you've had it the whole time?'

'Not the whole time, just since Isaac's escape from Sandstone Springs in '76. Really, you should see the advances he made towards the end of the last millennium! The drug you persuaded the unfortunate Mr Steele to thieve for you is barely deserving of the same name.'

Humboldt let out a low growl and raised his dagger again, but she shoved Sebastian aside and stepped forward, the pistol aimed at his head.

'What is it you want then, traitor?'

'As I've explained, it is not our way to take life. But my father always stipulated that if you were to die of natural causes, or the consequences of your own misdemeanours, it should not be prevented.'

'My brain tumour?'

'It is your destiny, Michael, and you must not be saved from it.' She took another step towards him, the pistol unwavering. 'This timeline cannot be allowed to continue in its current trajectory. It must be reset to prevent you from finding Tetradyamide, Rayner and a cure for your tumour. I need you to instruct Captain Litchfield to divert the flight.'

'No chance! Without the kid I won't live to see April.'

'Then I'll shoot you and do it myself,' she said. 'The end result is the same.'

'Really?' Humboldt sneered. 'Ever heard of decompression? Miss and you'll kill us all, the kid included.'

'If you think this is the first time I've held a gun, Michael, you're sorely mistaken. I'll shoot if I have to, and I won't miss. Now, I won't ask you again, put the dagger down.'

Sam held his breath as he visualised being sucked from an aeroplane tens of thousands of feet above the ocean. The moment seemed to drag on and on as Humboldt weighed his options.

'So die now or die later?' he said eventually. 'It's not much of a choice, is it?'

'It's the only one you have,' the woman who called herself Donna said.

At that moment a pocket of turbulence rocked the cabin and, as she staggered back a step, Sebastian sprang forwards, knocking the gun from her hand.

16

What happened next seemed to take place in slow motion. As Sebastian and Nora Rutherford tangled, Steele's pistol tumbled to the floor. It hit the carpet barrel-first and bounced, cart-wheeling down the aisle before coming to a rest a few inches before the toes of Humboldt's shoes. He let out a bark of laughter, transferred his dagger to the plastic hand of his prosthetic and bent to lift the gun.

Sebastian and Nora both froze as he straightened up and took aim at them.

'Looks like we won't be diverting the flight after all,' Humboldt said, his voice rich with glee. 'Sebastian, move out the way, would you?'

Sebastian released Nora and turned, his body positioned between them. 'Sir, don't do it! Remember what you said about decompression.'

'You think I'm going to let her live after what I've just heard?'

'Please,' Sebastian pleaded, 'you don't need to kill her. Think about everything we've been through to-gether!'

'All the more reason. Now get out the way, damn it!'

Sam clambered to his feet, his heart hammering. If he was going to act, it had to be now.

'Do what he says, Sebastian,' Nora said, her head held high.

Sebastian glanced at her over his shoulder, then looked back at Humboldt. 'No,' he said. 'I don't care what she's done, she's been my friend for over forty years and I'm not going to let you shoot her like a dog.'

'Fine then,' Humboldt said, and pulled the trigger.

The sound the gunshot was deafening in the confined space of the cabin. Sebastian lowered his arms, took a step back and gawped down at the bullet wound in his chest. After a moment he looked back up, opened his mouth as if to say something and then toppled sideways onto the sofa at the rear of the cabin.

'I told you to move,' Humboldt said with a sorry shake of his head.

Sam charged forwards, all thought of his personal safety absent. He dipped his shoulder and, as Humboldt took aim again, barged into him from behind.

The old man expelled a loud huff as the impact drove the air from his lungs and then, as he crumpled under Sam's weight, the gun sounded again.

17

Sam lay over Humboldt on the cabin floor, waiting for the roar and tug of pressurised air escaping the hull. But as the ringing in his ears subsided, all that remained was the hum of the aircraft's engines.

He lifted his head to see Nora Rutherford staring back at him, her eyes stretched wide. The bullet had carved a graze along her cheek before ending its short journey embedded in the frame of the kitchen door.

'Are you okay?' he asked.

She raised a trembling hand to her cheek and inspected the dabs of blood on her fingertips. After a quick glance at Sebastian's body, she nodded, heaved herself up and then helped Sam to his feet.

Humboldt was still face down where he had fallen. An expanding circle of blood was beginning to soak through the cream carpet beneath him. Nora crouched and rolled him over. The dragon's-head handle of his dagger protruded from his stomach, the blade buried deep within his abdomen. She rested her fingers on the side of his neck and then shook her head.

'Is he dead?' Sam asked.

'It wasn't supposed to end like this,' she muttered, and closed Humboldt's eyelids.

'What was that?' Captain Litchfield asked as he burst from the cockpit. He stopped in his tracks, his gaze darting from where Hinds lay unconscious by her chair to the scene at the rear of the cabin, and then removed his hat and pressed it to his chest.

Nora eased the pistol from Humboldt's lifeless grip and drew herself up. 'There's been a change of plan, Captain,' she said. 'I'm going to need you to plot a new course.'

Chapter VIII

Reset

1

Frances blew into her steaming mug of coffee as she gazed at Sam Rayner across their corner table in the café of the near-deserted terminal of Kuujjuaq Airport, Quebec. The place wasn't much bigger than the airfield in Dorset where, several hours earlier, George had tried to kill her before being felled by a police marksman's bullet. Through the glass wall to her left, she could make out the tail of the private jet against the dark sky. Somewhere onboard, covered by blankets, lay the bodies of Michael Humboldt and his scientist, Sebastian.

After being knocked unconscious, Frances had missed the moment Sebastian had snapped and tried to stop his boss. Apparently Humboldt had wrenched the pistol from Donna's grip and shot Sebastian before Donna and Rayner had managed to tackle him, causing him to fall on his own dagger. Although the exact details remained hazy, Frances had been so relieved to escape with her life that she hadn't really pushed the matter, and after touching down forty-five minutes ago she'd gladly deferred the responsibility of alerting the local authorities to Donna. In any case, the deaths had occurred in international airspace, far outside Frances's jurisdiction, and although she would provide a witness statement if required, the question of whether any blame was to be attributed to the pair was a matter for Interpol to decide.

'How are your wrists?' she asked, and took a sip of her coffee.

Rayner swallowed the last mouthful of his cheese and ham croissant and glanced down at the two red bands where the cable tie had cut into his skin. 'A bit sore,' he said, and then looked up and smiled, 'but I don't think there's any permanent damage. So, I was wondering, what now?'

'Between you and me, you mean?'

He nodded.

'Listen, Sam, I know you didn't kill Malcolm Fairview, if that's what you're asking. As for what happened at Knotsbridge, I think we both know who was responsible for that. Once we get home I'll help you clear your name through the correct channels, you have my word.' She paused and flattened her hair, which still contained the odd clump of dried blood in spite of her best efforts to make herself look presentable in the mirror of the airport toilets. 'After that, I think I'm through with policing.'

'*Really*?' he asked.

'For a while at least. I've put my job before everything else for so long that the rest of my life is a mess.' She laughed and shook her head. 'I suppose our brush with death just put that into perspective. I could do with a break, a chance to re-evaluate what's important.'

He nodded again. 'Actually, talking of home, I should probably ring and, you know, let them know I'm alive and everything. Have you got any of that Canadian money left?'

Frances dug into her pocket and pulled out the remaining dollars that Donna had given her. 'I saw a payphone over by the entrance,' she said, pressing the loose change into Rayner's hand. 'Just don't go running off anywhere, okay?'

'Wouldn't dream of it,' he said.

2

Chrissie lay dozing on the living room sofa, the telephone in her lap and her feet propped on a cushioned stool. She still wasn't sure whether or not Sam's escape from Knotsbridge had been part of his plan, but one thing was for certain: if her brother were free, he would make contact at the first opportunity.

Since starting her vigil over the phone, it had rung a total of eleven times. The first had been a reporter asking if Chrissie would like to comment on Sam's escape (to which she had promptly slammed the phone down). This had been followed by calls from Lewis and Auntie Laura, both wondering if Chrissie knew what was going on (which she didn't, obviously). The day after, three more reporters had contacted her in addition to an automated call saying that there was still time for her to claim back her mis-sold PPI. The trend had continued into Tuesday, when, as well as another automated call about seeking compensation for her injuries in a car accident that had never happened, four more reporters had rung.

So when the phone rang for a twelfth time, waking her from a fretful slumber in the early hours of Wednesday morning, Chrissie had all but given up hope of it actually being Sam.

For a moment there was nothing but static on the other end of the line, and then, in a voice that sounded weak and distant, she heard her brother say, 'Chrissie, can you hear me?'

'Sam, it's actually you!' she squealed, and jumped up from the sofa. 'Where *are* you? Is everything all right?'

'Yeah, everything's fine now,' he said. 'I'm in Canada.'

'*Canada*? What are you doing there?'

'I'm with Sergeant Hinds. Trust me, it's a long story, but the main thing is it's over now and I'm safe. I'll tell you all about it when I'm home.'

'So you are coming back then?'

There was a pause at the other end of the line. 'Soon,' he said after a moment. 'There's something I need to do first.'

3

Sam placed the receiver of the payphone back on its hook and turned to find the woman who had saved his life standing by his side.

'Thought I'd better call my sister,' he explained, 'just to let her know I'm okay and everything.'

Nora gave a slow nod. 'And Sergeant Hinds?'

'She's waiting in the café,' he said, glancing to the far end of the terminal, where Hinds was talking to a waiter who'd stopped at the table to refill her coffee.

'Good. I just finished meeting with my brother's contact. He knows someone on the local police force who can help with the bodies. He also managed to secure me a plane.' She pointed through the wall of glass at the back of the terminal to a row of small, twin-engine propeller planes. 'Perhaps not as comfortable as the jet, but it'll get us to where we need to go.'

'What about Captain Litchfield?'

'The man's a pilot for hire specialising in clients involved in disreputable activity of one kind or another, which means it pays to be discreet. Once his payment goes through at the triple rate Michael promised him – which I'll make sure it does – I doubt we'll ever hear from him again.' She paused and smiled. With the submissive stoop straightened out of her stance, she appeared several inches taller than she had as Donna. 'So, have you given any more thought to what we discussed yet?'

Sam bit his lip and stole another glance at Hinds, who was still talking to the waiter and didn't appear to have noticed Nora's return. As exhausted as he was and as much as he wanted to get home, see his family and begin the process of clearing his name, the opportunity offered to him might never present itself again.

'I have,' he said, turning back, 'and I want to come with you.'

'What do you say we make a quick exit before Sergeant Hinds notices your absence then?'

'Where are we going?'

Nora Rutherford smiled again. 'The family home, of course.'

4

It was almost ten o'clock the following morning when Sam and Nora touched down in Greenland, but so far north the sun was scarcely more than a suggestion on the eastern horizon. In spite of the thick, fur-lined coat Nora had given him, Sam felt his teeth begin to chatter the moment he climbed from the plane.

The airfield was just a strip of flattened dirt carved into the snow and surrounded by several low buildings. There was an ancient Land Rover parked up nearby. Standing by its side was a man with long white hair that had fused together with his beard to form a single mega-dreadlock.

Sam stopped and stared: it was the person he had seen watching him on the day he and Eva had visited the Prince Regent pub back in the December-only-he-could-remember. Nora hurried over and threw her arms around the man's neck, hugging him tightly.

Eventually they separated, and he stepped forwards, offering his hand. 'You must be Sam,' he said. 'I'm Isaac.'

'Pleased to meet you,' Sam said. It was only then, standing before him, that he realised there was another reason Isaac looked so familiar. Although much older now, he was the same man Sam had seen in a faded black-and-white photograph behind Lara McHayden's desk at Thames House. 'Hang on, *you're* Isaac?'

'The one and only.' Isaac grinned, then narrowed his eyes. 'Judging by your reaction, I'm guessing we've already met in a different timeline.'

Sam hesitated. On Christmas Eve, Isaac had provided Lewis with the vial of silvery Tetradyamide that had saved everyone in the Tempus Research facility and brought Chrissie back to life after Agent Steele had shot her.

'Not so much met,' Sam said, 'more like seen from a distance. Either way, I think I've got a lot to thank you for.'

Isaac laughed and opened the rear door of the Land Rover. 'Very cryptic, but don't mention it, Sam. Although I've also been known to start them now and then, putting out fires across multiple timelines is what I do best. Now hop in and let's get going. We've got a three-hour drive ahead of us, and I for one want to make it back in time for lunch.'

5

Sam was so tired that he fell asleep in the Land Rover, which was an impressive feat given that the suspension was even shoddier than Lance's Volvo. He woke shivering in an icy breeze blowing in through a hole in the canvas roof. Pulling his coat around his body, he stared out of the window. They were shuddering along a rough track cut into the side of a hill. The landscape was a desolate blanket of snow in all directions, with mountains to their left dropping down to a choppy sea spotted with huge chunks of floating ice.

After a while the track forked before them. Isaac followed the right-hand branch for a couple of miles before arriving at a rusty gate, which he climbed out to open and then steered them through.

There was a wooden farmhouse with a slanting slate roof about half a mile ahead; pretty much the first sign of civilisation they'd encountered since leaving the airfield. As they parked outside, an old man with sparse white hair and bushy eyebrows stepped out onto the front porch, where he stood waiting with his arms folded.

Nora clambered from the rear door, dashed over and wrapped him in a tight embrace. 'Marcus!' she cried. 'I can't tell you how wonderful it is to be home! The place hasn't changed a bit.'

'It's good to see you too, sister.' Marcus eased Nora back and held her at arms' length. 'What happened to you? You've grown old!'

'You're one to talk!' She gave him a playful slap on the arm and beckoned Sam over. 'Marcus, I'd like to introduce you to Sam Rayner, Joseph Rutherford's great-great-grandson. Sam, this is Marcus, my twin brother and the current head of our family.'

Sam climbed onto the porch. The man before him was almost the spitting image of his own grandfather, Alfred Rayner.

'An honour and a pleasure,' Marcus said, and rested a hand on Sam's shoulder. 'Please, come in out of the cold. I hope you like seafood. Lunch is almost ready and we have a great deal to discuss.'

6

From his chair at the head of an age-stained wooden table, Sam glanced around at his elderly companions. With Nora and Isaac sitting on one side, Marcus on the other and Marcus's wife, Katherine, dishing up bowls of fish stew at the stove, it felt a little like he'd dropped in for lunch at a retirement home.

The interior of the Rutherford house resembled that of a large cabin. It was surprisingly bare, and the mishmash of furniture looked as though it had been accumulated at a car boot sale several decades ago. The unpainted timber walls bore little by way of decoration besides the occasional stretched animal fur, the exception being the far wall, where the portrait of a young man hung. Apart from the early-1900s clothing, formal side-parted hair and stern expression, Sam might as well have been looking into a mirror.

'Stephen Rutherford, painted in 1920,' Katherine said, and placed a steaming bowl of stew in front of him. She had the hooded eyes of a native Greenlander and, despite her advancing years, not a strand of grey in her jet-black hair. 'You look a lot like him, you know.'

'I was just thinking the same thing,' Sam said.

Marcus offered him a slice of bread from a wooden chopping board and then took one himself. 'I'm not sure how much my sister told you already,' he said, dunking it in his bowl, 'but I expect you must be curious about the history of our family.'

Sam swallowed a spoonful of stew. It may have been the combination of hunger, exhaustion and relief, but it was pretty much the best thing he'd ever tasted. 'Yeah,' he said once his mouth was empty. 'Curious is an understatement.'

'Very well.' Marcus rested his elbows on the table and clasped his hands together. 'In that case the most logical place to start is at the beginning. Both of our families, in addition to that of Michael Humboldt, are descended from two brothers, Stephen and Joseph Rutherford.'

'I think I know this bit already,' Sam said, remembering what Nora had told Humboldt on the plane. 'They were sailors on a boat that sank a hundred years ago.'

'That's right. The *Northern Star*, it was called. Stephen – Nora's and my father – suffered a cranial injury similar to those both you and Humboldt sustained. As he recovered from his injuries, he began to experience seizures during which the flow of time was disrupted and he found himself transported into the recent past or future. He started documenting these in a series of journals which he continued to pen up until his death in 1989.'

'I know a thing or two about seizures,' Sam said, and filled his mouth with another spoonful of stew.

'I'll bet you do.' Marcus smiled and nibbled at his bread. 'Anyway, in the years after his injury, Father learned that his seizures were often brought about by changes in his mood or emotion. Using meditation and training, he came to realise that it was possible to induce such episodes at will, bringing back information gleaned from the future in order to alter events in the past or present. With practice he was able to gain greater control over his ability, choosing when his seizures occurred and extending the length of time he could travel to almost one month in either direction.'

'You mean like Michael Humboldt without Tetra-dyamide?' Sam asked.

'Exactly,' Nora said, 'although Michael had neither the patience nor the innate ability to fully master the techniques. The thing is, Sam, our father believed his power to be a gift from above that should only be used for the greater good of humanity, and never, under any circumstances, for personal gain. After the Second World War, he made several investments that continue to bring in a significant income to this day, but we use this to maintain the network of contacts that help facilitate our operations, such as the man I met with back at the airport back in Canada.'

'There's something I don't get,' Sam said. 'If your father was so interested in the greater good of humanity and all that, why didn't he just stop World War II from taking place? History was never my strongest subject, but I'm pretty sure something like sixty million people died. How could he allow that if there was something he could do? I mean, why didn't he just use his power to stop it from happening in the first place?'

'A noble sentiment,' Marcus said, 'but there's only so much a single person can do. There are tragedies and disasters around the world every day, Sam. It's something that caused me great distress as a younger man, but even with the power to alter the flow of time, it's impossible to prevent loss of life in every earthquake, motorway pile-up or political coup that takes place. You see, it's one thing to possess knowledge of a future event and quite another to use it to influence the actions of other people in order to prevent that event. In spite of these limitations my father and I have helped shape the late-twentieth and early-twenty-first centuries for the better.' He dipped his bread in his bowl again and took another bite. 'Secrecy has always been our family's greatest defence, you see. How do you think the rest of the world would react if they knew we were out here, invisibly shaping their destinies?'

'If it's for their own good, I would've thought they'd be grateful.'

'If only.' Marcus shook his head and gave a wry smile. 'In my experience, human nature makes people remarkably reluctant to have decision-making taken out of their hands. The notion of free will, no matter how illusionary, is a powerful lure, which is why we keep our location hidden. In fact, you're the first visitor we've had in many years, and you're only here because you're family. If word were to get out of our existence, how long do you honestly believe it would be before we're hunted down and turned into some sort of scientific curiosity, or worse?'

'I think I see your point,' Sam said, remembering everything Lara McHayden had done in an attempt to harness his ability.

'But things aren't as bad as all that,' Marcus went on. 'While human history under our stewardship has still been rife with injustice and bloodshed, things could have been a lot worse. Hitler was defeated in World War II, wasn't he? And the Cold War never descended into the nuclear apocalypse everyone expected. Had it not been for our work, the outcome of both events would have been decidedly different.'

Until then Isaac had been steadily devouring his food, but now he pushed his empty bowl away, dabbed the bristles of his beard with his napkin and turned to Sam.

'After I joined the Rutherfords in 1976, both Stephen and Marcus began using Tetradyamide to enhance their powers, travelling farther and with greater accuracy than ever before. But there's always more we could do, and that's why you're here.'

'Me?' Sam said. 'What could I do?'

Marcus laid his right hand on the table, palm up. 'Tell me, what do you see?'

'Er, your hand?' Sam replied, suspecting it was a trick question.

Marcus nodded and looked across to Nora. 'Now your turn.'

She glanced to the ceiling and gave an exaggerated sigh, but laid her hand on the table too. Running across her palm was the line of an ancient scar.

'What happened to you?' Sam asked.

'The same thing that happened to me,' Marcus said. 'When we were children, our father performed a simple experiment, slicing both our palms shortly before our thirteenth birthday.'

'Within a week Marcus's cut had almost completely healed,' Nora said with a touch of bitterness, 'whereas mine...well, you can see for yourself.'

'You don't have the healing gene Humboldt told me about?' Sam asked her.

'The genetic trait that enabled you to recover from your brain injury and created your ability to alter the flow of time is shared only by the men of our family, specifically those who share a direct paternal line of decent to either Stephen or Joseph Rutherford. I, as a woman, missed out.'

'Not that she's sore in the slightest,' Marcus said, an impish twinkle in his eye.

'Less than an hour in your company and you're already beginning to grate on my nerves,' Nora said, and gave him a scathing look before turning back to Sam. 'After it was confirmed that Marcus shared the family healing ability, our father performed surgery to recreate the cranial injury he had sustained in the sinking of the *Northern Star*. While my brother has spent his life perfecting Father's techniques and continuing his work, I was reduced to more of a supporting role, which is how I wound up babysitting Michael Humboldt for the best part of fifty years.'

At that point Marcus reached across to his wife, who had taken the chair beside him, and squeezed her hand. 'Unfortunately Katherine and I were never able to have children of our own,' he said. 'I'm an old man now, and I don't know how many years I have left. When I die, my bloodline will die with me. Until recently I'd consigned myself to the fact that our family's brief guardianship over humanity would soon come to an end. But then, as a result of Nora's insights into Humboldt's family tree, we discovered the existence of Bernard Humboldt's illegitimate child – your grandfather, Alfred Rayner.'

All four of Sam's elderly companions were now watching him in a way that made him distinctly uncomfortable. He shifted his weight in his chair and looked from one expectant face to another.

'Apart from my brother, you're now the only living person that we know of with a direct paternal line of decent to either Stephen or Joseph,' Nora said. 'That makes you the last person we know of to have inherited the healing gene they both possessed.'

'What about Grandpa?' Sam asked. 'Surely he's a direct descendent too, isn't he?'

'True,' Isaac said, 'and in his youth he would have been an excellent candidate for surgery. However, as the brain ages it loses plasticity, meaning that surgery is no longer viable after a subject reaches full adulthood. The same would apply to your father, were he still alive.'

'Michael Humboldt was nineteen when he sustained his injury,' Nora said. 'The very upper boundary, which explains his limited ability.'

'That's what makes you so important,' Marcus said. 'We'd like you to join us, Sam, and take your rightful place in our family. I'd train you in the techniques both my father and I have used to alter the flow of time, and with Isaac here you'd have access to an unlimited supply of Tetradyamide. With our guidance, you and any sons you might have could continue the work we've started, safeguarding the future of the human race for generations to come.'

The atmosphere around the table had grown so thick you could probably smash it with a hammer and use the pieces to grit your drive. Sam broke eye contact and looked down at his hands, once again noticing the thin white scar on the ridge of his knuckle. No matter how honourable all this talk of the greater good was, it reminded him a little of what Dr McHayden had promised him when he'd first joined the Tempus Project, and although he had no reason to believe the Rutherfords might have ulterior motives, he didn't need any re-minding of how that had turned out.

'And what about my old life?' he asked, looking back up.

'If you did decide to join us, it would mean relocating here to Greenland, where I could begin schooling you in the techniques my father passed down to me. Given our need for secrecy, I'm afraid it would mean leaving your old life behind. But then personal sacrifice has long been ingrained in what we do.'

'You can say that again,' Nora put in.

Sam gulped. His bowl was still half-full, but his appetite had suddenly deserted him. 'You make it sound like I've got a choice,' he said.

'You always have a choice, Sam. It wouldn't be right to impose such a responsibility on someone who doesn't want it. So, what do you say? Will you join us?'

'Can I think about it?'

Marcus smiled and spread his hands. 'I would expect nothing less.'

7

The next morning Sam woke curled under a thick eider-down quilt in one of the upstairs bedrooms of the Rutherford farmhouse. After more than twelve hours of sleep, the shock and exhaustion that had plagued him since his ordeal at the hands of Michael Humboldt had at long last loosened their grip, and he finally felt something approaching his normal state of mind.

Climbing out of bed, he saw that the filthy, blood-stained clothes he'd been given back at the house in south Wales had been moved from the chair where he'd left them and replaced by a neatly folded flannel shirt and a pair of khaki trousers with patches at the knees. They were both a couple of sizes too big, but he rolled the sleeves up to his elbows and was able to stop the trousers falling down by buckling the leather belt he'd been left to its tightest hole.

Once he'd finished dressing, he descended the wooden staircase to the ground floor and entered the kitchen to find it scented by the smell of freshly baked bread. Marcus and Nora were at the table, each cradling a mug of coffee. Nora wore a dark turtleneck jumper and had her hair tied back in a way that accentuated her cheekbones. With the last remnants of Donna erased, Sam could make out the traces of the beautiful young woman she must have once been.

'Good morning,' Marcus said, and stood to fill another mug from the pan on the stove. 'Have you given any more thought to what we spoke about yesterday?'

'I have,' Sam said. He took a chair at the table, accepted a mug of coffee and stirred in two heaped teaspoons of sugar. In truth, he had been able to think about little else. He glanced back and forth between Nora and Marcus, then sucked in a breath before slowly releasing it. 'I'm sorry, but I don't think I can do it.'

'Oh,' Marcus said, and lowered his head.

'I want to help, really I do, it's just…'

'It's okay,' Nora said. She reached across the table and rested her hand on Sam's arm. 'Like my brother explained, joining us is not a responsibility we'd wish to impose on anyone. It must be something you choose freely.'

'It…it's not that. Well, it is, but it's more what you said about leaving my old life behind.' Sam sniffed in an effort to hold back the tears that were for some reason trying to force their way out of the corners of his eyes. 'You've got to understand, I never asked for any of this. Before the plane crash last year I didn't know a thing about healing genes, time travel, Tetradyamide or any of that stuff. I was just a normal teenager going about my life and, although I might not have realised it at the time, I was happy that way. That's all I've ever wanted – my old life back, like it was before.'

'What exactly are you trying to say?' Nora asked.

Sam took another breath and laid his hands flat on the table. 'Humboldt promised me something in exchange for saving his life. He said that he would reverse the plane crash that killed my dad and caused my injury. He was lying, obviously, because that would have created a paradox and I wouldn't have been able to find a cure for his brain tumour. But if he'd really wanted to, he had the power to do it. That's what I'm asking. I want you to give me what Michael Humboldt wouldn't.'

Nora glanced to Marcus, who stared back, stony-faced.

'Father would have never permitted altering history for something so trivial as personal bereavement,' he said.

Sam sighed and let his shoulders drop. Saving his dad had been too much to hope for, it seemed, but at least once Hinds had helped clear his name he might have something resembling a life to return to.

'Fortunately I'm not my father though,' Marcus added.

Sam looked up again. 'Sorry, what?'

Marcus leaned forward in his chair, a smile on his lips. 'Remember, Sam, secrecy is our family's greatest defence, and if you *do* chose not to join us, I'll have to alter the timelines in order to remove your memory of our meeting.'

'But I'd never tell anyone, I swear it!'

'I don't doubt that, but there are people out there who might wish to use the information against you, and even promises made with the best of intentions have a habit of being broken under torture or coercion.'

'I see,' Sam said. 'I suppose I understand.'

'No, I'm not sure you do. The point I'm trying to make is that, if I'm going to have to alter the timelines anyway, it might be possible to kill two birds with one stone.' Marcus turned to Nora, his smile growing. 'In fact, while I'm at it, it might also be beneficial to clear up the mess Humboldt created with his research into his ancestry. After all, we can't leave anything that might eventually lead back to the family, can we? What do you think, Nora? Could we bend the rules slightly?'

'Hmmm,' Nora said, and placed a fingertip over her lips. 'Now that you mention it, there might be something we could do. If you were to travel back to last summer, Marcus, you might be able to destroy the paper trail linking Bernard Humboldt to Sam's grandfather, his illegitimate son. In the new reality this would create, you would still know about Sam and his family, but Michael would never find out, meaning he'd never find a cure for his tumour and Esteban Haufner would have no reason to sabotage Flight 0368.'

Marcus laughed and slapped his hand against the surface of the table. 'You know, that might just work! If we could arrange a small fire at the General Register Office in England, or even a burst water pipe in the right place, then Alfred Rayner's birth certificate could be made to conveniently disappear. In fact, I think I already know just the person for the job! Well done, Nora. A neat and tidy solution to both problems!'

At that moment the door opened and Isaac bustled in, huffing and stamping clumps of snow from his boots.

Nora leaned over to Sam. 'Marcus may have inherited the healing gene,' she whispered, 'but I got the brains of the family.'

'Fresh eggs from the chicken coop,' Isaac announced, holding up a basket. He slid his boots off by the door, unzipped his coat and approached the table on socked feet. 'I make a mean omelette, if I do say so myself. So, Sam, will you be staying long-term then?'

'Unfortunately not,' Marcus said.

'So you'll do it?' Sam asked. 'You'll give me my old life back?'

'If it's a side effect of alterations I would need to make anyway then it would be my pleasure. Isaac, bring me a vial of Tetradyamide, please.'

'Shame,' Isaac said, 'but I guess we know where to find you if we need you.' He laid the basket on the table, passed through a door to a side room and returned a minute later with a small glass vial. 'I've continued to tweak the formula over the years,' he said proudly, handing it to Marcus. 'The effects are now almost instantaneous.'

Marcus held the vial up: a bar of thick, silvery liquid wavered inside, sealed under a red screw cap.

'You know, I think I've seen something like that before,' Sam said.

'Have you now?' Isaac arched an eyebrow. 'Don't mind me asking where, do you?'

Sam considered how to explain, then wished he hadn't said anything. In this reality Lara McHayden was an innocent victim of the Thames House bombing, not the twisted control-freak who had tried to kill his family and friends. And if Isaac were really the same person Sam had seen in the black-and-white photo behind McHayden's desk, it might be best if he didn't know what she had become.

'Never mind,' Sam said. 'It's not important.'

'Intriguing,' Isaac said. He shrugged, but thankfully didn't press the matter.

Marcus twisted the cap from the top of the vial and held it to his lips. With a grimace, he downed the silvery liquid inside. As he lowered the empty container, his eyes glazed over.

'I don't know how I can ever thank you,' Sam said, tears gushing down his cheeks as he lost the battle to hold them back. After everything that had happened since last summer, at long last things were about to be set straight. Really, it was all he'd ever wanted.

'No thanks necessary,' Marcus said softly. 'It's been a pleasure to meet you, Sam. Goodbye, and good luck.' With that he closed his eyes. A couple of seconds passed and then his body started convulsing.

Sam watched on, fascinated to view the process in another person. He felt a sudden moment of disorientation and then, in a single instant, his memory was wrenched away like a rug pulled from beneath his feet.

8

Four months later

Sam was woken by the sensation of his mattress rippling. He rolled over, lifted his head and forced his eyes open. Eva was sitting on the end of his bed, beaming down at him.

'Oh good, you're already awake,' she said.

'Ugh.' He let his head drop back to the pillow and raised an arm to shield his eyes from the radioactive sunlight pouring in through the floor-length window at the end of his room. 'What time is it?'

She jabbed a finger into the exposed flesh of his upper arm and scowled. 'That's nice, asshole. I missed you too.'

'Sorry,' he said and sat up, rubbing his face. 'I'm a bit jet-lagged still. I missed you loads and loads. In fact, every minute was agony without you.'

'Much better,' she said. Her scowl softened into a smile again and she leaned forwards to kiss him. 'It's good to have you back, Sam. So good I'll even forgive the sarcasm. Now,' she glanced at her wristwatch, 'it's almost ten thirty. Are we going to make the most of Memorial Day weekend, or were you planning on laying about in bed all day?'

'I don't know,' he said and pulled her to him. 'All day in bed sounds pretty good to me.'

'Uh-uh.' She pushed him back, wriggled free from his arms and stood up. 'There'll be plenty of time for that later. Now, in the shower with you! It smells worse than Doug's gym bag in here.'

Sam emerged from the bathroom fifteen minutes later with a considerably clearer head and made his way down-stairs. Eva was sitting with his parents at the table out on the deck beyond the kitchen.

'And here's Chrissie in the hospital with baby Matthew a few hours after he was born,' his mum said, thrusting her phone under Eva's nose before swiping to the next photo. 'And here's Sam with his little nephew. And here's big Matthew and little Matthew together. Isn't he just so cute you want to eat him up?'

'And then some,' Eva said, tilting her head back so that she could get a proper look at the screen. 'Reminds me a bit of his uncle, especially around the eyes. You know, Rebecca, I wish I'd been able to come too. I can't wait to meet him and give him a big squeeze.'

'Next time, sweetie. You're coming to the wedding in July, aren't you? After all, you're practically family now.'

'Wouldn't miss it.'

Sam took a chair at the far end of the table. There was a hint of summer in the air, and the warm sunshine on his skin made a pleasant change from the drizzle-filled week he'd taken off school to visit Chrissie and the baby in London.

'I still don't get why they had to call him Matthew though,' he said. 'I mean, couldn't they think of some-thing original?'

His dad tucked a strand of long, greying hair behind his ear and puffed out his chest. 'Don't knock it, it's a fine name that. Strong. Regal even, some might say. I'm sure the boy will go on to achieve great things.'

'Yeah, right,' Sam said, and rolled his eyes.

His dad stuffed a piece of toast in his mouth and stood, tucking his shirt into his trousers. 'I better get going,' he said. 'My first lesson's at eleven thirty.'

Towards the end of last year he had set up his own music school, teaching piano lessons to children between the ages of six and eighteen. After a slow first couple of months things had begun picking up and he was now working all weekend and every evening after school.

Sam watched his dad leave, then turned to Eva. 'So, what's the plan for today?'

'I've got Collette's car and Stef's got the keys to her parents' place on the coast,' she said, and rose from her chair. 'First pool party of the year, Sam, and Susanna, Rodrigo, Chris and a few others are going too.'

'Sounds good,' Sam said, standing to join her. 'See you later, Mum. We won't be back late.'

They left the house and strolled down the drive towards Collette's car. Eva climbed into the driver's seat and, as Sam slid in next to her, started the engine.

'So, tell me truthfully,' she said as they turned onto the road, 'how was London? Are you sad to be back in Montclair?'

'Truthfully? No, not really. Don't get me wrong, it was great to meet baby Matthew and to see Chrissie and Lance and my grandparents, but...'

'What?'

'It's not the same. Lewis has got new friends now, people from college. I hung out with them one night, but it felt weird, like I was an outsider or something. I know he did his best to include me, but it was obvious we've both sort of moved on. This is my home now. Here, with you.'

She dropped a hand from the wheel and squeezed his knee. 'Good answer. I know it's kind of dumb, but I couldn't help worrying—'

As if from nowhere a man stepped into the road before them.

Eva hit the brakes, propelling Sam against his seatbelt. The man just about had time to look up at them with wild hazel eyes and put both hands on the bonnet before he disappeared under the front of the car.

'Oh my God!' Eva yelled. She flung her door open and jumped out.

Sam unclipped his belt and followed after. 'Is he okay?'

The man (a homeless person, judging by his filthy, mismatching clothes) was on his backside in the middle of the road, blinking and rubbing his elbow. His white hair was so long and matted that it had fused together with his beard to form a single mega-dreadlock.

'I am *so* sorry,' Eva said and pulled her phone out. 'Are you hurt? I'm calling 911.'

'No, don't do that! Really, I'm fine. There's no need.' The man clambered to his feet and began dusting himself down, which seemed a bit pointless given the state of his clothing. 'It's Sam, isn't it?' he asked. 'Sam Rayner?'

Sam frowned, thinking it unlikely he would ever forget such a person if they'd met before. 'Do I know you?'

'Not in this timeline,' the man said, offering his hand. 'The name's Isaac Barclay.'

Sam stared down at the hand: it looked like it hadn't seen a bar of soap in a long, long time. He looked back up without shaking it. 'What do you want, Mr Barclay?'

The man remained standing there for a moment with his hand outstretched before drawing it back. 'That's a bit of a humdinger. I'm afraid there's no easy way to say this, Sam, but the end of the world is coming, and you're the only person who can stop it.'

About the Author

Damian Knight lives in London with his wife and their two daughters. He works in a library and, being surrounded by books, probably has the best day job ever. When not writing, reading, parenting or working, he often falls asleep fully clothed on the sofa.

The Pages of Time Series includes *The Pages of Time (Book 1)*, *A Trick of the Light (Book 1.5)* and *Ripples of the Past (Book 2)*. A new book is currently in progress.

To find out more or get in touch, please visit www.damianknightauthor.co.uk or email damianknightauthor@gmail.com

If you enjoyed the book, reviews on Amazon and Goodreads would be very welcome.

Acknowledgments

I would like to thank my friends and family, without whose support and encouragement these books would not be possible. Once again I am hugely indebted to my editor, Will Wain, whose advice, expertise and general ability to act as a sounding board were instrumental in the process of getting the book from rough draft to finished product. I would also like to thank Mahalia Smith for her eagle-eyed ability to spot the mistakes that I have become blind to, and Phil Patsias for his beautiful cover art throughout the series. Finally, I must reserve a special mention for my wife, Francesca. On top of her unswerving love and patience with my writing obsession, her feedback and insights into early drafts helped shape the book into what is today.

The Pages of Time
Book 1

After suffering a traumatic brain injury in a shocking terrorist attack, sixteen-year-old Sam Rayner wakes from a coma to discover that he has developed seizures during which he is transported into the body of his past or future self. Can Sam and his friends somehow defeat the sinister forces that want to use his powers for their own ends? Can they manage to save Sam's family from violent deaths that are already in the past – and maybe also win the girl he loves – by turning back the pages of time?

Available now on Amazon!

A Trick of the Light
The Pages of Time Book 1.5

It's the summer of 1969, and as Apollo 11 touches down on the moon, Michael Humboldt, a soldier horrifically wounded in the Vietnam War, uses the strange and disturbing powers he has developed to escape a secure military hospital in San Francisco. Seeking to become the master of his own destiny, he travels the backroads of California in order to evade the police and military authorities who are searching for him. But before the year is out, Michael has fallen for the beautiful Rachel and returns to San Francisco to find the doctor who can help him control his powers. He is ultimately thrown into a deadly game of cat and mouse, the shockwaves of which will change his and many others' lives for decades to come.

Available now on Amazon!

Printed in Great Britain
by Amazon